DARK RENDEZVOUS

The night breeze was chilly, penetrating Colleen's thin, flowered dress. She gathered her courage, then quietly slipped between two wagons and climbed over the earthen breastworks to walk out into the darkness.

She had walked only a few hundred feet when she felt a gentle hand on her arm. He was as tall and handsome as her dreams had showed her. His long black hair hung loose about his shoulders, draping to his waist and fluttering in the chill breeze.

He wrapped his arms around her. Then he picked her up, cradling her in his arms, and carried her further away from the wagons to a sandy knoll, then gently laid her down and stretched out beside her.

"I feared you wouldn't come," he whispered.

"I had to." She reached out to touch his hair. Then she felt his mind reach out for her. She closed her eyes to let his soul seep inside. It was like being the sand, and feeling the rain permeate your grains. Together they soared, spinning weightlessly in a timeless world, their souls free . . .

Kathleen O'Neal Gear

Sand in the Wind

TOR

A TOM DOHERTY ASSOCIATES BOOK
NEW YORK

This is a work of fiction. All the characters and events portrayed in this book are either products of the author's imagination or are used fictitiously.

SAND IN THE WIND

Copyright © 1990 by Kathleen O'Neal Gear

All rights reserved, including the right to reproduce this book, or portions thereof, in any form.

Cover art by Royo

A Tor Book
Published by Tom Doherty Associates, LLC
175 Fifth Avenue
New York, NY 10010

ISBN-13: 978-0-765-35726-7
ISBN-10: 0-765-35726-7

First edition: December 1990
Second edition: October 2006

Printed in the United States of America

0 9 8 7 6 5 4 3 2 1

To Itrice R. Sanders

For all the stone circles and kivas,
cathedrals and temples,
campfires and long dusty trails.

I haven't forgotten.

• CHAPTER 1 •

GLACIAL WINDS HOWLED OVER THE MOUNTAINS, TEARING at the pines and rushing headlong down the narrow valleys of the high country.

Wounded Bear pulled the red blanket tightly around his shoulders, blinking against the storm. Snow creased his face, making him look much older than his twenty summers. He'd lost track of days; the fasting and praying made his time on the mountain seem endless. How long had he been sitting here, crouched uncomfortably before the long-dead campfire? Were the four days of his vision quest over? His mind rambled through the questions. No, he shook his head, remembering this was the fourth day. The hunger pains had subsided after the second; now he floated in euphoria.

"Spirits?" he called in the shimmering night sky. "I beg you, hear me!"

He tried to concentrate his wavering mind on the Great Mystery, shutting his eyes and clearing all thoughts from his head. He prayed.

The voice of his brother, Little Deer, came to haunt him,

rolling over his weakened body like one of the giant boulders scattering the mountain slope. "Wakan Tanka has abandoned his people!" his brother had yelled, raising his coup stick to the heavens and shouting a shrill war cry. Wounded Bear covered his ears; the sound of Little Deer's voice tore the air around him. He opened his eyes with a start. Was his brother here now? He shuddered, searching the white world with blurred vision. No, it was only the wind, he reassured himself—only the terrible freezing wind.

He stood, clutching the thin red blanket to him, and walked through the dizzying torrent to a nearby pine. He let his hand trace the patterns in the mottled bark.

"We are one, my brother," he whispered, his voice seeming far away and unfamiliar. His eyes drifted across the endless stands of trees. "Once my people were as numerous as you, but now we are dying . . . dying . . ." His voice trailed off, lost in a rush of wind and snow.

Wounded Bear dropped his hand to his side. His body seemed to float, lifting lightly off the ground. He flowed with the feeling, trying to block out the chilling ache stabbing at his moccasined feet. He bowed his head, long black braids dangling limply in the damp air.

"Please, Maheo?" he pleaded. "Send me a spirit helper."

Tomorrow he would have to return to his people, would have to face the medicine elders and tell them that once again he had failed to have his prayers answered—his vision quest had been for nothing. A gnawing emptiness spread through him, leaving him hollow and sick.

Faint voices called out to him. He tilted his head to the wind, listening. The soft strains of singing arose. Spirits. Three of them. He smiled, letting their song fill him. Their voices twined together, creating a harmony so stunning it tugged at Wounded Bear like a lover's gentle hands, pulling him closer, closer. Shutting his eyes, he chanted in unison. He and the spirits sang of their battles against the Shoshoni and the People's bond with the vast, undulating plains. They sang of the prophet, Sweet Medicine, and his journey to the sacred mountain. Wounded Bear's heart ached as he repeated the prophet's last words: *". . . I am troubled. Listen to me carefully, carefully. You will meet a people who are white. They will be looking for a certain stone. They will travel everywhere looking for it. They will bring sickness to you. There will be many of these people, so many, many . . ."*

A sound made its way to Wounded Bear's numb ears. He jerked his eyes open. Behind him some creature passed through the bare branches, its thick fur catching on the twigs. He spun around, legs trembling.

On the other side of the blazing fire a huge white wolf sat motionless, staring into the orange flames. Wounded Bear struggled to think. Had he lit a new fire? He couldn't remember, but in his euphoria, he might have without knowing it. He clenched his fists to bolster his courage. The wolf hadn't seen him yet. Its huge eyes were riveted to the flames; reflected flickers danced in the black depths.

Then the wolf looked up at him—and suddenly the warrior knew.

Wounded Bear shuddered under the penetrating gaze and looked around him. The snow had stopped, the howling wind quieted. He shuffled toward the beast on leaden legs.

"Grandfather," he murmured hoarsely, "have you come to help your people?" He swayed, the effects of four days of fasting taking its toll on his strength. But still he did not sit, would not, until asked to do so.

Strange eerie lights glowed in the spirit creature's eyes. They drew Wounded Bear closer, bathing him in a stillness and serenity. He felt warm, warm for the first time in days. He let the ice-encrusted blanket drop from his shoulders.

"Yes, grandson," the wolf answered, its deep voice echoing from the forested slopes. "Come—sit with me. We have much to discuss and little time."

Gratefully, Wounded Bear sank to the frozen ground.

"The people are lost," the wolf said. "They have forgotten the prophecies of Sweet Medicine."

Wounded Bear shuddered at the terrible words. "Yes,

grandfather,'' he whispered. The voice of Little Deer came to haunt him again, shrieking that Wakan Tanka had abandoned the Cheyenne. He cringed against the pain in his breast.

The wolf breathed deeply, its shimmering white teeth revealed in the light of the fire. "I know what the young are saying, grandson. Do you believe the Great Mystery has forgotten?"

Wounded Bear shook his head fervently, causing him to sway again. "No, grandfather. Wakan Tanka would not forsake us."

The wolf walked closer, nodding his approval.

Wounded Bear's mind drifted to the images of his people camped at the foot of the Big Horn Mountains, faces pinched with want. He could hear the children crying out in his mind. Hungry . . . hungry. His shoulders slumped forward.

"Tell me," the wolf asked, its tone soothing and warm, "when have the people been hungry before?"

Wounded Bear thought of the old stories, the stories told by the elders around the blazing night fires of winter. Memories of Ehyophsta filled him. Silently he offered a prayer, begging forgiveness for his need to tell the story of the Yellow-Haired Woman aloud.

"In the beginning, grandfather," he said, voice strong and sure, "before Sweet Medicine was born to the people."

"Yes, warrior." The wolf's dark eyes sparkled brighter. "And how were we saved from famine?"

Wounded Bear swallowed, his throat dry. "The Yellow-Haired Woman came to us from the high peak to tell us of the buffalo." His mind grew sharper with the telling.

"You know the *Hee man eh*, grandson?"

"Yes," Wounded Bear replied. The dances of the halfmen-halfwomen society were well known to his people. But he was bewildered by the wolf's reference. He waited—knowing he was being taught.

"Tell me, warrior, what you remember of the prophecies of Sweet Medicine."

The creature's eyes had become so bright he could no longer gaze into the furred face.

Leaning to his right, Wounded Bear retrieved a handful of sage he had brought with him to the mountain. He threw it on the fire, purifying the air. The wolf deeply inhaled the fragrance.

"Grandfather," he began haltingly, "Sweet Medicine taught . . . taught that the whites would come to our sacred lands and kill the buffalo. The people would suffer for many winters." Images of starving children flashed before him; a wave of pain and anger tore his stomach. "He . . . he taught that if the people were unfaithful to the Old Ways they would be pushed out by the whites, and the whites would cover the ground as thickly as the spring grasses."

He looked up at the wolf, but its face was turned away, eyes closed, listening to some spirit song the warrior could not hear. He kept silent, waiting for a sign that he should continue.

At last the beast opened its eyes and turned back to Wounded Bear. Tears glistened in the blackness. "Do you know the prophecy of how the whites will come to dig up our lands?" Its smooth voice rang with sorrow.

He nodded gravely. Sweet Medicine had foretold that the whites would come to desecrate the earth by tearing at her surface with sharp sticks until she cried out in anguish. If the people let that happen, he had foreseen the Cheyenne swept away like grains of sand in the wind. A ragged pain coursed through Wounded Bear's body. He gritted his teeth and closed his eyes. "Yes, grandfather," he said.

The fire blazed furiously, sparks scattering through the still air to curl in the pine branches overhead.

The wolf stood and walked closer, standing only a few inches from the warrior, its huge furred nose pointed at Wounded Bear's forehead.

When the helper spoke again, its voice pounded against his ears like the sacred drums of the Sun Dance.

"There is a wagon train coming, grandson. The men of the train are digging a road through the last hunting grounds of the Cheyenne. They must be stopped—lest the prophecy come true.''

Wounded Bear could feel the warm breath of the creature on his face. He slowly nodded his understanding. The train must be stopped.

"Soon," the wolf breathed, seeming farther and farther away, "you will be called upon to sacrifice a great deal for the People."

Wounded Bear sat silent, his heart throbbing in his ears. He could feel the bristly fur of the spirit wolf brushing against his buckskin shirt. He stared intently at the enormous paws beside his crossed legs. The wolf laid one of the white paws on his thigh.

"You must open your heart for the People." He paused, tilting his head. "Are you willing?"

"Yes, gran . . ." he began as a blast of icy wind splashed his face. He raised his arms to shield himself. The trees moaned and jostled violently in the gale. Even before he let his arms down, he knew the snow had started falling again.

Golden rays of light streamed through the pines, dappling the forest floor like an irregular patchwork quilt. Wounded Bear studied the wavering patterns as he weaved between trees, his moccasins crunching on snow. He'd seen such a blanket once at Fort Laramie. A pretty redheaded emigrant lady had traded it for flour. He remembered standing for over an hour at the post store staring at the intricate swirls and brightly colored squares of cloth.

Stepping into a broad meadow, wind gusted around him, whipping the fringes of his buckskin pants until they cracked like whips. He shivered, snugging his blanket tightly around his shoulders as he gazed across the vast plains below. The high desert was a sheet of white, interrupted here and there by the dark brown of windblown hilltops. Thin puffs of clouds drifted through the turquoise sky, heading southward to the lands of the Shoshoni, the enemies of his people.

Wounded Bear stood for a moment, looking toward the eastern horizon. Still low in the sky, the sun sent out a

milky wave of light to flood the snow-covered plains. Hills
touched by the light shimmered a pale yellow.

He exhaled and watched his warm breath form an icy
cloud before it was whisked away by the freezing wind.
Trudging across the meadow, he headed down the mountain
to the flatlands where his village nestled along the first terrace of the creek.

As he walked, his exhausted mind rambled over the words
of the wolf. They came back one by one, the helper's deep
voice interspersed with the crunching of snow beneath his
feet and the shrill caw of bluejays. The birds hopped from
branch to branch as he passed.

"There is a wagon train coming, grandson . . . a wagon
train coming . . ."

As he wandered through a copse of bare-branched cottonwoods along the creek bottom, he heard laughter. On
the terrace above him over fifty conical lodges sprouted. He
could see the tops of the tipis. Curling gray ribbons wafted
from the smoke holes, tumbling before they vanished in the
wind. He inhaled a deep soothing breath before climbing
the icy lip of the terrace to stand at the edge of the com-
munity. He would tell the chief, Dull Knife, and the withered medicine man, Box Elder, of the wolf's words. Then
his people could prepare.

"Wounded Bear?" The soft feminine voice came from
behind a nearby pine tree.

He turned slowly, feet unsteady, to see Yellow Leaf. Her
long black hair fluttered in the wind. She was bundled in a
heavy buffalo robe, gathering kindling by breaking dead
twigs from the trunks of live trees. A pile rested in the
crook of her left arm. She walked toward him, smiling.

He tried to smile back, but his frozen jaws made it more
of a scowl. His eyes wandered over her beautiful face. She'd
loved him for three years—turned down four marriage pro-
posals from warriors more respected than he. The old
women of the village whispered that Yellow Leaf would be
an old maid forever. She was already twenty. He snugged
the blanket to his throat, wondering why she waited—and

why he didn't love her. She was kind and his friend, but his heart was too worn and cold to love any woman.

She stopped only a foot from him and gazed up into his numb face. Her large brown eyes were warm. "Your vision quest," she murmured, "did—"

"Yes," he responded, eyes drifting over the tufts of snow weighing down the pine branches.

She nodded, dropping her eyes, a smile of pride on her lips. "The people will be grateful."

He took a deep breath and held the chilling air in his lungs. A lightness filled his head. He swayed, staggering sideways. She quickly reached out and gripped his forearm with her free hand, steadying him. A few twigs fell from her other arm to sink into the snow.

"You're going to the chief's lodge?"

"Yes—and Box Elder's."

"I'll help you."

As they entered the village, a tangle of laughing children scampered around them to weave between the lodges, barking dogs close on their heels. Wounded Bear smiled wanly and continued forward, watching the erratic course of the boys, noting their frequent falls. Though the morning was still new, a broad path of tiny footprints already compacted the snow in front of the lodges. They followed it, listening to the feminine voices that came from the tipis. Most of the women would be working inside today to avoid the cold. Already he could smell the fragrance of pemmican stew seeping through the closed door flaps. The concoction of buffalo, fat, and berries was all the village had left to consume after the long, bitter winter. And these days the stews were thinner and thinner, barely enough pemmican to sustain a man. No animals had given themselves for food in over a week; and the last large game, an elk who had chanced proximity to the village to gnaw the bark of the aspens along the creek, had been eaten in a single day—two weeks before. The people were hungry, yet no one complained. Soon the snows would be gone and the buffalo would return. At least that was the spoken hope. But the future looked different to him. The great beasts were dwindling rapidly, their ranges cut by the white man's roads and limited to a single basin now: the Powder River Basin. And all the tribes, friend and foe alike, were condemned to hunt them there, avoiding each other or waging war to maintain hunting rights so that their people could eat.

The thoughts and smells of food made Wounded Bear's stomach growl miserably. This was his fifth day without eating or drinking, but soon it would end, as soon as he delivered his message—the wolf's message. He dropped a hand to his shrunken belly and patted gently.

"Just a little longer," he whispered reassuringly.

Yellow Leaf looked up at him, frowning. A gust of wind sent a veil of black strands whipping over her face. She pulled it back, tucking the hair behind her ear. "Perhaps you should eat before you talk to the chief. I have a pot of stew in my—"

He lifted a weak hand and smiled, shaking his head. "No—thank you."

As he approached the chief's lodge at the other end of the village, he heard laughter coming from within. He stopped a few paces outside. His brown eyes surveyed the location. Dull Knife's lodge was stationed up and away from the creek on a low rise overlooking the rest of camp. Wounded Bear turned halfway around to gaze down at the village. The lodges formed an irregular crescent moon, the opening facing east so that the warming rays of the rising sun could heat them. And so that the people could offer daybreak prayers to the source of light and life.

"I'll be all right," he said, meeting her soft eyes.

She reluctantly released his arm, nodded, and backed away. He watched her walk down the hill to her parents' lodge and duck inside. A puff of warm air seeped out, sending a cloud of ice crystals to swirl around the entrance.

He shifted positions. Cold pierced his moccasins like a sharp knife. The snow screeched at his movements. Inhaling deeply, the burst of cold air in his lungs made him cough.

The voices inside the lodge ceased and the hide flap was pulled back slightly. Wounded Bear was surprised to see the wrinkled face of Box Elder peek out. The flap was opened wider and the aged medicine man stepped into the cold, the flap dropping behind him. His sightless eyes focused on Wounded Bear. He hobbled forward, a mostly toothless grin on his lips. The shaman was a small man with long gray braids that hung below his waist. He wore a heavily beaded buckskin shirt adorned with orange porcupine quills; the fringes lining the arms flapped in the biting wind. He walked to within two feet of the warrior, his white-filmed eyes fixed on Wounded Bear's tired face.

"I saw you climb the sacred mountain," he said in a rusty voice, pointing a gnarled finger to the ragged snow-clad peak.

"Yes."

Box Elder tipped his chin to the turquoise sky and murmured a hushed prayer. "And the spirits came to you." It was a statement, not a question. The aged head tottered in a nod.

"Yes, Holy One."

"Come inside, warrior." The shaman waved a hand at the chief's lodge. "We have been waiting for you." He strode back and entered the doorway.

Wounded Bear gazed through the village again, watching the children play, then walked numbly forward. When he lifted the hide flap, warmth struck him like the blow of a fist, making his face sting wildly. He entered and let the flap fall closed.

Darkness swelled around him, his eyes, used to the glare of sunlit snow, blinded for a moment. He stood still, blinking until the fire in the center of the lodge blazed normally and other things appeared. Buffalo robes were spread out across the floor, buffering the chill from the ground. The chief's round shield sat in the back, men and running horses painted across the front in red. In the firelight, the honey-colored tipi walls flickered orange, shadows dancing over the faces of Dull Knife and Box Elder.

The chief sat cross-legged by the fire. Though a middle-aged man, his hair was still black, eyes sharp. Strips of white tradecloth were woven in the braids that dangled over his chest. He had a round face with a broad flat nose and full lips. A blue and yellow blanket was draped over his shoulders; the chief unwrapped it and waved a hand to the place on his left. The warrior gratefully dropped to the thick warm buffalo hide.

"Here, son." Dull Knife handed the dry blanket to him.

He took the ice-cold one from his shoulders and replaced it with the chief's, shuddering for a few moments as the warmth seeped through his hide clothing to touch his skin.

Box Elder laid out a thick bundle. Murmuring a series of prayers, he unfolded layer upon layer of cloth until the contents were revealed. Wounded Bear swallowed convulsively, eyes widening. The sight of the sacred Straight Pipe struck fear into his heart. The long pipe rested on the fine cloth beside a buffalo wool and sinew tamper. Braided sweet grass scented the bundle.

The warrior averted his eyes, focusing on the flickering flames while the shaman prepared the pipe. Wounded Bear was confused, uncertain as to why his presence warranted such special treatment. The Straight Pipe was used only at Sun Dance or when the Mahuts, the sacred arrows, needed renewing and occasionally when the survival of the people was threatened. Through the corner of his eye, he saw Box Elder use a carved stick to retrieve a red glowing coal from the fire. The old man carefully placed the coal into the pipe, then offered it first to the earth, then Maheo, and finally the Four Sacred Persons. Cupping his hand beneath the pink stone bowl, the shaman smoked. Inhaling deeply, he closed his eyes and tipped his face heavenward to slowly blow the blessed smoke out to the four directions.

Wounded Bear's breathing quickened, his fasting euphoria returning in a rush. He felt light, as though his flesh barely touched the kinky hide beneath him. His eyes followed the shaman's puff of smoke as it was drawn up through the smoke hole and out, carrying a message of renewal and rebirth to the earth, humans, and all living creatures.

The aged medicine man's hands trembled as he passed the pipe to Dull Knife and bowed his head in private prayer. Wounded Bear carefully observed the delicate transferral. The chief's hands remained level, unmoving from the height at which the sacred artifact was given. Before touching it to his lips, Dull Knife imitated the ceremony performed by Box Elder, lifting the pipe to the appropriate spiritual agencies. Then he smoked.

Taking a deep breath, Wounded Bear pulled his broad shoulders straight in preparation. He felt warm now, too warm. Blood raced in his veins to throb at his temples. At last his turn came. The chief passed the pipe.

Stretching out his arms to touch the ancient sacred device, a tingle pricked his spine. He kept the Straight Pipe perfectly level and slowly brought it even with his eyes. Squeezing his lids shut, he whispered a personal prayer to the wolf, then offered the pipe to the earth, Maheo, and the Four Sacred Persons. When he placed it against his lips, Wounded Bear's entire body quaked, the instrument's power filling him, raising him to the sky until he felt he could no longer contain the divine power. He held the blessed smoke in his lungs for as long as he could, then gently blew out to the four directions.

When he handed the Straight Pipe back to Box Elder, the revered medicine man smiled. He tenderly stroked the device, then laid it across his lap, gnarled fingers caressing the stem.

Wounded Bear waited. The mixture of tobacco and sweet grass had gone straight to his head, making him dizzy. He dropped both hands to the buffalo robe to steady himself.

"I had a dream," Box Elder cackled at last, breaking the profound silence. "I saw you talking to a spirit wolf." He pointed toward the mountain peak.

"He came . . . Holy One."

Dull Knife folded his hands in his lap and gazed intently at the flickering orange flames, brow furrowed in thought.

"In my dream," the shaman continued, tilting his head precariously to the right, "I could not hear the words the helper spoke, but I knew you understood."

Wounded Bear nodded, swaying slightly. He pressed his hands harder into the robe. "I understood."

He watched Dull Knife clench his fingers together, the knuckles growing white, but still the chief kept his eyes downcast, his chest rising and falling erratically.

"And what did the wolf tell you, my son?" Box Elder leaned forward, gray braids sweeping over his knees. The old man's seamed face flickered eerily in the firelight. Wounded Bear studied his haunting eyes.

"He . . . he told me the people will be swept away like grains of sand in the wind . . ."

His words were cut off when Dull Knife sucked in a sudden breath and jerked up his eyes to stare. Fear and pain lined the chief's face.

"And?" Box Elder prompted.

"There is a wagon train coming. The men of the train want to dig a road through our last hunting grounds. We must stop them . . . If we cannot, Sweet Medicine's prophecy will come true."

Box Elder nodded slowly and leaned back. His buckskin shirt glistened, the blue and red beads reflecting the wavering flames.

"So," Dull Knife whispered hoarsely, "another battle is forced upon us."

Wounded Bear dropped his gaze. "Yes, my chief."

"When? When will they come?"

Box Elder answered, his withered face turned heavenward. He clutched the Straight Pipe with crooked fingers. "They will come during the moon when the buffalo bulls begin to rut."

Wounded Bear blinked. Somewhere inside of him the timing rang strangely ominous. During the moon when the buffalo were creating new life, the Cheyenne would be threatened with final destruction. His gut tightened, stomach muscles going rigid. A sign?

"I will organize scouting parties," Dull Knife murmured and stood.

Wounded Bear started to follow, but the chief held up a hand and shook his head. "No, my son. You must rest now and later eat." He paused, anxiety clear in his strained voice. "I will call a meeting for tonight. Then you can tell them."

"I will."

Dull Knife pulled back the door cover and slipped out. A gust of cold wind splashed Wounded Bear. He shivered.

"Lie down, warrior," Box Elder said gently. "Sleep."

Wounded Bear followed instructions, curling on his side in front of the fire. He yawned deeply and closed his eyes. In the back of his exhausted awareness, he heard the shaman start singing. The old man's voice was soft, the tune lilting to swirl through the tipi.

Just before sleep overpowered him, Wounded Bear recognized the words. Box Elder sang the wolf songs.

· CHAPTER 2 ·

COLLEEN MERRILL ROLLED TO HER SIDE, HER THIN ARMS thudding dully against the bed of the wagon. A web of long blond hair fell over her heart-shaped face, fluttering softly with each incoherent phrase she mumbled. Her brown eyes opened suddenly but quickly closed again, her mind still deeply asleep. The recurring dream was powerful, the images of the crystal blue mountains and the man with long black braids more real to her than the world of wakefulness.

"N-No!" she shouted, her arms flailing against crates and barrels—and her husband.

"Colleen!" Robert Merrill was abruptly wide awake, his yardstick-wide breast heaving as he rubbed the cheek where her frantic fist had landed. He reached over and shook her hard. "Wake up! Damn it, Colleen!" She seemed oblivious to his stern efforts, still mumbling shrill half sentences. He picked her up by the shoulders and shook her harder. Her waist-length curls bounced silver in the moonlight streaming through the rear curtains of the wagon.

"What?" she said, her eyes opening wide as she felt his hard grip on her shoulders. "Robert, what—"

"Get dressed and get out of this wagon now!" he ordered, shoving her back against the sideboard.

Her spine hit hard, a jab of pain flashing through her. A small cry escaped and she snaked a hand up her back to the injured spot. "But I—"

"I said get out! I ain't got to sleep a whole night in two months 'cause of your dreams," he growled, pointing to the rear curtains. "I plan on getting to tonight!" He picked up her yellow muslin dress and threw it at her. "Put it on!"

She complied, her mind not really here in the wagon on the sandy Nebraska plains, but far away in some distant beautiful land. "Robert, I don't want to leave. Can't I just—"

"No!" he yelled and flung open the rear curtains, then forcibly shoved her out into the night air.

She stood awkwardly, the chill evening breeze making her shiver, not knowing where to go or what to do. In her sleepy mind, anger was rising and waking her, but it hadn't quite completed the process yet. She still felt numb and tired. Putting a hand to her mouth, she yawned deeply, then aimlessly walked out over the sands and into the moonlit hills.

The wagons in the train stretched endlessly to the west, looking like a lumpy slithering serpent as they undulated with the sandy plains, their white canvas tops glistening in the lunar glow. She hugged her arms against the chill and continued walking until she found a high knoll that overlooked the entire camp, then she sat down and pulled up her knees to cradle them in her arms. Her thoughts reluctantly turned to her husband.

Robert had been a prosperous—if greedy—farmer in New York. It was the man's wealth rather than his integrity that had prompted Colleen's father to force her into marrying him. When she had objected, her father had been stern. "He'll provide well for ye and me grandchildren, girl!" he had insisted, slamming a freckled fist against a mahogany table. "What more can a lass of yer status in life ask?" He'd spoken in his usual heavy brogue. Only twenty years before, her parents had emigrated to America from Ireland. They were still acutely aware of their lowly foreigner status, despite the fortune her father had made in mining.

But no grandchildren had come. She sighed. Robert blamed her for that, saying she had a "problem." She rubbed her chin over the soft fabric covering her knees and stared across the camp. Probably that was the major reason he was gradually becoming more and more unkind, hurting her when he touched her. But the dreams were another reason. She shuddered, staring up at the full moon high overhead and the ring of faint stars surrounding it. The breeze tousled her blond hair, sending strands to flutter before her eyes.

Her mind drifted. Robert had heartily objected when she'd begged to accompany him to Montana Territory, but she had sweetly insisted, utilizing all of her feminine wiles to convince him.

They'd been sitting in the huge parlor of her parents' home. The hardwood furniture was ornately carved and beautiful; it glistened in the late afternoon light streaming between the blue velvet curtains.

"Robert?" she'd begun, sliding to the floor at his feet and taking his big hand in hers. "Maybe if I come West with you . . ."

"Now, Colleen, we've already discussed that and—"

"But, well . . . you know they say the climate of the West encourages health, and . . . maybe, if I take care of myself, it won't be too long 'til a baby comes." She'd dropped her eyes demurely to stare up at him from beneath her lashes.

He'd shifted uncomfortably, irritated by her reference to the lack of a child after nearly a year of marriage. But a light had flickered in his green eyes and he'd nodded. She'd known at that moment that he'd let her go.

And she *had* to go. The dreams were becoming overwhelming. Every night the vision of crystal blue mountains taunted her consciousness . . . and there was the man. The man with long black braids who looked into her eyes and made her heart swell with longing and a curious sadness.

At the thought of the dreams, her hand went immediately to the silver crucifix around her throat. She clutched the broken body of her savior tightly and murmured a silent prayer begging His forgiveness and understanding. In New York, when the dreams had first come to her, she'd poured out her fears and terror to Father Donovan in the privacy of the confessional. But here, on the barren Nebraska plains, there was no such solace. The train didn't even have a Protestant chaplain, let alone a Catholic priest. So her soul remained burdened, the vaguely adulterous dreams like a sword slash in the heart of her beliefs.

She crossed herself and uttered a fervent Hail Mary, hoping the blessed Virgin Mother would hear her humble pleas for guidance and release her from the torment of the dreams.

Her thoughts shifted back to Robert. When she'd begged to come along, she'd not counted on his abrupt change of character. They'd only been traveling for three weeks, yet he seemed increasingly insecure and frightened. It was as though the trip through the wilderness scared him more than it did her. He compensated by hurting her.

Her eyes drifted to the desert. Though the sand hills posed near insurmountable obstacles for the wagons, the grains shimmered like dew drops in the silver light, glimmering in waves over the open plains. She looked down at a heavy freight wagon mired up to its hubs in sand. It was canted at an awkward angle, leaning precariously to the left. They'd lost two oxen yesterday, the great horned beasts sagging to the ground in death after futilely pulling for hours to free the wagons. The road-building expedition was large, consisting of over eighty wagons and two hundred people. Thirty-six of the wagons were owned by a grocery store company from Sioux City, C. E. Hedges and Co., and were filled with food and supplies to start a branch store in Montana. The nineteen-year-old man in charge of the freight wagons was named Nat Hedges. She'd met him nearly a week ago. He was a dapper, self-confident man. The military escort pulled twenty-five heavy wagons with U.S. written in large black letters on the sides. The road-building crew, led by Colonel James Sawyers, had only fifteen wagons. But those were filled to overflowing with picks, shovels, tents, and supplies. Sawyers had been appointed by the Congress of the United States to build a road from Sioux City, Iowa, to Virginia City, Montana, and he was taking his job seriously. He was generally in a hurry and rude, riding through the train as though he were in charge of the world. And, after watching the road crew "build" the road for the past two weeks, she could not understand why they called it that. The crew didn't really "build" a road, they just smoothed an occasional rocky spot or constructed a stream crossing here and there. For the most part, the crew seemed idle and bored. But the eighty or so wagons in the expedition did leave a clear trail for others to follow. The iron-rimmed wagon wheels cut a swath through the desert by churning up the soil. Only a few of the wagons were filled with emigrants bound for the Montana goldfields. Hers was one of those.

Her anger with Robert was increasing, nipping at her like a rabid dog. She frowned as her fingers strayed to the swollen mounds on her shoulders. Cautiously she unbuttoned her bodice and lifted the fabric from her shoulder. Red splotches covered her flesh, mixing painfully with the pale yellow of bruises he'd inflicted a week before. She caressed them, then rebuttoned her dress. He'd never hurt her before—only since they'd joined the train . . . and her dreams had grown so vivid.

The darkness grew thicker as a cloud passed over the moon. She waited for the light to be renewed. Leaning back against the sand and extending her legs, her skirts rustled against a prickly rabbitbrush. As she started to relax in the silence of the night, she sighed audibly.

"Who's there?" a deep voice demanded from the darkness.

Colleen jumped, turning to see who the intruder might be. Finding her voice, she said, "I'm part of the train."

A blue-clad form approached, his rifle pointing at her chest. The man's boots moved silently in the deep sand.

"Oh, pahdon me, ma'am," he drawled.

She could tell now that he was one of the soldiers with the military escort. A "Galvanized Yankee," Robert had criticized. Her father had referred to them as "Goddamned White-Washed Rebels!" To the unbiased they were U.S. Volunteers, Confederate prisoners of war recruited from the prison camps to fight Indians on the frontier.

"You really should not be gallivanting around," the soldier scolded. "The talk of Indian attack isn't just funnin'. I—"

"I'm not gallivanting, soldier, I'm sitting," she replied curtly, annoyed by the intrusion.

He extended a hand to her. "Then I'm sure you won't mind if I escort you back to your wagon."

"Yes, I would!" she said hotly. Why were men always ordering her around? "I plan on staying out here until I'm good and ready to go back, and I don't happen to be ready yet, soldier!"

"Yes, ma'am," he said, spreading his feet into an at-ease posture. He looked down toward the wagons. Another soldier was walking slowly through the sand.

Cupping a hand to his mouth, he called, "Harper?"

The approaching man turned, saw the lieutenant, and started up the sand dune. Colleen looked at the officer beside her. He was tall, well over six feet.

"Sir?" Harper asked timidly, saluting. He was a short, stocky man with bright red hair.

The lieutenant returned the salute. "Take over these rounds, Private. I'll relieve you shortly."

"Yes, sir." Harper saluted again and walked off, circling the edges of the camp.

The officer turned back to Colleen, an amused look on his face. "Reckon that makes my job a sight easier."

She squinted in confusion. "How's that?"

"Well, since you insist on exposing yourself to danger, it's my duty to protect you. So, I'll just plant myself here and keep my eyes peeled." He sat down next to her and extended his long legs.

Dear Lord! she thought silently, what was she supposed to do now? She sighed gruffly, giving him a sign of how she viewed his unrequested presence. Being alone with a strange man did not put her at ease. Who could he be? With over one hundred and fifty military men accompanying the expedition, it was difficult to get to know any of them.

As the cloud passed from in front of the moon, the silver light exposed him to her speculation. He was really quite handsome. Brown wavy hair hung over his ears and he had a drooping mustache. His broad shoulders narrowed to a slim, muscular waist. His face wasn't particularly clear, but she made out a straight nose and squared jaw.

"What's your name, soldier?"

"Lieutenant Matthew Douglas, ma'am." His drawl came out light and airy.

"I'm Colleen Merrill—"

"Yes, ma'am. I know that."

"How, Lieutenant? We've never met, have we?"

"No."

"Well?"

"I make it my business to know the names of the attractive ladies under my charge."

He turned away to stare out across the moonlit sands, but she knew he was smiling, could hear it in his voice.

"Don't you think that's presumptuous, Lieutenant?"

"Uh-huh," he commented laconically, sounding utterly bored.

She stifled the lecture on proper conduct that rose to her lips and changed the subject. "Forgive me for asking, but what's an officer doing walking guard duty? I thought—"

"I'm not a regular officer."

"Well, what—"

"I'm a scout. I do pretty much as I please."

"Oh." She was confused. "I didn't think they let White-Wash . . . uh—volunteers—be scouts."

He turned to give her a wry grin, raising his brows. "I didn't ask for the commission. They gave it to me after they found out I'd spent a lot of years in this part of the country."

"Umm," she murmured. "You're scouting at this time of the night?"

"Indians frequently steal stock at night, ma'am."

"But I thought you soldiers had decided not to guard this train anymore? That's why we've been sending out our own guards and scouts."

"Yes, Mrs. Merrill," he said, leaning back against a bush. "That is quite correct. However, Captain Williford remains concerned for the safety of the emigrants."

"I'm surprised. There seems so little military discipline on this expedition, I'd assumed we were all on our own."

He looked at her from the corner of his eye. "You'll be better off if you keep thinking that way. This is the frontier army, ma'am. We're lucky we've all got matching uniforms."

"Of course, they had to give you something to wear when they let you out of prison."

"Reckon. Naked soldiers aren't seemly."

A silence fell between them. She could see he was drumming his fingers on his sky blue pants.

"So," she continued, "why aren't you guarding Mr. Sawyers' engineers?"

The lieutenant turned to stare, his eyes rudely appraising her from the tip of her toes to the top of her head. In defense, she sat forward and hugged her knees to her chest.

"You have no manners, sir!" she said stiffly.

"Never claimed to. Besides, you're mighty nosy for a woman."

"Why, I . . ."

A broad insolent smile creased his face as he studied her abashed response.

"But, since you asked, the debate goes something like

this: Seems the colonel—you know that's an honorary title. He's a civilian—doesn't understand my commanding officer's orders. He thinks the escort was sent along to build his road for him, but Captain Williford claims he heard it different. Captain says he was told to *guard* this train, not brush down the colonel's horses—if you get my meaning?" He paused, his smile still lingering, then continued. "So, we're camping in a different place from y'all and proceeding as if only loosely attached to this expedition. That is, until the colonel comes to his senses."

"You think he will?"

Douglas shrugged.

Colleen thought about it. She instinctively disliked the train's leader, James Sawyers. He had a prissiness about him that gave her the fidgets and his long narrow face reminded her of a misshapen watermelon. As well, no man could be trusted who had colorless eyes and a constantly scraggly beard.

"And what will happen," she asked crisply, "if we are attacked some night by Indians, Lieutenant, and you brave boys in blue are camped a half mile away?" She raised her brows and scowled.

He canted his head at a provocative angle and gave her a rude flashing smile that made her glance down to make sure she'd remembered to rebutton her dress.

"Well, ma'am," he replied in a slow, concentrated drawl, "reckon we'll hear the shooting and come arunnin'."

"Uh-huh," she mumbled. "I do hope we're not all shot up with arrows by the time you arrive to rescue us."

"Me too, ma'am."

"Sir, you—"

"So," he interrupted, changing the subject, "why don't you answer a nosy question for me?"

"Depends," she said cautiously, afraid from the looks he was giving her that it might be rather personal. "What?"

"Tell me what a beautiful woman like you is doing heading for a godforsaken hole like Virginia City?"

She furrowed her brow as she studied him. "Mr. Douglas, the city has only been in existence for two years. Have you ever been there?'' Obviously this former Confederate prisoner could know little about the place.

"Yes, ma'am," he replied, as though anticipating her intentions. "I have."

That shifted her line of thought. She'd hoped to humble him based upon his ignorance, but clearly that wouldn't work.

"We're heading there to mine for gold."

He frowned. "Your husband ever mined before?"

"Well . . . no. But Robert says it can't be that hard, he—"

His loud laugh stopped her. She crunched her teeth together, setting her jaw at an awkward angle.

This time the silence lasted for several minutes, punctuated only by continuing chuckles from the lieutenant.

"Uh—forgive me, ma'am." He squeezed the bridge of his nose, shaking his head. "But swinging a pick into solid granite isn't like dropping seeds into a furrow of soft earth. It's a might more arduous."

"Ardu . . ." She blanched, having no idea what that meant. "I'll have you know, sir, that my father was a miner and he said there was nothing to it!" She pulled back her shoulders to show indignation.

"What was your maiden name, ma'am?" He rolled to prop his head on one hand and stare at her as though he was hanging on every word she spoke.

"Meara," she replied, wondering what possible reason he could have for asking.

"Just as I thought."

She furrowed her brow, her eyes darting around. She had the feeling she'd missed something important. "What?"

"Your father's Irish!"

"Well, I hardly see what that has to do with—"

"Kissed the blarney stone one too many times."

"I beg your—"

"Now, tell me the truth. What the hell are you doing out here?"

"Don't curse!" she reproved, gripping her silver crucifix again in case God had any questions about who the foul-mouthed blasphemer was. "A gentleman—"

"I'm not a gentleman."

She sat quietly. She'd never known a man who willingly admitted a lack of breeding. "You're not?" Her mind went back to that strange word he'd used. "But you seem educated, Mr. Douglas."

"My father was strict about reading. Can't help but learn if you read. Education does not, however, make a man a 'gentleman.' " He said the word as though a profanity.

She raised a brow, hesitating. "What kinds of books did you read?" She'd attended a finishing school in New York for a few months. It had been so boring she'd begged her mother to let her leave.

"Mostly classical literature."

"Oh!" She was somewhat taken aback. He didn't seem that educated.

"So," he stubbornly persisted. "Why are you here?"

"I . . . I already told you." Suddenly the dream images burst in upon her. She shivered.

He straightened slightly, staring, but she ignored him, lost in her own thoughts. She couldn't tell this stranger that something had pushed her to come—intruded upon her sleep and forced her to undertake the long journey despite her husband's objections. Her skin prickled at the thought.

"You all right, ma'am?" His voice had changed completely, taking on a softness.

She nodded and swallowed, then steered the conversation elsewhere. "Where . . . where are you from, Lieutenant?"

"Virginia."

"Did you . . . live there all your life?"

Apparently realizing she wanted desperately to change the subject, he played along. "No, Pa and I left when I was ten to roam the western territories. I only returned a little over a year ago to offer my services to the Confederacy."

She examined his face curiously. "Why? Surely you knew the war was lost."

He sighed audibly, fumbling with his navy blue jacket. "Seemed the thing to do."

The face of her brother David came to her, his brown eyes warm and soft, his blond hair tousled. He'd been her only playmate for most of her life, as well as her fierce protector against other children's taunting. At fifteen he'd run away to join the army, throwing the family into frantic turmoil. Only two weeks after his disappearance, however, they'd received word that he'd been killed at Shiloh. His body had never been recovered from the mangled mass of dead.

She squeezed her palms nervously. The pain of losing her brother was still sharp. "Where were you captured, Matthew?" The thoughts of David had made her forget proprieties. Her eyes went wide. "Oh, I'm terribly sorry, Mr. Doug . . ."

"Egypt, Mississippi, Colleen," he answered familiarly.

She bowed her head, grateful for his indulgence, but a little disturbed at his usage of her first name. Her thoughts returned to David. A soft reverie swept her face. Her voice was strained. "I lost a brother at Shiloh." She pulled up her chin and leveled her eyes on his, accusing.

He arched a brow, giving her a questioning grin, but his tone was gentle. "I wasn't there."

"I . . . I didn't mean . . ."

He waved a hand, dismissing her apology as unnecessary, then picked up a handful of sand and let it trickle through his fingers. "Did your husband fight in the war?"

"No, he stayed home to farm."

"He just hurts women folk then?"

She flushed suddenly, dropping her eyes to play with a fold in her yellow dress. Of course the lieutenant had seen, his guard position overlooked her wagon. He'd also undoubtedly heard everything Robert had said. Had he witnessed other times Robert had hurt her? A wave of discomfort washed through her.

"I . . ." It was a weak attempt, barely audible. She tried again. "Sometimes."

"Hmmm." He recrossed his legs and bit off a comment before it could erupt.

She glanced at him from the corner of her eye. He was twisting one end of his brown mustache and staring down at her wagon. The white canvas top glowed silver in the moonlight.

"Well," he said, "nothing is ever as glorious as we imagine. Is it, Colleen?"

She pushed up from the sand to stand, his continued usage of her first name grating. "You are ill-bred, sir."

He remained lounging and fixed her with a bold, indecent stare. "I've been called worse."

"No doubt." She tugged up the hem of her skirt and started down the sands to her wagon, not bothering to say good night.

• CHAPTER 3 •

WOUNDED BEAR CHASED THE WILY CREATURE, DODGING back and forth across the forested slope to avoid the razor-sharp claws, but the underbrush was so dense the badger eluded him again.

"My brother," he called, his chest heaving from the race, "I need your help. Please allow me to catch you?" He sat heavily on the grassy hillside. The raspberry vines bristled sharply against his bare back as he sat next to a pine. Leaning forward, he searched the lush green environment for movement. But there was none. The badger was gone, his hopes of receiving a vision from the animal disappointed.

He was hungry, his empty stomach echoing in a long rumble. But that desire would have to wait. First he had to sanctify his badger quest by smoking. He unfastened the sack tied to his waist, then took his pipe out and filled it with tobacco. When he lit the mixture, a rich musty smell filled the air. Ritually, he held the pipe out to the earth, then the sky and the four directions before inhaling deeply of the smoke and blowing out to the four directions again.

The gray swirls rose and vanished in a gust of wind, carried upward to the Great Mystery and the spirit of the badger. Now he could seek food.

He took the buffalo jerky from his pouch, held it up to the sky, and whispered, *"Ma ah ku tsit o miss i."* He hoped the badger had heard and would come to eat with him. "Please, brother? You must be hungry too after the chase." He broke off a piece of his jerky and laid it in the tall grass.

Settling himself back against a swaying pine, he surveyed the new wildflowers that covered the steep slope. They wove a multicolored tapestry through the tall grasses. He let his brown eyes drift over the tall trees to the turquoise sky above. Fluffy clouds sailed aimlessly. If it weren't for the dreams his life would be almost perfect. But in his sleep a yellow-haired woman walked at his side, stroking the muscles in his arm with delicate white fingers. She looked up at him with tear-blurred eyes and he woke trembling—night after night.

Something stirred in the heart of the raspberry tangle. He sat forward. The badger?

"I have seen my soul, brother," he called softly. "It came to me as a shadow and beckoned me to follow." He was silent for a few moments, hoping the badger was listening and would come to talk with him as it had in the old days.

"Brother?" he murmured, his voice forlorn, troubled. "I must know the meaning of the vision. Will you help me?"

The question lay heavy on the fresh air of the forest—unanswered.

He scratched his back against the bark of the pine, allowing the vanilla scent of the sap to filter through him, refreshing his tired body.

It worried him that the badger would not come to speak with him. In the days of his youth, the creature had bravely waddled up to him as he played alone on the plains and advised him on how he ought to live his life—now it refused him audience. Pain pierced his breast. He dropped his head. He knew why. His emotions led him rather than the teachings of the tribal elders. But he was changing that, cleansing himself in sweat baths and praying constantly. He had sought out the wolf, and soon would participate in the blessings of the Sun Dance. He would dance to renew his people, to bring them back to the Old Ways.

Yet, he could not fully concentrate on the dance unless he knew the meaning of his vision. Why had his soul beckoned him away? Somewhere deep inside he felt it was trying to separate him from his people—or life.

Suddenly the rustling in the raspberry vines resumed. Wounded Bear sat motionless. It must be the badger. He pulled himself around behind the tree and crouched for attack.

From beneath the prickly vines, the badger emerged and waddled to sit only five feet away. Wounded Bear was puzzled; surely the animal scented him. The badger made a soft grunting sound and looked toward his tree. Then he understood. The creature was offering itself to him that he might see into the future. He slipped the knife from the sheath at his waist and pounced, slitting the beast's throat, making the death painless and immediate. The badger only wriggled a few seconds.

Wounded Bear tenderly stroked the soft fur, then picked the creature up and cradled it in his arms as he walked through the trees and out onto a broad flat outcrop of granite. The rocky slab overlooked the valley of the Big Horn Mountains. Below, the sage-covered plains stretched endlessly, marred only by winding rivers and occasional sandstone buttes.

Gently he laid the badger on its back, then took his knife and slit open the creature's stomach. Removing the entrails, he carried them to a place in the grass where he hoped the coyotes and wolves would find them, then walked back to the badger. He braced it against a rock so it wouldn't fall over and watched anxiously as blood slowly trickled into the empty stomach cavity. Fear welled in his chest as he nervously backed away. If his vision quest was meant to be answered, the spirit powers would protect the badger from other hungry animals.

Raising his arms to the sky, he prayed, thanking the spirit of the badger for allowing itself to be caught. Praising its bravery and willingness to sacrifice for a warrior of the people.

Then he turned and trotted away up the slope to his camp. At sunrise he would return to fulfill his quest.

Wounded Bear rubbed fingers into his tired eyes. It was long before sunrise, the darkness still heavy. He'd slept poorly, his anticipation keeping his mind as jumpy as drops of water on hot rocks. He threw off his red blanket and sat up, rubbing his face vigorously. Overhead, stars still glistened, white pinpoints of light against a background of midnight blue. Pulling himself to his feet, he gathered his few possessions and wrapped them in his blanket. Tucking the bundle under his arm, he weaved through the darkly silhouetted trees, feeling his way with his feet. The morning air felt cold against his face and hands, but his legs and chest were still warm from sleep, his buckskin clothing holding in the heat.

It only took a short time to reach the granite slab, but he did not approach the badger. Rituals had to be performed first. His eyes drifted over the broad valley below. A pale blue stain was growing on the eastern horizon, chasing away the stars. But the undulating plains were still cloaked in blackness, looking like a dark rumpled blanket thrown against the sky. Patches of charcoal clouds dotted the blue, unmoving in the windless heavens. All around him the world was still and quiet. He absorbed the peacefulness, letting it soothe his growing fears.

Turning, he walked southward around the lip of the granite ledge. The falls were only a whisper of sound at the badger's location, but as he got closer the whisper became a soft purr. Wounded Bear laid his blanket bundle beneath a tree and studied the waterfall. The meager trickle fell over a precipice fifty feet above and glided down between two granite walls to splash into a small mossy pool. Long before it reached the pool, however, the water had changed to a shower of drops.

He pulled his shirt over his head and tossed it toward his blanket, then unbraided his long black hair and shook it loose; it hung in waves down his back, covering his arms as he unfastened his moccasins and slipped off his pants.

Standing naked, the morning chill nipped at him. Goose bumps rose on his arms and legs. He stepped into the slate-colored pool.

He gasped as the near-freezing water swirled around his knees and drenched his body from above. Wading forward, deeper into the spray, he folded his arms over his breast and allowed the cold mist to encompass him, then closed his eyes to wait. Beneath the falls, the sound was softer, more subdued, like the feel of a cotton blanket rather than wool. His mind focused on the gentle resonance of nature's voice.

When at last his body adapted to the temperature, he felt numb, but whole and full. Kneeling, he caressed the jade mosses covering the stones in the bottom of the pool. They were as smooth and soft as rabbit fur. He patted them, murmuring praises for their beauty, then stood and backed out of the mist. Calm pervaded his soul.

When he had first stepped into the pool, the rippling water had been slate-colored, but now, as sunrise approached, the surface sparkled silver. He turned his back to the falls and looked eastward. The horizon was hidden, but a lavender hue lit the spaces between the pine branches.

Stepping out of the pool, Wounded Bear squeezed the excess moisture from his long hair and left it hanging free to dry in the breeze. But he didn't dress. Clothing was a shield. He had to be vulnerable before the spirits. He picked up his buckskins and blanket and clutched them to his breast. They were warm against his chilled skin as he carried them back to the granite slab and the badger. Gently he laid them in the tall grass and walked forward.

From twenty feet he could see the reflection of aspen leaves quaking darkly in the pool of blood that filled the badger's stomach. He stopped, his knees trembling. He swallowed and forced himself to breathe deeply, rhythmically. Fear filled him. Clenching his hands into fists, he stiffened his spine, trying to gain control.

The questions burst in upon him. What would the badger show him? Would he see the death of the Cheyenne? The destruction of everything he loved and cherished? Could he bear it if that was his answer? Would it be better not to know? What if he didn't look? The question made him ashamed. If he refused to face the pool of blood, then the badger would have given its life in vain. In his mind he could see the creature waddling from the tangle of vines and offering itself. He clamped his jaw tight and turned away.

Clutching his arms over his bare chest, he stared at a tall ponderosa pine that stood just at the edge of the granite slab. The tree was a giant, its trunk the width of two men standing side by side. His troubled eyes drifted up the pine, resting on the pointed top and the clouds drifting above. They were dark puffs, their edges tinged with the palest of lavenders. Tears welled in Wounded Bear's eyes. Clouds were free—floating wild and vulnerable. But he was trapped, caught in a world changing too fast for him to anticipate the future. Was there a future? A future for the Cheyenne? He was suddenly tortured by a wave of doubt . . . of cowardice. The word stuck in his throat. He bit his lower lip and flexed his fists.

From the top of the pine, a bluejay emerged, diving downward, hurling itself toward him; he watched it swoop to the lowest limb and cock its black-tufted head, fixing him with a single harsh eye. It cawed loudly and repeatedly, hopping to the very tip of the branch nearest him.

His breathing stopped.

He nodded and hoarsely responded, "Yes, brother. I hear you."

Bowing his head, he offered a prayer of thanks, turned quickly, and strode back to the badger, kneeling before the pool. The blood was beginning to turn black around the edges, coagulating throughout, but in the center a calm crimson pool remained. He cleared his mind of all thoughts and concentrated on the pool. After a few minutes, his stomach turned sour, a bitter acid rising in his throat to choke him. But he did not turn away.

Time passed slowly. The peaks behind him glowed red with sunrise, the warmth of the morning touching his bare skin. His breathing was deep and rhythmic, his tumultuous mind calm like the surface of the crimson pool.

As he watched, the blood stirred, washing lightly back and forth in time with his breathing. His heart pounded like a sacred drum in his ears, strong and sure. His blood was becoming one with that of the badger, pulsing in union, reflecting the rhythmic harmony of the universe. The birds had stopped singing, the whisper of the waterfall gone. The sky around him blazed red, enveloping both him and the badger in a silent womb of blood, an infinite timeless cavern of birth and death.

He stopped breathing and the pool stilled, then quivered suddenly, as if touched by a breeze, and an image began to form. Wounded Bear felt his fear rise powerfully again. Tears glided down his dark cheeks, tracing salty paths to drop from his chin. The face in the pool was crystal clear and unmistakable—and his.

Bands of rich dark blood stained his face in hideous patterns, already umber from age. Where the scalp had been ripped off, flies circled hungrily, periodically landing on the bare bone. His skull gleamed golden, reflecting some soft source of light. A campfire perhaps? And he heard the growling of a wolf in the background—snarls and human screams of pain. Had the wolves found his lifeless body? Were they chewing his flesh? But who screamed? He stared into his own eyes and saw life there. The man in the vision was not dead—*he* was not dead.

"No!" It was a deep-throated cry. He pushed frantically away from the badger, struggling to his feet to run wildly through the forest.

But he didn't go far. In a few seconds the shock of the horrifying image faded. He halted. The early morning breeze gusted at him, blowing his long, loose hair over his face. He stared at the ground through a web of silky black strands, his eyes fixed absently on the bed of pine needles. A hollowness was building in his chest, an emptiness so vast and terrible it engulfed his very soul.

He tipped his face to the sky and spread his arms wide. "Must it happen this way, Maheo?" he pleaded, a faint hope in his heart that the future might be altered some way.

To survive scalping and be torn apart by ravening wolves was to live a nightmare.

But no answer came. The animals of the forest were silent. He dropped his arms and turned, letting the truth sink in before he returned to the badger. His steps back were slow and heavy.

He knelt next to the creature that had given its life that he might see. Emotion rose to choke him as he touched the badger's side and tenderly stroked the soft fur.

"Thank you, brother," he murmured unsteadily. "I will learn to face it."

He stood and walked to the edge of the granite slab, leaving the badger to the beneficent will of the Great Mystery. The body would provide food for the other creatures of the forest, maintaining balance and harmony. He looked out over the valley. Below him, antelope charged across the plains, tumbling into draws like tan waves of water, only to surge up the opposite bank and rush away in winding fluid patterns. He sucked in a difficult breath. From his vantage, the antelope herd resembled a giant serpent slithering methodically between eroded sandstone pillars and patches of pine. He let his eyes drift, giving his soul time. On the northern horizon, clouds loomed dark against the turquoise sky. A storm was on the way. The distant roar of thunder hailed its coming.

Slowly his mind began to function again and he could think about the vision's message through his shock. Perhaps the future shown was symbolic, not literal; a sacrificing of self to the cause of the people's survival. Many spiritual leaders gave totally of themselves.

And the wolf's words came back, flooding his mind. "Soon, you will be called upon to sacrifice a great deal for the people . . . are you willing?"

And his own answer rumbled in his mouth: "Yes, grandfather."

· CHAPTER 4 ·

COLLEEN CRAWLED OUT OF THE BACK OF THE WAGON AND jumped down to the soft sand, bringing her flowered bonnet with her. As she tied it beneath her chin, her eyes drifted over the camp. People were rising. Laughter and the smell of bacon frying wafted on the breeze. The sun hung just below the horizon, but golden rays illuminated the eastern sky, giving a yellowish hue to the line of white canvas coverings on the wagons.

She stretched her arms over her head and yawned. Robert had arisen much earlier, leaving without a word. Tightness rose in her chest as she thought of him. Where was he? Perhaps she should apologize, just to regain a semblance of domestic bliss if nothing else. Silence was his way of punishing her; it isolated her, making her feel empty and alone—a very effective punishment—she hated it. In the past she'd often tried outlasting him, maintaining silence herself. It had never worked. He was more introverted than she, taking pleasure in his own internal companionship, but she desperately needed other people to talk to, to laugh with, to comfort or be comforted by.

She sighed and started walking through camp looking for him. She stopped to briefly chat with the other emigrant families, then continued her search. No one had seen him that morning. He'd probably gone off to do something by himself. He wasn't the sociable type unless socializing offered a gain in status or opportunity. And he tried to keep her isolated with him. In the three weeks they'd been on the trail, she'd met only a few of the other emigrants. He'd made it clear she was not to speak to people unless he introduced her to them first. She hated it. Why did she obey? She bit her lip, feeling guilty for such thoughts. Her mother had always taught her that a wife's duty was unquestioning loyalty to her husband. Not even in the privacy of her own thoughts was she supposed to think him less than perfect. Memories bubbled up. On the day before her wedding, she had said something less than complimentary about her husband-to-be and her mother had turned suddenly to stare at her. "Ye mustn't ever say a thing like that again," she had gently admonished, putting a meek white hand on Colleen's shoulder. "Bad thoughts multiply themselves. If ye think that one today, tomorrow ye'll have two, and the next day four and so on. It's not the way of happiness." But Colleen had never been as strong as her mother. The bad thoughts came no matter how she tried to suppress them.

As the sun rose the heat increased dramatically. She braided her long blond hair and tucked it up in her bonnet. Perspiration trickled beneath her arms, soaking her fresh green dress.

She reached the end of camp and was almost to Colonel Sawyers' private tent when she finally spied her husband. He stood outside the corral with one of the soldiers. Robert was such a huge man. Six feet tall, his chest was nearly twice the size of the average man's. He had full lips, a broad flat nose, and a slanting forehead. His brown hair haloed his head in tight, tiny curls.

The infantryman had captain's bars on his shoulders. Was this Douglas' commanding officer? What had he said the man's name was? She thought about it as she strode across the warming sands. Williford! that was it.

As she approached she saw the captain stoop and touch his finger to something on the ground. He shook his head, his brow furrowed, and said, "I've never seen anything like this." He pushed the blue cap back on his head and wiped sweat from his brow, then cast a brief speculative glance at the already searing sun.

"Pack of 'em?" Robert questioned, turning halfway around to look at Colleen.

Her presence interrupted the discussion. Robert sniffed and glared his irritation.

"Mornin'," she said politely.

"Mornin', ma'am," the captain responded congenially.

Williford was a medium-sized man, around five feet eight, she guessed, with piercing, wide-set gray eyes and brown hair. He had a thin, deeply tanned, triangular face and the look of a man who'd seen too much of life's pain and anguish. There was a hardened squint to his eyes.

Robert reluctantly provided introductions, a pouting tone in his voice. "Captain Williford, this is my wife, Colleen."

Williford touched the brim of his blue cap. "My pleasure, ma'am."

She curtsied, smiling. "No, mine, sir. I've heard much praise about you from your men," she lied. The only conversation she'd had with any of the soldiers had been with Douglas and he'd said little.

Williford gave her a subdued smile. "That's always good to hear, ma'am."

Robert stared aghast. He clenched his fists at his sides. "You been talking to Galvanized Yankees!" He spat. "Why, half the scum have already deserted this expedition. They're cowards! I don't want you—"

"Begging your pardon, Mr. Merrill." Williford's voice was cool, his gaze hard. "To date only three of the desertions have been former Confederates. The other nineteen men who've run away have been Union soldiers.'' The statement was uttered as a fact, not a challenge, but Robert misunderstood.

''Well,'' he scoffed indignantly, crimson rising in his cheeks, ''it's difficult to tell with your command, ain't it? I heard Sawyers say that most of your men were former Union soldiers captured by the South, put in prison camps, and then turned traitor! Taking an oath to fight for the Confederacy! And that's how they were captured in Mississippi, wearing *gray* uniforms!'' Robert's chin was thrust out and he was breathing heavy.

Colleen could feel the tension in the air. Her own blood raced, her heart pounding like a hammer in her chest. But she kept her silence, eyes downcast.

''Mister,'' Williford calmly responded, spreading his feet and folding his muscular arms over his chest, and glaring. ''Did you fight in the war?''

Robert shifted uncomfortably, his jaw quivering in anger. ''No, I was needed at home. But—''

''Then, I suggest you keep your own counsel. The men in my command have seen hard times. Some of 'em fought the last two years straight without a breather or even soles for their boots, worrying the entire time that their families might be starving . . . or worse. They'd not take kindly to your ignorant criticisms.'' He paused to take a deep breath and cock his head threateningly. The harsh look he fixed Robert with made Colleen quake. ''Nor do I,'' he finished, enunciating each word clearly.

Robert stammered, clearly unsettled by the captain's reference to his ignorance. ''Well, I—I don't—''

''Perhaps . . .'' Williford glanced at Colleen's anxious face and exhaled audibly. ''Perhaps, it would be better, sir, if we ended this discussion and returned to our former topic.'' He knelt and pointed to the ground again.

Colleen blinked her relief at the soldier. He gave her a wan smile in return and outlined one of the doglike prints in the sand—spreading his palm and comparing the size. The track was huge.

"Well." Robert cleared his throat and pulled his head straight. "What do you think it was?"

Williford didn't deign to look up, he just pointed. "See here and here? These tracks were all made by one animal."

"That cain't be! There must be a thousand tracks around the corral!"

"Uh-huh." Williford nodded, pulling his cap down to shield his eyes from the blistering sun. "Appears the beast trotted around the corral four or five times, then came to sit here, facing the wagons." He stared across the shimmering sands to the train.

Colleen followed his gaze. A soft thread of fear wound through her when she noticed his line of sight led to her wagon. Coincidence, she convinced herself.

"A coyote?" she asked timidly.

Williford shook his head and stood, propping his hands on his hips. "More likely a wolf, ma'am."

"A damned big wolf!" Robert whispered harshly.

"But." Colleen was confused. She shrugged her narrow shoulders. "I don't . . . don't understand. Why didn't the cattle spook? Surely they must have scented—"

"I don't know, ma'am," Williford responded. "Looks like the beast didn't bother 'em at all."

A gust of hot wind whistled over the dune, pounding them with stinging grains of sand. Colleen grabbed her bonnet and turned her face away.

"Well"—Williford looked down at the military camp—"I'd best be getting back to my own duties, folks. Will I see either of you at the dance tonight?"

"We'll be there, Captain," Robert answered coolly.

Colleen was lost. Dance? Then suddenly it occurred to her that it was the Fourth of July. Of course there would be a celebration. Happiness bubbled up and she smile brilliantly at Williford. People! She'd be able to mingle with the rest of the train! He returned the gesture, tipping his hat.

"If it wouldn't be an intrusion, ma'am," he asked humbly. "I'd take it real kindly if you'd save a dance for me? Being as how there aren't many women with this—"

Her cheeks dimpled. "I'd be honored, Captain."

"Thank you, ma'am." He bowed slightly.

Robert bristled, taking Colleen roughly by the arm before she had a chance to say good-bye to Williford and dragging her down the hill.

"Robert!" She stumbled to keep up with his pace. "That was rude! The captain was just being pol—"

"Hush!" he commanded. "I don't like that man and I certainly don't want him dancing with you! How dare he ask your permission rather than mine!" His green eyes flashed.

Anger flared in her breast, but she clamped her jaw and held the hot comment inside.

"Matter of fact," he continued, "I don't want you near anybody today! You hear me?"

"I hear, but—"

"You just get on back to the wagon and stay there. You got plenty to do getting our clothes ready for tonight. I want both of us to look like the royalty of this expedition, so lay out our best."

"All right."

He released her arm with a shove and walked forward, his long strides leaving her far behind. She halted, watching him swagger toward Sawyers' tent. She'd meant to apologize for hitting him in the face, but hadn't had the chance. And now she was glad of it. She didn't feel like apologizing anymore—if she ever had. Bracing herself against a gust of hot wind, she clutched the bonnet bow beneath her chin, feeling hurt and unhappy. Robert always managed to keep her heart raw. She closed her brown eyes for a moment, letting the sensations of wind and heat filter through her, steadying her emotions. Her green skirt flapped around her legs. He worked tirelessly to keep her spirit wounded . . . and she didn't understand why. What had she done to make him resent her so? The lack of a child was part of it, she was certain. He considered it a reflection on his masculinity. But she had tried. Not having a child hurt her too, yet he seemed oblivious to her feelings. Butterflies fluttered in her stomach. She let her gaze drift to the military camp.

Men were such strange, unfathomable creatures. Sometimes they could be tender and kind and moments later fly off the handle and reverse themselves completely. Women were more consistent, she thought, kinder.

But then, when it came right down to it, she had only meager experience. She'd been courted by two other men before Robert. Sweet memories came to mind. She'd loved Nathan Schott. He was a shy boy with wide blue eyes and strawberry blond hair. But her father had uttered the final painful judgment. "Ach, lass! The boy's poor as a church mouse! Ye'll not be marrying his kind!" And she'd been forbidden from seeing him again. Her heart had been broken. She'd been listless for months, eating barely enough to keep her alive. Perhaps that's why when Robert came along she'd been so solicitous and eager. She was hungry for companionship—from any man.

She sighed and started back for her wagon, words from the Bible ringing in her mind. "Wives submit yourselves unto your husbands as unto the Lord." She'd do as Robert instructed and lay out their best clothes. Maybe she'd have time to pray the rosary and ease the hurt in her soul.

She slowly trudged down the sandy hillside.

Sunset was turning the western sky lavender and orange when Robert climbed into the back of the wagon to dress. Colleen patiently handed him a gray ruffled silk shirt and black trousers. He took them without a word, not even looking at her.

"Did you get to talk with Colonel Sawyers?" she asked softly.

He preened silently in front of a small hand mirror, checking his bearded face.

"Did the men get all the wagons freed from the sand? Can we go on down the trail tomorrow?"

When she still received no answer, she stopped trying and folded her hands in her lap to wait for him to finish dressing. After a half hour he climbed out of the wagon, leaving her alone. The festivities weren't, it appeared, going to be very festive. The hollowness in her chest expanded. She wanted to be happy. Why wouldn't he let her?

She fumbled uncertainly with her dress for a few minutes, smoothing her hands over the fabric. Finally she whispered hotly, "I don't care! I'm going to have fun anyway!"

Slipping the sky blue organdie gown over her head, she fastened the pearl buttons and tightened the cream-colored satin sash around her waist. The thirty yards of ruffles, she hoped, hid the slightness of her bosom and accented her tiny eighteen-inch waist. She brushed her long hair over her head until it snapped, then pulled it away from her face and fastened it with a large golden clasp. The graceful swirls of the clasp shimmered against the background of blond curls.

Picking up the hand mirror, she gazed at her image. She was a tiny, fraily built woman, but her brown eyes were large and her upturned nose added a dash of interest, she thought. Bringing the mirror closer, she frowned. The creamy skin she had flaunted in New York was long gone. A rich brown had replaced it. She clucked her tongue and accepted the fate, then bit her lips to make them redder and splashed rose water on her wrists and behind her ears. Feeling daring, she added a dash between her breasts. The liquid felt cool against her perspiring flesh. The scent of roses filled the wagon.

The curtains were jerked back suddenly. She jumped as Robert's hostile face peered in. "Will you hurry!" he growled, his mouth pursed. "The fiddlers are setting up!"

"Oh!" she exclaimed frantically, then smoothed her gown one last time. Had she taken so long? She accepted his hand, allowing him to lift her out of the wagon.

Arm in arm they strolled across the sand to stand in front of the musicians. Three of the men were cavalry soldiers dressed in dusty blue uniforms. Colleen studied their perspiration-stained jackets. Rumor had it that Williford's men had been mustered out without even an extra pair of shoes, the war-depleted budget so low the Department of War could barely keep cavalry units in the saddle, let alone provide spare uniforms or equipment. Given these men's disheveled appearance, she believed it. The remaining two musicians were part of Sawyers' road-building crew. One carried a banjo, the other a mouth harp.

As they began tuning up, people crowded the broad expanse of sand, some clapping, some tapping their feet in time with the rhythm. Her heart leapt with joy at the smiling faces. Mostly, she figured, the celebration was not so much in honor of the great national holiday, but to thank the Lord for deliverance from the sand hills.

She glanced up at Robert who was stiff-faced, staring across the crowd to where Sawyers stood surrounded by people. He wanted to be there, she realized, but didn't want to take her along. He fidgeted.

She suppressed the anxiety welling in her chest and let her eyes drift. Across the circle she noticed Matthew Douglas talking with Captain Williford. Her moonlight inspection had been correct; he was handsome. The sturdy line of his clean-shaven jaw accented his straight patrician nose and his drooping mustache framed his full lips. Strong muscles bulged from beneath his blue sleeves. He looked oddly like one of the Greek statues her mother had shown her in picture books. His face was a perfect oval and his broad shoulders narrowed triangularly to a slim waist. She tried to remember the name of the statue he reminded her most of, the one with a hand propped on its hip? She couldn't recall, but smiled admiringly at the similarities.

Before she could change the expression on her face, he turned in her direction. His eyebrows raised and his mouth contorted into a questioning grin. His look suggested there was something more between them than just a night of talking. A flush of pink lit her cheeks. She jerked up her chin and turned away, taking up Robert's arm. Her husband didn't seem to notice. His eyes were still glued to Sawyers' circle of friends.

Merciful heavens! she chastised herself. *Did anyone see me staring at the lieutenant?* She let her eyes dart around. No—no one paid her the slightest attention, except Douglas, whose gaze was still fixed on her. Unconsciously she crushed and recrushed the silken fabric of Robert's shirt, her fingers nervous.

"Quit that, Colleen!" he whispered harshly, pulling his arm away. "You want to wrinkle it?"

"No." was all she could muster. She let her hand drop to her skirt and fiddled with the sky blue organdie instead.

"Excuse me, Mr. Merrill?" She whirled at the sound of Douglas' voice.

Robert turned arrogantly, straightening his shoulders at the Southern accent. "What do you want?" His tone was contemptuous, but Douglas didn't seem to notice. He met Robert's gaze evenly, bowing with considerable grace.

"Would it be a terrible indiscretion, sir, for me to request the honor of dancing with your lovely wife?" His deep voice was soft and apologetic, just the thing to assuage Robert's sense of indignation.

Douglas threw Colleen a fleeting glance of interest before straightening up.

Robert stared back across the circle to Sawyers, then responded quickly. "I reckon that'd be fine." He returned the bow, not quite as artfully.

"You are very kind, suh." Douglas smiled and offered Colleen his arm. She took it, heart beating in her throat as he led her out to the sandy dance floor. The fiddlers played a waltz.

Robert immediately fled to Sawyers' group, a broad smile on his face.

Douglas, she found, was remarkably graceful for such a tall man. He never once abused her small toes the way Robert did. And, more importantly, he was conscious of her smaller steps and adjusted his to match hers. That was an odd thing, she thought. Robert always forced her to stretch to match his longer steps. As a result, she always felt exhausted and awkward. Dancing with Douglas was like putting on a pair of comfortable old shoes.

Shyly she glanced up at him. It was disconcerting to find his blue eyes focused on her face, his mouth twisted into an insolent and suggestive grin. Butterflies raged in her stomach. She quickly looked away, swallowing to ease her constricted throat. With some dismay she noted that he was steering her away from the rest of the crowd to the far side of the gathering—away from Robert!

She jerked up her eyes to meet his. "Mr. Douglas . . . I . . . I really think that perhaps we should . . ." She stopped, and started again. "I don't feel, sir, that it is appropriate for you to take me so far from my husband."

"Why not?"

"I'm married, Lieutenant. That makes—"

He interrupted, his deep voice lilting like the music. "Yes, your marital status is quite the pity—for both of us."

"Sir!" She gasped, her mouth dropping open. She struggled in his arms, embarrassment seeping to her bones. "Release me!"

"Do stop wiggling so, Colleen," he ordered, amused. "You'll draw attention to us. You don't want people to stare, do you?"

"Oh, my! No . . ." she breathed, glancing quickly around to see if anyone was staring. "Mr. Douglas, you must never suggest—"

"Oh, but I must," he said quietly, his blue eyes dancing. "I'd never try and delude you into thinking I had manners. That would be a travesty."

"A tra—ves . . ." She thought hard, but could not recall ever having learned that word. She frowned. Was he trying to confuse her so she'd forget his unseemly aggressions? What was the worst insult a person could hurl at a southerner? she wondered. Ah, she knew. She stiffened her back and hissed, "Sir, you are a scalawag!"

He pulled his head back, raising his brows questioningly. "I . . . why," he sounded strangely pained. "I assure you, madam, that the thought of turning Republican has never once entered my mind. I swear it!" He disengaged his right hand and raised it as though taking an oath.

"I . . . you . . ." She was exasperated. She gritted her teeth and glared. "That's not what I meant, sir."

"No? Pray tell, what did you mean?"

The fiddle music stopped. Colleen hurriedly tried to get

away, but he refused to release her, obviously waiting for her response. She struggled only a moment before deciding it was no use, he had no intention of allowing her to escape. She glared up at him from beneath her lashes.

"I declare, Mr. Douglas!" She stamped a foot in irritation. "Must you be so rude?"

His eyes danced in merciless merriment. "I don't recall calling you a scalawag."

People laughed and whooped around them as children dodged between dancers, squealing joyously. Standing stationary, as they were, gave Colleen a chance to really feel his hand on her waist and clutching her palm tightly. He was indecently warm. Not only that, but his warmth felt pleasant—which made the situation all the more uncomfortable. She argued with her conscience, trying to decide whether she should allow herself to enjoy the sensation or continue to just grudgingly endure it. Taking a deep breath, she met his eyes and started to relax in his grip, opting for the former solution.

"Well, you are," she said insistently, tossing her blond hair over her shoulder.

"I'll accept that assessment only so long as you mean it in the sense of a wholesome blackguard—and *not* a Republican sympathizer. I could not endure the latter, Colleen."

"A blackguard," she granted.

He released her suddenly and offered a deep, graceful bow. "At your service, madam!"

The action caught her off guard and she laughed.

The musicians played another waltz. Douglas quickly took up her hands to lead the dance. She reluctantly went along.

"Tell me about Captain Williford?" she asked, changing the subject abruptly.

Douglas moaned. "What? You'd rather hear about that decent gentleman than my scandalous ways? I'm gravely disappointed."

"Oh, hush and tell me!"

"Well, if you insist," he agreed. "Captain George Williford, my good friend, and the former commander of the

9th Illinois Infantry. His company saw almost constant battle from Shiloh to the end of the war, when he was mustered out to recover from wounds and exhaustion. In April he was appointed by General Dodge to his current position. He is probably, my dear, the best damned commander in the Union Army.''

"You say that about a man who was your enemy only a few months ago?'' She studied Douglas. His impudent demeanor was gone, replaced by a seriousness that made him somehow exciting. His blue eyes shone with a sudden vulnerability, a softness.

"George Williford was never my enemy. We just fought on opposite sides, that's all.''

"Technically, he was your enemy.''

"Technicalities have never interested me, darling.'' His eyes took back their mocking insolent quality.

So intrigued was she by his change of character that she overlooked the impetuous personal term. What an enigma he was!

"Now, wouldn't you love to hear about me and my—uh—exploits? For example—''

"No,'' she lied, sighing audibly as though terribly bored. "In fact—''

"Well,'' he said quickly, "then let's talk about you. You're nineteen, from New York and of Irish descent. Is that correct?''

"Yes.'' She cocked her head. She didn't recall telling him her age. Had he been asking around? Despite the evening coolness, perspiration trickled down her sides. The blue fabric beneath her left palm was getting clammy, soaking Douglas' shirt. Aghast, she shifted her hand to a different location on his shoulder.

He smiled at her as though reading her uncomfortable thoughts, but his question didn't reflect it. "And your father mined for gold?''

"Yes.''

"Where?''

"He spent much of his time in California.''

"Long way from New York," he muttered observantly, his blue eyes searching her face.

"Yes, we didn't see much of him in the early days."

"And he made money, you said, so he must have been in on the early strikes of the late forties?"

"He left in 1849."

"Ah." He nodded knowingly. His voice took on an edge. "And when did he return to be a father for his daughter?"

She probed his eyes. Were her feelings about her father that clear on her face, or was he guessing? His eyes didn't tell her. "He returned when I was twelve."

"His strike lasted that long?"

"Well, no. He took up freighting for a time, when it was still profitable."

"Hmm, must have been lonely."

He pulled her closer, whirling her around in the dance. She dutifully followed, watching his face change again, become soft. And he was holding her differently, more . . . tenderly. There was a comforting assurance in the strength of his arms and she felt herself sinking deeper until her eyes were barely three inches from the brass buttons on his shirt. When she realized the scandalous fact of his physical proximity, she frantically tried to push away.

"I like you there just fine."

Her mouth dropped open and she vainly struggled, but his muscular arms guaranteed she went nowhere. She was shamefully speechless; hot blood rushed to her cheeks. So closely were they entwined that she could barely move her feet around his. But the position seemed to have little effect on his gracefulness. He looked quite accustomed to having women pasted to his bosom while waltzing. They finished the dance in silence, she casting looks of umbrage, he smiling politely in return.

When at last the musicians finished, he released her. She felt a wave of relief and tried to rush away, but he grabbed her hand and kissed it. Bowing deeply, he began a loud speech thanking her profusely for deigning to dance with a lonely soldier forced to endure the hardships of the wilder-

ness and who would undoubtedly be killed at the hands of
the red devils before they reached Montana Territory. He
spoke so loudly and sounded so humble that she was forced
to genteelly respond that it had been her pleasure.

His insolent smile mocked her chivalry as he led her back
to the company of her husband.

After that she was never off the dance floor. Every man
in camp seemed dying to spend time with her, and her husband was only too willing to let them. Every man, that is,
except Williford, who stood back encouraging his men to
dance before he took his turn. When once she had asked
Robert if he would dance with her, he had responded coolly,
"No, the colonel and I are talking about ways to get the Indians
off this land so it can be put to some good farming use."

"Oh" was all she could think to say. She'd immediately
accepted an invitation from a scraggly bowlegged private who
talked her ear off telling her the horrors of Alton prison camp.

"My," she responded. "And I thought that was one of
the better ones?"

"Well"—he'd cleared his throat and stared at the
ground—"none of 'em were any too good, ma'am."

She'd nodded understandingly.

Finally she was exhausted and breathless, her legs wobbly from exertion. She excused herself from the celebration
to stride out to the cool hills. Because it was the Fourth of
July, everyone was in camp at the celebration; no guards
had been posted. Not that that was unusual. Except around
the stock corral, guards were an oddity.

The darkness wrapped coolly around her, refreshing her.
A breeze was blowing. She lifted her long blond hair over
her head so the wind could dry the perspiration. The chilling sensation was delightful.

Finding a sandy knoll overlooking the camp, she sat down
and heaved a tired sigh. From her position she saw dancers
lining out for a reel. She laughed softly. The mere handful
of women had little effect on the number of couples lining
out. Men just tied scarves on their arms when it was their
turn to dance female parts and the celebration proceeded.

She let her eyes drift over the moonlit hills. Many of them were forty to sixty feet high and jutted up like huge anthills to prod the dark blue sky. The peacefulness soothed her, smoothing the ragged edges of her mind. She marveled at that. When they had first emerged from the tree-filled regions of her homeland into the vast desolation of the plains, she'd been frightened. The trees somehow provided both an internal and external shelter. The open plains left her feeling vulnerable and insecure. But the fear had vanished. Now she looked forward to waking in the morning and staring out across the hundred-mile vistas to the lavender sunrise. The vast unfenced deserts extended their hands to her, offering solace in their dusty arms.

She breathed deeply of the cool, fragrant air and stared out across the sands. A small white dot on a far hill caught her attention. It seemed to shine with an inner light, not a reflected one like the sand and brush. She studied it for a moment, then her eyes wandered back to camp. The fiddle music carried her away, lifting and tantalizing her to come back. She hummed to the tune. It was "When This Cruel War Is Over." Idly she wondered if the people were mouthing "suit of blue," as they did in the north, or "suit of gray" as they did in the south. She strained to listen, but couldn't tell. Not that it mattered. *The War was over!* She pulled up her knees and cradled them in her arms.

Yawning, her eyes drifted again. The white dot had grown larger. She sat up, adrenaline rushing through her. What was it? An animal? No, silly, it couldn't be. It seemed nothing more than a solid dot. She studied it more closely; it wasn't moving. The perception must result from the changing patterns of light cast by the partially cloud-covered moon. She took a deep breath and relaxed, watching the moon wobble through misty clouds. Odd shadows formed on the hills to crawl across camp and disappear in the light of the lanterns. Yes, just the light.

Her thoughts drifted to New York. Her mother always wore her long blond hair in a single braid that hung down her back. Colleen smiled at the memories. Marie Meara was a strong and warm lady. In all the lonely years of her father's absence, Mrs. Meara had never once cried out in pain or anger. She had borne the entire affair with a wan smile, saying only, "It's his way, child. I could no more hold him here than hold back the wind."

She looked for the dot again, but it was gone. *There!* she scolded herself. *I told you it was nothing!*

And what of her father? His stocky frame filled her thoughts, his face red and freckled, his hair the color of a carrot. Would she miss him? Her mind shifted from memory to memory, but no affection was evoked. The only emotion called forth was a dim anxiety. He had never held her in his arms, never comforted her tears. His only interest had been that she marry a wealthy man and give him many grandchildren. She recalled clearly the harsh glare thrown over bifocals when she'd expressed hesitancy about marrying Robert. "Yer lucky to be getting him, girl!" he'd bellowed. "Ye should be thanking the saints for the gift!"

Would she miss him? No, though something deep inside wished she could.

She gazed up at the silver moon, pushing the painful thoughts away. Feathery clouds drifted slowly through the starry sky, stroking the face of the moon like thin transparent fingers. Her tired muscles ached. She stretched backward, dropping her head over her shoulder—and froze.

The sight stunned her. She stopped breathing. Running would be no use, the wolf was only ten feet away. She would never reach camp before it pounced and tore her to pieces!

The beast moved closer, threading its way through the brush—black eyes fixed on her face. She started to gasp as it approached, trying to scream for help, but no cry escaped her constricted throat. She fought to rise to her feet, but her weak legs refused. Terror threatened to make her faint.

The beast came closer still, stalking to within two feet. She stared at it, unable to tear her gaze from the snow white face. The blackness of its eyes seemed to mesmerize. A strange euphoria filled her; she floated free on the cool night air, no longer rooted to the sands.

Suddenly her field of vision changed. She reeled, her mind whirling until she found herself sitting in a hide hut. Beside her sat a man, the man with long black braids. She gasped, recognizing the Indian in her dreams. His face was painted hideously, but it was him. Another man, old and gray, threw sweet-smelling grass onto the glowing coals of a fire. The young man cleansed himself in the smoke that rose. He hadn't noticed her before, but abruptly he shot a glance to where she sat, his dark eyes probing. Her heart stopped. She stared into the brown depths, feeling both elation and fear. Controlled strength exuded from his eyes, but she also sensed a worry. Strangely, she wanted to go to him, to comfort his fears.

Then she was back on the sands, the moonlight bright around her. The wolf padded close, laying its forepaw on her leg. She struggled desperately to scream, but was unable. Clutching frantically at the tight stays beneath her basque, she tried to release some of the pressure on her lungs, but her hands only fumbled aimlessly at the blue organdie.

The wolf's eyes glistened brilliantly. "Go back," a deep soothing voice commanded.

. . . And she was with the man again. This time he knelt on the ground in the gleaming rays of afternoon sunlight. His kinsmen thrust a knife into his right breast, slicing a flap of skin through which they slipped a wooden skewer. Colleen could smell the rich earthy scent of blood that streamed down his brown chest. Then, suddenly, she felt his pain. The skewer tormented her own breast. In agony she tore at her flesh, but her hands seemed far away. She gritted her teeth to hold back the cry that rose savagely to her lips. Horrified, she watched the old man come forward with the knife again. She cried out as the cold steel ripped the soft tissue of her left breast, cutting a wide flap. The flap was pried back with the blade and another skewer slid through her flesh. The ropes tied to the skewers were attached to a pole protruding from a strange hide lodge.

She watched the man in her dreams stagger to his feet, feeling herself rise with him. He threw himself back against the tension of the ropes, trying to rip the skewers from his flesh. A jagged, overpowering pain splashed through Colleen as she realized she was inside the man, or he inside her. They shared each other's agony. She could hear the rapid thumping of his heart in her own chest, could sense his thoughts. He threw himself—and her—back again and again, the pain stabbing inhumanly as *their breasts tore, searing their mind.* They writhed under the convulsions of excruciating pain. Finally, he heaved them back against the ropes with all his strength and the skewers ripped loose. Hot blood covered their chest, but they were free, soaring together toward the stars. Pain vanished and a world of light engulfed them. Colleen felt his mind seeking hers, trying to touch her. Then she was wrapped in his gentleness. The power of his soul swelled like an ocean around her, comforting, protecting. Together they danced a dance of light and dark. Life and death.

Then all was blackness.

When she awoke, she found herself inside her wagon—back on the sandy Nebraska plains. The worried faces of Robert, Matthew Douglas, and Dr. Tingley stared in at her.

She sat up, frantically searching each of their faces, her eyes wide and frightened. "Did you see it?" she asked hoarsely. Her throat was so bitterly dry. "Did you?"

"What?" Robert shouted derisively, glancing at the other men.

"The wolf!" she cried, extending both of her hands pleadingly.

Memories flooded back and she felt again the tearing pain in her breasts. She ripped the fabric over her chest, exposing her soft white flesh as she desperately sought the wounds. Robert lunged inside the wagon, grabbing her hands and forcing them painfully to the bed.

Matthew Douglas politely turned his back and walked away.

"Stop it, Colleen!" Robert shouted. His grip was deliberately brutal. She winced and whimpered, lying down.

"Damn it!" he cursed. "You just danced too goddamned

much, went out to the sands and fell asleep. We heard you scream and came arunning. That's all there was to it! You understand? There was no wolf!'' His voice was contemptuous.

Tears welled in her eyes as he released her. She slid farther back in the wagon, searching for her rosary. Dragging it across the bed, she clutched it to her breast and cried. Her chest heaved as she made the sign of the cross and stammered the Apostles' Creed, ''I—I believe in God—God the Father Almighty, creator of heaven and earth. I believe—in Jesus Christ, his only Son, our Lord . . .''

She curled on her side, continuing to whisper the prayers. The words came spontaneously as she drifted off to sleep—just as spontaneously as the vision of the crystal blue mountains and the man with long black braids.

Douglas stood uneasily in the gray light of predawn. He could see clearly the place Colleen had sat the night before. Her skirt had left a broad patch of smoothed sand. Tiny hand prints pressed into the sand, surrounded on one side by wolf tracks and on the other by the boot prints of those who had come when she screamed; his own tracks were there. He pushed his blue cap back and wiped his brow, then began rolling up his sleeves. The temperature had to be in the nineties, and the sun had yet to rise.

He looked out across the sands. He had risen early to see if he could track the beast and kill it, but as he gazed at the winding tracks over the hills, he knew that goal had been misdirected. He fumbled with the Springfield rifle slung over his shoulder. He'd rechecked the wolf's route four times. It led from where Colleen had sat to a small knoll a hundred yards away.

He shifted positions, putting his hands on his hips. The sand hills sprouted up around him, shadows clinging to their tan faces. In the background the horizon was shading pink, golden rays spiking up. He twisted one end of his brown mustache. He could check again—but he'd find the same thing. The wolf had come from nowhere and gone to nowhere. There was no beast to track. He took a deep breath, studying the wagon where she still slept. Gusts of cool early morning wind made the wagon's white top undulate. Anxiety rose, a hollowness filling his chest. Memories stirred. He shook his head and fingered the stock of his rifle. No, he reassured himself. There couldn't be a connection. The Cheyenne and the Big Horns were still three hundred and fifty miles away. Yet . . . a spirit wolf? Here?

He spread his long legs and stared out to the rising sun. A sliver of gold shimmered over the hills.

Now he knew the nature of the wolf, but he had no answers to his questions of "why?" He took off his cap and wiped his brow with his blue sleeve. His gut felt tight, as though his body understood something his mind refused to believe. More memories rumbled—winter stories told around blazing sagebrush fires. Old and bittersweet voices encircled him: *"Old Crazy Mule,"* Grandmother Beaver Tail whispered, *"he's one of them, one of the* Eehyoim. *He can kill or make people do things no matter how far away they are. I think we should whack him over the head and let the wolves have his evil carcass. His witchcraft is too strong. He's getting ideas about his power."* She'd lifted a fist and shaken it in the face of Grandfather Crescent Moon. He'd waved it off. *"He's not the one, you foolish old woman."* He lowered his frail voice and leaned around the fire to whisper. *"It's Broken Star. He's the one. His soul flies everywhere. Or sometimes he changes himself into animals and stalks his enemies. He murdered two Shoshoni last week. I heard about it . . ."*

Matthew massaged his forehead. Behind his eyes, a headache was building, making him sick to his stomach. Spirit power had no bounds. A true Eehyoim could travel through space faster than the wind. And he rode time like an eagle, soaring here and there, wherever he wanted—whenever he wanted.

A prickle like tiny teeth eating him from the inside out stung his chest. He exhaled heavily and strode back to the train. The wagons would be ready to roll soon.

· CHAPTER 5 ·

THE SUN DANCE WAS BEGINNING.

Box Elder stood beside the sacred fire in the Lone Tipi. He stood over the flames, his sightless eyes remembering how the orange flickers looked. Fragments of the eighteen Sun Dances he had participated in drifted through his mind. He bent down to fill his hand with cedar. His braids hung like gray ropes over his white beaded shirt. He wiped the sweat from his long hooked nose and sighed as he threw the cedar on the flames. The blaze was smothered and smoke filled the interior of the tipi, the rich tangy scent enveloping him.

He picked up his buffalo robe from its place by the doorway and wrapped it around his shoulders. Crouching over the smoldering coals, he made a tent of his robe to capture the purifying smoke. The power of the Great Mystery filled him as he inhaled the sweet fragrance. He allowed himself the indulgence of basking a few moments longer—of feeling the presence of eternity in his soul—then straightened up and hobbled to the southeast point of the tipi. Moving slowly to each of the cardinal directions, he came back to the center and stood still—absolutely still. The peace of the Great Mystery flowed into him, stroking his soul like a huge gentle hand. He heaved a sigh of contentment and threw back the lodge flap to emerge into the subdued light of the late afternoon. He walked a circle around the camp, his blind steps slow and easy, toes feeling a path through the sage.

"The Pledger has taken pity on you!" he called. "He has given his wife to the Above Powers, to the Below Powers, and to the other *maiyun* he has called upon!"

When he reached the Lone Tipi again, he spread his arms to the reverent, excited faces of the villagers, smiling broadly as he returned to the scented interior of the lodge and closed the flap. Soon he would call the dancers.

Wounded Bear waited anxiously at the outskirts of the village. There were many warriors gathered to participate in the dance, both Cheyenne and Sioux. But his medicine lodge would contain only four. He and these other young men sat alone and quiet in a grove of aspen trees. They wore their finest clothing. He touched his soft doeskin shirt. Across his chest, red, blue, and yellow beads formed a brilliant starburst. A single red bead was tied to the end of each fringe lining his sleeves and pants.

He let his eyes drift over the other dancers. Red Hawk, Willow, and Running Elk had their eyes downcast, focused absently on the long spears of green grass that spread out like a soft blanket through the trees. Running Elk plucked a blade and put it in his mouth, chewing slowly. Each man was nervous, knowing what to expect, but not knowing what it would feel like. Only Willow had danced the Sun Dance before. He wore the scars on his chest proudly; they were a badge of courage, a symbol of his faithfulness and dedication to the Old Ways. Yet even he showed signs of anxiety. He fiddled with his sleeve fringes; starting at his shoulders and moving down his arm, he tugged each strand of buckskin individually.

"Sometimes," Willow whispered, "the ancestor spirits come to the dances."

Red Hawk's eyes widened. "What do they do?"

"They sit in the medicine lodge and make strange animal sounds in your ears. They make the sounds so often that you think you've become the animal and you start making the sounds yourself."

"And what happens?"

"Sometimes nothing. Other times the dancer never again thinks he's a man. He lives his whole life as an animal. His family has to treat him like a beast."

"H-How?" Red Hawk's voice faltered, fear plain on his face.

"They feed him only raw meat and make him sleep outside even in the winter."

"But—but he has great spirit power?"

"Oh, yes."

Wounded Bear looked askance at Willow. The story was colorful, but he'd never heard anything like it before. He strongly suspected Willow made it up on the spot to scare Red Hawk, the youngest dancer.

"That must be what happened to you," he commented dryly.

"How's that?"

"You're still a beast. Your wife says—"

Willow jumped on top of him, laughing. They wrestled in the grass for a few seconds, seeing who could stay on top the longest. Willow won. Wounded Bear gave up.

"So it's not true?" Red Hawk asked hopefully, brows lowered at the knowledge he'd been taken in.

"I didn't say . . ."

Wounded Bear gave him a disgusted look.

"Well, maybe not completely," Willow said.

Time seemed to drag. Wounded Bear let his gaze drift upward to the changing sky. Sunset smudged the clouds a dark purplish gray. Through patches of quaking aspen leaves, he could see a golden eagle circling. The giant bird glided on the wind currents, its wings wobbling to maintain balance in the erratic gusts.

"It won't be long now," Willow assured.

Each dancer nodded, shifting positions to sit straighter. Wounded Bear's heart pounded thunderously, blood rushing through his veins. He glanced at Red Hawk. The sixteen-year-old sat rigid, the vein in his neck throbbing a dark blue. Perhaps Red Hawk was even more frightened than he? A bare smile crossed his lips. The thought made him feel better, bolstering his courage.

The singing was soft at first, wafting like a meadow lark's trill on the wind, but then it grew stronger. Box Elder was calling them, his aged voice lilting and melodious.

"Come in, you young men," he sang. "Bring the sacred drum to the Lone Tipi."

Anxiously the dancers got to their feet and formed a line. Willow led the group, Wounded Bear bringing up the rear. They walked forward through the center of the village. People were gathered in front of the lodges, smiling and whispering to one another as the dancers ambled by. Children hugged their parents' legs and pointed excitedly. Through the corner of his eye, Wounded Bear saw his brother, Little Deer, and family standing tall and proud. His three-year-old nephew, Black Bird, bounced up and down as his uncle passed, a hand over his mouth to cover his giggle. Little Deer wasn't a believer, but he abided by the tradition in deference to his brother, nodding his respect as Wounded Bear passed. Yellow Leaf stood at the end of the line of people, head high, long black hair blowing. Her heart-shaped mouth was curled into a soft smile. In the grove behind her, cottonwood leaves rustled. The shoulders of her doeskin dress were intricately beaded, the red flowers against the yellow background beautiful. She was one of the finest artists in the tribe. He lifted his head to smile at her as he passed. She nodded her approval, watching him with gentle eyes. A glow warmed him. His decision to dance was good—he felt its rightness in his soul. He would renew the people, restore them to the path of harmony and beauty taught by the Old Ones. Then the buffalo would return and hunger would vanish. Their lives would be peaceful again.

The Lone Tipi sprouted at the edge of the village, its hide covering the color of a newborn elk calf. He bowed his head as they approached, fear and excitement mixing to form a sweet brew in his mind. Willow led them into the lodge.

As Wounded Bear entered, the darkness disoriented him. Blinking, he followed Red Hawk around the central fire and to the rear where they sat side by side. Only the glow of the fire and the embers in the sacred pipe lit the interior. He breathed deeply of the cedar-scented air, cleansing his lungs and preparing for the next four days.

Outside an awesome stillness descended. Only the muffled sounds of children disturbed the silence. Wounded Bear blinked into the darkness and touched the eagle-bone whistle around his neck. It had absorbed the warmth of his chest and felt comforting in his cool fingers. Soon he would put it to his lips and make the eagle cry echo through the heavens, telling the spirits and the Great Mystery of his pledge to renew the people.

Box Elder's footsteps could be heard outside. He shuffled around the Lone Tipi, then pulled the sides of the lodge back to reveal the dancers to the darkening heavens. Stars dotted the black sky. In the increasing breeze, the lodge flaps fluttered, slapping softly at the pine poles.

Wounded Bear stared out across camp. People sat quietly in the grass around the Lone Tipi, their faces reverent, waiting. The drumming began, faintly at first, then increased in intensity to echo from the surrounding mountains. He let his spirit sway with the rhythm, bending his knees. Touching the whistle to his lips, he blew softly, the shrill blasts chiming with the cadence of the singing and drums. He closed his eyes. The icy pit left by the vision in the pool of darkening badger blood had faded from his mind, hope filling the space. Hope that his people would live, that the wagon train would be stopped.

He sang the wolf songs four times, stopping after each recitation to feel the cool night breeze brush across his hot

skin. The starlight seeped inside him, brightening his spirit
and sending the snow white face of his spirit helper to him.
Throughout the first night, the wolf's face returned again
and again, nodding its furred nose and telling him the people had forgotten the prophecies of Sweet Medicine. They
must be made to remember if they were to survive.
Wounded Bear prayed to the wolf, promising he would make
them see, would not let them fall into the fatal trap Sweet
Medicine had foreseen.

The scents of lush vegetation drifted on the wind, encir-
cling him. He breathed deeply of the fragrant air.

Finally the dancers filed out of the Lone Tipi. At sunrise
the next morning they would enter the Medicine Lodge and
be painted. Wounded Bear would not eat, drink, or sleep
for the next four days; he had to be pure for the final dance
around the pole, had to purge his soul of all wrong thoughts.
Ecstasy loomed on the horizon for those who sought ear-
nestly.

On the fourth day of the Sun Dance, Wounded Bear's
senses awakened. His vision seemed clearer, his hearing
more sensitive. His fingers traced the beads on his moccasins. The colors jumped out at him, flashing brightly before
his eyes. Untying the laces, he removed the moccasins and
laid them aside. He would not need them for the rest of the
Sun Dance. The cool air was good on his bare feet. Then
he turned his attention to the Medicine Lodge, counting
each pole, letting his brown eyes absorb the infinitely de-
tailed patterns carved into the wood by worms. The patterns
held a message of life and death that he'd never understood
before. All things left their mark, some more intricate and
beautiful than others. He prayed his would be as glorious
as the worms'.

The scents of men, cedar, and sage entwined inside the
lodge to form an intoxicating fragrance. It was the odor of
devotion and prayer. He filled his lungs as he watched the
Painters spread robes in the form of a crescent moon on the
floor. They outlined the man-power design on the ground

and covered it with the sacred white sage, then they faded back, leaving a way clear for him. He stepped lightly into the center of the bed of sage, feeling it prickle against his feet. The pale green leaves were cool.

The priest threw sweet grass on the burning coals, and Wounded Bear knelt to bathe in the blessed smoke. He rubbed it into his arms, legs, and chest, then nostrils, eyes, and ears; the sweet tangy fragrance permeated his soul, purifying him. He felt light, his mind floating over the flames, drifting upward with the sacred smoke toward the hole in the top.

Suddenly his mood changed. His consciousness was jerked down to earth. He looked carefully around, peering into the warm darkness, searching. But for what? Some *thing* demanded his attention. He looked to his right. It was there! He knew it, though his eyes perceived nothing. His heart felt the presence. Then, just as suddenly as it had come, it vanished, gone like a wisp of smoke in the wind.

He shook his head and blinked wearily. A fragment of a vision? Maybe. He would wait. If the Great Mystery wanted him to see it fully, it would return.

The Painters moved slowly to slip a blade of sacred grass in his hair. He bowed his head. The last moments of the Sun Dance were nearing; joy and fear welled in his breast. His eyes cleared. He wanted to get to the pole.

Box Elder walked in front of him, singing the final songs of the dance, his aged voice rising strong and sweet. The glare of harsh sunlight burned his eyes, sending stabs of pain through his head. He squinted, allowing the organs to adjust after the long days inside the lodge. The pole stood before him—a wealth of relief flooded his veins.

The entire village gathered around the Medicine Lodge, faces somber and anxious. They wore their finest clothing for this last moment. Bright blue and yellow beads shimmered in the sun. Yellow Leaf sat silent in the midst of a group of children, watching.

Wounded Bear knelt down and bowed his head, closing

his eyes. The priest came forward with the bone-handled knife and thrust it into his right breast, cutting a flap of skin. He winced from the sharp thrust of pain, but no sound came from his lips. They passed the wooden skewer through the flap and lowered the knife toward his left breast.

He jerked his eyes open. The awareness struck him like a bony fist. The vision had returned. He searched the grounds in front of the Medicine Lodge for the presence, but could not find it. But as the priest punctured his left breast, he knew. The presence had come to reside inside him. He probed the other soul. It was a woman! The Great Mystery had sent her to share his quest. But she was bitterly frightened. Her soul cried out to him for comfort and he soothed her, telling her it was all right, that the pain was good. The agony renewed the people.

He staggered to his feet, blood streaming down his chest in bright red bands. He held the woman close and could hear her breathing, sense her pain and terror.

"Shhhh," he whispered to her. "You will see. Together we will fly to the stars." A contented smile graced his lips as he threw himself hard against the tension of the pole. The flesh of his chest tore under the strain. The pain helped him see more clearly; he repeated the process over and over and over. The agony seared his mind like a sharp burning knife. He tried to speak to the woman, but she could not hear. Her fear prevented her from knowing him fully—but that was all right. Soon the pain would end and they could talk.

He mustered all of his strength and jolted his body against the pole. The skewers ripped loose and he was free, soaring to Seyan, the Land of the Dead. He stroked the woman's soul, searching her consciousness until her fear subsided and they could merge. Their souls entwined and danced as the ancestors pulled them upward, away from the earth.

Wounded Bear lay prostrate in the late afternoon sun. The soil was warm beneath his bare back, the wind fragrant and cool over his face. When he breathed, he felt the essence of the world flowing through him, in and out with the motion of his lungs. Beneath his half-closed eyes, his lips glistened in a smile.

"Are you all right, brother?" Little Deer questioned tenderly, bracing his hands beneath Wounded Bear's body and lifting his head to his lap.

"I have seen Seyan," he rasped, his voice barely audible. His lips were dry and cracked, the taste of blood in his mouth.

Little Deer leaned closer, face taut with worry. "Say again, brother. I couldn't hear."

Wounded Bear smiled and blinked tiredly as he met Little Deer's soft eyes. "Seyan, brother. The ancestors told me . . . told me . . ." Sleep was overpowering him. He fought to stay awake.

Little Deer patted him on the shoulder and nodded. "You must sleep."

"No!" Wounded Bear raised a trembling hand. His eyes fluttered open and closed. He saw a woman's beaded skirt flapping in the wind behind Little Deer. A woman? "They told me that . . . that our people will live. The white woman . . . will help. Will . . ."

In the back of his exhausted mind, he heard Yellow Leaf's sweet voice. "White woman?" she asked. "Who does he mean?"

"I don't know," Little Deer said, then leaned down and cooed soft reassurances in his brother's ear. But Wounded Bear's attention wavered; the days of fasting and praying had drained his strength. He could no longer battle sleep. He felt himself being drawn upward, floating over his body.

His soul was free—free at last.

· CHAPTER 6 ·

MATTHEW DOUGLAS SAT ALONE IN HIS TENT, EYES FO-
cused on the dingy white canvas over his head. The wind
howled and tugged at his shelter, buffeting the thin walls.
Methodically he sorted through the events of the past two
weeks. There was a pattern; he could sense it just beyond
his grasp. He clenched his fists as he struggled with the
puzzle.

He stood and walked to the coffeepot, pouring his tin cup
full again. The liquid was cold, stone cold, the pot having
been made hours before, but he didn't notice. He sipped
absently at the stale brew, his mind locked into a round of
question and answer. Why would a spirit helper come to
Colleen Merrill? Because she was somehow tied to the Indian spiritual world. How could she be tied? She'd never
been out of New York, never even met an Indian. Perhaps
her father had established a relationship when in the West?
Answer: unknown. And the round began over again.

He set the cup on the dirt floor, then stretched out and
shoved his bedroll beneath his head. Spirit helpers were

difficult to obtain, yet this frail little woman from New York had one taunting her—much to her dismay. His face wrinkled in seriousness remembering her terror after the appearance of the wolf. He'd wanted to go to her the following day, to hold her protectively and tell her not to be frightened, that the spirit creature meant her no harm—but he couldn't do that. He shook his head, squeezing his eyes shut. She was a virtual stranger—and a Catholic. She'd never understand what it meant to have such a creature at her side. More than likely she'd consider the helper a "demon" sent by Satan to torment her, rather than an agent of God.

For an instant, his heart seemed to stop beating. Maybe . . . An *Eehyoim*? Broken Star's voice rasped wickedly in his memories. Could the medicine elder have touched the patterns of time and woven his and Colleen's strands of destiny together. *Why?* Old hatred?

Through gritted teeth, Matthew whispered, "No. No!" He slammed a fist into the ground and squeezed his eyes closed. "Grandfather, no, *please*. Haven't I paid enough? Let me go . . . let me go."

He rolled to his right side. Tan soil clung to his blue uniform. For the first time in years he allowed his mind to drift past the barriers he'd painstakingly erected to a time twelve years before. The pain caught him off guard, the memories like a blunt blow to the stomach. His wife, her face pale and twisted in pain, peered up at him—and he could barely stand it.

"You'll see her again," he softly promised himself, trying to calm the roiling in his gut.

Yes, he'd walk the pathway of stars and meet her in the afterworld. He brought up a hand to touch the scars over his breasts. He could still feel the agony of the struggle against the pole and the ecstasy of breaking free. He knew about Seyan. He'd been there.

He deliberately forced his thoughts back to Colleen. She'd told him she was having nightmares, but refused to elaborate. He impatiently scooped a handful of dirt and let it trickle through his fingers. If the wolf was a spirit helper and not one of the *Eehyoim*, perhaps Matthew had nothing to do with Colleen's mystical experiences. Or, perhaps their fates had been tied for reasons other than the hatred of a bitter old man. Undoubtedly the dreams were the wolf's method of communication, but Colleen was too frightened to understand. If he could just find a way of getting her to tell him the details, he could interpret for her. And then maybe the pattern would be revealed.

. . . And maybe I'll be able to tell what games the spirit world is playing with our lives.

An alarm rang frantically inside of him, as though his soul was shouting, "Go back! Get out of the West!" But he couldn't go back. He'd tried running away from the northern plains and had managed to succeed until a few months ago. But when the recruiters came to Alton prison camp saying any man who would swear an oath of loyalty to the Union and agree to frontier duty would be freed, he'd jumped at the chance. Avoiding starvation and disease appeared wise. And the possibility that he'd be returned to Dakota Territory seemed so small. It wasn't until after he'd signed on that the army found out he'd lived in the west and commissioned him as a scout.

. . . the strands of destiny.

He had to know. But would Colleen talk to him, trust him? He was a stranger. A wave of futility and anger washed over him.

Well, she'd need a friend sometime. Perhaps he could arrange to be there. Silently he offered a prayer to the wolf.

The rapid clopping of hooves outside camp disturbed his thoughts. With Williford and the other upper echelon officers in meetings with Sawyers, he was in charge of military operations. He got to his feet and strode outside into the bright glare of midday. The temperature was well over a hundred and still rising. Even the normally turquoise sky had been seared a pale blue. Douglas shielded his eyes to watch the rider approach. Though it was Sunday and Sawyers insisted on a day of rest, soldiers were still assigned duty.

Private Will Lacey dismounted and ground reined his

horse, saluting stiffly. Matthew gave him a lazy response. A sheen of sweat and windblown dirt streaked Lacey's young face.

"What is it, Lacey?" He propped his hands on his hips.

"Fresh Indian sign, sir." He pointed northwest toward the river they'd been following for days. The water flowed through a winding canyon eighty to a hundred feet deep. Scrub pines, cottonwoods, and aspens dotted the banks. "About two miles up yonder."

"War party?"

The boy raised his brows uncertainly. "I—well, sir—I guess I don't know how to tell. There was maybe five or six ponies in the—"

"Hunting party," Matthew affirmed. Almost none of the men in the escort had been west of the Mississippi. As a result the only thing they knew about the tribes of the plains was what they'd read in the papers. "How recent?"

Lacey ran a dirty hand through his brown hair, pushing it off his forehead. "We didn't see 'em, but from the sign I'd say they was up and about this morning."

"Just fresh tracks or something else?"

"Found an antelope carcass. They musta killed it yesterday, but there was still fresh carving on the haunches, like they'd had it for breakfast this morning."

"Coyotes hadn't been at it?"

Lacey shook his head a definite "no."

Matthew nodded. In this part of the world coyotes and wolves were experts at locating downed animals. If they hadn't gnawed the carcass it was because somebody'd been close enough to keep them off. He slapped a hand on the boy's shoulder. "Good work. I'll let the captain know when he gets out of his meeting."

"Yes, sir." He saluted again.

Douglas returned it halfheartedly, hating military protocol, and grunted. "Dismissed."

Lacey pivoted crisply and strode back to his sorrel. Taking up the reins, he mounted and wheeled away, heading back to the dusty plains.

Douglas frowned, smoothing his mustache. A hunting party that close? Didn't seem right. They'd have seen the train's dust during the day and dozens of fires at night. The tribes weren't on the best of terms with the U.S. government after the Sand Creek Massacre only eight months before. A small hunting party would be keeping its distance.

He surveyed the trees along the river and let his mind wander. Maybe it wasn't a hunting party. Scouts? He ground his teeth and folded his arms over his chest. The hot wind blew strands of dark hair into his eyes. Which tribes would want to scout the train? And for what purpose? The days of caging handouts from the military were gone. Indian-White relations had undergone too much trauma in recent years with too many broken promises. Neither side trusted the other.

He rolled up his sleeves and unbuttoned the top three buttons of his blue shirt. It wasn't particularly professional for an officer, but it *was* cool. Dark hair sprouted from the open vee. He put a hand to his chin and rubbed gently. Too bad Lacey didn't get a look at the warriors. He might have been able to identify which tribe they belonged to.

He dropped his hand to his side as anxiety built in his chest. His eyes scanned the high points, seeking the warriors.

The question came unbidden: They were too far east for the Cheyenne . . . weren't they?

Matthew strolled across the starlit sands, his rifle slung over his shoulder. The news of the Indian scouting party had left him uneasy and unable to sleep. Even though he wasn't assigned guard duty, it made him feel better to walk the perimeters of the camp—especially since only one other guard was out, and he was stationed by the stock. Sighing, he gazed up to the moonless sky, studying the constellations. The Big Dipper hung low over the horizon, tipped to pour its contents down onto the world below. The sandstone buttes beneath glowed darkly, looking like ebony blocks scattered across the flat plains.

Shoving one hand into his pants pocket, he continued around the camp, eyes vigilantly scanning the wagons and the sands. They were entering Sioux territory, a thought that made his gut roil. Raids on the train for horses were not far distant and Sawyers' lax security made matters worse. When the Sioux arrived and found only one man guarding the corral, they were sure to kill him, then waltz away with the stock, whooping their triumph over white ineptitude. Williford had tried repeatedly to point out this fact, but Sawyers had insisted the dangers were minimal so far east. That's why the wagons were rarely circled at night and few guards were posted. And James Sawyers was the leader of the expedition. Williford's orders had merely said he was to accompany the train and provide military support—the captain was not to presume any authority over the civilian road-building crew, since he had none. Though the expedition had been funded by Congress, it was still a civilian operation designed to build a road from Sioux City to the newly discovered goldfields of Montana Territory.

Douglas chuckled to himself as he walked, shaking his head in dismay.

"What fool," he whispered, "could possibly think of building a new road through the heart of the last buffalo grounds?"

The regional tribes were certain to object. The roads drove away the game and brought white settlers, both of which made Indian existence more precarious. The tribes would have no choice but to use every means at their disposal to stop such a road. First they'd try talking—then they'd kill to protect their hunting grounds.

Just after he left Texas to head east and volunteer his services to the Confederacy, he'd heard that the Bent brothers, George and Charley, had taken to the warpath with their half brothers the Cheyenne. He'd never met the Bents, but they were well known in all Cheyenne camps. Their father, William Bent, had come to the Arkansas River and built a trading post, later marrying the Cheyenne maiden, Owl Woman, and after she died, marrying her sister, Yellow Woman. In all, the Bents had had three sons and two daughters. And, though they lived most of the time with their mother's people, George and Charley had been educated in

St. Louis. As a result, they knew both the red and white worlds. Their choice to fight on the side of their mother's people had been a blow to many of their white friends.

"Can't blame 'em," Douglas whispered to the cool night wind.

From what he'd heard, George had been wounded at the Sand Creek Massacre and Charley had been saved only because Old Medicine Calf Beckwourth had concealed him in a wagon with a wounded army officer. The soldiers had wanted to kill all the half-breeds on "principle."

Douglas stopped, staring out across the undulating starlit hills. He squinted his eyes, picking up movement. Quickly and quietly he unslung his rifle and knelt down, bracing the gun against his shoulder. But his caution was unwarranted. A coyote climbed to the top of a hill and yipped a song to the heavens. He smiled at the beautiful serenade, then stood and proceeded on his way.

As he came close to the Merrill wagon, he heard soft muffled cries. He frowned and halted his steps, staring down from a hillock fifty feet away. Nightmares again? He clamped his jaw tight, grinding his teeth. There was nothing he could do. Hushed voices wafted out to him.

"Damn it, Colleen!" Merrill whispered. "Wake up! Wake up!"

"Hmm," her soft sleepy voice called.

"Get up! I can't get any sleep with you carrying on like this!"

"Oh! I . . . I'm sorry. I didn't know . . ."

"Go take a walk or something!"

"All right," she murmured.

Douglas held his breath. Maybe the wolf had heard after all? He waited, folding his arms and spreading his legs.

At last she stepped out of the wagon, pulling a white crocheted shawl snug around her green cotton dress and carrying a book in one hand. Her brow was knit in bewilderment. She spotted him almost immediately, a weak smile replacing the look of confusion. He saluted and smiled back. She walked slowly toward him, yawning.

"Rather late for an evening stroll, don't you think, Mrs. Merrill?"

Her eyes strayed to the darkness. "Nightmares, I'm afraid, Mr. Douglas." A shiver played over her body.

"Here," he said, waving a hand to a nearby windblown hillock. "Come and sit down." He led the way to the smooth sandstone platform, out of hearing range of the wagons. In the daytime the sandstone was ochre, but in the starlight it shone a dull gray.

Douglas sat and patted the flat stone beside him, indicating she should sit too. Smiling awkwardly, she complied and heaved a tired sigh.

For a few moments they sat in silence, staring up at the star-pitted black bowl over their heads. He fidgeted. Having her close and alone made him want to reach out and cradle her in his arms, but he suppressed the urge, realizing she'd feel obliged to leave if he tried.

"Nightmares?" he questioned softly, his voice deep. "About what?"

She shrugged, a faraway look stealing across her face. "Odd things." She hesitated, glancing at him with pain in her eyes. She clutched the book to her breast. "I . . . I'm sure you wouldn't find it very interesting."

"Try me."

She stared absently at her bare feet. He stared too, noting the small broken blisters; they were in the process of forming calluses. He nodded to himself. The feet of a woman who walks hundreds of miles across country. Delicate feet, torn by the sands and heat of the prairies.

"It's a . . ." She swallowed, not meeting his eyes. "A dream I've had before."

"About the wolf?" he guessed, leaning back against the gritty sandstone.

She looked up suddenly, searching his face. "No. No—a badger."

His muscles went rigid, memories from the past welling up like a tidal wave. He quelled his response, forcing his voice to remain calm and intimate.

"And?"

"A face," she said, strain evident in the tone. She pulled her shawl tighter around her throat and stared out across the sands.

He shifted, moving closer, but stopped when her shoulders tightened. "Whose face?"

"I . . . I don't know. A warrior." Her eyes widened and drifted to the northwest, a thoughtful expression on her smooth face.

He followed her gaze, seeing in his mind the dark blue choppy peaks of the Big Horns. Tender emotions haunted his memories. He glanced back to Colleen. Her breathing had become erratic, fearful.

"Don't worry," he whispered conspiratorially, patting the pistol at his side. "I'll shoot him if he comes looking for you."

She gave him a tortured smile, closing her eyes and propping her chin on her knees. The black book lay alone at her side. He could see now that it was a Bible.

"May I?" He reached for the holy text.

She nodded.

A golden ribbon marked a passage in the book of Matthew. Gently he opened it to the ribbon and lifted the book close to his eyes. In the starlight it took time to make out the words.

"Which passage were you reading?"

"Chapter seven, verse fifteen," she replied nervously.

He squinted at the dim words, reading them haltingly. " 'Beware—of—false prophets—who—come to you in—sheep's clothing—but in—inwardly they are—ravening wolves.' " He closed the book and gently laid it down beside her.

"Seems to me," he said lazily, "the wolf you saw wasn't making no pretenses."

"But . . . ." She turned to face him, then quickly crossed herself and mumbled something under her breath. "Saints preserve us! Don't you think that means the beast was a false prophet sent to deceive me? I mean—even—even if it wasn't hiding behind a disguise."

"No, guess I don't."

She blinked and started to say something, then thought

better of it and kept silent, but her pleading expression stayed. He met her gaze evenly.

He broke the silence, casting his gaze heavenward. "Did it try and lead you astray?"

"Yes! It . . ." she blurted, then stopped, suddenly fearful of telling him the rest. She pulled her white shawl over her chest and stared uncomfortably at her hands.

"It did?" he mused, giving her a skeptical grin.

"Well," she clarified tersely, backing off her former statement. "I guess, Lieutenant, that I . . . don't know for sure."

He smiled. The tone in her voice was heating up, telling him her fears were fading.

"Did it tell you Jesus wasn't your savior?"

"No, but—"

"Did it tell you Catholicism was a false religion?"

"No!"

"Did it beg you to commit yourself to Satan?"

"Blast it, Lieutenant! No!" she said, pounding a fist against her leg.

He shrugged and brushed his fingers over the rough sandstone as he let his eyes drift to the dunes. "Hmm. Doesn't sound like a false prophet to me. Doesn't even sound like a run-of-the-mill demon. Did it lust after you?"

He laughed as her abashed jaw gaped open.

"You are the rudest, most ill-bred . . ."

"Scalawag!" he finished helpfully.

She laughed. It was a tinkling bell-like sound.

"Yes," she insisted flatly, giving him an askance look.

"Well, tell me what happened?"

"Well, I—it." She swallowed. "It made me see things, Matthew." Relief shaded the statement, as though she was glad to be discussing it with someone.

He smiled at the use of his first name. "Like what?"

"Like—like a man with—with . . ." She halted, fear creasing her face again.

"With a *what*?" he asked, his voice seductively suggestive.

She scowled, pursing her lips. "Not a *what*, Mr. Douglas!"

"Well?"

"Well—he had wooden skewers in his chest and they were attached to ropes . . ."

She stopped abruptly as he sat bolt upright and moved closer to her, eyes suddenly hard, entire body tensed.

"What else, Colleen?"

She recoiled at his intensity, hunching her narrow shoulders forward and dropping her gaze to stare at the ground.

Seeing her response, he forced himself to relax and breathe deeply. Some of his tension fled.

"Forgive me," he mumbled, tugging his blue cap. "It's a . . . ritual I'm familiar with."

She jerked her eyes back to him, searching his face. Then she reached out a hand and touched his shoulder. The tiny fingers felt cool through his blue shirt.

"Tell me?" she pleaded, her eyes wide.

He put his hand over hers and squeezed gently. She blinked and dropped her eyes again, trying to pull the hand away. But he refused to release it. Instead, he shifted positions to sit cross-legged beside her and wrapped both of his hands around hers. The fingers were cold in his tight grasp.

"Sun Dance," he murmured softly, focusing on her downcast face. "It's a summer ceremonial."

She looked up, anxiously waiting for more. "What else?"

He leaned forward, looking calmly down into her brown eyes. She'd stopped trying to tug her hand away. It rested cool and unprotesting between his palms. "You tell me."

"I—we—do you know what the final . . . flight means?"

He nodded slightly, his face deadly serious. "It's a journey to the spirit world."

"I . . . !" She whirled around to face him. "I think . . ." But she wouldn't let herself express it. She only closed her mouth and breathed shallowly.

"Colleen," he said sternly. "It is *not* a journey to hell, my dear. It's a journey to God."

"But, Matthew," she begged, "the Indians are pagans. Their gods are false!"

"Indeed?" He abruptly released her hand, raising his brows as he stretched out and crossed his legs at the ankles. Powerful memories stirred in his breast. He had to apply great effort to keep his voice unemotional. "I think if you asked one of the dancers, he'd tell you the journey was very pleasant. Not like hell at all."

"I—know."

He scrutinized her pinched expression.

"I know!" she stressed the words and touched his shoulder again.

He let his eyes briefly examine her delicate hand, then returned to her face. "You—know?"

"Yes! I—the wolf . . ."

"The wolf—took you there?" he asked, furrowing his brow.

"Yes." She dropped her hand and slowly brought it back to her lap.

He reached over, clasped the tiny fingers, and clutched them to his chest. Thoughts roiled in his head. Why would the Indian spirit world bestow such a great honor on this white woman from the East? What was the wolf trying to teach her? *And why?*

"You believe me?" she whispered.

"Of course."

"I—I was beginning to think that Robert was right that I wasn't . . . you know? All right."

"Poppycock! You're perfectly sane."

Her eyes poured out gratitude.

"More, tell me more," he insisted, rolling to his side and propping his head on his hand. Her palm was still pressed to his shirt.

Her eyes drifted northwest again, seeing something in her mind. He followed her gaze. Stars glistened brilliantly in the western sky.

"What are you seeing?"

"Mountains," she whispered. "Ragged and blue."

"Um . . . Big Horns, I suspect."

"Big Horns," she repeated, nodding slowly.

Her hand against his chest was warming, the fingers absently moving beneath his palm, caressing his blue shirt. He tried to divert his mind from the sensations called forth.

Patting her hand, he reluctantly released her fingers, then sat up. "So"—he cleared his throat and smiled awkwardly—"I think God's just provided a different kind of angelic messenger for you."

Turning, her long blond hair fell in curls over her shoulders. Her face was soft as she tipped up her chin. "You do?"

"I do."

"But what's the message, Matthew?" She retrieved her Bible and pressed it to her heart.

He shrugged. "That, Colleen, is something only you can determine. Listen to the dreams."

"To wolves?"

"If that's the form God chooses."

"You're very kind, Matthew—to listen."

He raised his brows lasciviously. "Purely selfish, I assure you." His eyes drifted leisurely over her body.

She looked askance at him. "Stop that!"

"Yes, I'd better," he said, then pulled the cap down on his head and twisted one end of his mustache. "Besides, I should get back to my walk."

He pushed to stand up and offered her a hand. A crescent moon was rising in the distance, casting a silver light on her blond hair; he watched the curls glint as he pulled her to her feet.

"Matthew." She bravely left her hand in his. "Please don't—mention . . ."

"Dear lady!" he reproved, sounding pained. "I may have faults but private discussions are *private*!" He paused, tilting his head provocatively. "Of course, someday I'll expect compensation."

She squinted, disbelieving. "You may kiss my hand."

He sighed and complied. "Crumbs are better than nothing, I suppose."

* * *

Colleen shook her head and watched him disappear into the darkness, then turned up her palm and examined it. The hand still felt warm from when he had held it. She flexed the fingers open, then shut, holding the warmth in. It was as though by closing her hand she could keep him with her for a time longer.

"Strange man," she whispered as she walked toward her wagon.

His blunt self-confidence made her feel safer. The way, she supposed, a husband should. Pink rose in her cheeks as she acknowledged the fact. It frightened her a little.

Unwrapping the shawl from her shoulders, she crawled into the back of the wagon and undressed, then slipped her pale blue nightgown over her head. Robert lay still beside her. She studied him, frowning. He didn't even look like he was breathing. She assumed he must be deeply asleep. Folding the shawl, she tucked it under her head, curled on her side, and closed her eyes.

The hard hand on her arm shocked her. He rolled over.

"Robert!" she cried. "What—"

"Did you think I'd be stupid enough not to know you been dallying with that damn soldier!" he said, his face inches from hers.

"We just talked!"

"Just talked!" he spat, tightening his grip until his fingers dug holes in her flesh.

Colleen cried out in pain. "Robert, please!"

"Please?" He grunted, grabbing her by the shoulders and pulling her frail body against him. He kissed her hard, deliberately bruising her lips.

She pushed away from him and wiped at the trickle of blood that ran down her chin.

"Come here!" he growled, dragging her back.

She fought him, pushing hard to free herself from the brutal grip. He grabbed her hands and crushed them against his chest.

"Please, Robert," she whimpered as he tightened his arms around her back. "Stop it, please! You're hurting me!"

His huge arms roughly shoved her away. Her shoulders slammed against the opposite side of the wagon, her head cracking dully on the sideboard.

He jabbed a stiff finger at her, rage making his voice breathy. "You'd sneak out and see that damned soldier, then refuse me my rights as your husband?"

"No, Robert! You were just—"

"Then come here!"

Tears came to her eyes. A wave of trembling overpowered her. He was going to hurt her! She had to get away! She lunged for the rear of the wagon, scrambling for the opening, but his huge hand reached out, the fingers entwining in strands of blond hair. He jerked her head, dragging her back across the floorboard.

"Thought you'd get away?" he whispered insanely, his hot mouth pressed against her cheek. "You'll never get away." He smashed her against the bed and rolled over on top of her, pinioning her beneath him.

She tried to scream, but only a vague whimper came out before he clapped a hand over her mouth. With his massive three-hundred-pound body, he pressed the air out of her lungs. She gasped for breath, struggling.

A killing rage swept over her. Frantically she clawed at his face with her one free hand. Warm drops of blood dripped from the scratches onto her forehead.

"Damn you!" he cursed as he forcefully spread her legs, then ripped away the clothing that barred his entry. The jagged sound of tearing fabric rang like thunder in her ears.

Deliriously her hand fluttered over boxes and barrels, searching for something, anything, to strike him with. Finally her fingers rested on cold metal—smooth steel. She tightened her fingers around the wooden butt of the pistol, then struck out madly with the barrel, slamming it against his head again and again.

"Ach!" he screamed in pain, his hand still pressing hard

against her mouth. His massive arm reared back, a fist forming to pound her face.

The gun blast boomed deafeningly through the still night air, slashing hideously into the peaceful dreams of those nearby.

Douglas whirled on cat feet, pulling up his rifle and crouching to the ground. A wave of excited voices crackled through the train. He ran, eyes searching the dark terrain quickly and deftly for the unseen threat. By the time he reached the location of the blast, the ·Merrills' wagon was surrounded by people. His heart leapt into his throat as he rushed forward.

''Move!'' he commanded, charging the wagon.

Men cleared a path for him, but before he reached the white-topped vehicle, Robert Merrill thrust his head through the rear curtains. His brown hair was soaked in blood, red streaking down his face.

''Get away from my wagon!'' he shouted, waving his arms insanely.

Douglas raised his rifle and pointed it at Merrill as he approached. ''What's wrong here?'' he asked in a cool, steady voice.

''Nothing!'' Merrill screamed shrilly. ''Go on! Get away from here! Accidental discharge, that's all!''

Matthew could hear muffled cries from behind the big man. Silently he appraised the possibilities.

''Go on, folks,'' he said softly. ''We've got some heavy traveling to do tomorrow.''

The crowd grumbled as they dispersed, taut looks on their faces. He lowered the barrel of his rifle and stared at the wagon. Merrill had quickly retreated inside and the sobbing had stopped. Threatened her, probably.

For the remainder of his watch, Douglas paced back and forth in front of the Merrill wagon, glaring contemptuously.

• CHAPTER 7 •

WOUNDED BEAR LOUNGED LAZILY OUTSIDE LITTLE Deer's lodge. The noon sun was warm against his bare chest, the wind cool on his upturned face. Sparrow, his brother's wife, stood close by scraping a fresh buffalo hide. The task was laborious and time consuming, but the first step to a warm winter robe. Once the connective tissue and bits of flesh had been removed, she could begin the tanning process. Sparrow was a plain woman, eyes too large, face too round, but the wealth of coal black hair that draped over her shoulders made her seem almost attractive.

"He'll be here soon." She smiled, tugging at a stubborn bit of transparent tissue.

Wounded Bear nodded, knowing that Little Deer's morning hunt could not take much longer. They'd seen the antelope just after sunrise and the day was half over already. But antelope ran like the wind. If he'd spooked the herd, he'd have to circle around and cautiously approach from another side.

In the meantime, Wounded Bear enjoyed the sun and

watched his nephew, Black Bird, and his twelve-year-old
friend, Crow Foot, play in front of the lodge. Black Bird
was thin and weedy, small for his three years. To make up
for his size, he ran harder, rode faster, and played more
frantically than any other boy in the village. Crow Foot was
a tall, muscular boy with shoulder-length black hair. He
always wore a red and blue beaded headband. He was a
good boy, well respected by the people of the tribe, always
deferential to elders, always reliable. Old women whispered
that someday Crow Foot would be a great chief—Wounded
Bear didn't doubt it.

He smiled as Black Bird marked a spot on the ground,
then trudged back fifty paces and marked another spot.
Looking up, he waved.

"You count, uncle!"

"I'll count," Wounded Bear granted and rolled to his
side to get a better view of the upcoming race.

Black Bird sucked in a deep breath and blew it out hard,
then perched on his toes and spread his arms. Wounded
Bear chuckled. The boy looked an eagle ready to drop off
a cliff in flight. Crow Foot smiled at his younger companion
and took his position beside him.

"Ready?" Wounded Bear called to Black Bird, lifting a
hand in preparation.

"Ready!" the child yelled.

Wounded Bear chopped the air with his hand and both
boys lunged forward, feet flashing, chests thrown out. When
they were halfway through the race Crow Foot slowed down,
barely trotting along beside Black Bird's ferociously pounding legs, obviously letting the child win the race.

Black Bird swept over the finish line first, gliding to a
stop and turning anxiously to Wounded Bear, his chest
heaving. Crow Foot wasn't even breathing hard.

"How—long?" Black Bird asked.

Wounded Bear held up three fingers. "Three breaths."

The boy put his hands on his hips and frowned. "Maybe
just a little less?"

"Maybe."

Black Bird smiled broadly, his eyes sparkling. "It's a record!"

"Sure."

"No, really! It is!"

"Can you beat Little Owl?"

Black Bird tilted his head uncertainly and scuffed a bare toe into the ground, looking embarrassed. Wounded Bear nodded knowingly. Little Owl was ten and the fastest child in the village.

"If I go find Little Owl will you be here to count?" It was a hopeful question.

"I'll be here."

The boy beamed and raced away through the village. Spurts of tan dust sprouted behind him. Wounded Bear followed his route down the hill.

Crow Foot sauntered over and sat beside Wounded Bear, a smile on his young face. He pointed his chin at Black Bird. "He is fast for his age."

Wounded Bear chuckled. "Yes, especially when his competition lets him win!"

Crow Foot shrugged and leaned back on his elbows, extending his legs. "It makes him happy to win."

It was a lazy day. Women laughed and talked outside the conical lodges as they scraped hides or hung strips of meat to dry on broad wooden racks. The rich scent of drying buffalo filled the air. The wind gusted periodically, sending long tendrils of black hair fluttering over their faces.

He turned to Crow Foot, looking him up and down. The boy was gazing absently at the clouds. "I hear you have asked to ride with the Dog Soldiers?"

Crow Foot smiled. "Yes, and they might let me. First I have to prove myself worthy."

Wounded Bear looked up at the clouds too, his thoughts drifting. The Dog Soldiers waged constant battles against the bluecoats. It made his heart sting to think of a boy this young riding with them. "Why are you in such a hurry to be a warrior?"

"Because . . ." He hesitated, shifting his wide eyes to

Wounded Bear. ''The whites are bad. They are trying to wipe the Tsistsistas from the face of the earth. I love my people.''

He sighed, eyes drifting as his own thoughts turned to the wagon train. ''I understand.''

At the other end of camp old men sat in a circle making arrow points from fine orange chert. The constant tap-tap-tap of antler hammers against stone carried on the breeze. Most men used iron points now, but not these elders. They believed the new iron points brought bad luck and that only the stone points could be imbued with spirit power.

''What will you do to prove you're worthy?''

Crow Foot shifted positions, pulling up one knee. He had a secretive smile on his face. He whispered, ''I'm going to steal many horses from the Sioux.''

Wounded Bear cocked his head. ''That's not easy. They guard their horses heavily.''

''Yes, but I can do it.''

''I believe you. Just remember they won't let you ride with the Dog Soldiers if you're dead.''

The boy laughed. It was a high-pitched childish sound. ''I'll remember.''

''Good, I never want to find out if my medicine power is strong enough to remove Sioux arrows from you.'' He gave the boy an askance look. Crow Foot laughed again.

''You won't,'' he said as he stood up.

''You're going?''

''I told my mother I would bring a rabbit home for dinner.''

Wounded Bear waved him away. ''Shoot a great big one.''

The boy waved back and trotted down to his family's lodge.

He looked to the gray-haired old men again. They sat in the shade of a towering cottonwood tree where the constant wind made leaf shadows dance over their withered brown faces. Soft voices bubbled up from the group, punctuated by occasional loud laughs and the crack of a hand slapping a knee.

Sparrow moved to the other side of the hide, her stone scraper making rough sounds.

"Has—the woman come back?" she asked hesitantly, not meeting his eyes.

The question fragmented Wounded Bear's peaceful thoughts. His sister-in-law knew how delicate the subject was. It showed bravery that she would ask—bravery and concern. He bowed his head to stare at the healing wounds over his breasts.

"No," he answered softly.

A gust of wind whistled through the village. Grains of sand sprayed him, stinging his face before he could turn his head. Sparrow's black hair was whipped around her throat. She shielded her eyes with her hands.

When the wind subsided, she reached down and patted him on the shoulder. "She will, don't worry."

He stared uncomfortably at the fingers knitted over his stomach, then nodded once. He had prayed for her return, but in the eight days since the Sun Dance, he had been alone inside. She had not come back.

"Maybe," he murmured.

At the bottom of the hill, Black Bird jumped up and down, waving his arms and pointing out to the plains. Wounded Bear furrowed his brow and stood up, trying to peer between lodges to see what the child was so excited about. The boy was shouting something into the wind, but the words were swept away.

Wounded Bear stood up and put a hand over his eyes to shield them from the glare of the sun. In the distance a trail of dust lined the sage-covered hills.

"Riders," he mumbled.

Sparrow stopped scraping and came to stand beside him, following his gaze. "Coming fast."

"Yes." A thread of fear wound through him. He lowered his hand and started walking down the hill toward Black Bird. The boy raced up to meet him.

"Uncle! The scouts!" he shouted breathlessly, tugging Wounded Bear's leg fringe.

"You sure?" He continued walking, the boy still clinging to the buckskin fringe.

"Yes! Gray Squirrel's horse is in the lead!"

"Let's see." He strode out to the edge of the lodges and looked again. The boy was right. The big bay was in the lead, pounding rapidly over the hills. He reached down and ruffled Black Bird's sweaty hair. "Can you go and tell the crier?"

"I can!" He smiled brilliantly and raced up the hill toward the circle of old men.

Wounded Bear waited, his hands dropped to his sides, his fingers fumbling aimlessly at his palms. The wind teased his braids, making them slap repeatedly at his bare chest. The riders were hurrying. He watched the ponies bound down one hill and up over another.

The big bay sped toward him, lather soaking its withers. Anxiety welled in his chest. The message was so urgent?

Gray Squirrel raced to the edge of the village, then brought the horse to an abrupt halt and dismounted. Waving a hand to a boy, he instructed the child to cool down the horse. Wounded Bear waited, breathing shallowly. The scout strode forward, his face tired and serious. He put a strong hand on Wounded Bear's shoulder and met his gaze.

"They are here, brother."

"The train?"

"Yes."

Wounded Bear swallowed, shifting his gaze to the other riders. Only eight led their horses to the corral.

"Scouting parties are still out?" he questioned softly.

Gray Squirrel nodded. "Watching to see what they do, where they go."

Behind them the voice of the village crier split the air. "Come! I have told the chief you are here!" He waved a hand up the hill toward Dull Knife's lodge. The middle-aged man was dressed only in a breechclout, his hard muscles shiny with perspiration.

Gray Squirrel wrapped an arm around Wounded Bear's shoulder. Together they climbed the hill.

"There are many soldiers."

"How many?" The wolf had not told him about the blue-coats.

"Over a hundred."

A tendril of anxiety taunted him. "We will have to gather a bigger war party."

Gray Squirrel sighed. "Much bigger. The soldiers are also dragging two of the big guns that blow huge holes into the ground."

"Howitzers?" Wounded Bear had learned the term at Fort Laramie. Speaking it made him quake.

"Yes."

"And—there are others—with the train. Women?" He didn't want to ask straight out if his friend had seen the yellow-haired woman.

"Not many—but some. And children too."

"Children?"

"Yes."

His eyes dropped to the ground. He didn't want to kill children. A hollowness swelled in his chest.

The afternoon was bright and hot, a searing wind rushing down from the west to pepper man and beast with sand and tiny rocks.

Colleen clutched the bonnet bow beneath her chin and tried to look forward, but couldn't. The fierce wind kept her head canted left. Through slitted eyes, she saw that the dust kicked up by the gale swirled devilishly around the jolting wagons, shooting eerie fingers into the pale blue sky.

The train was heading due west into the sinking sun, the golden rays reflecting so brilliantly from the sands that they almost blinded. She squinted at the western horizon, then back to the wagon banging and creaking beside her. The traces on the oxen jingled like bells. Robert sat stiffly on the seat, trying to keep the animals from stumbling into the jagged drainage channels that lined Rush Creek.

"Hyah!" he shouted, cracking his whip over the cattle's cream-colored backs. "Move, damn you!"

Colleen watched him, but tried to conceal the fact by canting her bonnet so that it looked like she was facing forward. For more than a week he'd punished her by silence, speaking only when absolutely necessary, so that now she was starved for companionship, her heart sore. Still the punishment continued. She'd pleaded with him to say something, to shout at her, but he'd refused.

Her thoughts drifted. Somewhere up ahead, Matthew was riding advance guard. He'd come by early that morning to talk with her, but had left abruptly when Robert returned, a look of intense dislike twisting his handsome face. It was odd, she thought, that since that night a week before when they had talked about her nightmares he had been the one truly kind person in her life. He always seemed to sense when she was feeling lonely or confused, and would appear out of nowhere, tipping his dusty blue cap and giving her that insolent grin.

She smiled to herself, turning her face away from the wagon so Robert couldn't see. Matthew seemed inexplicably interested in the content of her "visions," as he called them. And the chance to share the troubling dreams relieved much of their alarming urgency.

She sighed. Douglas had a wildness about him that made her feel unsettled. Underlying his controlled exterior, she sensed a fire raging and the awareness affected her in strange ways. Often when they talked together she found her heart fluttering madly, like that of a trapped animal suddenly freed to wander home again. To make matters worse, she was growing attached to him, thinking of him constantly. Once, a few nights ago, she had awakened from a particularly powerful dream and instantly called his name. A wave of staggering relief flooded her when she realized Robert was sound asleep.

Her thoughts were disturbed when the wagon beside her suddenly stopped rolling, the brakes screeching in the dry air. She looked up to where Robert stood on the seat, shielding his eyes from the dust storm.

"What is it?" she shouted, hoping her voice could be

heard over the tumult of wagons and wind. The entire train was coming to a halt.

He glanced down at her, then back over the plains and finally yelled, "Rider—coming at us hell-for-leather!"

She stood on tiptoes but could see no one. Then his frantic cries met her ears. "Indians!" he was shouting. "Indians!"

Colleen gasped and raced for the rear of the wagon, climbing in as it began to move hurriedly to join the circle. She flattened her body against the floorboard, feeling the jostling vehicle turning to line up behind another wagon and interlock wheels.

"What's happening?" she shouted to Robert when the movement stopped, but he didn't answer. Throwing down the reins, he jumped from the wagon and disappeared.

The rider's voice had ceased. All she could hear were her own shallow breaths against the floorboard. A mass of blond curls had tumbled down over her face. She pushed her bonnet off and smoothed the locks behind her ears as she waited.

Abruptly a ragged staccato of shots rang out and terrifying Indian war cries erupted. The shrieks of the warriors seemed to pierce her soul, cascading over her in waves. An overpowering sorrow built inside her. Confused, she rolled over on her back and stared up at the white canvas, trying to determine the source of the sadness. The shots came nearer, each blast like a knife blade in her heart. She pressed her hands over her ears and curled into a ball on the floorboard. As she lay there, she felt some awareness seep in. Jerking her hands down, she sat bolt upright. Was *he* with the warriors?

She scrambled for the rear of the wagon, climbing out and hitting the sand running, then she raced across the circle. She barely heard the shocked voices that called her name. When she was out beyond the wagons, she pulled up her yellow hem and ran across the open plains with all her might. The voices behind her were harsh now, demanding, but she kept going. She had to reach him!

Up ahead she saw the battle site. In the midst of the dust storm, figures whirled, horses racing. She extended a hand, calling out to the warriors, but her voice was lost in the rumbling gusts of wind and the rattle of gunfire.

"Mrs. Merrill?" a voice behind her screamed. "Stop! Stop!"

Her lungs hurt but she couldn't obey. She picked up her feet and ran harder, her blond hair flying in the wind.

Suddenly someone knocked her to the ground. Colleen kicked and screamed at the man, trying to escape, to crawl to the Cheyenne braves. But he wouldn't release her. He just kept shouting words she didn't understand. She struck him with her fists, pounding his back and face, then scrambling in the sand to crawl away.

"Stop it, Mrs. Merrill!" the man yelled, wrapping his arms around her waist and holding tight. "Stop it!"

She clawed at the sand, her face searching the storm for the warriors. Then she saw them, riding away, retreating. Tears filled her eyes. Through the blur she could see the blue-clad soldiers pursuing.

She stopped struggling to lay her head in the warm sand and close her eyes. The shots continued—but she knew she couldn't reach them.

The man slid forward on his stomach to stare disbelieving into her face. She recognized him then. He was Nat Hedges, the nineteen-year-old leader of the civilian freight wagons. He planned on opening a store in Virginia City.

"What's the matter with you, ma'am?" he shouted, pulling his wide-brimmed hat down over his brown eyes. "You trying to get yourself killed?" His voice was concerned and angry.

"They were . . ." She hesitated, the words caught in her throat. "We mustn't build this road!" She raised her arms to shield her face as a gust of wind splashed sand into her eyes.

Then the wind stopped and she was floating. The wolf was beside her, its gigantic black eyes glowing. A tendril of fear wound up her spine. The man with long black braids appeared, his body bare, revealing pink scars over his breasts. He was pouring water over hot stones and bathing himself in the steam that rose. She stood beneath a crumbling sandstone overhang. He called out to her, voice soft and soothing. Joy replaced her fear. She wanted to go to him. He held his arms wide to receive her and she struggled to walk forward, but something held her back.

Nat Hedges was shaking her, covering her body with his own as the booming rifle shots came closer.

"Stay down!" he commanded into her ear. "Down!"

She stopped struggling and concentrated on staying here, here on the dusty Nebraska plains.

Then the firing ceased and she closed her eyes again. In her mind she could see the soldiers capturing two Indian ponies as the braves raced away through the tangles of sage.

Hedges dislodged himself from on top of her, looking shy and embarrassed. His ears burned crimson in the sunlight.

"Sorry, ma'am," he apologized. "I couldn't figure no other way of keeping you safe."

Her breathing came in unsteady gasps as he helped her to her feet and supported her arm as they plodded back to the wagons. People watched her suspiciously, their faces drawn and taut. She heard harsh whispers as she passed. She made out some of the words: "crazy," "addled," and "sick."

By the time Hedges delivered her to her wagon, she was sobbing, tears streaking through the dirt on her cheeks to leave muddy trails. He stood uncomfortably, not knowing what to do. Removing his hat he rolled and unrolled the brim waiting for her to calm down.

"Can I do sumpthin'?" he asked quietly, moving to shield her from the prying eyes of the train. When she didn't answer he made his decision. "I'll go find your husband," he muttered and started away.

The impact of his words hit her like a fist. "No!" she pleaded, whirling around and holding out a hand. "Please, no!"

He came back and patted her gently on the arm, then spoke in hushed tones. "Ma'am, I won't if you don't want me to, but . . ." He paused, glancing over the growing crowd. "But I wasn't the only one who saw you run out there. He'll find out soon enough anyway."

"I know—Mr. Hedges." She forced a wan smile. "I just need some time."

He tipped his brown felt hat and nodded. "All right, ma'am." Then he trotted away through the milling crowd.

Colleen eyed the onlookers numbly for a few moments, then turned her back and stared at the covered wagon. She was so tired, so very tired; she leaned wearily against the wagon, feeling as though she'd run a hundred miles.

She pulled a handkerchief from her skirt pocket and lifted the lid on a barrel of water hanging from the side. Wetting the cloth, she washed her sage-scratched arms and face. The coolness was soothing, filtering through her like the autumn winds of New York. In her mind she could see the brilliant leaves and the wet snows clinging to the eaves of buildings. She closed her eyes and tried to imagine herself there, watching the snow fall through the front windows of her parents' home.

A strong hand gripped her arm and flung her around.

"What the hell did you think you were doing?" Robert bellowed, his green eyes boring into hers.

"I—I," she stuttered, knowing she couldn't tell him the truth. Suddenly the image of Matthew riding advance guard filled her mind. The question formed long before she could consider the implications. "Is Matthew all right?" she asked.

Robert released his grip and stood stiffly over her. The glare of rage made her shrink back until she hit the wagon with a dull thud.

"You ran out there," he said, "to see if Douglas was hurt?" He clenched his fists.

"No! I . . . no!" she whispered, stumbling over the words as she tried to move farther away.

Robert's face contorted in rage. He glanced cautiously

around at the increasing number of bystanders, obviously
trying to fathom their opinions of him in light of his wife's
insane behavior. He reached out and grabbed her by the
shoulders, then shook her ferociously.

"The Indians!" she cried, cowering. "They said we can't
build this road!" Tears streaked hotly down her cheeks.
"We can't—"

"How the hell would you know?" he screamed. "Those
savages were speaking Cheyenne! Not a one of 'em knew
any English!"

His words hit her with the power of a bolt of lightning.
She straightened up, searching his face. "But—that—can't
be." Shock numbed her senses. "How do you know? Were
you out there?"

"No," he fumbled, his eyes darting through the crowd
again. "I wasn't—I—I was over yonder tending to the
stock." He pointed to the rear of the circle. "But I heard
it from someone who was!"

The crimson rose hot in his cheeks and his fingers relaxed
on her arms. His anger was dwindling, being replaced by a
new emotion.

Puzzled by the guilty look on his face, Colleen asked,
"You were in the rear while the other men were up front
with their rifles ready? Why . . ."

The fist appeared out of nowhere, slamming into her
cheek and hurling her to the ground. She scrambled to crawl
away, but he picked her up and struck her again. Faintly
she heard her own voice crying for help. Then lights flashed
before her eyes, her head rolling back on the hot sand from
another blow. She entwined her fingers in a sage, pulling
weakly, but her strength had vanished.

And the warrior reached for her again, his eyes warm.
She tried to run to him, but couldn't. Something held her
back.

Robert reached down and grabbed her by the hair, lifting
her off the ground. Feebly she raised her arms to protect
herself, screaming and cringing against the blow she knew

was coming. But abruptly he let her drop. She fell softly to the sand.

The voice was cool and deep. "If you touch her again, Merrill, I'll blow a hole in you so big they'll be able to drive a goddamned train through it." There was a cocking sound.

Robert's feet shuffled backward, his pants catching on prickly sage and making a scratchy sound. His voice cracked, fear lacing it. "You—you stay away from my wife, Douglas!"

Matthew? Her mind cried out for him, but she couldn't make her mouth utter the words.

"Easy, mistuh," he drawled coolly. "In my opinion any man who'd hit a woman don't deserve to live. I'd be mighty careful if I was you not to tempt me to prove that."

Matthew's steps advanced as Robert's pattered away, then he knelt beside her, stroking the tangles of blond hair from her face.

"Colleen?" he asked. "Can you stand up?"

She tried to move, to lift her arms, but they fell weakly back to the sand. Then she felt muscular arms slide beneath her and carry her away. The soft swishing of boots in sand was the only sound of movement.

She slept.

Cool blue mountains rose up from the sage-covered plains. She kicked her tan and white pony and rode as fast as she could to the foothills of the granite peaks. When she dismounted, she noticed she was dressed in soft buckskin clothing. Curiously she touched the supple fringes on the shirt, then began to climb, her feet padding silently over beds of fragrant pine needles. The pony whinnied behind her, nodding its white nose.

As she moved up the steep slope, the coolness of approaching evening made her shiver. Winding between towering trees, she came to a lush meadow. Grass stood tall and straight, stretching up her thighs to brush her fingertips. She let her hands play with the blades, stroking them.

Stopping, she extended her arms wide to the heavens . . . and the awareness struck her dull mind. *She was with him.* Once again she and the Cheyenne warrior shared minds and bodies. His gentleness swirled around her, encompassing her like a warm blanket. She drifted, reaching out for him, and he pressed closer, his spirit sending out tendrils to find her. They floated together, their souls touching, entwining, in a vast ocean of eternal silence.

Until suddenly he pulled away.

Colleen found herself standing beside him in the dwindling light of the forest. He knelt down before her, his brown eyes soft and pleading.

"Mistai?" he called tenderly. "Speak with me?" A breeze tousled his black braids.

She wanted to go to him, to lie down in the meadow and merge her soul with his until no difference remained. She walked forward, stretching her arms to meet his.

"Colleen?" another voice echoed from somewhere behind her. "Colleen?"

And she felt sand beneath her, could smell the rich tang of the sage and feel the wind blowing through her hair. She opened her eyes, a touch of eternity lingering in her soul. Matthew sat next to her on the sand. He'd carried her out away from the wagons to a small knoll behind the military camp. Below, she could see soldiers in blue strolling between tents.

"Colleen?" he asked again, sponging her face with cool water. His eyes were concerned. "Are you back with me yet?"

She struggled to sit, but the pain halted her movement.

"Oh!" she murmured, bringing a hand up to the mounds of blue on her face. She had a terrible headache.

"Here." His strong arms reached around her and helped her to a sitting position.

She put her head in her hands, feeling every muscle ache. Tangles of blond hair fell over her face. With numb hands she pushed them back and looked up at Matthew.

He stared at her for a few moments, then leaned against

a sage and pushed the dusty cap back on his head. His face slackened in relief. "Thank God, I was afraid he'd hurt you worse than it seemed."

"No," she whispered, her spirit still far away, ahead of them somewhere on the trail. "I'm—all right." She pulled her knees up and cradled them in her arms. The yellow fabric of her dress was soiled, the hem torn, ripped by some thorny bush in her flight toward the braves.

Matthew put a hand beneath her chin and turned her face toward him, carefully studying her eyes. Apparently deciding she really was all right, he stood. "I'm going to my tent, but I'll be right back. Don't move, hear?"

She nodded and he left.

Alone on the desert sands, she propped her chin on her knees and gently stroked the leaves of a white sage that thrust sharp branches into her side. Her eyes drifted westward. The sun was setting, she realized with a start. How long had she been away? Delicately she touched the bruises on her face, then squeezed her eyes shut. She could not think about Robert now; if she did she would cry again. She shoved the thoughts away, dropping her hand to the sandy hillside.

The wind was vanishing with the fading sunlight, a coolness growing in the air. She hugged herself and looked to the clouds on the horizon. They floated lazily across the sky, blazing orange as they approached the golden ball sliding below the hills. She breathed in their quiet beauty.

From the camp below, Matthew emerged, carrying a canteen and two cups. He trudged up the hill and sat down beside her, a worried look on his face.

Pouring two cups of amber liquid, he handed her one and ordered, "Drink."

She peered over the edge of the blue tin cup and sniffed. The potent smell of alcohol made her crinkle her nose. She glanced sideways at him as he stretched out across the sands, leaning back on his elbows—but she drank, slowly at first, then in great gulps. The hot liquid burned a pathway down her throat, choking her and bringing tears to her eyes. She lowered the cup and coughed, then wiped her mouth with a dirty hand.

"Good!" Matthew said, refilling her cup from the dented canteen. "You'll feel better."

She drank more, her stomach tingling pleasantly. Already the amber saint was lighting a fire in her veins, percolating through her body until even her toes felt flushed.

"What a blessed feeling." She sighed. The benevolent fire softened the jagged edges of the world.

"Now," he said, his swarthy face appraising her condition once more. "Tell me what happened today. I heard from Nat Hedges that you ran out toward the battle—and gave him quite a licking for trying to stop you." He cocked his head in disbelief, his skeptical smile mocking her supposed fragility.

She sighed, peering in at the film of liquor on the bottom of her cup. The silken flush in her veins bolstered her courage. She extended the cup. "More?"

He looked amused, one brow arched. He refilled it, then shook the canteen and frowned. "I'd no idea, my dear, that you had such a fondness for whiskey. Why, it's a sign of breeding I hadn't—"

"I'm well bred!" she insisted, missing the point, her brow furrowed in confusion.

"Uh . . . yes." His blue eyes twinkled.

"Where were you today?"

"Scouting. I spotted the war party. Incidentally"—his mouth twisted into a jeer—"I heard that your beloved thinks you ran out because you feared for my safety. But we both know that isn't true. So . . ." his voice softened, "why did you?"

"You brought back two ponies."

He eyed her curiously. "I did."

"Cheyenne ponies."

He nodded, twisting his mustache thoughtfully.

"They don't want us to build this road."

His sat forward, his eyes cauldrons. "No, they don't."

She played with a fold in her yellow dress, forming it

into a peak, then smoothing it away. He watched her every movement.

"How do you know that?"

"I . . . I . . ." She swallowed, recalling Robert's words. "I heard them tell you."

"You speak—"

"Not 'til today," she blurted unhappily. Her eyes drifted to the northwest. He was there somewhere. The warrior was real and waiting for her.

Matthew followed her gaze, periodically glancing at her from the corner of his eye. "He's talked to you? In the dreams, I mean?"

She made another peak from the fabric of her skirt and nodded.

"And you understood?"

"Except one word."

"What?"

"He called me . . . *mistai*."

Matthew blinked, tilting his head knowingly. He scooped a handful of sand and let it trickle through his fingers as he studied the darkening western horizon. The clouds were charcoal now, hanging unmoving in the sky. Colleen watched him sip absently at his cup.

"What does it mean?"

"Ghost."

"Oh . . ."

The fact that the warrior would see her as a phantom made perfect sense since she saw him in the same light. Not only that, but the fire in her belly was leading her thoughts away from anything serious. She let her eyes study Matthew's lazy posture. There was something about the easy way he carried himself that made her feel comfortable. Her whiskey-befuddled mind was suggesting things to her she'd never thought of before, making her see him clearly for the first time. She widened her eyes and stared unblinking. He was a *remarkably* handsome man. Even with the contemplative frown on his face, his straight nose and dark blue eyes were vibrantly masculine. She studied the blue shirt stretched across his broad chest and the way the muscles bulged through the fabric over his legs . . . and extended a hand to touch his thigh.

He glanced at her, raising his brows as she smoothed her fingers across the muscle. Reaching over, he pulled her cup down to look inside.

"Hmmm."

"What?" she asked innocently, tossing her head so that her hair fell over her shoulders in glistening blond waves.

He watched the action with amusement. She saw his chest vibrate softly with repressed laughter.

"What?"

"Well, I was thinking"—he gazed up at the stars poking through the blackness overhead—"that you're on the verge of making a request of me that you'll regret terribly tomorrow morning." He gave her a dazzling smile.

"Well . . . maybe not."

"But probably."

She dropped her gaze, pink rising in her cheeks despite the boldness lent her by the whiskey. "Matthew, I—I can't go back to my own wagon tonight. I—want to . . ."

"Yes, I can see that you do"—he nodded—"and I cannot tell you how much I'd like to take you up on that offer, but . . ." He frowned, looking like he hated himself for saying it. He tugged hard at his blue cap and sighed. "But I think, my dear, that what you need most is—er—rest."

She jerked her hand back, feeling slighted, then gritted her teeth at the roar of laughter that greeted the action. "You are the most—"

"Don't worry, Colleen," he said softly, a new seriousness creasing his swarthy face, "I've no intention of letting you spend the night with that—uh—coward you call your husband."

"Coward?"

"Yes," he shifted. "I thought you knew and that's what started the—"

"No, tell me?"

"One of the teamsters had a hell of a time prying your

beloved from beneath a wagon after the skirmish was over today. Seems he ran like a jackrabbit at the first sound of shots.''

She blinked. So that's why Robert had reacted so violently when she'd questioned him about his location during the fight.

She bowed her head to stare into her empty blue cup. She didn't want to think about Robert, she wanted to think about Matthew.

"I'm not going back to my own wagon?" she asked.

"No."

Abruptly he cleared his throat and got to his feet, extending a hand to her. She rose, pressing close to him, her chin tipped up.

He shook his head and sighed. "You're not making this any easier, you know?"

There was a fire building in his eyes. She slipped her arms around his neck and pulled gently. The amused look on his face faded as he bent to kiss her. His mouth was warm and moist, his arms around her waist tightening to bring her closer. Her heart pounded in her ears as he parted her lips with his own, kissing softly at first, then with a rush of desire, harder. She noticed curiously that his arms had begun to tremble and then suddenly he pushed away, taking a quick breath and holding her at arm's length. His face glistened with perspiration.

"Don't stop." she whispered, leaning toward him. She was slightly disgruntled by this unexpected disappointment.

"Don't . . . ?" he asked loudly, throwing his head back. "Dearest, what's happened to that starched morality of yours?"

"It was never starched."

"Never?"

"No!"

"Could have fooled me."

He slipped an arm around her narrow shoulders, then led her down the hill, not toward his own tent but toward a strange wagon.

As they approached the camp, she saw a plump matron with starkly white hair and a broad rosy face throw a stick of wood into a small fire.

"Maureen?" Matthew called as they rounded the wagon. "I want you to meet Colleen Merrill, the woman I told you about."

The elderly woman's eyes quickly went over Colleen, noting every bruise and scratch before she rushed over and patted her gently on the shoulder. Matthew reluctantly dropped his arm and took a step backward.

" 'Tis a pleasure, Colleen," she said in an Irish brogue. Her face was lined with worry. Obviously Matthew had explained Colleen's situation. "You'll be needing a place to stay for a few days, Mr. Douglas says. We'd be honored if ye'd stay with us."

"Oh! I . . . ." She cast a confused glance at Matthew. He smiled wryly in return. "I'd be very—grateful," she continued, understanding seeping in. Matthew had planned this all along. "If you're sure I'm no trouble."

"Heavens, no, darlin'! Mr. O'Brian and I want ye to stay for as long as ye need. You'll be sleeping next to our daughter. I hope you don't mind?" She bent over and pointed to a redheaded girl rolled in a blanket beneath the wagon. The child smiled.

Colleen bent over and smiled back, then asked, "What's your name?"

"Elizabeth."

"You won't mind if I sleep next to you, Elizabeth?"

"No, ma'am."

"Thank you."

Matthew put his hands on his hips and yawned audibly. Mrs. O'Brian gave him a sideways glance, exchanging a knowing look with him, then took the hint.

"Well, Colleen, dear, I'll be heading to bed. I've laid yer blankets out beside Elizabeth, so ye can retire when ye've a mind to."

"You're very kind, Mrs. O'Brian. Thank you."

"Good night to ye both." She curtsied slightly and headed for the back of her wagon.

"Night, Maureen," Matthew called.

Walking to the wagon, he knelt down and peered under at the freckle-faced child. "Lizard, Mrs. Merrill and I are going to take a short walk, but we'll be right back. Okay, honey?"

The child giggled. "Yes, Uncle Matthew."

Taking Colleen by the arm, he led her out to the darkness, then put both hands on her shoulders and gave her an impertinent smile.

"This—er—isn't my preferred arrangement," he pointed out. "But someday when you're sober, you'll thank me."

She stamped her foot, pouting. "I will not."

"No?"

"No!"

He grinned broadly. "I'll make a promise; do you want to hear it?"

"What!" she whispered hotly, feeling dejected.

"The next time you suggest we be—close, I'll absolve myself of all gentlemanly conduct and accept. Understand?"

She thought about it, frowning, then nodded curtly.

He nodded back once, as though they'd shook on it.

"Get some sleep," he whispered, releasing her and striding off into the darkness toward the military camp.

She stood still for a time, looking out to the darkness where he'd disappeared. Stars glistened overhead, a coolness creeping up around her. She hugged herself and started back for the wagon. It took a concerted effort to keep her path straight. Her feet wanted to weave.

· CHAPTER 8 ·

DARK RUMBLING THUNDERHEADS SHROUDED THE MASSIVE peaks of the Big Horns. Wounded Bear stared longingly at the forested slopes. The wind was increasing as the storm approached, whipping the fringes on his shirt and tugging at his braids. The rich smell of vegetation wafted on the damp air. He took a deep breath, trying to still his raging emotions. The Cheyenne were moving, pushing southward toward the summer root grounds along the Powder River, leaving the sacred peaks where his visions had come. He didn't want to go—but it was necessary. The train was only days away. They had to move closer to the whites' path to intercept and stop them.

The pinto pony beneath him stamped its feet, pawing frustration at the grass. The horse was ready to move with the rest of the herd. He tugged his eyes from the slopes and looked southward, over the long dusty line of horses pulling travois. People walked beside them, reins in their hands. Children played on the fringes of the line. Tinkling laughter mixed with the rolling growl of thunder.

"Ho, little one," Wounded Bear said soothingly, stroking the pony's long neck. "We will be going soon enough. Give me just a while longer."

The horse blew and relaxed. Wounded Bear continued petting the silken mane and cooing soft words as he stared upward. He could not drag his eyes from the places on the slopes where the wolf and the badger had helped him. Would they come to him out on the open plains of the south? Would the sandstone cliffs soothe his worried heart the way these granite giants did? A tired ache spread through him. He pulled his eyes away and bowed his head.

The soft clopping of hooves came slowly up behind him. Lifting his head, he saw Little Deer. A smile brushed his lips as his brother rode the spotted pony closer.

"You are sorry we are moving?" he asked, his brown eyes concerned.

"Yes," he said, letting his gaze stray back to the massive ragged peaks. The word sounded pained, but he could not keep the emotion from his voice.

Little Deer nodded and looked down at the tan soil as drops of rain began splatting. Wisps of dust sprouted up at the wet disturbance.

Wounded Bear's thoughts turned to the woman and his eyes unconsciously drifted to the old village site and the location of the Medicine Lodge. The chasm left by her disappearance yawned wider, leaving him hollow. He didn't realize that his face had taken on a softness, his eyes seeming far away and lonely.

But Little Deer noticed. "She has not come back." It was a statement. "And you fear you will lose her forever if you leave this mountainous place?"

Wounded Bear filled his lungs and spoke through a long exhale. "I fear that her spirit resides only here." Pain glazed his eyes.

He turned his pony to follow the rest of the band southward. Little Deer trotted beside him. They kept silent for a time, listening to the thunder roar and feeling the warm drizzle soak their buckskins.

"Brother?" Little Deer began awkwardly, looking away to the undulating plains. "You must take care. The religious elders are saying . . ." He stopped and sighed as though trying to decide whether to continue. Turning to meet his brother's eyes, his face hardened. "They are whispering that this woman you feel in your heart is a *ho ho ta ma itsi hyo ist.*"

Wounded Bear whirled to face Little Deer, anger rising hotly. "She has not shot an evil arrow into my heart, brother! Who is saying this?"

Little Deer remained quiet, meeting his brother's hostile glare.

"Who!"

"Many."

Wounded Bear turned back around, gripping the reins of his pony tightly. He fought to control his anger. How could the elders say such a thing? Had he acted any differently since the woman appeared? Had he done anything that would harm the people? She was not evil!

He swallowed his harsh tone and made his voice soft. "Why are they saying these things?"

Little Deer shrugged. "Perhaps because they do not understand why she comes to you, brother. If she is a spirit helper, then she should bring you a message and leave. In that case, you would not feel this torture of loneliness. If she is a ghost"—he hesitated, shaking his head—"then she tortures you for a reason. Ghosts do not come to the living with good intent." His eyes had grown cold.

"I . . . she . . . !" Anger rose like a tornado. He clamped his jaw; he did not want to scream at his brother. Kicking his horse hard, he rode away toward the mountains, leaving Little Deer far behind.

He prayed as he flew across the sage, begging the wolf to send him the woman so that he might ask her intentions. The revelation that the elders were whispering she might be an evil spirit came as a shock. Her presence made him feel so wonderful that he'd never considered the possibility that she might be using him for some wicked purpose. Wouldn't the wolf have warned him? Yes! his mind shouted. The helper would not let him be deceived so.

He dismounted and tethered the pony to a pine, then went about gathering dead twigs from the bottom branches of the trees to build a fire. He would purify himself, then he would beg Maheo to send her to him.

He threw rocks into the fire, letting them heat as the flames died down. Taking his hollow gourd to a nearby rock where rain water trickled over the stones, he filled it. Walking back, he laid the gourd beside the fire and stripped off his clothing, hanging his shirt and pants over the branches of a young aspen. The misty rain chilled his bare skin.

He prayed, singing the wolf songs to the heavens. His voice carried on the wind, lilting melodiously through the trees. He sang until his heart opened and his mind cleared of thoughts, leaving him vulnerable and afraid. Then he poured the gourd of water over the coals and bathed himself in the steam that rose. Closing his eyes, only prayers disturbed the stillness of his mind.

He did not know how long he sat there, huddled before the dwindling fire, his mind centered on the Great Mystery and the woman, but a rush of adrenaline signaled him that his prayers had been answered. He opened his eyes and looked to the sandstone overhang ten feet in front of him. His soul calmed. The wolf had heard. She stood there, her long blond hair hanging to her waist, her eyes frantically seeking out his. Blinking slowly, contemplatively, he extended his arms and called, "Please, talk with me? I need . . ."

But she vanished.

He gasped and pounded his fists into the rain-soaked soil. He knew why she refused to speak with him. He was too impure! His life too cluttered with emotion and hostility! He hadn't yet learned the lessons of restraint and control taught by the ancestors. He dropped his head to his hands.

He looked back to the empty sandstone overhang. He would try again. Perhaps if he were closer to the Great Mystery, she might return. He let his eyes drift up the forested slope. Yes, he would climb higher, as high as he could before the darkness halted him.

He dressed and untethered his pony, riding as far up the mountainside as the animal could go, then he dismounted and secured the reins around a small pine. The pony whinnied when he walked away.

As he weaved through the trees, the coolness of the afternoon permeated his moist clothing, the chill of the shadows touching his skin. He shivered. Then the rush of adrenaline returned and he closed his eyes, inhaling suddenly. She had returned. He could feel the softness of her breathing in his own chest. The hollowness that had haunted him for days vanished, replaced by a tingling warmth. He probed her mind. She was tired and cold. He fingered the fringes of his shirt, hoping the clothing would be warm enough as he climbed to higher elevations.

The rocky slopes felt rough against his moccasins, but his movements were silent. At last he reached a small meadow filled with blue, white, and yellow wildflowers. Tall grass waved in the breeze.

Wounded Bear walked out to the center of the meadow and spread his arms wide, asking the wolf to show him the point of connection between his soul and the woman's. Slowly his mind encircled her presence, mentally stroking her hair and whispering that she should not be afraid. He felt her fears fade as she opened her heart to him, inviting him to merge his identity with hers as he had that day at the Sun Dance.

He concentrated, sending his soul inward to meet her. And she held him, spinning threads of her essence with his, floating weightlessly in the bosom of Maheo. Time vanished as they danced, whirling together through an infinite sea of light and silence.

But he had to talk to her. Gently he pulled away. She grasped frantically for him, but he forced himself to separate. Opening his eyes, he saw her standing in the meadow, her blond hair blowing in the wind. He knelt and held out his arms.

"Mistai?" he called softly. *"Mistai*, speak with me?"

She smiled at him, her eyes yearning for his companionship, and extended her arms to meet his. But as she walked forward, her smile faded, her face growing taut—and disappeared.

"No! Come back!" he shouted to the silent mountains, his breast heaving in anguish. "I—must—speak with you!"

The sound of his cries rang hollowly through the forest.

Colleen was awakened by loud voices. Rain had pattered steadily all night, the drops sending trickles of water to invade her blankets. In an effort to stay dry she'd spent much of the night carving drainage ditches with her hand to lead the insistent water in another direction. As a result, she hadn't slept much. Yawning, she rolled over on her side to see what the commotion was.

At the movement, her head pounded, her stomach threatening to empty itself. She sucked in a slow breath and put a hand to her forehead. It was hot. The harsh voices didn't help; each shout was a hammer clang in her brain. She squinted as she located the angry disturbance.

Captain Williford slouched nonchalantly in front of Colonel Sawyers, his arms folded. In the distance, the horizon was shading lavender and pink with sunrise.

"Damn you, Williford!" Sawyers lowered his voice to a hiss as he noticed the growing crowd. "You *will* obey my orders! This train is continuing on!"

Williford looked up calmly to meet the angry eyes. "Colonel, my men cannot walk barefoot through prickly pear, rattlesnakes, and greasewood. Their shoes are just plain worn out, man!"

"I—well . . . !" Sawyers stumbled over the words, his long narrow face quivering in impotent rage. "Find some half measure to fix them, Captain! Surely there must be—"

"No, sir." Williford shook his head sternly. "Either my men will have decent shoes to carry them the rest of the way to Montana Territory, or I'll get on my horse and ride to Fort Laramie to request we be relieved of this duty and assigned there.''

Sawyers thrust out his chin. "You—you'd leave women and children without military protection in hostile territory, Captain?''

Williford's voice took on a deceptively smooth quality, but his eyes were hard. "Are you telling me, Colonel, that you'd continue on into the heart of Sioux and Cheyenne country without an escort?''

Sawyers ran a trembling hand through his graying beard and tipped his chin indignantly. "Sir, I have been commissioned by the Congress of the United States to build a road to the goldfields of Montana. I will do that no matter what the dangers. The emigrant wagons may return to the safety of Fort Laramie if they want. But my road-building crew isn't as fainthearted as you and your—uh—*men*. We're going on!'' Sawyers took a hostile step toward the captain, his chest thrown forward.

Colleen cringed at the baiting quality in Sawyers' voice. He was clearly trying to shame Williford into continuing by suggesting any other course would be cowardice.

Williford lowered his arms and tightened his hands into fists at his sides. His gray eyes slitted. "Colonel,'' he warned, "I'd take that step backward again ifn I was you.'' The look in his eyes was deadly.

Sawyers swallowed and reluctantly complied, his mouth puckered.

Williford stabbed a finger at him. "What I'd like to recommend is that you halt this train for a few days while I send a party to Fort Laramie for supplies. I think that Lieutenant Dana can be back—''

"I can't afford that kind of delay, Captain! We're already behind schedule!'' He gritted his teeth and set his jaw at an awkward angle. His elongated face looked like a misshapen potato. "I won't let army incompetence cost me more time!'' He turned to walk away.

Williford called after him, his voice clipped and cold. "I'm sending Dana for supplies, Colonel. My command is going to halt here for ten days until he returns. If you decide to continue on, you'll do it alone."

A fever-pitch tenseness spread through the crowd, anxious voices rumbling like distant thunder. Colleen glanced around. The blue-clad soldiers stood stiffly, their faces stern. Obviously they supported Williford. Their feet had endured hell over the last week as their boots finally gave out and they were forced to tramp, mostly barefoot, across searing sands and cactus. But the physical discomfort was only one element of the debate. Williford did not want to move his men into a danger zone unprepared. One hundred and fifteen out of the total one hundred and forty making up the escort were *infantry*! Pursuing mounted Indian warriors on foot was ludicrous anyway, but forcing men to do it without soles in their shoes was suicide. The taut, uncomfortable faces of the soldiers showed their fears.

Sawyers halted his steps, but kept his back to Williford. Colleen, however, could see his face. He looked like a scolded child, his scrawny nose quivering and his lips pursed. "Do you give me your word, Captain, that this train will be moving again in ten days?"

Williford sighed heavily and stared at the ground, smoothing a patch of upturned dirt with the toe of his boot. "No, sir."

Sawyers whirled, his face near geranium with anger. "What!" he demanded.

"I can't make those kind of promises, Colonel. Dana might run into a war party on his way—"

"You . . . !" Sawyers was on the verge of name calling.

Williford held up a hand for silence, fixing the colonel with a threatening glare. "What I will say, however, is that if Dana is not back in the specified amount of time, my command will *attempt* to proceed forward with you. Dana can follow our trail to find us. But you'll have to slow your pace considerably, Colonel."

Sawyers digested that bit of data, chewing his lower lip. "Send the lieutenant to Fort Laramie, Captain!" He spun and strode quickly away.

Williford offered a lazy salute to the retreating back and murmured, "I was planning on it, Colonel."

The crowd began to disperse and Colleen rolled over on her back. The stationary wagon over her head moved as if alive. She closed her eyes and groaned softly as she patted her rebellious stomach.

"Not feeling well?"

Matthew's voice made her jump. She opened one eye to stare at him. He knelt down by the wagon, his lips twisting into a impetuous, but sympathetic, grin.

"What did you do to me?" she moaned.

A wide flashing smile filled his face. "It's what I didn't do that I regret."

She'd been so concerned about her physical well-being she'd forgotten the content of the evening. His words brought it back vividly. Her eyes widened as her cheeks went crimson. Slowly she pulled up her blanket to cover her face. Only tendrils of blond hair protruded from beneath. The humiliation was worse than the throbbing pain in her head.

"My dear!" he said in frank enjoyment, deliberately misconstruing her actions. "Don't tell me that our failure to have a liaison disturbs you?" He dropped his voice to a suggestive whisper and pulled down the corner of her blanket. "I could remedy that?"

She writhed at his words. "You are the coarsest man I've ever known."

He laughed uproariously, fixing her with bold appraising eyes. "Think how much worse this meeting would have been if I'd—uh—complied with your request? As a matter of fact, the meeting would have occurred much earlier when you awoke to find yourself—"

"Matthew!" she whispered insistently, pulling the blanket off her face to glance quickly around and see if anyone else was within hearing range. No one was. A wave of relief cascaded over her.

"What?"

She pursed her mouth in anticipation of her next retort, but when she met his merry, mocking eyes all she could do was laugh. Unfortunately her stomach resented the action. She sat bolt upright, clutching a hand to her abdomen.

He surveyed her from the corner of his eye. "That bad, huh?"

She nodded weakly and swallowed, pure misery lining her heart-shaped face.

"Colleen." There was a teasing, caressing note in his voice. He reached out to stroke the blond hair away from her face. "I've a pot of coffee at my tent. If you can keep a cup down, you'll feel much better."

"Oh, Matthew, I'd never make it to your tent."

He gave her a wry smile. "And last night you were so eager."

"Will—you . . ." She stopped, tasting that horrifyingly familiar acidity in her watery mouth. The worst thing she could imagine would be vomiting in front of a man. Carefully, she swallowed. "I—I'll be fine—thank you. Go away."

"If you insist, but I'll be back." He stood and strode away toward the military camp.

Colleen heaved a sigh of relief, then rolled to her side, glanced cautiously around, and started digging a shallow hole next to her. At least if she was going to lose the contents of her stomach, she wanted to know where they went.

No sooner had she finished the hole than her recalcitrant belly decided it was time to use it. She pulled her blanket over her head and made a tent over the hole to shield herself from prying eyes. Then her stomach turned inside out. When the tumult ceased, she felt remarkably better. But before she lowered the wool shield, she pushed the dirt carefully back into the hole and smoothed it flat. Except for a slight soil discoloration, it looked as though a hole had never been dug at all.

Sighing, she lifted the edge of the blanket—and cringed. A muscular calf sheathed in sky blue was stretched out beside her.

"Better?" his amused voice asked.

"How long have you been sitting there?"

"Long enough."

She straightened up, slowly lowering the blanket to see a coffeepot and two cups sitting on the ground in front of her. Pulling the shreds of her dignity around her, she took a deep breath, straightened her shoulders, and responded, "What a marvelous idea, Mr. Douglas. Please?"

His stifled his laughter and poured, then handed her a tin cup.

She sipped gingerly, unsure how the brew would rest in her stomach. As the steaming liquid went down it roiled a little, but made no moves to escape. She sighed and crawled out from under the wagon to sit beside him. Tucking her yellow skirt around her ankles, her eyes conveniently drifted to the sunrise. Already the wind was coming up, blowing golden clouds across the horizon. Cautiously she glanced at him.

His eyes smiled cynically at her over the rim of his coffee cup. "You look better."

"Better than what?" she questioned, aware of her tousled, unbecoming appearance. Her yellow dress was smudged with dirt, torn at the hem, and looked like she'd slept in it—which she had.

He twisted his mustache and looked her up and down. His voice sounded lusty. "Best-looking woman I've seen in months."

"Of course," she muttered skeptically, frowning. "You just got out of prison."

"Technicality."

They fell silent, each staring out to the glistening sunrise. The sun was above the horizon now, its brilliant rays making the sage glimmer a silverish green. The clouds had blown into thin wisps that streaked the azure sky like strips of white lace. Eagles drifted on wind currents, their brown bodies soaring and tumbling as they played.

Colleen was feeling much better. Matthew'd been right about the coffee. Her stomach was sore and grumbling, but not dangerous. She propped her chin on her knees and watched the hustle-bustle of camp. Breakfast fires blazed; the smell of bacon and bread carried on the breeze.

"Hungry?" he asked.

"You think food is safe?"

He lounged back lazily, a glint in his eyes. "Hard to say."

She studied him as he gazed out at the military camp. Williford's resupply party was being outfitted with horses and wagons. Matthew leaned back on both elbows, his long legs extended and crossed at the ankles. His oval face was dark brown, the tan extending down his neck and into the vee formed by his half-unbuttoned blue shirt. Dark hair curled out of the opening. The drooping mustache that framed his full lips hung almost to his chin. But it was his blue eyes that fascinated her, drew her to him like a thirsty animal to water. There was a wary self-assurance there—the eyes of a man who's seen too much danger and suffering to ever be quite comfortable in the world.

He turned to look at her and smiled. "Cat-at-a-mouse-hole look. Thinking something devious?"

She made an airy gesture. "Just wondering."

"About what?"

Her face puckered, feeling uncomfortable about broaching personal topics.

"Ask. I'm not shy."

"I was—wondering why you've been so kind to me. Why someone with your 'experience' would care?"

He gave her a ravishing smile. "I told you. Someday I expect compensation."

"Oh, Matthew, be serious! You can't just be interested in my—favors." Her mind jostled, spurs of doubt poking her. She whirled around to face him. "Can you?"

"Why, Colleen, what an ill-bred question. I'm shocked."

She gave him a sideways appraisal, poorly concealed irritation seeping out in her voice. "You? I'll bet."

His eyes twinkled, fingers entwining over his stomach. "I don't like this."

"What?"

"You having the upper hand—it's unnatural."

She grabbed her yellow skirt and started to stand. "If you're not going to answer . . ."

He reached up and clasped her arm, pulling her back to the sand. "I'm interested," he said resignedly, "because you're young and vulnerable—and I find you very attractive."

"Oh!" She fumbled with her hands, wrapping them in her skirt. "I—I'm married."

"I'm aware of that, Mrs. Merrill."

She let her eyelids flutter as her mother had taught her to do when she wanted to demonstrate her modesty and simultaneously make men notice her charms.

"Do stop that, Colleen," he ordered, brows lowering. "You look like a demented goose."

"I . . . well." She fumbled with her chin. Why was he always so blasted disconcerting? "I mean, Mr. Douglas, that it's—it's not appropriate for you to . . ."

He stood, his mouth pursed in annoyance. "If you're going to start that again, *I'm leaving*!" He turned abruptly and started away across the sands.

Colleen lifted a hand, but he was gone, his long legs rapidly putting distance between them.

She watched him stalk back to the bustling hive of soldiers and lost sight of him in the eddying knots of blue uniforms. The military camp was located a hundred yards from the rest of the train under a broad canopy of cottonwoods.

Why was it that he could be so exciting and repulsive at the same time? She always felt odd when he was near, as though she were perched on one foot atop a narrow pole— always struggling to keep her balance. It was like he came from another world and had a deep scorn for the things her world told her were sacred, like feminine coquettishness and masculine childishness.

Her thoughts drifted to New York. After her father had returned from California, life had been difficult. Marie Meara had been quite accustomed to making difficult decisions alone and had done so effectively for ten years. But with the reappearance of Patrick, those skills of independence had to be immediately abandoned; the task wasn't easy. Colléen recalled her father's blustering rage one day when Marie authorized the family banker, as she'd been doing for years, to transfer funds from one account to another. Patrick had stamped through the house, throwing things and shouting, ''Ye'd think ye wore the pants in the family, for God's sake! Money's a mon's doing, woman! Ye'll not put yer fingers in it again!'' Marie had followed along behind him, bewildered, wringing her hands and apologizing. Then later, in private, she had whispered to Colleen, ''Men are just little boys in grown-up bodies, darlin'. They need pettin' and coddlin' and guidin'—but you must never let them know ye'r doing those things. Oh, heavens, no! If they think ye can take care of yerself, well''—she'd shuddered, a grave look on her face—''they just might make ye!''

Colleen fiddled with a fold in her yellow skirt and thought about it. Her mother—of course—was right. Being an adult woman without a man to take care of her would be a terrible fate.

''Saints preserve us!'' she muttered thoughtfully and bit her lip. Of course, she had to admit silently that women were quite capable of taking care of themselves, but no one wanted to endure the criticism of a Susan B. Anthony. She remembered reading about Miss Anthony and her band of suffragettes on the front page of the *Seneca County Courier*. The newspaper hadn't been kind, calling the advocates, ''sour old maids'' or, more scandalously, ''divorced women!'' And, Lord knew, such women were ostracized from every civilized social occasion and only allowed grudgingly into uncivilized ones! Being an ''independent woman'' meant *a near complete loss of social status*! Colleen shook her head.

She looked back to the milling men in blue. The encampment was alive with activity, soldiers running pell-mell to gather rifles and supplies for the trip to Fort Laramie.

Williford stood in the midst, hand on hips, hat pushed back on his head. His triangular face was creased in seriousness. There was an air of control about him, as though he knew quite well every detail of every situation that might be encountered by the small party headed south.

She caught a glimpse of Douglas; he was leaning lazily against a tree, arms folded across his chest, talking with another soldier. His impudent cackle made it across the sands to her ears. She furrowed her brow in confusion and irritation. He wasn't a child, as her mother had proposed. But neither was he a typical adult male. He rarely did things she could term "gentlemanly," and often seemed intent on behaving just the opposite, as though deliberately offending her sense of proprieties to make a point. Unfortunately, she had no idea what that point was. The only thing clear was that he felt a sort of impersonal contempt for all things "civilized."

He was puzzling indeed—like a wild bird dropped in the midst of a chicken coop. It was as though he felt it his sacred duty to throw the chickens over the fence and, if they refused to run at the chance of freedom, to break their silly necks to demonstrate the error of their ways.

She smiled to herself, then laughed out loud, a hand over her mouth. She could see Matthew in the form of an eagle in a chicken coop, routing dumb birds with his beak. Then she stiffened. Is that what he was doing to her? Routing her to make her see the squalor of the pen?

She shifted uncomfortably. Her proprieties . . . a pen? But proprieties were the heart of all things good and civilized. Everyone knew that! She frowned. Civilization . . . a pen? It was a strange new thought. She drummed her fingers against her knees.

He'd unlocked a door in her head and handed her a key to others. She crawled over to the wagon wheel and leaned back against it. The iron rim was cool. She needed time to think.

· CHAPTER 9 ·

WOUNDED BEAR CROUCHED HIDDEN BENEATH THE STREAM bank, his heart pounding like thunder in his chest. Dream voices echoed from the tableland above—white voices. Army ponies whinnied. The streambed was slick as he picked his way carefully along the bank, his moccasins sliding in the mud. The babbling water sounded loud, the spirit of the stream urging him to hurry, to flee the blue-clad soldiers.

"You! Halt!" a voice shouted as a rifle hammer was pulled back with a loud *click*!

He whirled, pressing his back against the crumbling muddy bank. His breathing was erratic, terrified.

"Cain't hide, Injun!"

Wounded Bear closed his eyes, swallowing convulsively. He slowly swiveled his head to look above him toward the voice. There, standing on the first terrace was a red-faced soldier, grinning maliciously. The man spat brown juice down at him and laughed.

"Here he is, boys!" he called over his shoulder.

A loud pounding of hooves and feet filled the air. A hundred white faces leaned over the bank to stare at him. He closed his eyes, praying desperately to the Great Mystery, begging for help.

"Well, get him up here!" a man with captain's bars said and turned to walk away from the bank.

Fear overwhelmed Wounded Bear. He could only stand like a statue as ten men climbed down over the bank and shoved rifle barrels into his sides to make him scurry back over the terrace and toward their camp. The barrels were cold, bitterly cold against his bare back.

He sucked in shuddering breaths as he stumbled forward, taunting white voices surrounding him. Then he reached the tent where the captain stood stiffly outside, his jaw grinding in the bright light of the sun.

"What tribe?" he signed, his hands moving rapidly.

"Tsistsistas," Wounded Bear murmured, his eyes darting around, then made the sign for his people. The army camp was large. Hundreds of dirty white tents dotted the flat tableland. How had he missed it! How had he gotten so close without smelling the thousand horses and campfires?

"Hmph!" the captain grunted, folding his arms and squinting. He signed, "You with war party?"

Wounded Bear shook his head quickly. He couldn't tell these men he'd been out seeking a vision. They wouldn't understand.

"Sure, you ain't!" a short private with missing front teeth yelled. "You cain't trust no Injun, Cap'n. Hell! there could be a thousand savages over the next hill and he'd never tell us! I say we kill him now so's we don't have to worry 'bout him!"

A rumble of agreeing voices echoed through the cottonwoods.

In a sheer act of will, Wounded Bear forced his body to quiet its shuddering fear. He would meet death like a warrior—not crawling and begging. He stiffened his back and threw out his chest, staring hard into the captain's gray eyes.

The officer nodded. "Reckon that's the way to do it."

The short private raised his rifle gleefully, pointing it at Wounded Bear's bare chest. His muscles went rigid in preparation for the bullet's impact.

"Wait!" a new voice came through the clamor.

A dark-haired lieutenant stepped forward, one hand held high. The toothless private reluctantly lowered his rifle, grumbling under his breath. The lieutenant was a big man, his shoulders broad and heavily muscled and he wore a long mustache that touched his chin. Wounded Bear met his blue eyes squarely, no fear showing on his face. The lieutenant tilted his head suddenly, squinting, studying Wounded Bear as though he knew him, cared for him. A softness came over his face.

"What band are you with?" the lieutenant asked in Cheyenne.

Wounded Bear sucked in a quick breath. The soldier knew the language of the people! "Dull Knife's," he whispered back solemnly.

The lieutenant glanced surreptitiously around at the glowering men in blue, then spoke in a hushed voice. "I'll see you're not killed, then, tonight, I'll cut you loose. Wait."

Wounded Bear nodded. Why would a white soldier help him? The man's actions made no sense. Yet; in the back of his mind there was something hauntingly familiar about the lieutenant, something painful and buried deep in his unconscious—but he couldn't place it.

"Captain?" the lieutenant called. "If he is with a war party, our shooting him will only bring the whole Indian camp down on us. I suggest, sir, that we tie him up and scout this area thoroughly. If we find he's alone, we can always kill him tomorrow."

The captain shrugged and waved an impatient hand. "Do it!"

The toothless private trotted forward and shoved his rifle barrel brutally into Wounded Bear's back. Pain shot through him . . .

. . . and he woke with a start, jerking forward, the dream images still powerfully real. His red blanket fell to coil in folds around his waist. The cool breeze flooded over his bare chest as he stared into the ebony night, searching . . . searching. The sky was covered with dense clouds, leaving the world dark and barren. He shivered and hugged himself, his gaze roaming over the black rolling hills. The dream had been so vivid. It stayed with him, lingering to taunt his awakened mind.

Cold sweat dripped down his forehead to sting his eyes. He lifted a trembling hand to wipe it away, then got to his feet. His legs were unsteady—wobbly from sleep and fear. The dream was important. He could feel the tug of the wolf behind the images. There was a message hidden in the story—a lesson to be learned. He knew the difference between ordinary dreams and symbolic dreams sent by his spirit helper to show him a fragment of the future. Symbolic dreams left him feeling anguished and hollow—like he did now.

Who could the dark-haired lieutenant be?

He picked up his blanket and strolled silently through the village. The lodges were dark and quiet, only occasional snores and the whimpering of babies disturbed the night. Wounded Bear forced his lungs to inhale deep breaths, trying to chase away the terror and emptiness left by the dream. The cool breeze flicked his loose hair, sending black tendrils fluttering over his face. He ignored them, staring absently through the web of black and out across the conical lodges of his people.

Was the soldier a part of the wagon train that threatened the future? Would he help the people—help Wounded Bear?

An odd muffled voice echoed in the depths of his memories, but he couldn't make out the words. Yet he knew they were tied to the soldier. Was he a man from the people's past?

The indistinct voice shouted at him again, trying desperately to make itself heard through the layers of mental cloth that muted its message. Wounded Bear halted his steps and listened. But the voice faded, leaving only a dull ache to twist his gut.

Wounded Bear squeezed his eyes shut and felt the pain, the turmoil of his body. The voice had spoken to him—even though he couldn't hear the words.

He strolled past the last of the lodges and into the darkness to a sage-covered hill. Sitting down, he sighed and snugged the blanket tight around his throat as his eyes drifted across the rolling hills. The moon was rising, casting a subdued silver shadow over the clouds.

Spreading his arms, he opened his heart to the night and the wind and the moon, seeking their wisdom, asking for help in understanding the mysterious meaning of his dream.

He prayed long into the night, letting the light of the moon filter through him and the strength of the wind caress his aching soul. He prayed until at last he knew—knew that the soldier was with the train . . . and the yellow-haired woman.

Matthew Douglas and George Williford lounged beneath the towering cottonwoods that lined Hat Creek, watching the water flow by. The stream wasn't particularly impressive; it was seventy-five feet across and a single foot deep. But it ran swiftly over slate bedrock, providing some interesting eddies and splashes as it tumbled over protruding stones. The real draw to the location, however, was the road-building crew busy with picks and shovels on the east side of the creek. A granite-hard, perpendicular clay wall jutted straight up from the water. Sawyers had ordered his men to dig the road from the tableland to the creek bed— through the clay wall.

Douglas leaned back against a cottonwood and pulled his cap down over his eyes, yawning.

"How long you think, George?" he asked lazily, his eyes half-closed.

"For what?"

Douglas flipped a hand at the laborers. "Them to dig that crossing through the clay."

Williford frowned. He swatted a fly on his shirt sleeve. "Oh, reckon a week."

"Um," Douglas said dryly. "Only if it don't rain."

Both men turned to look westward. Dark thunderheads built castles over the orange sandstone bluffs in the distance.

Williford chuckled and shook his head in disgust. "Man's a damn lunatic, Douglas."

"Who?"

The captain thrust out a hand at the sweating road crew. "Sawyers! Hell, even if they manage to knock a hole through that wall, it's clay!"

"So?"

"The runoff next year will take this crossing out in a single season."

Douglas removed his blue cap and beat the dust out on his leg. "Won't make much difference. This road is mostly a ditch anyway."

Their attention was drawn away. One of the road-builders had thrown down his pick and was cursing loudly. He'd made barely a dent in the clay before his pick split in two. Williford laughed lightly at first, then louder as the disgruntled laborer began including Colonel Sawyers in his colorful tirade. The man paced back and forth, shaking both fists in the air and kicking the broken pieces of his pick like a child's ball.

"Sawyers ever built a road before?" Matthew asked as he put his cap back on his head and tugged the brim down over his eyes again. Bright sunlight was filtering through the leaves and dappling his face.

"Heard tell he built some forts in Iowa a few years back."

Matthew looked askance, tilting his head so he could see from beneath the blue brim. The sunlight hit him again and he squinted. "This isn't Iowa, George. Terrain's a might different."

"Couldn't prove it by the colonel. This is his first trip to the northern plains."

Matthew choked in mid-yawn, straightening up. "What!

What fool would assign a tenderfoot to head an expedition into the heart of Cheyenne and Sioux country?''

"Fellow by the name of Congressman Hubbard."

Matthew shook his head and settled back against the tree. "No wonder this road is a ditch! Politics!"

"And money."

"Whoa up, there, George." He rolled over on his side, a hand up to halt the discussion while he thought. "You telling me this road is just coins jingling in somebody's pocket and not part of the glorious cause of Manifest Destiny?''

"I'm sure the citizens of Sioux City think it is." Williford picked up a black rock and tossed it in the air, watching it rise and fall.

"How's that?"

"If this road is successful—"

"And that rests with the Sioux and Cheyenne."

Williford nodded lazily and scratched his cheek. "Anyway, Sioux City stands to make lots of money, since they'll be the eastern supply base for the road."

"Ah, and that's why Congressman Hubbard pushed for it?''

"Pushed like there wasn't no tomorrow, 'less Iowa got to build a road to the Montana goldfields."

"And who, pray tell, decided on the course of this road? I mean, winding up through the last hunting grounds of two of the most powerful tribes left in the country doesn't seem particularly bright. Better to take a straight shot from Duluth to Virginia City than—"

"Congress gave Sawyers complete discretion in locating the route and doing the work necessary to—"

"Jeezzz!" Douglas shifted uncomfortably back against the tree, lacing his fingers over his stomach, a disgusted look on his face. "First they hire a man with no road-building experience or familiarity with the northern plains, then they give him a free hand to put it in the wrong place?''

"Now, wait a shake," Williford objected, holding up a hand. "This road would be just fine if we took half the goddamned hills and dumped them into the goddamned drainages.''

"Ain't enough hills to make it come out. It'd still be a ditch.''

Williford nodded resignedly. "Reckon you're right.''

The more Matthew thought about it, the funnier it seemed. He started to cackle, laughter rising from the bottom of his belly. Williford squinted at him out of the corner of his eye, snickered softly, then burst into a side-splitting roar. So loud was their fit that the road crew halted in midswing to look across the stream. When Douglas noticed the gaping faces, he hooted louder, pointing and kicking his feet. Williford followed his insistent finger, saw the contemptuous faces, and squealed as he slapped the ground. In their mirth they missed the arrival of Colonel Sawyers.

Seeing them, the colonel scowled, then climbed down the clay wall, waded the shallow stream, and came to stand in front of the two infantrymen. His oblong face flushed as he stared down at the lounging soldiers, translucent eyes growing cold. He tugged roughly at his scraggly beard, wiped a sweaty hand over his red shirt, and spread his legs.

"Captain? I'd like to speak with you.''

"I'm right here, Colonel.''

"I'm going to call a camp meeting to explain our—delay to the train. I'd appreciate it if you and your command could be present in case there are questions concerning military matters.''

"When?''

"Tonight.''

Williford nodded, his eyes locked with Sawyers'. "I'll post the appropriate guards and order the remainder of my men to be there, Colonel.''

"Thank you, Captain.'' Sawyers turned crisply and tramped away.

"Hmph!'' Williford grunted as he watched the man cross Hat Creek. "Wonder what the meeting's really about?''

Matthew pushed his cap back and wiped the sweat from his brow. "Mud slinging.''

* * *

Colleen finished the last of the supper dishes and shook her hands to make them dry faster. Lawrence O'Brian smiled at her from beside the fire. He was a stocky, freckle-faced man with bright red hair and flashing green eyes. His round face was adorned with a crooked nose, broken in one too many fights, and paper-thin lips.

"So, lass, are ye ready to go to the grand meeting?"

She smiled wanly, frightened that Robert might be there and try to force her back to his wagon. "You'll be there?"

He nodded. "Aye. And I'll not be letting anyone make ye do anything ye don't want."

"You're very kind, Mr. O'Brian. I don't know how I can ever thank—"

"Ach!" He waved a hand. "Yer no trouble, Colleen. And yer teaching me tomboy daughter how to be a lady. That's worth whatever it takes to keep ye here!"

Colleen smiled. She and Elizabeth were becoming fast friends. Already the girl had started leaving her long red hair to flow free in the wind, rather than restricting it to severe braids.

Lawrence stuck the stem of his pipe out at Colleen. "Do ye know what she asked me a little while ago?"

Colleen shook her head.

"She wanted to know if she could wash her face before the meeting." He sat up straighter, shaking his head. "Ach, lass! That girl has never *asked* to wash her face in all her life. Aye, yer having a positive influence!"

Colleen laughed and looked out to the large bonfire that Sawyers had ordered built in the midst of the cottonwood grove. Leaves reflected the light of the fire, flickering golden as they rustled in the wind. People were starting to gather. She studied the wide variety of slouched hats, caps, and panamas that bobbed as men talked and crowded closer to the fire, their plaid- and solid-colored shirts weaving a tapestry over the background of tree trunks. A large crate had been set up in front of the fire for Sawyers, and as he emerged, winding through the trees, he walked straight to it, but didn't climb on top.

O'Brian followed her gaze.

"Ye know," Lawrence said, pointing his pipe stem at Sawyers. "The expedition may be a shambles, but I'm glad we came along."

"Why's that?"

"Because we're going to be part of building this new land, lass. Me and me family." His voice had grown soft, his freckled face somber. "Aye, there's nothing left in the Old Country. It's all filled to burstin' with people and farms and cities. But this new land—now that's a different matter."

"It's certainly got open spaces," Colleen said, looking back to the milling group of people at the bonfire. The soldiers had started to arrive and were crowding around beneath the cottonwoods, but she hadn't seen Douglas yet.

"Aye, and open spaces mean freedom. Freedom to make something of yerself, without the jolly king putting a noose around yer neck. I could tell ye some stories about that." He laughed loudly, his green eyes wide as he rolled back on his elbows and nodded vigorously.

"You got the law of Ireland after you, Lawrence?" she asked with interest, her head cocked skeptically.

"Anybody with any guts in the Old Country has the law after them."

Colleen laughed. "Why?"

"Oh, I suppose it's because the land is too crowded. There's too many folks hungry and too many others living off their misery. That!"—he poked his pipe at her—"is why this new land is the place to be. You can grow the way you want here, without crowding somebody else's roots." He stuck the pipe stem between his teeth and spread his arms to the dark prairies. "Here, a mon can be wild as he wants."

"Wild?" Her thoughts instantly turned to Matthew. He was certainly an example of that.

"Aye, and a mon's got to be wild if he's gonna be a mon."

She nodded absently, her thoughts still on Matthew and his excitingly wild—and gruff—ways.

"Sure, lass. You break a mon to harness and you ruin him! He loses the courage to fight. And that's what life's really all about girl: fighting for what ye believe. Just like an animal. Fer example, if you take a wild deer who's been used to kicking coyotes in the belly to survive and force it into a set of traces, then make it pull wagons—well, after a while its spirit withers. Men are like that."

"I suppose." She smiled, completely confused as to what he meant. Animals and men alike? God forbid! But she kept quiet, knowing if she disagreed or asked questions he'd tell her more and she was anxious to get to the meeting. It looked like everyone was there but them!

Lawrence's eyes studied the gathering. Sawyers climbed on top of the crate in front of the fire and people were starting to quiet down in anticipation.

"Time we were agoing, it seems."

"Guess so."

"I'll go fetch Elizabeth and Maureen," he said, getting to his feet and ambling off to the other side of the wagon.

Colleen sucked in a breath, her brown eyes scanning the crowd for any sign of Robert. He'd left her alone for the past twenty-four hours, but there was no telling how long the peace would last. Her stomach tightened in fear of that inevitable meeting.

"All right!" Lawrence's voice boomed as he returned with his wife and daughter in tow. "Let's go hear what the colonel has to say."

Elizabeth trotted forward to slip her hand into Colleen's.

"You look pretty!" Colleen whispered into her ear as they walked.

The child put a hand over her mouth and giggled in pride. She had put on one of her best dresses, a green and red plaid with ruffles down the front. "So do you!" she whispered back.

Colleen raised her brows and shook her head. Unfortunately, she knew what a mess she was. Though she'd washed her long hair and bathed, she still had no fresh clothing. The torn yellow dress would have to do until she felt she could go back to her own wagon. Maybe tomorrow she'd have the courage.

As they entered the circle of people, Colleen spied Matthew. He leaned against a tree with his hands in his blue trouser pockets. He looked quite bored, eyes drowsy. She looked around for Robert, but could not see him. Some of her tension fled. She dropped a hand to Elizabeth's shoulder and took a deep breath.

Colonel Sawyers cleared his throat loudly, his long narrow face and red shirt flickering orange in the light of the flames. As he raised both hands for silence, his salt and pepper beard quivered with words that were lost in the hubbub of over two hundred people shushing their neighbors.

Finally the gathering grew silent and the colonel lowered his hands and looked out over the crowded assembly. The soldiers were grouped together in a dusty blue tangle on his right, the rest of the expedition scattered in front and off to his left. Overhead, the towering cottonwood trees rustled softly in the cool evening breeze. He put his hands on his hips.

"Friends, I've called this meeting tonight to let you know that we'll be delayed here a few days. Captain Williford tells me his men can no longer accompany this expedition . . ."

A clamor of worried voices rose, all eyes fixing on Williford, who stood with his arms folded and legs spread near Douglas, a smooth, unreadable expression on his face. Sawyers waved his hands.

"Because!" he shouted over the angry buzz. "Because his men no longer have soles in their shoes." The buzz faded. "So, he dispatched Lieutenant Dana this morning to Fort Laramie to retrieve such supplies as he needs for the rest of the expedition. As a result, we will be spending the next few days in this vicinity awaiting Dana's return. I suggest that everyone take advantage of the creek for washing clothes, etc. However, you should all be aware that we are entering Sioux and Cheyenne territory and those tribes will undoubtedly have scouting parties out. Go nowhere alone and stick as close to the train as possible. If you—''

Nat Hedges interrupted, his young face lined in disbelief. He tugged the brim of his brown slouched hat. ''Hell, Colonel! We got over two hundred guns, two mountain howitzers, and enough ammunition to lick any war party them tribes can send out!''

Cries of ''of course!'' and ''certainly!'' rang through the assembly. Impassioned conversations grew up among the milling men, fists shaking in the air as confident laughs cackled.

''Bunch of blasted fools!'' Lawrence leaned over to whisper to Colleen. She nodded.

''Now, hold on!'' Sawyers shouted. ''Hold on!'' Voices quieted. ''That's true. We're well equipped to defend ourselves, but I don't want any of you taking chances. The Indians don't know the ways of civilized people. They're liable to sneak up on you when your plumb nekked—er—uh—excuse me, ladies—and shoot you in the back! We've been sending missionaries for the last few years, but these Indians haven't yet learned to appreciate Christian values. They still worship bestial gods and practice the most abominable morality. So, I don't want . . .''

The clamor rose again, and Colleen saw Lawrence pull Maureen and Elizabeth close. ''Don't ye worry none,'' he said, patting the pistol at his side. ''Those red devils won't even get close!''

Colleen looked across the circle to Matthew. His navy jacket and sky blue pants shone brightly in the orange light of the huge fire. He was squeezing the bridge of his nose, a pinched expression on his face. He shifted positions, bracing his other shoulder against the broad cottonwood trunk. He looked like he was struggling not to get involved in the discussion.

''Well . . . why haven't they learned Christian virtues?'' Hedges called out, waving an emphatic hand. ''Everybody here knows why! It's because they're savages who don't want to give up their perverted ways!''

Pink rose in Colleen's cheeks as her breathing quickened. Why, these men acted like they were looking for a fight! Eager to kill Indians, as though the act was somehow sanctioned by God. She clutched her crucifix and crossed herself.

"Devil Spawn!" someone behind Hedges shouted. He turned around to look through the crowd. "That's what they are! Why they've killed enough of our decent young boys in blue to—"

"Sure!" Hedges yelled back. "Just ask the captain!" He pointed to Williford.

Williford shifted uncomfortably, his eyes drifting nervously through the crowd.

They were working themselves up, getting in a shouting rage in preparation for the fight they hoped would come. Colleen felt her own blood rising. Her eyes darted over the excited faces. Williford stood with his jaw clamped, his eyes focused on Sawyers. Douglas, however, wore a contemptuous smile—contempt as though he listened to a passel of fools.

He stuffed his hands back in his pockets and propped one foot against the tree trunk. "Colonel," he called in his airy drawl, "I know something of the tribes in this part of the country. Could I comment on this discussion?" His manner had turned suddenly polite, but his eyes still gleamed.

Sawyers nodded curtly, his disdain for the officer apparent. "Go on."

Douglas removed one hand from his pocket and twisted his mustache, his manner still overly polite. "Gentlemen, has it occurred to you that there are only two hundred of us and at least ten thousand plains Indians? If the tribes decided to attack this train, I'm sure they'd wipe us out to the last man."

"Oh, dear Lord!" Colleen murmured to herself, her eyes darting around at the confused faces. Women gasped behind her, while men clenched their fists. Hostile glances were exchanged throughout the assembly.

Dr. A. M. Tingley, who served as the train's physician,

geologist, and botanist, stepped forward to stand by Colonel Sawyers. His white hair gleamed brightly in the dwindling firelight. He raised both hands to the crowd, reminding Colleen of a preacher ready to deliver a hell-and-damnation sermon. His thin face was filled with a righteous fervor, as was his voice.

"Listen, folks!" he said. "My brother William, whom many of you know, is the pastor of the Congregationalist Church in Sioux City and he and I have talked long hours about the Indian problem in this country. I want to stress that Christian charity commands us to generosity in this manner. We don't want to have to fight these Indians."

Douglas swatted a mosquito on his sleeve and gave the man an exaggerated nod.

"Bah!" Hedges exploded, striding forward. "The best way to handle savages is fight fire with fire! We've got to—"

"No, please!" Tingley pleaded at the top of his lungs. His wrinkled face shone golden in the firelight as he looked at Hedges. "God has planted in the heart of the Indian affections and feelings that only require molding and direction to noble aims! He is our brother, erring and benighted though he be, but still our brother!"

Sawyers walked close to Tingley, shaking his hands in the air to silence the growing clamor of dissenting voices. His red flannel shirt flickered. "The good doctor is right!" he agreed. "It is our duty to reclaim the Indian race to the path of godliness—not kill them."

"Yes!" Douglas' deep voice rang out. "We must reclaim these savages from their perverted concept of a beneficent God. It's bestial!"

Stutters echoed around the assembly, his mocking tone sinking in. Indignant men threw out their chests, slitting their eyes.

Williford cast Douglas a sideways warning glance, then walked over to lean against the same cottonwood. The captain's lips moved in some inaudible comment to which Douglas chuckled rudely.

"Sir!" Nat Hedges stuck out his chin, wiping sweaty palms on his blue plaid shirt. He looked shockingly young in comparison to Douglas and Williford. His round face was as smooth and wide-eyed as a babe's. "Are you suggesting these perverted devils are—"

"Ah, perversion!" Matthew's blue eyes widened. His airy drawl turned deceptively smooth. "Sir, I would never suggest that the Cheyenne's strict emphasis on female chastity and modesty was virtuous; why, I much prefer our own system of setting up clandestine cathouses—er"—he bowed deeply to the handful of ladies, making a gesture of self-reproach, then changed his voice to a conspiratorial whisper and winked at Hedges—"houses of ill-repute."

Hedges stammered, his face shading crimson, "I—I—sir! You—you know I wasn't referring to . . . I meant that they kill wantonly and wouldn't scruple to inflict the worst torments on our helpless women and chil . . ."

Colleen jumped. It was amazing how much noise only a few gasping women could make. Hedges turned quickly, his mouth gaping.

"I'm terribly sorry, ladies!" He bowed deferentially. "I didn't mean to startle you. I was just . . ."

Douglas raised his brows high and gave the young man a cynical smile. "Yes! I'm in complete agreement, Mr. Hedges. Indians do kill wantonly." Then suddenly the expression on his face changed, becoming so contemplatively polite, almost naively sweet, that Colleen thought the manners an affront in and of themselves. He continued. "But the reasons they are barbarians is precisely as Dr. Tingley says. Their naturally good inclinations need molding. And God knows, there aren't enough heroes like our glorious Colonel Chivington to set the kind of examples the Indians need." He put a hand over his heart and pursed his lips as though saying "the shame of it all."

The audience was back on his side, heads nodded graciously throughout the gathering, people acknowledging their Christian duties to provide better examples for the savages. Colleen rubbed her chin. Hadn't she read somewhere that Colonel Chivington was under congressional investigation for the battle at Sand Creek last November? That some folks were raising serious questions about whether his actions were glorious or just plain murder?

"Just the same"—Nat Hedges' voice rang out—"we can't spend all our time trying to teach red devils the finer things in life. We got a mission to settle and develop this great land, to—"

"Yes, the devils just don't understand that we Christian folk need this land."

A loud shout of "That's right!" rang out, followed by a series of conflicting emotional outbursts, some for the Indians, most against.

Sawyers had perceived the mocking tone in Douglas' voice. He looked up suddenly, his long face tensing. "Lieutenant, the Indians do not know how to use this abundant land." He waved a negligent hand. "The gold and silver, rich farm and grazing land are going to waste. It's essential that we gain access to this country so that our own can grow. There are civilized people in this country starving. Starving while fertile fields lay fallow in the West!" His voice had risen to a quavering crescendo, his translucent eyes gleaming.

An ominous silence descended.

Colleen swallowed. She could feel her fluttering heartbeat in her ears. She looked back to Matthew. He had a disagreeably confident smile on his face, white teeth shining beneath his mustache. His low chuckle was like an impertinent blow to the stomach of the Manifest Destiny devotees in the audience.

"Yes, Colonel"—his deep drawl pierced the air with an unexpected slap—"most of us here know well the starvation in the South." He extended an open hand to the men in blue who shuffled nervously, their faces showing pain and anger.

A new and anguished rattle rose up from the soldiers. Colleen watched as their expressions turned sour and they waved hands in disgust. Matthew straightened up, his smile changing to a hard glare, then turned and strode out into the darkness. It seemed only moments until every soldier at the meeting had followed him, leaving road-builders and emigrants behind.

Sawyers fidgeted, grinding his teeth. He clenched and unclenched his hands as he stared after the retreating soldiers. "It's all right, folks! This road we're building is good for the country. It will open this great land, hastening our expansion from sea to sea. Why, as soon as we've contained the hostiles and can use these rich regions the way God intended, everybody will benefit—even the Indians. Once they're safely on reservations, we can teach them how to farm and live decent lives."

"That's right!" Nat Hedges affirmed, lifting a fist and slicing the air. "If these tribes knew what we was doing for them, lending a hand to help 'em out of barbarism, they'd be grateful!"

Nods and sighs of relief swept the assembly. With Douglas' departure, things were running smoothly again, people's minds clearing.

"Well." Sawyers sighed, looking out over the fifty people still left. "Let's get some sleep, folks." He stepped down from his crate. "We'll have a few days' rest here, but Virginia City is still four hundred miles away."

The crown began to disperse, Colonel Sawyers joining a small group of teamsters, while the emigrants gathered their few children and sauntered off toward their wagons.

Colleen lagged behind the O'Brians, her thoughts on the meeting. Matthew was such an offensive sort. Didn't he realize people wanted this land opened up and that the Indians were being cantankerous not accepting the reservation land the government offered? It seemed so obvious that they'd be better off learning to be civilized. She was wrapped in her thoughts when the voice startled her, making her jump sideways.

"Colleen!"

She whirled. Robert stood stiffly between two freight wagons, his face stern and uncertain.

"Git on back to our wagon!" He anxiously looked around to see if she had any hidden protectors.

"No." She shook her head. "I need more time to—"

"Git!" he shouted, stabbing a hand down the line of wagons.

She clutched her arms over her breast and stared at the ground. "No, I . . ."

He stepped out from between the wagons and rushed toward her. She backed up, looking frantically for Lawrence. To her relief he was stamping back toward her, his red face hostile.

"Damn it!" Robert cursed. "You're my wife! It's your duty!"

"Ye'll leave her alone now!" Lawrence ordered as he walked to stand beside Colleen. "She'll come back when she's ready and not before!" He canted his body so that the pistol on his hip was clearly visible. A silent threat.

Robert kept his fierce eyes on her, giving O'Brian the barest of acknowledgments. "You're my wife!" he repeated insistently. "Get back!" His arm trembled as it jutted out again, pointing toward their wagon.

"Give me . . . give me another day, Robert. Then we'll talk."

He lowered his arm reluctantly, his nostrils flaring in embarrassment and rage. He glanced to Lawrence, who eyed him with disdain.

"One more day!" he agreed through clenched teeth, then pivoted and walked quickly away.

Colleen heaved a relieved breath.

"I don't care what ye think, missy," Lawrence commented passionately, fists clenched at his sides, "I don't like him."

She nodded wanly—not sure she did either.

· CHAPTER 10 ·

HE'D BEEN HUNTING, THROWING STONES AT GROUSE HIDden in the trees along the riverbank. Two hung from his left hand, their grayish brown feathers ruffling in the breeze. He swung them as he walked, his thoughts on the train—and the yellow-haired woman. What day would the invaders arrive—the battle begin? When would he meet her?

The air was fragrant, thunder rumbling through the dark clouds. The strong breeze blowing down from the north murmured mournfully through the brush. A light rain fell. He lifted his face to the mist, letting the cool drops caress his skin.

As he approached the village, he frowned, steps slowing. Women scurried, dark hair flying out behind them. Dogs scampered between the tipis, barking as people rushed by. Anxiety welled suddenly. He gripped the thin necks of the grouse tighter as his dark eyes went over the scene. A group of strange horses whinnied and stamped in the corral. Children huddled in knots beneath the cottonwoods, frightened by the turmoil.

Wounded Bear stopped, confused. A lilting wail rose on the breeze, high and sharp. And shouts—bitter shouts of rage and pain.

In the distance, riders approached the village, travois dragging behind their horses. A solid line of tan dust marked their trail from the south. He shielded his eyes from the rain, studying the horses. Red Dog's black and white mare led the procession. Fear shot through him. Red Dog had led the wagon train scouts! He stumbled forward, his feet catching on sage; then, as the shrill moaning from the travois met his ears, he ran, rushing headlong for the lodges, his heart in his throat. Battle? Had there been a battle? With the train?

Yellow Leaf met him as he entered the village, brown eyes wide and tormented. Her beaded doeskin dress was splattered with red, the blood filling in the spaces between the white and blue diamonds. Her black hair fluttered in the wind.

"Hurry!" she said, gripping his forearm tightly. "Box Elder has been calling for you. He needs your help with the wounded!"

He squinted, his voice soft with fear. "What happened?"

"The Dog Soldiers fought the bluecoats at Fort Caspar. Many were killed. Ours was the closest village so they brought—"

"Where is Box Elder?" he asked quickly, understanding now. Their scouts had joined forces with the raiding Dog Soldiers to fight the fort. The casualties from the fight had been hauled for days, their wounds tended only by fellow warriors on the run.

She raised a trembling hand and pointed up the dirt path between the lodges. "There, beneath the trees."

He threw the grouse beside a lodge and strode forward, his steps heavy. He weaved between people who rushed to find strips of cloth for bandages or medicinal herbs. Tears streaked their brown faces, mourning for the dead already thick on the rain-soaked wind.

He worked his way to the grove, searching for the small

frail form of Box Elder. The injured were scattered through the shade of the towering cottonwoods. Wounded Bear stepped over a delirious warrior, careful not to disturb the silent, still forms around him. Most of the injured were pale and drawn, too weak to whimper their agony.

"Wait!" the fevered man breathed, eyes glassy as he blinked at the medicine bag hanging from Wounded Bear's belt. The beaded bag contained a pipe and a few precious sacred objects. The injured warrior nodded, sweat coursing down his cheeks. The buckskins over his left leg were torn and clotted with blood. He reached an exhausted hand out to grip the fringes on Wounded Bear's pants, then tugged weakly. "You're a—holy man—sing—sing for me?"

Wounded Bear knelt, clasping the warrior's fingers between his palms. The hand was hot and clammy, the stench of decaying flesh strong. His stomach rose acridly in his throat.

"The battle?" he asked anxiously. "Did we win, brother?"

The warrior smiled faintly, closing his eyes. "We killed many."

Wounded Bear bowed his head—a victory. He lifted his voice in song, pleading with the Great Mystery to heal this brave fighter. As he sang, he studied the injury. Flies swarmed hungrily over the blackened blood, their buzzing so loud it seemed to dim the cries of the suffering. The wound was infected, swelling the leg to twice its normal size. The buckskin pants bulged. He swallowed—this warrior would die. The knowledge left him hollow. He squeezed the man's sweaty palm, pushing away his raging emotions to murmur tenderly, "There, brother—you will live. Rest easy."

"Cold," the warrior mumbled, shivering suddenly. "Cold . . ."

Wounded Bear reached for a green and red blanket lying on the ground—it probably belonged to the warrior—and tucked it around the man, then brushed damp hair from his forehead. Hot. The warrior was so hot.

His legs were weak as he straightened and surveyed the grove of trees. At the far edge, away from the stream, the dead were wrapped in brightly colored blankets. Women wandered hauntingly through the bodies, searching for husbands, brothers, or sons. When relatives were identified, they were carried back to their lodges where they were cleaned and prepared for burial. High-pitched sobs undulated on the wind.

Under one huge cottonwood, a group of mourners wailed as their hair was cut by relatives; it was a badge of pain, a symbol of loss. Long strands of black fell to scatter on the ground like autumn leaves.

And through the agonized tapestry of sound, Wounded Bear heard the rhythmic rattle of a medicine gourd. His eyes searched the frantic scene, touching each possible source. Down the hill, hunching over a young boy, was a fragile figure. Box Elder's white-filmed eyes were cast heavenward, the rattle in his hand shaking in time with his prayers. His long gray braids swept about as he sang, dragging through the blood covering the child's bare chest.

Wounded Bear forced his numb feet forward, trying to prepare himself. Comforting injured children was the hardest task of a healer—and he was only just learning. He'd worked on three dying children, held their hands and murmured soft words to soothe their fears. Was the song of the aged shaman a death wail or a prayer for healing? He couldn't tell through the clamor in the village. He quickened his pace, clamping his jaw in preparation for the worst—that the child was alive.

As he neared the shaman, he heard the boy mumbling incoherently and recognized the voice. It was Crow Foot. Pain welled strong in Wounded Bear's breast, memories flashing. He remembered playing whoop-and-stick with this boy, spinning tops for him, scolding him when he was bad . . . judging a race only weeks ago.

One of the young warrior's arms thrashed about, striking the medicine man in its senseless flight. Wounded Bear knelt down opposite Box Elder, on the other side of the child-warrior, and grabbed the flailing arm, holding it to keep the boy from injuring either himself or the shaman. Splintered bone protruded from the child's shoulder. The warrior slipped in and out of awareness, sometimes looking up imploringly at Wounded Bear, other times falling abruptly limp and quiet.

Box Elder finished his prayer, his voice trailing off into stillness as he turned blind eyes on Wounded Bear. His withered face was tired, aged head tottering.

"The bullet is lodged in bone," he said unsteadily, pointing to the bloody hole in the boy's shoulder. "We must take it out."

Wounded Bear nodded, squinting at the torn flesh. Crow Foot was twelve, yet he rode like a man with Dog Soldiers, fighting the bluecoats, trying to drive them from Cheyenne lands. Box Elder pulled back the battered flesh around the wound. The boy was in a half-conscious state, his eyes fluttering open and closed, whispering incoherent, urgent half sentences.

"Coming . . . they're coming . . . across the bridge . . . fight! Kill!"

He shuddered as the medicine man's gnarled fingers probed beneath the skin for the bullet. Wounded Bear gripped the young arm tighter to prevent him from lashing out.

"N—No!" the boy suddenly screamed, rising up off the ground. Fresh blood flowed from where Box Elder had probed.

"Shhh, *warrior*," Wounded Bear murmured into the child's ear, saying the last word with pride.

The boy writhed, forcing Wounded Bear to throw a leg over his stomach to hold him still as Box Elder worked.

"Hurry!" Crow Foot growled frantically, ". . . bluecoats . . . more, more coming!"

"Warrior," Wounded Bear whispered, pressing his mouth to the boy's ear. "You must not move. We're going to take out the bullet."

The child looked up with pained, wavering eyes, his fevered mind still lost in the battle. "Run!" he shouted hoarsely, struggling with Wounded Bear. "Hide!"

"Hold him still!" Box Elder ordered hurriedly, jerking blood-encrusted fingers from the wound before more damage was done.

Wounded Bear laid his full weight on the boy's chest and whispered, "We will hide here, all right? Together—they won't find us."

"They will!" the boy screamed and broke into sobs, struggling bitterly. "They will!"

"No," Wounded Bear murmured into Crow Foot's ear, gripping his arms so tightly he knew the flesh would be bruised. "I have spirit power, brother. The wolf told me we will live—both of us."

Crow Foot's rigid muscles relaxed some, his frantic eyes resting on Wounded Bear's face. Some recognition flared and his frightened look faded. "Wounded Bear?"

"Yes, brother."

The boy relaxed. Once again he felt safe, protected by the spiritual powers of this man. "The wolf?"

"Yes, my brother. The wolf came to me on the mountain. He told me of your bravery—said you would live." It was a lie, he'd had no visions of the Fort Caspar battle, but the words seemed to comfort the boy.

"Live . . . live . . ." The boy forced a swallow and murmured the reassurance over and over. Rain splashed his face, but he didn't seem to notice, eyes wide. "Hide . . . we will hide here." His tone had changed, taken on a glimmering of hope. His young head nodded in fragile relief.

"Yes, brother. We will be safe. But you must lie still."

Wounded Bear felt hollow. This child believed he could save him, that his frail spiritual powers could assure another day of life—of seeing another sunset or hearing the trill of the meadowlark. But Wounded Bear knew how shallowly founded that faith was . . . the wolf had not spoken to him in weeks.

The child-warrior clamped his jaw against the fear of the

soldiers and stared blindly at the roiling clouds over his head.

"Bullet mold," Box Elder said, his weathered mouth pursed. "Get me a pair!"

Wounded Bear stroked the boy's arm and gazed quickly around, knowing he could not get up to comply with the medicine's man's request. Yellow Leaf stood next to a tipi, arms crossed protectively over her breast. She watched an elderly man lift the lifeless body of his son from the area of the wounded and carry it down through the village to his lodge, legs wobbling under the weight and emotional strain. Her brown eyes were empty.

"Yellow Leaf," he called. She jumped, startled, and turned to face him. "Quickly! Find a bullet mold!"

She raced away, the bells on her moccasins clinking as she ducked into a tipi. Wounded Bear waited anxiously. The rain had stopped, but dark clouds still thundered over the mountains, the wind increasing to whistle through the cottonwoods. The fringes on his pants snapped against his legs.

In seconds, Yellow Leaf emerged from the tipi, a bullet mold in her hands, and ran headlong to him. Wounded Bear quickly took it from her outstretched fingers.

"I have the mold now, Holy One."

Box Elder extended a quaking hand to accept the tool and Wounded Bear laid the mold in his warm, withered palm.

"Hold the boy," the old man gently instructed, opening and closing the scissorlike mold.

"I will," Wounded Bear answered softly, his gut tightening as he pressed his chest against the boy's and squeezed the young arms hard.

Somewhere on the mountain a rifle boomed, and boomed again. Probably someone hunting food. But in Crow Foot's mind they were shots from a white soldier's rifle. He twisted frantically, kicking his legs.

"They're here!" he screamed. "They're here!"

Wounded Bear tried desperately to hold him still. Turning around to Yellow Leaf, he asked, "Can you hold his legs?"

"Yes." She knelt down and grasped the boy's knees, pressing them firmly to the ground.

"They're passing by us, brother," Wounded Bear murmured into his ear. "See? They don't see us. The power of the wolf makes us invisible. Lie still—still."

Crow Foot's muscles tightened, his breathing growing shallow. "The wolf?" he repeated.

"Yes, the wolf has blinded their eyes to us—we are safe. Just don't move."

The boy's fevered eyes were glazed, but not a muscle in his body moved.

Box Elder probed the wound again, his fingers moving like worms beneath the skin. Crow Foot seemed oblivious to the pain.

"There," said the medicine man. "The lump of lead . . ." He wriggled the mold inside the warrior's bloody shoulder, then fastened the cupped ends around the protruding metal of the bullet and pulled . . . and pulled again—and again.

Wounded Bear's heart ached as he watched the futile action. The bullet was lodged too deeply in the bone. They'd have to try something else. Box Elder removed the mold, sighing as he tenderly patted the warrior's injured shoulder. Bits of tissue clung to the iron device, blood dripping from the mold to run down the medicine man's arm.

"Your knife has been blessed?" he asked Wounded Bear, his aged face grave. The white-filmed eyes shone darkly in the cloudy daylight.

"Yes," he answered, pulling the sharp blade from its sheath and laying it in Box Elder's hand.

Crow Foot's muscles cramped and quivered as if he were suddenly aware of what was happening—aware enough to know what came next.

Box Elder wiped tired blood-encrusted fingers over his wrinkled brow as he took a deep breath. His forehead smeared with crimson.

He lowered the knife to the boy's flesh.

Wounded Bear pressed harder on the boy's arms, and

signaled Yellow Leaf to do the same with his legs. She
looked up, meeting his impassioned face. They exchanged
a soft look before he pulled his gaze away. As always, there
was love in her eyes when she looked at him. It made him
sad—the knowledge that she loved him. He returned his
attention to the young warrior.

"Sing," Box Elder whispered.

Wounded Bear's voice rose strong and full, his praises for
the warrior's bravery carrying on the wind to filter through
the trees and drift upward to God. Rain patted steadily
against the silver sage. People throughout camp turned to
look and listen. The mourning wails quieted for a tense
moment. Somewhere in the trees a drumbeat began, the
rhythm timed to his voice. His song faltered as the child-
warrior flinched—muscles straining against pain. Wounded
Bear sang louder, trying to project strength to the young
man. Box Elder was slicing through living tissue, going
down for the bullet. Blood oozed up, bright red and thick,
flowing over the boy's breast to soak the ground. Crow Foot
barely whimpered.

Wounded Bear glanced at Yellow Leaf. Her face was
puckered, tears glistening on her lashes as she pressed firmly
against the boy's quaking legs. Sorrow filled her eyes.

Box Elder held the bloody flesh open with his fingers,
then took the point of the knife and worked it beneath the
bullet, levering up, trying to pry the lead loose. The knife
made a shrill scraping sound against the bone.

"The bluecoats," Box Elder whispered as he worked,
"did they follow?"

Wounded Bear looked up suddenly—the thought hadn't
occurred to him. His eyes drifted anxiously over the sage-
covered hills, half expecting to hear the call of bugles as
the soldiers rode down upon them. He turned to Yellow
Leaf, his gaze questioning. She shook her head. He closed
his eyes for a moment and sucked in a relieved breath. "No,
Holy One."

Finally the flattened ball came loose and the medicine
man dug bloody fingers through the ragged hole to lift it

out. Clutching it tightly in his palm, he stared blindly at Yellow Leaf. "Bandage his shoulder," he ordered and stood up.

Reaching down, he put a hand on Wounded Bear's shoulder. "There are others," he said.

"A moment, Holy One?"

The old man nodded and hobbled resolutely away, giving him time.

Wounded Bear leaned down again, brushing his cheek against the boy's. "You make me proud, warrior," he said.

The boy swallowed, relieved, and closed his eyes.

Wounded Bear got to his feet and looked at Yellow Leaf. Her black hair fluttered wildly in the wind, strands wet from rain. "Will you be all right?" he asked her. "Do you need help?"

"No." She shook her head slowly. "You go. Heal the others."

He nodded, touching her shoulder lightly. The grateful look she gave him made him tired. His eyes traced the lines of her beautiful face, resting on her heart-shaped mouth. He did not know why he didn't love her. He flexed the fingers at his sides, thinking. His heart was just cold. Smiling wanly, he held her warm gaze. "You're sure?"

"Yes." She timidly reached up to pat the hand on her shoulder, dropping her eyes before he could see the emotion well. "Go."

He turned and strode away, the hollow feeling in his breast stronger now than five minutes ago. He balled his fists as he walked, telling himself it could not be otherwise, that the spirit world had condemned him to a solitary life. Yet, somewhere below his consciousness, a voice cried out that he was wrong.

He tugged his thoughts away from Yellow Leaf and back to the village, opening his eyes and ears. The dull roar of thunder mixed with the piercing wails of the mourners to sound hauntingly like the howling and growling of wolves. His thoughts returned to his spirit helper and the deep voice of the wolf whispered in his mind ". . . are you willing?" He nodded to himself, turning his eyes to the dark, roiling clouds as he picked up his feet and trotted forward, running to help Box Elder.

Night was heavy when the last of the injured was carried home by his family. Wounded Bear stretched his exhausted muscles, raising his arms over his head. His limbs were leaden, his back aching as though it had been pounded with a hammer. Box Elder sat propped against a cottonwood, his head bowed in sleep. The old man had worked feverishly with the badly wounded, yielding to the sweet oblivion of sleep only when he knew Wounded Bear could handle the remaining men. Should he wake him? he wondered. No, he shook his head, Box Elder's lodge would be only a little more comfortable than the warm night breeze.

He walked out away from camp. He was numb, his hands and clothing stained brown with dried blood. Dessicated clots formed irregular mounds on his pant legs. Six men had died in his arms that day, their haunted eyes growing suddenly still, their pain quieted as the last breath seeped from their lungs. *His soul hurt.* He gazed up at the shimmering stars. The clouds had blown by, leaving the black sky crystal clear.

He crossed his arms over his blood-stiffened buckskin shirt, mind rambling. Perhaps that was the only real freedom men had—the freedom to die honorably. The rest was just a scurrying to escape suffering—to outguess the cruel judgments of the spirit world. He dug his fingers into his arms. All of existence seemed nothing more than facing death.

His thoughts soured. He furrowed his brow and strolled toward a high knoll overlooking the eastern horizon. A thin sliver of moon was rising, silver light dotting the highest hilltops. Emptiness filled him, deadening his physical senses and opening his mind to forbidden questions. The spirits fought on the side of his people, informing, protecting . . . didn't they? He climbed the sandy hill, thoughts hauntingly riveted to the reasons for life and the roles of the spirits. When he reached the top, he stopped. There was already someone sitting on the opposite side. He sighed and turned to walk away.

"Don't go," Yellow Leaf said timidly, standing. Her tall body was straight and willowy in the moonlight. "I'm leaving."

"No"—he held up a hand and walked toward her—"stay."

She smiled awkwardly and sat down again. He dropped beside her, stretching his exhausted legs and leaning back on his elbows. His tired shoulders cried out. He shifted positions, lying flat on the cool sand. The white beads on his moccasins gleamed in the moonlight. He stared at them, trying not to notice how Yellow Leaf's hands fumbled with her doeskin skirt.

"Seventeen lived?" she asked, gazing out at the rustling sage.

"Yes." His tongue was heavy with the words, *but six died*! He couldn't say them. To utter the sentence aloud would be admitting his spiritual impotence. He was a medicine man! He was supposed to *heal*.

Yellow Leaf seemed to sense his anxiety. "Crow Foot is sleeping soundly. Box Elder says his fever is down. Is that what's worrying you? He'll be all right."

"It's not Crow Foot. I *felt* he would live."

"You're a very great medicine man. I never doubted he'd—"

"Don't say that." He shifted uncomfortably, plucking a sprig of sage and twisting it in his hands. "Death tramps tirelessly through our camps—no matter what I do. If I were truly—"

"If the Great Mystery decides to take someone, not even the greatest healer can stop it. It's not your fault."

"But it makes no sense. Those warriors—"

"Should it?"

He looked up at her. Her beautiful face was blank. He

lightly beat the sage on his fringed pants. "Yes—yes, of course it should."

Her voice was soft and high, sweet. "Should the Great Mystery reveal all things to us?" Her hair fluttered in the night wind. He watched the strands dance in the moonlight. Somewhere in the distance a pack of coyotes serenaded the darkness.

He rubbed his fingers over the rough bark of the sage branch. "Not everything—but more."

"What don't you understand?"

"Pain," he answered wearily. "Its purpose . . ."

She wrapped her arms around her knees and gazed north-ward at the dark mountains. The ragged edges of the peaks were softened by the night, looming tall and rounded against the background of stars.

"And—and the yellow-haired woman?" she asked tim-idly, a twinge of jealousy underlying the words. She fum-bled with her moccasin ties, her nervous movements making the bells jingle.

He blinked thoughtfully. The rumors of how the woman returned again and again to haunt him had spread like wild-fire through the village. He leaned his head back and stud-ied the stars. They looked like ice crystals strewn over a black blanket.

"Yes—and the yellow-haired woman."

"She still comes to you?"

"Yes." He swept the branch nervously over the sand. "She was gone for a time—but she's come back."

"In your dreams?"

"Every night."

Yellow Leaf shifted to sit cross-legged facing him. Her fingers smoothed the sand by his arm. "The wolf sends her?"

Wounded Bear squinted at the crescent moon, unsure how or whether to answer. He plucked a sage leaf from his branch and put it in his mouth, biting down on the pungent plant. "I—don't know."

"But probably?"

He made an uncertain gesture with his hand. "I think so."

"You love her?"

He hesitated, thoughts whirling tiredly through his mind. Did he? He watched Yellow Leaf from the corner of his eye. Her brow was furrowed, eyes lowered to stare at the sandy ground.

"She is not my friend—not like you."

A faint smile glimmered on her lips, then faded quickly, replaced by a frown. She fumbled with her skirt again. "As your friend, may I tell you something?"

Her anxious tone made his muscles go rigid. He propped his head on one hand and rolled to his side. "What?"

"Some—some of the elders are saying this white woman is a witch who comes to harm us—through you."

His mind returned tiredly to Little Deer's words weeks before. His brother had said they were calling the woman a "ghost," not a witch. The latter was a far more serious charge. Adrenaline flushed his system at the news. "Who—who says this?"

Yellow Leaf tilted her head awkwardly and lowered her voice. "Even Box Elder."

"You—you lie! You say that only because you . . ." He stopped himself just short of accusing her of spiteful jealousy—and clenched his fists to still his emotions.

She got to her feet, keeping her face turned away, and started down the hill.

"No—*wait*!" he pleaded, extending a hand. "Please— I . . . I'm just—tired. I don't know what I'm saying—or thinking."

She stopped, her back to him, listening. The silver light made her white dress shimmer.

"I know you would not say it, if it weren't true."

The hands at her sides trembled. "Be careful, Wounded Bear," she said softly. "Tell no one about her again. Already old men are whispering you need a shaman to take her out of your heart."

He got to his feet, his mind reeling. The people wanted

to *force* him—a *medicine man*!—to undergo a witch ritual! He tried to calm himself. If such rumors were being passed it meant the tribe was gravely worried about the yellow-haired woman.

"Yellow Leaf?"

She turned halfway around to look at him. Tears sparkled in her eyes. He felt shame for having hurt her when she was trying to help him. He shrugged futilely.

"I thank you for telling me."

She nodded and walked quickly away toward camp. He watched her go, confusion and hurt strong in his soul.

"A witch?" he said aloud, turning his attention to the stars again. "She isn't . . ." He paused, studying the pinpoints of light. Doubt crept through him, searing his thoughts.

"Couldn't be . . ."

Colleen sneaked out of camp, hiding between wagons until the few sentries were far enough apart they wouldn't see her, then crossed downstream from the road crew and followed a deer trail up a rocky hillside. Not that it mattered much. Though Sawyers had warned people to stay close to camp, few obeyed. The river had become a place of both work and play, where people gathered to wash clothes and talk or fill water barrels. And the guards seemed to care little, usually ignoring the actions of the civilians.

The path she followed wove around scrub pine and over sandstone ledges. She let her mind wander as she walked. She needed time alone. Though the O'Brians were very kind, they were always close, especially Elizabeth, who had become her constant companion—and the company kept her mind occupied and off the painful decisions she had to face.

When she was about a quarter mile from the train, she found a place in the shade to sit and settled herself against a large boulder. Below, on the banks of Hat Creek, the road crew was collecting its tools and heading back to camp for supper. The dust from the men's difficult labors filled the air like fog, glowing dimly lavender in the fading rays of daylight.

She let her eyes drift over the desert. The winding ribbons of plateau furrowed their black brows at the coming nightfall, yawning dark against the pastel sky. A cool evening breeze was blowing, playing with the wisps of blond hair that fell over her shoulders.

Her mind rambled. Fresh Indian sign had been spotted by the scouts that morning. The tracks said that the warriors had stopped suddenly and retreated after sighting the train. Colleen crossed her arms against the increasing chill. She felt a little fear of the Indians, but not enough to prevent her from seeking the solitude necessary to think out her problems.

She was confused about Robert. She didn't love him and never had, though she'd always hoped the emotion would come. Now she was certain it wouldn't. Yet, she was still his wife and her marriage vows were unbreakable, the bond between them sacred. She could still hear Father Donovan's ominous tone when he'd pronounced them man and wife. It had been a threat. Instead of saying ''I now pronounce you man and wife,'' he could just have as easily substituted, ''And if you've a notion to break this bond, remember that hell's fire is just over the horizon!''

She wiped a strand of blond hair from her eyes and tucked it neatly behind her ear, then gazed out to the sunset. The horizon had grown darker, shimmering a deep blue. A herd of mule deer grazed warily a few hundred feet away. The lead doe eyed her curiously, ears pricked, ready to bound away at the first hostile movement.

And there was Matthew. She cringed, knowing her feelings toward him verged on adultery, and though she hadn't yet sinned in the flesh, she'd certainly sinned in her mind. What was it Jesus had said about lusting in the heart? She couldn't recall, but it was just as bad as sinning in the flesh— that much she remembered. She sighed uncomfortably and smoothed her yellow skirt. It was curious that the words ''sin'' and ''Matthew'' were inextricably linked in her thoughts, like "good" and "morning," or "holy" and "Bible," they just seemed to go together. It was disturbing.

She'd been thinking so seriously that she hadn't noticed the sun had slipped well below the horizon and darkness was swelling around her. Crickets chirruped nearby and stars were poking through the dark blue overhead. She blinked suddenly and jumped. Campfires sparkled across the creek. She had to get back!

She put a hand on the sandstone boulder and pushed up. A ripping sound greeted her efforts.

"Oh, blast!"

Her skirt was caught tight on a thorny bush. She tugged hard and more fabric tore, the abrupt sound silencing the crickets.

"Well!" she said, tugging harder, but the dress wouldn't come loose.

She knelt, pushing yards of dirty yellow material out of her way to find the location of the snag. Her hands thrust into a stiff prickly pear cactus. She cried out sharply and jerked her fingers back, putting them in her mouth and pulling tines out with her teeth.

Standing up again, anger took hold and she threw all of her weight against the snag. With a loud shriek the fabric pulled loose and she tumbled to the ground, landing on her stomach.

Exasperated, she swore under her breath and stood yet again. The countryside took on a different character at night, becoming ominous. She clutched her ruined skirt, lifting it slightly off the ground, and started quickly down the rocky slope. The wind grew stronger as she walked, making the pines creak and whistle eerily. Fear welled in her breast.

"Shhh!" she hissed to herself, hoping the effort would hush her inner sense of panic.

A stick cracked behind her. She froze, her heart beating like a kettle drum. She wanted to turn around but wouldn't let herself for fear that any shadow would send her mind reeling in terror. Instead, she sucked in a deep breath and stiffened her spine, then proceeded down the slope.

The stones became slippery in the darkness. Her feet repeatedly slid off the black rocks to land hard against the rough ground, jarring her whole body. Her ankles were raw from rock scrapes and her knees had begun to tremble. To make matters worse, clouds were rolling in, thunder rumbling jaggedly across the plains. Darkness grew heavier until she could no longer make out her feet. She started to rush, her fear increasing.

As she swept down the hillside, unseen objects reached up to trip her. Her foot caught on an exposed tree root and she toppled to the ground, striking her knee on a rock. Pain flashed through her, bringing tears to her eyes. Fumbling with her skirt, she snaked her hand to the injured area. It felt warm and moist. Blood.

As she lay there, her eyes darted frantically over the darkness, her breathing growing more shallow and hurried by the second.

"Stop it!" she commanded, but her mind wasn't convinced. Her eyes continued their search.

Her injured knee ached miserably as she got to her feet. Gingerly she put her weight on it and felt with her toes for purchase, then picked her way carefully toward the creek bed.

Another sound met her ears. It was a soft, rhythmic panting, the sound a man would make after running, or an animal . . . Cold fear traced fingers up her spine as she whirled. There, coming down the slope was a white form.

She screamed as she turned and ran headlong down the hill. The underbrush tore savagely at her skirt, but she couldn't stop. The panting came closer, she could almost feel the hot breath on her exposed legs.

An icy wind swept across her face as she approached the stream. The sides were incredibly steep and in the darkness she couldn't see the crossing she'd climbed up. She ran back and forth in front of the bank, tears streaming hotly down her cheeks. Stumbling, she fell flat against the hard-packed clay. A dull thud echoed.

She jerked her head to look behind her. The animal was

gaining. She could see its black eyes glinting in the dim light. And another sound reached her ears—a voice. Was it calling her name? Terror ravaged her mind, the fear so blinding and powerful that she could not think. All she could do was run.

She scrambled over the steep bank, clawing at the crumbling walls and falling several feet to the water below. Splashing into the stream, her face was smothered in cold liquid. She gasped for breath, coughing as she came to the surface.

She looked up. A huge white face leaned over the bank; the wolf stared down at her and crouched to jump into the water.

A ragged scream was torn from her throat. She crawled through the water to the other side of the stream and dug her fingers into the wall to pull herself up.

On the other side of the bank, the wolf dove lightly into the water and padded to stand below Colleen as she climbed. Standing up on its hind legs, it pawed at her, catching a piece of her skirt and pulling.

"No!" she shrieked at the beast and tugged her skirt loose, then climbed higher.

"Colleen?" a deep, smooth voice called.

Fear filled her mind. "Leave me alone!" She pulled herself up over the bank, and ran blindly for the wagons.

Campfires glowed ahead. She turned her back to the creek. The wolf leapt gracefully to the tableland and trotted behind her.

"Colleen?"

She ran wildly but it was catching her, its gallop cutting the distance between them to a dozen feet. "Matthew!" she screamed hoarsely. *Matthew!*

Her lungs were bursting, the heaving sobs choking her until she couldn't breathe.

A dark form ran toward her from the camp.

"Colleen?" Matthew shouted.

"Colleen?" the wolf called.

· CHAPTER 11 ·

SHE THREW HERSELF INTO HIS ARMS, SHOUTING "RUN! Run!"

He held her fast, coolly ordering, "Stop it, Colleen!"

Her arms flailed as she struggled to get away. He gripped them and forced them to his chest, holding her tighter. She wept, tears soaking his blue shirt.

"Shh," he whispered. "You're all right." He stroked her tangled blond hair.

"Is it gone?" she asked, fear sparkling in her eyes; she jerked her head around to stare back into the darkness. Only the moaning of the wind through the pines disturbed the quiet.

He tilted her chin up to meet her frightened brown eyes. People were starting to gather. The entire camp had heard her terrified screams.

"What, Colleen?" he asked softly. "Is what gone?"

She clutched furiously at his arms, her nails digging into his flesh. "The wolf!" She buried her face in his shirt.

"He came back?"

She nodded, pleading, "Hold me!"

He disentangled her frantic grip and pressed her harder to his chest. "It's all right," he soothed. "I'm going to take you back to my tent, all right? We can talk there."

She stared up at him, eyes wide with terror, and nodded.

He held her close as they walked back through the crowd, his arm over her narrow shoulders. Toward the end of the murmuring mass of people, Robert Merrill pushed through to block his path. The big man stood stiffly, his hands clenched at his sides, barrel chest beneath the green plaid shirt rising and falling rapidly. When he looked at Colleen there was embarrassment and contempt on his face. Matthew walked straight forward, his path not veering in the slightest. Colleen raised her head and saw her husband. Her petite body went rigid. She pressed closer to Matthew, wrapping one arm around his waist.

"Move," Matthew ordered calmly as they approached Merrill.

Robert's nostrils flared at the command, sweat beading on his sloped forehead. He licked his lips nervously. His hand dropped to the .44 Army revolver on his hip.

Matthew studied that quaking hand, but made no moves for his own gun. It was a personal rule. If his hand ever dropped to his pistol, he pulled it and aimed to kill. He wasn't certain at this point, however, how Colleen would react to him killing her husband.

A slow smile crept over his face as he stopped where Merrill blocked his path. He stared hard into the man's green eyes, his gaze icy. Colleen put a hand to his chest and tugged aimlessly at one of his brass shirt buttons. The arm around his waist tightened, trembling.

"Gonna use that?" he asked congenially, pointing to Merrill's gun.

Robert stammered, eyes darting around the whispering crowd. "I—I might!"

Matthew took a deep, irritated breath and lazily propped his hand on his hip, still making no moves to the pistol dangling below. "Then do it."

Merrill looked confused, uncertain. He licked his lips again, trying to hold Matthew's penetrating gaze—but he couldn't, his eyes dropped.

"Then get out of my way," Matthew said and started forward again. Merrill grudgingly stepped backward, shame clear on his face. His hand still rested on his pistol.

As they walked, Matthew forced his back muscles to remain relaxed. His mind was tensed for the impact of a bullet and his body wanted to respond.

They strolled slowly through the center of camp, past a dozen freight and Conestoga wagons. People whispered harshly as they watched them, folding their arms in disapproval. Matthew smiled in exaggerated politeness, tipping his cap to the ladies.

He leaned his head down to murmur to Colleen. "Despicable things, reputations. You didn't want one anyway."

"Hmmm?" she asked innocently, looking up at him. Blond tangles fell in damp ringlets over her shoulders. She'd been watching her feet, her attention focused inside, and was unaware of the contemptuous glares from the other members of the train.

"Did you?"

"What?"

He waved a hand to the scornful spectators, flashing a broad smile. "Want a noose around your neck?"

She shook her head, completely confused. "A what?"

"A noose—to strangle you."

She frowned. "Are you talking to me?"

"Not really." He smiled, pulling her closer.

As they reached the emigrant section, Maureen O'Brian ran out, white hair flying. Lawrence kept Elizabeth back by the wagon. His red face was wrinkled in concern. Matthew held up a hand to Maureen, telling her he'd take care of the situation. Maureen gave him a worried look and extended her hands. He shook his head, smiling confidently. The middle-aged woman reluctantly stopped and walked back to the wagon.

Dingy white tents sprouted beneath the cottonwood grove,

campfires sending sparks to curl through the leaves. Dozens of men were gathered around each fire, finishing dinner and talking. Conversations were halted abruptly as Douglas strolled through the tents. A variety of looks were cast his way, some lustily approving, others disgusted. He ignored them all and guided Colleen beyond the military camp to his tent that was staked a goodly distance away from the others. He liked his privacy.

The coals of his fire still glowed orange.

"Here, sit down," he said, gently lowering her to the ground.

He retrieved more firewood and threw it on the coals, then blew softly for a few minutes to get the blaze going again.

Colleen shivered, rubbing her arms as she stared hollowly into the fire. He frowned, eyes drifting over her. It was the first time he'd had a chance to take a good look at her muddy yellow dress. He reached over and felt her skirt.

"My God, Colleen. You're soaked clear through. Get out of those clothes."

Her brown eyes widened. A sinking expression came over her face. "Now? Here?"

"Of course!" He stood and walked to his tent, pulling the flap back so she could enter. "Come on."

She rose and walked to him, staring up with embarrassment in her eyes. He pursed his mouth disapprovingly and pointed inside. She ducked down and entered. He dropped the flap and returned to kneel before the fire. The coffeepot sitting off to the side was still hot. He picked it up and shook it—half a pot left. Idly he retrieved his cup from an hour before and looked inside. A brown film stained the bottom. He poured a bit of fresh coffee in, swished it around and tossed it out. The stain was gone.

"Matthew . . . I . . . ." She hesitated.

"Everything!" he ordered.

"Everything?"

"Even your shimmy."

"Oh, but I couldn't."

"Want to catch pneumonia?"

"Matthew, I don't think—"

"Coyotes'll dig you up. They prefer aged meat."

Silence.

The sound of rustling clothes drifted out. He smiled to himself.

"Well!" she demanded hotly. "What am I supposed to put on? Or should I walk out—unclothed!"

He raised his brows and stared first to the military fires a hundred yards away, then back to the closed tent flap. "Darling, if you walk out naked I'll never be able to protect you. There are over a hundred frustrated men in this camp." He paused, caressing his jaw. "Or do you have fantasies of the Myrmidons?"

"The . . ." She stopped short, as though annoyed and running every name in camp through her pretty head. "Are they kin to you?"

"Uh—well?" He tilted his head in contemplation, but decided to ignore the arguable behavioral kinship. "Not blood relatives."

"Well, what'd you bring them up for?"

He sighed and stretched out on his back in front of the fire, clasping hands beneath his head. "I'm not sure anymore."

"Matthew!" She stamped her foot. "What should I—"

"Oh! uh—wrap my blanket around you. It's rolled up in the rear corner."

He gazed lazily into the rustling cottonwood leaves and rubbed his brow. The evening breeze was cool, gusting to scatter sparks from the campfire across the grove. He watched orange flickers blaze and disappear as they whirled through the thick smoke-colored limbs over his head.

She emerged shyly from the tent, his gray wool blanket wrapped securely around her. He smiled and sat up. She'd constructed it so that one shoulder was bare, like a toga. Her hands clasped the blanket at her waist in a death grip. Her hair was beginning to dry, the ringlets tightening.

"Scandalously beautiful!" he said, bold eyes raking her.

She pursed her mouth, furrowing her brow. "I—wouldn't have . . . but I couldn't figure any other way of . . ." She pulled tresses of blond hair over her bare shoulder.

"Here"—he extended a hand—"come and sit down."

She walked to the fire and sat beside him, tucking the gray wool around her ankles.

"Feeling better?"

She nodded, smiling faintly.

"Good." He poured her a cup of hot coffee, then stood and entered his tent.

She gasped when he walked out with her dress and undergarments and spread them over the roof of the tent.

"Matthew! I'll die of embarrassment."

"Then you'll die dry."

Her gaze went to the men in the distance. They were too far away to see. She relaxed some.

He pulled another tin cup from his tent and walked back to sit beside her, pouring himself a cup of steaming coffee. He stretched out again, leaning back on his elbows. Carefully he examined her face, noting every change of expression. She seemed calmer.

"So." His tone grew serious. "Tell me about the wolf?"

"It—came after me," she said, voice quaking, and dropped her eyes to stare unblinking into the fire. "I ran."

"Did he call out to you?"

She jerked around to face him, eyes wide. "Yes—how did you . . ."

He sighed, took off his dusty cap and beat it out on his pants. Then he tossed the hat toward his tent and gave her a disappointed stare. "My dear, why didn't you talk with him?"

Her mouth dropped open, a look of utter incomprehension on her face. "What—are you . . ." She lifted a hand to the silver crucifix around her neck and swallowed, eyes glazing over. "It's a—beast! A—"

He shook his head in disgust. She was on the verge of quoting the Bible to him. He shifted uncomfortably, recrossing his legs. "A sheep in wolf's clothing?"

"Well—"

"Ah, Colleen," he exhaled the words, squeezing his eyes shut to think. "Where is it?" he asked tiredly. "You'd know better than I—somewhere in Ezekiel, I think. God comes to the prophet out of a whirlwind and shows him four faces. One is the face of a man and the others are animals." He dug deep, it had been years since he'd seriously read the Holy Scriptures. "One of the animals is a lion, another an ox . . . and what the hell is the third?"

"Don't curse!"

"Well, what the hell is it?"

"An eagle."

"Yes!" he cried and sat up, pointing a finger at her. Tan dust clung to his uniform. He swatted the sleeves; dirt jumped from the fabric. "Well?" he asked expectantly.

She cradled her knees in her arms and looked at him from the corner of her eye. "You mean," she began feebly, "that God can appear in many forms—don't you?"

"Exactly."

"But, Matthew, I don't want to talk to God. Why should He want to—"

"You're a goose!"

She frowned indignantly. "I'm not!"

"How many times a day do you pray?"

"Well . . ." she murmured. "Several, I suppose."

"About what?"

"The . . . dreams . . ." Her face slackened as understanding dawned.

"Yes, God sent you a personal angel to discuss your dreams and look how you treated him."

"Oh, no. Matthew, I—I—didn't know."

He smiled faintly and gazed at her askance. A warm rush of relief filled him. The creature couldn't be an *Eehyoim*. Witches didn't give their victims the luxury of refusing to talk. The wolf was obviously a dedicated spirit helper. But what was he trying to help her with? Did some future event demand this undivided attention? If it had nothing to do with Matthew, then what had Colleen done—or what *could* she do—that warranted such dogged pursuit? It didn't make any sense. Visions of Enanoshe had filled his dreams of late, making him feel lonely and vulnerable. Somewhere deep inside him, tendrils of foreboding twined around his soul.

He swirled his coffee, watching the dark brew wash the sides of the tin cup. Flickers of firelight danced in the liquid. No matter how hard he tried, he couldn't convince himself that his past, his expulsion from the Cheyenne tribe, Broken Star's rabid curses, and Colleen's mystical attachment to her dream warrior had no hidden connection. All the signs pointed to the fact that Colleen's path and his had been linked long ago in the misty nether worlds of spirits and witches. Matthew tightened his shoulder muscles to suppress the shiver that climbed his spine. Spirits either saved or damned. There were rarely in-betweens. Which would it be this time? *Both, maybe.*

He reached out and gripped her hand, holding it tightly. His heart had begun to pound.

"Matthew?" She wet her lips anxiously. "Will the wolf be back?"

"Don't worry," he said. "God loves fools and Irishmen. You've got both covered."

A look of quiet horror came over her face, as though she were contemplating how she'd respond when the beast next appeared. She bit her lip and released his fingers to pull the blanket more tightly around her waist.

"Cold?"

"A little."

He moved closer and put his arm around her, pulling her against him.

She sat still, gaze darting absently over the cottonwoods.

"Now that we have that settled," he lowered his voice, "let's discuss your husband."

She bowed her head to stare at the tiny hands folded in her lap. "All right."

His eyes glimmered darkly watching her awkward movements. "You want to go back to him?"

She fiddled with her fingers, squeezing each one individually, then she abruptly slipped from beneath his arm and stood up. He watched her walk away from the fire to stand next to the dingy tent. She acted like she was trying not to look at it. The flames cast wavering shadows across her face. She turned halfway around to look at him, then changed her mind and strolled farther away from the tent into the trees.

He reached for his tepid cup of coffee and sipped quietly, observing her over the brim. She folded her arms over her stomach, keeping the gray blanket in place as she gazed up to the starry night sky. Her blond hair dangled over the smooth curve of her hips.

He pursed his mouth, silently cursing himself for being so blunt. Maybe he should have given her more time? He leaned back, rolling to one side. He didn't want to give her more time—that's why he'd pressed. He was falling in love with this frail little woman from New York and the thought of her going back to her husband was like a sword thrust in his belly and turned slowly.

He looked back to her. She was watching him, her eyes wide and vulnerable, fingers clutching the blanket stiffly. She dropped her gaze and started back. His gut tightened, but he didn't change positions, remaining stretched out on his side.

She gracefully knelt beside him, head bowed, blond hair falling over her shoulders. "Matthew." Her voice was soft, strained. "He's my husband."

He nodded, fumbling to retrieve a long stick to poke the dwindling fire. Sparks flitted and whirled in the draft, rising upward to vanish in the darkness. He watched the flames, keeping his breathing even. His heart pounded like a drum in his chest.

Hesitantly she reached over and touched his shoulder. He looked up. Moisture glistened in her eyes as she searched his face.

"But . . . I don't want to be his wife anymore."

He sat still, listening to the fragile tone of her voice,

waiting anxiously for the rest. She sniffed softly and ran a hand beneath her nose. Then, abruptly, a fierce defiance lit her face. He raised his brows in anticipation.

She pounded a fist into the ground. He jumped at the spray that shot up. "I'll probably go to hell, but I . . ." She turned uncertain eyes on him. "I—want to be with you."

His gaze was alert as he evaluated her expression. Her eyelids fluttered in authentic insecurity. She pulled her hand back, afraid.

He sat up, a smile creeping over his face, reached for her arm, and pulled her across the sand to him. Pressing her to his breast, he kissed her.

"You're sure? You're not afraid of hell?"

"Well—only a little. And you'll be there with me after all. So—"

"Wonderful!"

He kissed her again, then stood and pulled her to her feet. The night wind was increasing, whipping the tent flap back and forth and whistling through the cottonwoods. Her hair fluttered wildly in the gusts as he wrapped an arm around her shoulder and led her into his tent.

When he awoke, he found her lying in his arms, her bare body pressed softly against his. Long tresses of blond hair tumbled over his chest. He touched them, winding the strands around his fingers quietly, trying not to wake her with his movements.

The wind gusted outside, sending the tent flap fluttering back. He rubbed his eyes and stared out to the darkness. The sky looked like a sequined ebony blanket, stars glimmering brilliantly. Only the wind through the cottonwoods gave voice to the stillness. He listened to the evening sigh and moan as he thought.

He was tired. He'd lain awake most of the night, listening to the broken parts of conversations Colleen spoke in her sleep, many of them in Cheyenne, most of them to a warrior. Why would a Cheyenne warrior send his soul to touch

Colleen's? Or perhaps she did the sending? The possibility left a curious tingle in his chest. Her voice had been soft and anxious, as though the dialogue were hurried, urgent.

He reached down and picked up a long tendril of hair to brush over his face. It was like gold silk on his cheeks. He made a web over his eyes and gazed through it to the sky. The strands glistened dimly in the starlight.

She stirred, absently bringing an arm across his stomach and snuggling her head into his shoulder. Her fingers flitted over his side in a soft caress. He watched her sleepy movements, noting the serenity of her smooth face and frailness of her body. She was like a spun glass figurine: willowy and fragile. That delicate quality stirred something inside him, some masculine need to protect, to pet.

He brought a hand up to brush the hair away from her face. "You awake?" he whispered.

"Um."

He smoothed a hand down her arm. "Tell me about the warrior?"

Sleepily she opened her eyes and rolled over to prop herself on her elbows. An embarrassed expression creased her face. She blinked and gazed at the canvas walls. The tent shuddered and crackled under the impact of the wind.

Her voice was timid. "Did I—talk about him?"

"Yes."

"Oh, Matthew—I . . ."

He smiled. "Am I that inept? In my vanity I'd assumed you'd be dreaming of my tender caresses."

"Oh, be serious."

"But I am! I take great pains to see that you . . . " He paused, tilting his head and flashing a wide smile, letting his expression finish the sentence. "And your dreams are filled with another man."

She leaned over and kissed him carelessly, her hands on his chest. Abruptly she stopped, fingers resting on the scars over his breasts. In the dim starlight, he could see her expression change, the smile fading to an anxious question.

He reached up and gathered her hands in his, trying to head off her line of thought.

"Tell me about the warrior," he repeated softly.

Her eyes flickered over his face, hunting for something. He concentrated on keeping his eyes warm and his expression blank. The time was not yet right for her to know about his past. It would only complicate things—make their relationship harder and more uncertain.

"He—comes to me in my dreams—and sometimes when I'm awake." Her voice floundered, fingers wiggling against his palm.

"In daydreams?"

"No—not exactly. They're more like . . ." She frowned and tucked a lock of hair behind her ear. "I guess I don't know what, but something else—more vivid and real."

He nodded, squeezing her hand. "Do you know who he is?"

"No," she whispered.

"But he's Cheyenne. You do know that, don't you?"

"I think he is. I don't know for certain, Matthew."

"Tell me about him. What kinds of designs are on his clothing, his shield? Are there any paintings on the lodges in his village?"

She blinked, straightening up. "Yes—one tipi—has a buffalo head painted on it in bright colors. It—"

Before he could stop himself, his body went rigid, hand tightening on hers. Images of the sacred Buffalo Hat Lodge sprang up crystal clear in his mind. Is'siwun had been given to the people by the Suhtaio hero, Erect Horns, before the Tsistsistas and the Suhtaio became one tribe. Her presence in the village promised that the supernatural power of the buffalo resided there, that the Cheyenne would be protected from starvation by the blessings of the buffalo. So, Colleen's visions *were* of the Cheyenne. The warrior . . .

"What is it?" she asked insistently, eyes wide. She was struggling to disentangle her fingers from his.

In a sudden burst of awareness, he realized he was crushing her hand. He relaxed his grip, took a deep breath, and stroked her fingers. "Nothing," he mumbled, closing his eyes. "Just—images."

"Images?"

He opened his eyes and met her bewildered gaze. Pulling her to his chest, he hugged her and smoothed her long hair down her bare back. Her skin was like velvet, warm and soft.

"There's still a few hours before daylight. Let's sleep."

"All right," she responded, confused. She laid her head against his shoulder and her fingers drifted back to the Sun Dance scars. He didn't try to stop her.

But she didn't ask. Her resigned tone told him she understood he didn't want to talk about it, but that timidity would vanish the more she got to know him—and then she'd ask. He feigned sleep.

But sleep was the furthest thing from his mind.

· CHAPTER 12 ·

THE PUMPKIN BUTTES ROSE LIKE SQUARE TOWERS FROM the undulating plains, their sandstone faces glistening orange in the afternoon light. Wounded Bear reined the pinto to a stop and shifted positions, looking down over the flat basin below. From his vantage on top of the grassy knoll, the Powder River was visible as a winding emerald ribbon of cottonwoods and aspens.

He sighed and murmured to his horse. "They are there, little one." His eyes drifted over the vast expanse of sage and greasewood. "There somewhere."

Though his village was camped near the Powder River, the war council was being held farther south. If they were discovered by soldiers, the old people, women, and children would still be safely away from the fighting.

The pony grazed leisurely on the grass, occasionally swiveling a brown ear in his direction to listen. He gave the animal free rein to wander as he stroked the cream-colored mane and patted the long neck. The camp of the Dog Soldiers lay below along the river. Already Dull Knife would have laid battle plans and readied his forces. Tonight would be a time to talk and pray.

Eagerness and anxiety welled in his breast. He squinted out across the plains, thinking about the yellow-haired woman. He had asked the wolf to tell him her role—but no answer had come. It was as though the spirit world had grown suddenly quiet and brooding. The silence left him moody.

Virile gusts of wind tugged at his braids, whipping them over his shoulders to pat against his bare back. He cast his eyes heavenward and watched the eagles as they dove and circled. Somewhere above, the wolf waited.

He grabbed up the reins and kicked his horse forward, down the slope and toward the river. He had to make camp before nightfall.

As daylight dwindled, shadows dawdled across the faces of the buttes, flowing into the crevices like honey and casting a subdued golden hue over the sage. Scattered puffs of clouds glowed on the western horizon, looking like a handful of prickly pear blossoms strewn over an azure lake. He guided his horse down into the river bottom and wound methodically through the trees, heading northward.

His thoughts drifted to the woman again and a hollow anxiety prodded him. He tried to shake her image from his head so that he could concentrate on the upcoming battle, but it wouldn't leave him, returning again and again. His sister had told him once, many years before, that he wasn't like other boys, that he lived in his head too much. Memories of her teasing smile blotted out the yellow-haired woman but brought him pain. Even twelve years of death could not dim her image.

"Enanoshe," he whispered her name aloud.

Her face rose strong and powerful, black hair hanging straight down her back, her eyes shining bright and brown. Nine years older than he, she'd cared for him like a mother after their parents' death at the hands of the Shoshoni.

A tendril of pain worked its way through his chest. Enanoshe had died when he was eight, been carried away by the terrible diseases of the white man. The last time he'd seen her face, she'd looked pale and weak, her eyes dim. He'd wept in misery as she was hauled out of camp, burying his face in the buckskins of his grandfather. The old man's words that night so long ago still haunted him, wafting through his dreams like wind: "The spirits remember, grandson. *The loss will be restored.*"

He shook himself again, trying to focus his attention on the muddy thread of water that flowed beside him. Gradually the memories ebbed away, leaving him numb and tired. He kicked the pony into a trot, anxious to get to the war council.

As the sky dimmed and stars poked through the faded blue, Wounded Bear saw campfires on the riverbank ahead. He worked his way through the cottonwoods until he reached the edge of camp, then he dismounted and hobbled the pony.

There were many warriors here, many more than his dreams had shown him. He stared wide-eyed, knowing the numbers must approach a thousand. He walked forward into the milling, laughing men.

"Eh! Wounded Bear!" someone called.

He looked around, trying to locate the familiar voice in the crowd. Above the heads, a hand waved. He lifted a hand in response and wound through the tangle of people toward the unknown friend's location.

"Bent!" He slapped the warrior on the back. The man was tall with a square face, wide-set eyes, and straight nose, and sported a black mustache over his lip. He was half-white, his father a trader on the Arkansas River in the south. The mustache, a distinctly white characteristic, was the brunt of jokes at gatherings such as this. But no one questioned his loyalties. He'd fought far too many battles against his own white brothers for such questions to arise. His bravery was the subject of campfire stories.

"You're alive, brother. I'm surprised!" Wounded Bear taunted.

"You'd heard different?"

"No, but I'd feared a bullet might have found you."

"None that were deadly." The smile faded from his face.

In the background, the rough sound of Box Elder's singing called the warriors to the central circle of chiefs. As they started off, Wounded Bear noticed Bent's stiff-legged limp.

"A bullet?" he asked, concerned.

"In the hip."

Such wounds took a long time to heal. His friend undoubtedly had trouble riding, yet still he was on the war path. Together they made their way to the circle.

Dull Knife was the first to sit before the blazing fire, his round face serious, his full lips moving in a low song. A fox skin was draped around his neck, falling over his red and blue beaded shirt to reach his stomach. Grizzly bear claws were sewn along the edges of the fur; they glistened darkly in the orange firelight.

He was followed by the great Oglala chief, Red Cloud. Wounded Bear's eyes went wide at the sight of the Sioux chief. He wore a long warbonnet of many eagle feathers that draped down his back. Porcupine quills covered his shirt in horizontal rows, interspersed with yellow and white beads. He was an impressive man, tall, with a large hooked nose and thin face. A quiet air of dignity and power surrounded him.

Around the two main chiefs, minor leaders came to sit. Some were Cheyenne, most were Sioux. Wounded Bear pushed closer, looking between people to see the Sioux chiefs. Why hadn't his dreams shown him that another tribe would come to help the people fight the wagon train? The presence of the Sioux was a good omen. They had far more warriors than the Tsistsistas, as well as more horses and weapons.

Small talk broke out among the headmen as the aged Cheyenne medicine man, Box Elder, hobbled into the flickering light of the fire, his long gray braids dangling freely over an intricately beaded shirt, the sacred pipe clutched in his hands. He was singing powerful and lilting pipe songs, his voice caressing the air. Gently he delivered the pipe to Dull Knife. The chief nodded his gratitude, then lifted it to the earth, the sky, and the four cardinal directions before he inhaled deeply and blew out to the four directions. When he lowered the pipe, his black eyes were thoughtful, his face seamed with worry. He nodded tiredly to the young men assembled around the fire.

"It is good that you have come, brothers." He smiled wanly and handed the pipe to Red Cloud.

The pipe passed easily from hand to hand, moving first around the circle of leaders, then ceremoniously through the gathering of warriors. When at last it came to Wounded Bear, he gripped it tightly and looked up at the starry heavens. His long braids hung down his back, patting softly against his skin. He chanted a private prayer to the wolf before he smoked. Then he touched the sacred device to his lips and inhaled deeply, letting the smoke fill his lungs, cleansing them, making him pure for battle. His spirits soared, the smoke rising to his head as he passed the pipe to Bent and stared up into the waving branches. They were dark with night, whispering.

For an hour or more, the chiefs talked among themselves, discussing the wagon train and what should be done to stop it, then, finally, they opened the discussion to the eager warriors.

"Brothers"—Dull Knife's deep voice pierced the silence—"the wagon train is two days' ride from us. The white men are even now tearing at the earth with sharp sticks, building a new road through our hunting grounds. Who will speak?"

"I will speak!" an anxious voice sounded from behind Dull Knife. He turned around to watch a young Sioux warrior push through the dense crowd.

"I am Lame Coyote," the stocky man announced, a pinched look on his triangular face, his hands were clenched into tight balls at his sides, "warrior of the Bad Faces. I have single-handedly stolen fifteen horses from the Crows and counted twelve coup against my enemies." Mumbles of praise spread through the warriors for his achievements. His introduction was impressive, marking him as a man to be listened to. He continued, "I want to know what we plan to do with the whites who dare to invade our lands!" It was a demand rather than a question.

Red Cloud answered, his words slow and clear. "We will stop them."

Lame Coyote looked hopeful, a dark hatred in his eyes. "We will kill them all?"

Red Cloud shook his head, a quiet look of confidence seeping from his intent eyes. "There is no need. We must stop them from building the road; that is all."

Dull Knife and the other chiefs around the fire nodded their agreement, several leaning over to whisper opinions or reservations.

A potent gust of wind whistled down the river bottom as Lame Coyote stepped closer to the circle of chiefs, his face contorting in rage. "My chief, we must rid our land of the white disease! Look around you!" he shouted. "Our people starve because the white roads drive away the game—and the trains bring disease! There are so many mourners in Sioux villages that no one's hair grows these days! The whites must all die!"

War whoops rose, drifting in waves across the river. Wounded Bear cringed, sucking in a breath. Even Bent added his shriek to the call for obliterating the train.

"Lame Coyote is right," Bent leaned over to whisper. "I know the whites. The only way to stop them is to kill them!"

Wounded Bear frowned and exhaled tiredly. "No, brother. I don't think so."

Bent shrugged, giving him a hard look as he shifted his weight to his uninjured hip. The wound was hurting.

The gathering buzzed with dissenting opinions. Finally Red Cloud held up a hand and stood, propping his feathered war lance beside him. The yellow and white beads on his shirt shimmered golden. His expression was hard, the look of a man with too much pain inside to be ignored. A man of wisdom. The crowd grew gravely silent.

His voice carried the iron ring of authority, though it was soft. "I am not a peace chief," he acknowledged and extended a hand to Dull Knife, "not like my friend here. My people are hungry. Each year the hunting grows worse and the whites grow stronger." He waved his war lance to the hills surrounding them. "This place is still home to the buffalo. Because of that, the Sioux live. We must kill all the whites who try to take it from us—but only if they will not leave us in peace. Let us bargain first.'' He reseated himself and leaned over to whisper something to Dull Knife, who nodded quietly in return.

Others came forward to speak, but Wounded Bear's thoughts drifted. Red Cloud's words about the buffalo made him think of the story of Ehyophsta, the sacred Yellow-Haired Woman who saved the Cheyenne by giving them the buffalo. His mind whirled with new thoughts. Did the wolf think the yellow-haired woman on the train would save them in the same way? Give them the buffalo? The thought had never occurred to him and now drew his attention away from the war council. Was that why his soul joined with the woman's? He turned the possibilities over in his head.

Dull Knife's loud voice brought him suddenly back. The chief was standing, tall and straight, his words doleful. ''We must close up all the white roads through our country and stop them from building new ones.''

Bent pushed to the circle, his long black hair glistening in the light of the fire, his mustache strangely out of place. ''It is not only the roads that are the problem, my chief. The whites are building forts to protect the roads. Once they are finished and filled with bluecoats, many Cheyenne will die trying to close them up. We must kill the whites now, before their numbers grow too large for us!'' His enraged voice cut the air like a knife.

A new rumble of voices spread through the assembly, warriors shouting concurrence and emphasizing their opinions with loud shrieks.

Dull Knife bowed his head for a moment, letting the fervor die down, then he responded. ''You know the whites better than I, my son,'' he exhaled heavily, putting hands on his hips. ''But it seems to me that the whites will have no need for forts if there are no emigrants crossing our lands. And the emigrants will not cross without roads. It is the roads that are the problem—they must be closed.'' He stared knowingly into Bent's hot eyes until the warrior's gaze wavered and fell.

Wounded Bear folded his arms over his chest, smoothing his fingers over the red, blue, and yellow beads that formed concentric diamonds. Should he tell these warriors that his dreams had revealed a new fort was being built even as they talked—that it was only a few miles to the south? He considered it, mulling the effects the news would have. It might shift the council's emphasis from the train to the fort. That would not be good. The wolf's warning had been about the train. The fort, he decided, could wait.

The discussion continued long into the night, with each warrior who could reach the circle of chiefs speaking his mind. Wounded Bear waited in the background, yawning as he listened to the opinions tossed back and forth. A merging was taking place, a consensus that the train would not be massacred if they agreed to leave the lands of the Cheyenne and Sioux.

To his surprise, after hours had passed and stars that had originally dotted the sky had rolled to the western horizon, Dull Knife called out his name. Wounded Bear jerked himself awake and walked forward into the light of the blazing fire, rubbing fingers into his tired eyes.

"Tell them about the wolf, my son," Dull Knife gently instructed.

Wounded Bear swallowed and began the story, leaving out no details, except his visions of the yellow-haired woman, and stressing that the wolf had only told him that the road must be stopped, not that all the whites had to die.

A heavy silence descended when he'd finished. He stood still, his legs spread apart and his head bowed.

Red Cloud broke the silence. "When did the wolf come to you, warrior?"

"During the Spring Moon."

Dull Knife waved a hand and added, "Not long after it led the women who survived the Sand Creek Massacre to safety."

Red Cloud raised his black brows and nodded slowly. Nearly everyone knew the plight of the women, how they'd fled the brutal battle into the frozen grounds of winter and almost starved until a wolf came to them and brought them food. The wolf guided them past their enemies and back to the camps of the Cheyenne, then the spirit helper disappeared into the hills.

In his mind, Wounded Bear saw the wolf nod its furred nose in approval and he knew that the Sioux would believe him. He closed his eyes and met the gaze of the wolf, softly singing thanks to the helper for taking pity on the people, for saving them from the atrocities committed by the whites.

Red Cloud stood, his warbonnet flickering orange in the firelight, and raised both hands to the sky in a silent prayer. The assembly watched his reverent actions, murmuring softly, waiting for his words. When he lowered his hands, silence descended.

"The wolf taught you well, warrior. I will fight to close the roads—not to wipe the whites from the face of the world." He turned and strode out into the darkness.

Dull Knife grunted, pulling himself to his feet. "I have no more to say," he announced. He stretched his arms over his head, yawning deeply, and followed behind Red Cloud.

The assembly dispersed, warriors seeking their blankets.

Wounded Bear watched them go, each drifting in a different direction, then walked to his pinto pony where it had joined the horse herd and retrieved his blanket. Throwing it out in the soft grass a short distance away, he rolled up and closed his eyes.

His dreams were of the yellow-haired woman.

He was still sound asleep the following morning when the gentle shaking on his arm began. Opening his eyes, fear shot through him. The blue-clad soldier jumped on top of him as he scrambled for his rifle. They wrestled, rolling over and over through the tall grass, the soldier laughing hysterically. Suddenly Wounded Bear realized he knew that voice. He stopped struggling and stared at the man in the officer's uniform.

"Bent!" he said. "You are braver than the stories tell. But this time it wasn't a white bullet that almost got you."

The tall man stood up, spreading his arms to display the

blue treasure. His black eyes glowed in pride. "I took it while raiding in the south!"

Wounded Bear nodded, exhaling, and studied the uniform. It hung awkwardly over his friend's shoulders and the sleeves and pant legs were much too long. "It doesn't fit very well, brother," he observed.

"Watch!" Bent chuckled, then leaned down to roll up the legs and proceeded to the sleeves. Adjusting the shoulders, he threw out his broad chest. "See? Now it fits perfectly. You, too, will have one after we attack the wagon train."

Wounded Bear sat up and smiled dimly. "No. Already I fear I act too much like the whites. My emotions lead me more than the teachings of the Old Ones. A soldier's uniform would not ease my conscience." He rubbed hands over his sleepy face.

Bent punched him in the shoulder, shoving him back to the grass. "You are missing a great gift. In battle the whites are never sure whether to shoot at me or not. I'm certain this uniform has saved my life many times."

"I'll take my chances."

Getting to his feet, he headed for the muddy Powder River. Bent limped to catch up. The bottoms along the river were rich with grass and cottonwoods. Massive dead logs lay tangled on shore. The river in flood stage was powerful, tearing trees from the banks and sending them bobbing and twirling through the opaque water to come to rest here, on the first terrace, when the water level dropped. They wound around the tangles.

Together they walked out to the white sandy beach that lined the oxbow in the river and began undressing. Wounded Bear tossed his skin clothing on a fallen tree and waded into the water. He gasped at the cold, his muscles stiffening. Bent whooped behind him and dove beneath the surface. Wounded Bear watched, chuckling, then followed his example. Soon the muddy waters were alive with screeches and laughter.

When they finished their bath, they waded out of the chilling river and stretched out on the warming sand bracing their backs against the fallen tree where Wounded Bear's clothing hung, flapping in the early morning wind.

"Brrr!" Bent sputtered, wiping hands down his arms and legs to throw off the excess water.

"Lets you know you're alive." Wounded Bear shivered in the early morning breeze as he pulled his long black hair over his shoulder and squeezed out the water.

Mosquitoes swarmed around their naked bodies, buzzing in their ears. Slaps sounded.

"Ah, Wounded Bear, this is a good life. If we can just keep the whites from taking it from us."

Sweet Medicine's prophecies echoed in his mind and he reached down and scooped up a handful of white sand. The grains glittered in the light of sunrise. He cupped both hands together as a fierce gust of wind whistled by. But no matter how hard he tried, grains were torn from between his fingers and scattered out across the roiling muddy river. He watched the water carry them away. Something inside cried out.

"What is it?" Bent asked. He'd seen the change of his friend's expression.

Wounded Bear turned to him, letting his eyes drift over the man's square face. The bristly mustache glistened with beads of water. He dropped his eyes and shook his head. "Nothing."

Bent leaned back against the tree trunk and ruffled his wet hair. A spray of water spattered the trunk. "I've heard stories," he began, his voice soft as he looked out across the roiling river.

"Stories?"

"I didn't believe them."

"What stories?"

He shrugged, turning back to meet Wounded Bear's eyes. His face was blank, unreadable. "Before you arrived last night, some of the elders were whispering that a witch had put a spell on you."

Wounded Bear leaned forward, sighing audibly. Pain welled inside him. "She is not a witch, brother."

Bent's eyes went wide, his brows raising. "It's true then? A woman comes to haunt you?"

"Not to haunt," he murmured, letting his eyes drift across the river to a grove of aspens. Their leaves quaked in the wind, sparkling dark green in the morning light. Surrounding the grove, a series of low sage-covered hills rose in rounded humps.

"Then why?"

"I—I don't know." He bowed his head, looking back to the white sand that warmed the bottoms of his feet. He dug his toes in and watched the grains cascade over the top.

"Is she a helper?"

He shrugged.

"You don't want to talk about her?"

"I do. I just don't know how." That wasn't the reason, though. He was hesitant because the more people knew of the yellow-haired woman and her powerful effect on him, the more they came to believe she was a witch. Yellow Leaf's advice long ago about not talking had been sound. But his heart cried out to tell someone about his love.

"Ah, well—let me help. Tell me what she looks like."

He lifted his eyes to gaze eastward. A glowing orange ball peeked over the low hills, sending a flood of copper light across the sage to touch the river. The white caps shimmered, the water changing from slate to a dull green.

"She is white." He turned to meet Bent's black eyes. His friend's face was still expressionless, showing no signs of shock or dismay as he'd expected. He was encouraged a little and went on. "She has long yellow hair." Dropping a hand to his back, he slashed a line across his waist to show the length. "Her eyes are—like the people's."

Bent frowned, putting a hand to his chin and rubbing softly as he gazed out to the river in contemplation. "When did she start coming to you?"

"At Sun Dance."

"She came during one of our most sacred ceremonials?"

"Yes, she came to hold me during the flight to Seyan."

"Who is she?"

"I don't know, brother."

"Where is she from?"

Wounded Bear hesitated, anxiety building. He swallowed the lump that was growing at the back of his throat. "The wagon train."

Bent leaned back abruptly, eyes intense, face taut. "You are sure?"

He nodded.

"A white woman from the train we are about to attack comes to you—and you do not think it witchcraft? White witchcraft!"

"No! No!" he insisted, swinging around to face his friend. He extended both hands, palms up, and shook them in the air. "She—doesn't come—to hurt."

"How do you know, brother? She is white and with the train that is digging a road through our last hunting grounds."

"Yes, but—"

"Does she help you?" His tone had grown hard and skeptical.

"Yes . . . she—fills my heart."

Bent nodded knowingly, exhaling. "I'll bet! What better way to deceive a man of the people than to 'fill his heart'."

"Deceive?" Wounded Bear's mind raced over the possibility. Yellow Leaf's words came back to him—words he had put out of his mind as too silly to seriously consider. But now—with Bent suggesting—could the woman be a white witch who deceived him so that her train could hurt the Tsistsistas? Cold fear tingled in his belly. He sat back against the tree trunk.

"The whites have strange and powerful medicine, Wounded Bear." He leaned forward, stabbing a finger at himself. "I know! I went to their schools in St. Louis. I saw their magic."

"But . . ." he whispered, staring down at the Sun Dance scars over his breasts. They were pink mounds now, healed over on the outside, but inside they were still fresh and raw. "She flew with me to the stars. The ancestors in Seyan— they said she would help."

"Are you sure you heard the words of our ancestors, Wounded Bear? Or hers?"

He blinked, sucking in a suddenly uncertain breath. "I—
I . . ." The ramifications were staggering. If she was a
witch and had deceived him, then his love for her was a
trap—a trap designed to lead the Cheyenne away from the
prophecies of Sweet Medicine and the teachings of the Old
Ones. But how could that be? She'd never tried to tell him
things that contradicted the teachings. Nor had she ever
pushed him to perform acts he knew were wrong. All she'd
done was to come to him and make him happy—fill his
heart. He stiffened his spine, his mind set. "I heard *our*
ancestors, brother. And they would not lie."

Bent shook his head. "I hope you are right. I would not
like to ride into a trap, my friend."

"It . . ." He dropped his eyes again, uncertain. His voice
was soft. "It won't be."

Bent stood and looked down at him, his head cocked.
Wounded Bear held his stern gaze. There was reluctant be-
lief in his friend's black eyes.

"It won't be," he reassured in a stronger voice.

The wind blew Bent's black hair over his eyes. He brushed
it back and nodded slowly, jaw vibrating softly as he ground
his teeth. "I believe you, brother. Because I must. If I were
to go into battle worried that a white witch might affect the
outcome by casting spells . . ." He inhaled abruptly and
stared back through the cottonwoods toward camp. "How
many others know about the woman?"

Wounded Bear mulled the possibilities. "I'm not sure. The
elders, the chiefs, a few of the warriors—that's all, I think."

He put his hands on his naked hips and sighed. "Good."

"Why?"

Bent's lips curled into a sour grin, but his eyes didn't
smile. "A warrior who doubts is dead, brother."

Colleen combed her hair and threw back the tent flap,
walking out into the hot morning sun and weaving through
the cottonwoods into the military camp. The soldiers
lounged with their shirts open, caps pulled down over their
eyes, napping. As she strolled by, a few insolent grins

gleamed beneath the brims, knowing chuckles floating on the hot breeze. She ignored them, picking up the hem of her soiled yellow skirt and throwing her shoulders back as she proceeded across camp.

Her steps were hurried, fear lacing her stomach, as she headed for Robert's wagon. She paced through the sage as though it weren't there, making only minor attempts to avoid the snagging branches. Her skirt tangled in the brush, but she tugged it loose without missing a step. She had to do this thing now—before her courage faded.

The hot wind panted in her ears like some invisible prairie beast, fluttering the hem of her dress until it crackled. The sand was ankle deep in places and the heels of her button-top shoes sank abruptly, making her gait awkward, stumbly. She struggled to keep herself marching in a dignified manner, but it mattered only a little. Whatever the other members of the train thought of her, she felt happy inside—giddy like a girl with her first proposal. Though Matthew hadn't proposed, of course, but she knew he meant to. Despite his gruff insolence and biting comments, he had a curiously honorable streak.

The thoughts of Matthew brought her mind back to Robert. She bit her lip and plodded forward—hands planted firmly against her skirt to keep the wind from revealing her legs. The emigrant wagons were quiet as she passed, only children played beneath the wagon beds, their faces bright as they constructed castles from the dusty soil. She was glad no adults were out. Not that she cared what they thought! She jerked up her chin—borrowing for a moment Matthew's shield of insolent invincibility. It was just easier this way. The fewer harsh glares she had to endure on the way, the greater her confidence would be when she faced her husband. It was a chilling thought and left her weak-kneed and trembling. But she plodded forward.

As she neared the end of the emigrant wagons, Ethel Lory stepped out, her eyes going wide at the sight of Colleen.

"Get away from my wagon!" the woman shrieked, pointing a finger to the sage.

Colleen was stunned. Rather than complying she stopped completely and stared. Mrs. Lory was a forty-year-old woman with gray-laced auburn hair and deeply seamed skin. Her blue eyes were squinted hard as she spread her flowered skirt in front of the wagon to shield the children from seeing Colleen.

"Mrs. Lory, what—"

"I know all about your wicked ways, missy! And I don't want my children to lay eyes on the likes of you! Your poor husband is hanging his head on account of your running off to that—that . . ." She dropped her eyes, unwilling to speak the vile names she was thinking.

A shiver ran up Colleen's spine. The train already knew? Robert—knew? Fear choked her. "I'll be going," she said to Mrs. Lory and started forward again, not even feeling her toes against the sand.

"You walk around my wagon when you come back!" Mrs. Lory yelled behind her. "Harlot!"

She filled her mind with thoughts of Matthew to bring her courage back. He was so strong and gentle and his wry grin smoothed the edges of the world, making her take herself with less seriousness and straightening her crooked perceptions of reality so that she saw life more clearly. Thinking of Matthew worked for a while, at least until she got closer to Robert's wagon, then her courage drained. Disheartened, her feet seemed weighted down by lead bricks, her spirits flagging. She slowed her pace as her heart rose in her throat, edging forward rather than walking. His wagon was only fifty feet away.

Her gaze drifted to the barren rolling hills where hot wind kicked up fingers of dust to stain the azure sky a rust color. The vast prairies which had formerly given her pleasure seemed somehow just plain barren today—just as desolate and lonely as she.

As she got to the rear of the wagon, she mustered her courage and bravely called, "Robert?" She stood primly still, her shoulders stiff, even if her knees were quaking. "Robert?"

There was no answer.

"Oh!" she squeaked in frank relief, putting a hand to her sweaty forehead. It was a short reprieve, she realized, but she wanted to enjoy it just the same. Sooner or later she'd have to face him and tell him she wasn't coming back—ever. But in the meantime—cautiously she tiptoed to peer around the other side of the wagon—she'd accept Robert's absence as an act of divine intervention and take the opportunity to retrieve her belongings from the back of the wagon. Casting a quick backward glance, she pulled open the rear curtains and climbed inside, then quickly jerked them closed again.

She felt safer and dropped her trembling fingers from the curtains to her sides where she entwined them in her skirt and turned around, her eyes drifting over the things that belonged to "them." Crates were stacked in the right front corner and she knew from having packed them that they contained kitchen supplies, pots and pans, and a set of fine china that her grandmother had given her. Faintly her heart cried out. But it was a small cry. She crawled forward and patted the box tenderly, letting the china know that she wasn't leaving it because she didn't want it—it was just . . . just that she would no longer have a place to keep it. She couldn't very well ask Captain Williford to haul domestic items for her. Letting out a halting breath, she began gathering her clothing and placing it in two medium-sized satchels. One was technically Robert's, but that bothered her only slightly. She took comfort in the fact that she was leaving him everything else. How could he argue over something so insignificant when he was making out like a pirate! Of course, he would object, but she refused to think about that now. If she could get away before he returned, he'd have to come to Matthew's tent to ask for it back and she didn't think he'd be brave enough—at least she hoped he wouldn't. She reached for her box of "pretties" and gently clutched it to her breast. It was a small gold chest inlaid with a circle of blood red rubies. Inside were her hair clasps and brooches—things that would mean nothing to Robert.

Quickly she tucked it into her bag. There was little left that she could consider hers alone. A spear of anger rose abruptly. She frowned. In the year they'd been married all she'd accumulated were a few gowns and pieces of jewelry? It didn't seem possible—but it was true. Robert owned the land in New York, fine carriages and horses, stocks and bonds, and interest in the Montana gold mine. She owned nothing. It wasn't right somehow, she clucked to herself. But then, it was a man's world, there was nothing a woman could do about it except endure it as gracefully as possible.

Dragging the satchels back to the rear curtains, she took one last look around. It was then the sounds outside struck her. She'd been so thoughtful she'd missed them. Chains jangled at the front of the wagon as though someone was tending the traces. Her heart leapt, knowing who it must be. Quietly she parted the rear curtains and jumped down to the sand, then lifted out the first satchel and the second. They were made of a heavy red and gold brocade that glinted in the sun. But before she could reach down to pick them up, Robert strode around the back, almost running over her.

"What?" he gasped, taking a step backward. Then realizing what the scene meant, his face stiffened into a lined mask, eyes blazing.

"Robert, I . . ." she began, backing from between the wagons so she could run if she had to. From the corner of her eye she saw Matthew's tent. Was he back yet? she wondered frantically. She dared not take her eyes from Robert to see. "I came to tell you."

"Get out of here!" he yelled. His huge fists were clenched threateningly at his sides. He pointed a rigid finger at her, a bitter smile coming to his lips. "I'da never married you if I'd known you were a filthy whore!"

Her mouth fell slightly open, quivering at the word. She bowed her head as tears came to her eyes. How dare he call her such a thing! Why, she'd never—until recently—and only then because he was so nasty and treated her so badly. And Matthew was so charming.

Indignation flooded her veins, her fears fading. Fiercely

she grabbed up her skirt, tramped past him, and retrieved her satchels and started away. His low voice stopped her.

"You and your boyfriend better be right careful, Colleen. Nobody shames me—*not without paying!*"

She was going to reply, but he turned on his heel and vanished, a twisted look of hatred on his face. She shuddered as she picked up the bone handles on the satchels and stepped away from the wagon.

Before she'd taken ten steps Matthew was at her side, looking swarthy, his smile so recklessly self-assured that just looking into his jaunty eyes made her feel better. He took the bags from her hands, throwing one under his arm and carrying the other by the handle so that he had a free arm to wrap around her shoulders.

"Brave girl. I told you I'd go with you."

"No, I—I needed to do it alone, Matthew." There was a hint of bitterness in her voice, but she didn't know why. She wasn't sorry to be leaving Robert, nor reluctant about Matthew. Maybe, though, there was regret that it had to end so painfully. And regret that she no longer fit into any social segment of the train. Many of the soldiers would still accept Matthew, but they had to, he was an officer. But she would be an outcast wherever she went. She sighed and stared at her feet as they waded through the sagebrush back to the cottonwood grove.

"Well, what did he say?"

"You weren't close enough to hear?"

He shook his head forlornly. "Not a word."

"He said—that you and I—had better be careful—that nobody shamed him without paying."

Matthew's brows arched as he leaned down, watching her with mock anxiety as though he hung on every word. "A threat?"

"Yes," she said uncomfortably.

He burst into indecently loud laughter, throwing his head back. His blue eyes danced, but there was a hard, calculating glint too. The sound of his merriment was rich and guttural and boomed across camp full force. Which, she realized, was no doubt intended. But it made her cringe, wondering what the other train members must think.

"It's not funny!" she whispered insistently, her brow furrowed.

"Oh, but it is, my dear!" He laughed again, then put his arm around her and started walking again. "I can think of nothing more amusing than your husband in my pistol sights at twenty paces. It would be quite an enriching experience."

"Enriching?"

"Uh—for his character. And God knows he could use it. But I don't suppose I'll have the chance. He may be courageous enough to threaten a woman, but I doubt he's the stomach to challenge a man. A pity!"

"Oh, Matthew!" she moaned. "I just want to be left alone. I don't want any more trouble."

An odd look came over his face and he twisted one end of his mustache like a villain in some cheap play, then whispered menacingly, "Do be careful, dear! There's nothing more irritating to the common folk than someone who 'just wants to be left alone.' Saying such a thing is like throwing out a gauntlet. You'll have people on us like ducks on a June bug."

She stopped watching her feet to look up at him. There was a twinkle in his eyes. "I declare, Matthew! I wish you'd be serious sometimes."

"Ah, but I am, darling. From this point forward, you and I are going to be conspicuous."

"Conspicuous?"

"Yes, indeed. I plan on foisting our companionship off on anyone who isn't impolite enough to say they don't want it."

"But—"

"No buts!"

• CHAPTER 13 •

THE COLD RAIN FELL IN GRAY SHEETS, WIND HOWLING around his tent.

James Sawyers sat hunched over his plank desk, writing in his journal. He was dressed warmly in a blue wool shirt and had a gray blanket wrapped around his shoulders. The July night was chilly. Only an hour before, they'd measured the temperature to find it forty-eight and still dropping. He reached over and pulled his lamp closer for warmth.

"These high western plains are a strange place," he muttered to himself, watching the walls of his tent undulate. "Can be a hundred one hour and down to fifty the next."

The gale penetrated his tent, making his lamp flicker. He opened a book and propped it around the lamp as a shield.

"Colonel?" a gruff voice from outside called.

He sighed. It was undoubtedly Merrill. He'd summoned him two hours ago. He threw the blanket off his shoulders, letting it fall to the ground. No sense in looking like an old man—though these days he felt twice his forty-one years.

"Please come in, Mr. Merrill."

The tent flap opened and the big man stepped inside. Water cascaded from his hat and coat to pool on the dirt floor. He had an awkward look on his face.

"Won't you have a seat?" Sawyers extended a hand to a stool beside his desk.

Merrill took off his hat and shook the water off, then sat down. "I didn't make it earlier, Colonel, 'cause I was mending a worn harness."

"Quite all right." He laid his quill pen down and closed his journal, then shoved it to the side. "Leather goes fast in this dry climate." His words sounded odd in light of the ferocious storm outside.

"Yes, sir."

Sawyers brought his hands up on his desk and twined his fingers together, nervously wiggling them.

"Mr. Merrill, I called you here to have a talk—about your wife."

Merrill shifted uncomfortably, batting the water from his pant legs. "What about her?"

Sawyers breathed out his response. "I've had some—uh—complaints from other members of the train—"

"Complaints about her whoring?"

Sawyers raised his brows and looked into the big man's green eyes. Even if a gentleman thought such a thing about his wife, he'd never say it. "It seems that she is—has—taken up residence with one of our soldiers."

Rage gleamed in Merrill's eyes, his face growing hard. "Douglas." The name was a low growl.

Sawyers leaned back, hugging his arms. Without the blanket around his shoulders, he was becoming chilled. "People on the train are concerned that your wife's behavior might 'influence' their children."

"So?" Merrill asked, running a hand through his wet curly hair. "What am I supposed to do about it?"

"It has been suggested that perhaps you could convince her to come back to your wagon. At least for the remainder of the trip. That way—"

"You ordering me to drag her back? For the good of the train?" A hateful smile filled his face.

"No, no," Sawyers quickly clarified, staring uncomfortably at his hands. He'd already heard stories of Merrill's brutality toward his wife. He wanted no part of it. "At least, not until we've tried other things. What I mean to say is perhaps you might convince her to be more sensible. Maybe, if she won't stay in your wagon, she could stay with another family."

Merrill's loud laugh made him look up suddenly. The big man's barrel chest puffed in and out as he slapped his knees.

"You cain't ask a whore to jump up and become a lady, Colonel. Whores are whores."

Sawyers frowned, keeping silent for a time to collect himself. He wasn't accustomed to having men in his association use such a term so blithely. "Well, maybe if you—"

"Why don't you go parley with that Captain Williford. There must be some army regulation to stop soldiers from—"

"Behavior unbecoming an officer?" he mumbled, rubbing his bearded chin. Douglas was a lieutenant. It might work. That would settle the train down.

"Sure . . . or using army property for illegal things. Adultery is still a crime in New York. I don't know about out here."

"I believe, Mr. Merrill, that it is a crime anywhere—but that's between you and your wife. My only concern is halting internal bickering among members of this train."

"Ain't there some punishment for officers misbehaving?"

"That will be up to the captain." The longer Merrill sat in his tent, the more he disliked the man. He reached over and pulled his lamp closer, wrapping his chilly hands around the metal base. The warmth made his fingers tingle.

"And, if she won't come back and that captain won't make her . . . you want me to drag her back?"

Sawyers drummed his fingers against the base of the lamp. A hollow tinny sound filled the tent. "Perhaps a nudge like that might work. Sometimes all a woman needs is to see who's boss and all her fancy notions are forgotten." He looked up at Merrill. "But I want no physical harm to come to her, sir."

"Won't be none."

"Well, that'll be fine, Mr. Mer—"

"Besides," Merrill interrupted, frowning. "She needs somebody who won't dote on her crazy dreams. She ain't right in the head, Colonel."

Sawyers kept his eyes on the flickering lamp. "What do you mean?"

"She carries on like a banshee most nights, dreaming about Indians and such."

"Well, perhaps that's just a natural response to our coming into Indian territory."

Merrill shook his head vehemently. "No, she had these dreams before we even decided to come West. Way back last winter, when we was still in New York. She'd wake up moaning and carrying on; then, the next morning, she'd be down to church crying to Father Donovan. For a while he thought she might be possessed. Talked to me about it one time."

"Possessed?" Sawyers' eyes slitted, a little lump of fear growing at the back of his throat.

"Yes, sir. I never did mention it to Colleen. Just told Donovan to forget it, that I didn't want my wife being dragged through the mud that way. But"—he shook his head—"I might have been wrong. Probably should have let him do the exorcism."

Sawyers blinked thoughtfully, leaning back. Demon possession was not something he even wanted mentioned to the train members. Great gods! the terror and turmoil that could bring. "Mr. Merrill, I'd appreciate it if you didn't mention this to anyone else in the expedition. It might—well, you know—cause some unwarranted concern."

"I won't say a word, Colonel."

Sawyers met his eyes. The man's words said one thing, but his tone and facial expression said quite another. He wished he'd never opened his mouth at all. Now he'd have to prepare for the worst.

Merrill broke his concentration. "You'll let me know what Williford has to say?"

"I will, sir. Thank you for coming by."

Merrill put his hat back on, nodded curtly, and left. Sawyers breathed a sigh of relief and retrieved his gray blanket, draping it over his shoulders again. He shook his head. Superstition would be running rampant in a few days, he figured. He'd have to talk to the captain immediately. Maybe if Mrs. Merrill were back in her own wagon soon, the whole thing would come to nothing. He shifted uncomfortably. The idea of talking with Williford was unpleasant in and of itself, but to discuss the behavior of one of his officers was even more onerous. The captain didn't take kindly to any negative comments about his men—though God knew the rabble often deserved the worst a man could say. Sawyers pulled his journal back across his desk and opened it to resume his entry.

"Well," he murmured resignedly, "it has to be done."

Robert Merrill stood stiffly behind his ox, anger and humiliation searing him. The rain poured down, drenching him and rolling in rivulets off his hat brim. His green eyes darted around the quiet camp. Everyone was huddled inside out of the storm. His anger grew, trying to figure out who could be spreading stories of his private business! Probably one of the old women, or their puny husbands. They were all laughing behind his back. The soldiers especially. They wore rude smiles and snickered when he passed by.

"Damn rebel scum!" he cursed, pulling his hat down lower over his eyes to keep out the rain.

The road crew was just as bad. He'd heard them whispering he couldn't keep his woman home. Well, she'd be home soon enough. He laughed to himself, patting the ox. And with the colonel's approval! And he'd have time for revenge too. The moment would come. One day he'd find Douglas out alone and put a ball neatly through his skull. Or Colleen would take one of her walks by herself. And he knew how to hurt her. A smile creased his face. He'd make her pay for shaming him!

He shifted, leaning up against the ox for warmth and to let the beast block the whistling wind. Douglas might be a problem after he dragged Colleen back, but a fight between the two of them would make the whole train take up arms against one another—split the members right down the center. And he'd have Sawyers on his side.

And he could start passing rumors about her being possessed right now. That would put more people on his side when the final moment came. Nobody wanted to defend a witch. He chuckled to himself.

The three men stood in a small circle, Sawyers' red shirt and slouched hat looking awkward beside the two soldiers in ragged blue uniforms. Two freight wagons sat next to them, piled high with road-building tools. Shovels, picks, and jumpers poked up into the air behind them, a spiky iron foreground to the broad flat plains and turquoise sky beyond. Wind flicked their sleeves.

"No, suh," Lieutenant Daniel Dana responded laconically and leaned back against the freight wagon to let his eyes drift tiredly across the rolling plains. He was a short man with straight black hair hanging to his chin and lazy blue eyes. His hooked nose was canted at an angle, the result of a huge Irish fist in a bar in Boston, and he had plump dark cheeks. At the age of thirty-four, he was one of the oldest members of Williford's command.

The temperature was unbearably hot, well over a hundred degrees. He wiped his brow with a dirty red handkerchief, then stuffed it back in his shirt pocket. He'd just returned from a hard ride to Fort Laramie and was in no mood for civilian criticisms. His expression was appropriately disgruntled.

James Sawyers crossed and uncrossed his arms, indicating his irritation at the news. "You *foolishly* left the supplies behind!"

Williford's face hardened. "As the lieutenant reported,

Colonel, the commanding officer at Fort Laramie would not let him bring the supplies, saying that fifteen men were inadequate to guard the wagons.''

"So where are the supplies, Lieutenant?" Sawyers hotly demanded. His red shirt was stained with sweat, the dark splotches running down his chest and below his arms to his waist. The nostrils in his long face flared anxiously.

"The quartermaster with one of General Connor's columns said they'd be marching this way in a couple of days and would bring 'em along."

"You—"

"Lieutenant," Williford interrupted, seeing the hostile look on the colonel's face. "You did well. Go get some grub and rest up."

Dana exhaled disgustedly, saluted, and cast a hard sideways glare at Sawyers before he left. Williford propped his fists on his hips.

"The man had no choice, Colonel. He couldn't very well have disobeyed orders from a superior officer."

Sawyers' colorless eyes slitted. "You going to tell me your men can't go on?"

Williford spread his legs, adopting an at-ease posture with his hands behind his back. It took great effort to keep his voice calm, but he managed. "As I told you before Dana left, Colonel, my men cannot walk barefoot to Montana Territory. Not only that, their uniforms are in rags."

Sawyers' salt and pepper beard quivered. "I won't accept further delay! Your orders from General Dodge were to—"

"My orders, sir, were to escort this expedition and pick up needed supplies at the nearest forts. I am trying very hard"—he frowned—"to do both."

"Well, you're not succeeding!" Sawyers shouted. "The expedition is at a dead halt on account of your incompetence!"

Anger flared in Williford's chest, but he swallowed it, determined to remain civil and professional for as long as possible. "Colonel, I'm going to dispatch Lieutenant Tom Stull and some of the Dakota cavalrymen to Old Woman's Fork to meet the supply column when it comes up from

Laramie. It should not take more than a week to get shoes for my men—"

"A week!" Sawyers charged, his face flushing crimson. "A week, Captain?" He slammed a fist into the side of the freight wagon. The hollow thud echoed. "That'll make two and half weeks you've delayed this expedition!"

Williford's spine went rigid. He lowered his brows and dropped his hands to his sides. As he stared threateningly into Sawyers' grim face, he wondered what the precise wording of the regulations was. Striking a civilian was certainly a punishable offense, but could they bust him to buck private?

"Sir," he stiffly replied. "Let me remind you that this command arrived at the Niobrara River during the second week of May. It was *you* who kept us waiting for nearly a month while your road-building crew assembled."

"What's that got to do—"

"Just this, sir!" Williford shouted, balling his hands into fists. "That's when the real delay occurred—and it had nothing to do with military incompetence!"

Sawyers' breast puffed in rage, his eyes darting over the surrounding hills. A dim smile came to his lips. "Captain, you're—afraid to go into Sioux and Cheyenne country. That's it, isn't it? This has nothing to do with supplies."

Williford's triangular face went stony, his eyes staring unblinking. Afraid? The smell of peach blossoms wafted through his mind, blossoms mixed with the acrid scent of blood. Shiloh. Not even the heavy April rain could clear the sweet-sour odor from the air. He was running again, kneeling in the mud, bracing his rifle over the body of a fallen Confederate officer to fire. His rifle stock smeared with the man's blood. The troops whispered that General Wallace was dead. Dead? Fear laced his belly. Another promotion? More responsibility—more lives to pray for.

So shallow was his breathing that the blue fabric over his chest barely moved. His muscles had gone rigid. He blinked, bringing his mind back, and turned tiredly to Sawyers. "Colonel, I'm dispatching Stull immediately. My command will move forward in short increments each day until he returns. That's the best I can do.''

Sawyers threw up his hands, grumbling, "Very well, Captain.'' He turned on his heel and strode rapidly away, his slouched hat brim undulating in the breeze.

Williford stood still for several seconds, unable to convince himself to move. His mind was still only partially on the dusty plains. Finally, he managed to force a deep breath. He slowly walked back to the military camp.

As he paced, his boots striking heavily against the sand, his anger increased. Sawyers *dared* to accuse him of cowardice! He saw Douglas in the distance. The lieutenant was standing alone in the copse of cottonwoods, fiddling with some horse equipment. Probably putting away the things Dana had used on his trip to Laramie. There was only one more unpleasant task he had to complete today. He tugged his blue cap down hard over his eyes and headed for the lieutenant.

"Douglas?'' he called as he approached. "I want to talk to you.'' He strode past Matthew and deep into the cottonwoods to get away from the other men lounging about camp. He heard a mumble and then light steps behind him. He kept walking, weaving between thick trunks and across waving grass until he found a fallen log that would make a bench. The log sat at the edge of the grove and looked out over the vast washboard plains—and it was at least three hundred feet from eavesdroppers. He didn't want to embarrass Douglas—though he'd thought about taking off his captain's bars and punching him a time or two—he just wanted to have a good frank talk. He swung around and met Matthew's eyes.

"What'd I do, George?'' Douglas spread his arms wide. His shirt was unbuttoned to the middle of his chest and his sky blue pants were shaded tan from where he'd been kneeling in the dirt.

"You jackass!'' Williford pointed to the fallen log. "Sit down!''

"Yes, suh,'' Douglas responded and sat, crossing his legs

and scratching the patch of hair exposed by his unbuttoned shirt.

Williford spread his legs and stared down at him. The lieutenant looked truly bewildered—but Douglas could do that when he wanted—his blue eyes wide and his face slack.

"What'd I—"

"Lieutenant," he began, clasping his hands behind his back and pacing through the grass, "it has come to my attention that you are using army property for illicit purposes."

"Illicit?" Douglas asked, brows raising high as amusement glinted in his eyes.

"Goddamn it, Douglas!" Williford shouted. "I'm serious! What the hell do you think you're doing with a woman in your tent?"

Douglas took a deep breath and spread his arms again. "George, she doesn't have any other place to stay. All I'm doing—"

"All you're doing is having the time of your life and bringing the wrath of the train down on me!"

Douglas frowned, cocking his head. "What do you mean by that?"

"I mean, my friend, that I've had four different soldiers, nearly every woman on this train, and *Sawyers himself* hissing in my ear about you and your interesting sleeping arrangements! And I goddamn don't like it!"

Douglas pushed his cap back on his head and cradled one of his knees in his arms. "You don't like my sleeping arrangements or you don't like the hissing?"

Williford waffled between wanting to laugh and wanting to knock him off that log. "You're a damn lunatic, you know that?"

"George, I—"

"I want her out of your tent!"

Douglas jumped to his feet, fists clenched at his sides, looking like he was ready for a fight. "Where the hell is she supposed to go, George?"

He waved an unconcerned hand. "How do I know. Find a place. Wasn't she staying with that O'Brian family for a—"

"She was sleeping in the mud, for God's sake, George! I'm not sending her back to that!"

Douglas unconsciously took a step forward, but it set Williford on edge. His spine stiffened. "I know you didn't mean nothing by that step, Matthew, but—"

"The hell I didn't!" Douglas shouted, his face contorting in anger. His blue eyes flashed.

It was a toss-up as to which one ripped off his shirt faster, but Williford landed the first punch, his fist glancing off Douglas' right cheek and hurling him to the ground. He jumped on top of the lieutenant as a powerful right cross smashed into his nose, bringing tears to his eyes. He grabbed Douglas around the shoulders and Douglas grabbed him around the waist and together they rolled through the grass, looking like a couple of five-year-olds wrestling for fun.

After a solid minute, Douglas' wild raucous cackle disturbed the contest. The lieutenant was on the bottom at the time and abruptly released his hold on Williford. The captain looked down, frowning, to see tears of hilarity rolling down Douglas' cheeks.

"Damn you, Douglas!" he said, rolling off the lieutenant to sit beside him in the grass. He noticed his arms were scratched and bleeding, then saw the briar of wild roses they'd been rolling around in.

Douglas grabbed his stomach, his chest vibrating in laughter. Williford started chuckling softly, eyeing Douglas askance.

"You just struck an officer, George," Douglas pointed out, wiping tears from his eyes.

Williford nodded, wiggling his nose; he wasn't sure it was still in one piece. "Felt damn good, too."

Douglas gave him a wry smile. "Want to go at it again?"

"Hell no, Matthew. I didn't really mean to in the first place."

Douglas bowed his head, plucking a sprig of long grass and putting it in his mouth. The amusement in his eyes was part forgiveness for his superior officer's brash actions. "I know that, George."

"Bad day—that's all."

"You had to talk to Sawyers?"

Williford nodded and exhaled heavily, glancing apologetically at Douglas, then stretched out on his side and propped his head on one hand. "So." He grabbed a handful of grass and pulled it up. It made a screeching noise. "Give me an option, Matthew. Just . . . give me a way out?"

Douglas sat up, obviously thinking. The wind ruffled his brown hair, whispering through the grass and rustling the tree leaves. "What if I move my tent farther from camp?"

"Sure, I reckon the Sioux could use a long blond scalp for their coup sticks."

Douglas gave him an askance look and rubbed his chin. "Well, what if I . . . no, hell that wouldn't work."

Williford tossed down his handful of grass and touched his nose again. Blood was trickling down his chin. Tilting his head back, he pinched it while he talked. "Why don't you try buying a tent from the road crew? They came prepared for six months, so they've got lots of spare equipment. Or that kid from Ohio, Nat Hedges? He's got thirty-six wagons of goods to start a store. He sure as hell ought to have tents if he's going to a hole like Virginia City. Half the population still lives in tents."

"I could do that." Douglas nodded. "Will that solve the problem?"

"So far as I'm concerned." He hesitated, weighing his next words. "But it won't stop the talk. People are mighty upset."

"Don't expect it to." Douglas leaned over and retrieved his cap from the tall grass, then beat it out on his knee, eyes downcast.

"Hell of a fix, Douglas."

"Didn't seem I had a choice. She needed help."

"And you figured you were the one to give it." He shook his head, fingering the cool grass.

"Reckon."

"That, and you've never really cottoned to white ideas of

right and wrong.'' He looked up to meet Douglas' blue eyes.

The lieutenant raised his brows and gazed out to the rolling plains. "I always figured there was more than one way of judging things.''

"Indians have a different understanding of marriage, don't they?'' Douglas frowned and stared at the ground, not answering. Williford waited a few moments and continued. "Way I heard it is if a woman doesn't like her husband she just sets his things outside the tipi and they aren't married anymore.''

Douglas smiled. "Something like that. Depends on the tribe.''

"By most Indian ways, you'd be considered married to Colleen, wouldn't you?''

"By most.''

"Train'll never see it that way.''

Douglas shrugged.

Williford reached over the grass for his shirt and brought it back to his lap. "You don't care?''

"No.''

"But Colleen does?''

"I reckon.''

He and Douglas held each other's eyes for a few moments.

"You need money for that tent?''

Douglas chuckled softly. "Army hasn't paid any of us since we left Alton prison camp—where would you get money?''

Williford reached in his pocket and pulled out a twenty-dollar gold piece. He turned the coin over in his palm. "I've been saving this—I want the change.'' He threw it to Douglas.

The lieutenant caught it.

· CHAPTER 14 ·

COLLEEN AMBLED THROUGH CAMP, DOWN TOWARD THE trickle of water in the creek. She had two canteens clutched in each hand. That would be enough to take care of her and Matthew for another day. They'd started rationing, giving the animals most of the precious liquid. Train members were only allowed to collect water from two to four in the afternoon. It was almost two. She cringed at the thought of having to associate with people who scorned her, but she had no choice. Maybe no one would be there yet?

Her tan, flowered skirt flapped around her legs as she walked over the low sandy hills, eyes studying the pale blue sky. No clouds were visible anywhere. Only swirling hawks marred the heavens. The heat was nearly unbearable. Sweat drenched her legs. She'd been praying for rain, but it seemed God hadn't heard.

At the edge of the creek, a tangle of dusty children played, their high-pitched giggles drifting on the hot wind. When they saw her coming, they rushed around, hiding behind tall bushy stands of greasewood. She frowned a little, but figured they must be playing hide-and-seek and her arrival just coincided with the hiding part.

When she reached the trickle of water, she uncorked a canteen and knelt down, lowering it beneath the flow. The water felt cool as it rushed over her fingers, washing away the sweat and dirt on her hands. In the back of her mind, she heard a soft rustling in the brush, but thought nothing about it—just rabbits or horned toads probably.

The rustling continued until a stern-faced child reared up from behind a bush and screamed at her, flinging a large stone. The stone landed hard against her back. She dropped the canteen. It clanged as it smashed to the bottom of the creek. More children rose and more stones were hurled, landing on her arms, chest, and face. Blood streamed down her right cheek.

Terror filled her as the stoning continued, children shrieking and grabbing handfuls of rocks. "Stop it!" she cried, standing up and shielding her face with her arms. "Stop it!"

"My mama says you're a witch!" Sidney Lory's shrill voice knelled. He was twelve and bullied the other children in the train, telling them he was *their* leader. "They stone witches!"

"What?" she started, stunned and staring wide-eyed.

A blond boy perched on his toes, a large rock in his hand, posed for attack. His face was contorted into a scowl. "We're going to stone you to death just like they did in the Bible!" he shouted, flinging his weapon.

She sidestepped, anger rising like a whirlwind to soften her fear. She ran at the children, scattering them. "Get home! All of you—before I tell your mothers!"

They retreated a short distance, but continued their taunting.

"My mama wouldn't care!" a tiny girl in a blue plaid dress yelled, leaning over and spitting at Colleen to emphasize her words. "She says there's demons what lives in your head!"

The dreams? The children knew of her dreams? "I—I

don't care what your mothers say!'' Colleen screamed back, tears flooding her eyes. "I don't care, you hear?''

The brawny Lory boy threw out his chest and walked bravely forward. "God is going to punish you fer being a witch!'' he rasped. "He's going to kill you!''

"Kill you! Kill you! Kill you!'' the children chanted over and over in unison.

The chanting cut her heart, each word plunging like a jagged knife blade into her soul. Welts were rising on her arms where the stones had landed, stinging.

"Stop it!'' she screamed.

Her legs went weak, knees trembling at the hateful looks on their young faces. Who could have told them such a terrible thing?

"Don't you talk to no Indian demons in your head no more!'' the little girl screeched, picking up another rock. "Or we'll come back and kill you dead!''

The rock pounded her leg, sending a flash of pain through her. She winced. The children laughed and pointed cruelly, enjoying her agony, then Sidney Lory waved a hand and they all followed him, running away to the wagons.

Colleen stared after them, deeply shaken, heart beating so loudly in her ears she could no longer hear the moaning of the wind through the brush. Her feet had gone numb, feeling a part of the tan sand of the dry plains. She was rooted to the spot, her legs refusing to carry her away.

In a daze, she forced herself to turn around and finish filling the canteens, her hands trembling so terribly she could barely keep the spout beneath the trickle of water that tumbled over a large stone. When she'd finished, she splashed her face with the cool liquid and stood up, looking carefully over the route to the military camp. No children were in sight. She swallowed her fear and headed back.

As she strode quickly by the emigrant wagons a voice met her ears.

"Witch!'' it hissed. "Witch!''

She whirled around to see Robert, green eyes gleaming hatred. He rushed from between two wagons and grabbed

her arm, dragging her forcibly across the sands to his wagon.
Her canteens fell into the dirt as she stumbled.

"No!' she screamed. "Leave me—''

He pressed a hard hand over her mouth and jerked her to
his chest, whispering hotly in her ear. "I'm going to talk to
you! Colonel Sawyers told me to drag you back if Williford
wouldn't make you come.''

Her mind tingled with a sudden flash of adrenaline.
Colonel Sawyers? She tried to scream, but only a muffled
mewing came out. He shoved her against the back of his
wagon, his free hand reaching down to rip her bodice. Her
white breasts shone brightly in the sunlight, bared.

"Folks think you're possessed, that Satan is making you
be a harlot,'' he whispered insanely, his face only inches
from hers. A green fire burned in his eyes. His full beard
bristled against her chin. "Well, I don't want no harlot in
my wagon. So I ain't agoing to drag you back.''

She tried to scream again, but he pressed his hand tighter
over her mouth, leaning his massive body against hers to
keep her from squirming.

"But I want you to know who told folks you was a
witch—*it was me*. I told them all about your dreams and
how Father Donovan tried to get me to allow an exorcism
to rid you of the demons.''

Colleen went white, her muscles slackening. My God!
Could it be true? Why hadn't the priest told her? Despite
all of Matthew's assurances that the wolf and warrior were
good, doubts roared through her. Possessed . . . ?

Robert grinned, seeing the frightened pleading expression come over her face. "Yeah, I never told anyone, not
even you, 'cause I didn't want to suffer from folks talking.
But now it's a heap different, ain't it?''

He released her and shoved her out from between the
wagons. She landed on her back, breasts spilling from her
torn dress. She clutched at the bodice, pulling it tight as
she got to her feet unsteadily and retrieved the canteens.

Mrs. Lory came around the side of her wagon with a pan,
heading to the creek for water, but stopped suddenly on

seeing Colleen. Her mouth gaped open as her eyes drifted to the torn dress. "You filthy . . ." she began, pursing her lips, then rushed by Colleen in a whirl of skirt.

Stunned by Robert's words, Colleen drifted to Matthew's tent. He was out scouting and wouldn't be back until nightfall. She laid the canteens beside the canvas structure and ducked inside to change clothes. Then, huddling like a child in the corner, she forced her stricken mind to work. Should she tell Matthew what had happened to her today? She desperately needed his strength and comforting, but what would he do? He'd feel obligated to support her and might do something dangerous. Her mind whirled as she pulled her knees against her chest. And, if Matthew knew that Sawyers had told Robert to drag her back . . . The possible bloodshed made her numb.

She dropped her forehead against her knees.

Colleen coughed in the dust kicked up by the wagons. This section of the plains was bitterly dry. Every creek bed they passed was parched, as parched and thirsty as they themselves. It was Sunday, but Sawyers' customary day of rest had been called off. They were floundering in the arid country like aimless wanderers, their water gone.

She stumbled over a bristly sage, but caught herself before she fell. She'd been plodding along beside the O'Brians' wagon, Elizabeth playing hopscotch next to her, but she was suddenly too tired to keep up the pace and began lagging behind.

In the distance, square sandstone buttes rose. They wavered in the hot air, shimmering brassy against the pale blue sky. The country was rough and hilly, dissected by jagged drainages and filled with cactus and rattlesnakes. The land was so thickly covered by greasewood and sage that Colleen could barely take a step without snagging her green-flowered tan skirt. She had bent down so often that day to untangle her hem that her back muscles ached miserably.

As if in answer to her prayers, shouts of "Hold up!" and "Whoa!" rang out and the wagons slowed. Rusty squeaks of varying tones filled the air as the brakes did their jobs. She shielded her eyes from the blaring sun and saw Elizabeth running back toward her, her red braids bobbing.

"Lunchtime, Colleen! We're stopping to eat!" She waved her arms and jumped over a sage, her blue dress flying up to show bare knees, then ran headlong and grabbed Colleen by the hand. "Come on. Papa said to bring ye!" The child tugged her tired arm.

"All right, Elizabeth." She smiled, letting herself be pulled along.

The line of wagons seemed to stretch endlessly in front of her. She looked ahead and saw several road-builders pause over a deep dry gulch. The channel was maybe ten feet across and a half a dozen feet deep. It would have to be graded before the train could cross. As well, several men were unhitching cattle and letting horses graze freely on the grassy slope overlooking the gulch.

"Guess we're going to be here for a while, huh, honey?" she asked Elizabeth.

The child turned up a heavily freckled face to nod. "Papa says hours, 'cause that gully is so deep."

From behind, the sound of hurried steps echoed, but before she could turn around, Elizabeth squealed "Uncle Matthew!" and happily threw herself into his arms.

"Oh, Lizard!" He grunted as the girl squirmed up on his hip. "You're getting too big for such doings!"

Colleen smiled and waited for him to catch up, then asked, "What are you doing here? I thought Captain Williford had you on some sort of 'hard labor'?"

"He did."

She looked him up and down, glossing over the girlish legs around his muscular waist. "You look fine to me."

"Um, you look fine to me too," he whispered seductively, winking.

Elizabeth giggled and rolled her eyes. Colleen shook her head. Despite his smile, he looked worn. The elbows in his uniform were threadbare, his brown skin showing through, and he had deep lines around his eyes as though he'd been squinting all morning.

"What sort of hard labor?"

"The worst kind—diplomatic bantering."

"With who?"

"Our illustrious leader," he drawled, raising one eyebrow and pursing his lips like he wanted to spit.

"Oh." It was a hollow comment. She'd grown to hate the train's leader.

Ahead, overlooking the dry gulch, Maureen stood by her wagon and waved an arm. The vehicle was perched above the small canyon and the white canvas top ruffled in the hot wind. She'd lowered the tailgate and thrown a red-checkered tablecloth across it. Bread was folded in a napkin at one end to hold down the fluttering cloth and Lawrence was seated at the other, a sandwich of breakfast leftovers, bread and bacon, gripped in his freckled hand. He smiled between chews as they approached.

"Ho, lassy." He cast a disapproving eye at his nine-year-old daughter riding Matthew's hip. "Didna I tell ye ye're too big for that?" His wide-brimmed brown hat waffled in a potent gust and he quickly shifted his attention, smashing it down on his head before it sailed away.

Elizabeth disentangled herself from Matthew and jumped down, her blue dress flying up. "Yes, papa." She grinned shyly, a finger tucked in the corner of her mouth. Her green eyes were wide, waiting for either a reprimand or a forgiving nod.

Lawrence waved a negligent hand. "It's all right, I guess—for today!"

Elizabeth smiled and whirled around, letting the wind flood over her, then charged to the front of the wagon to pet the oxen.

"She's gonna be a tomboy all her life, if ye don't do something, woman." Lawrence shook a finger at Maureen.

The middle-aged woman shrugged, holding down her green skirt to keep the wind out, and walked to stand beside him, a hand on his stocky shoulder. " 'Tis the trip, darlin', she's too excited to care about being a little lady. We'll work on it when we get to Montana.''

"Might be too late by then," Lawrence commented dryly, "especially after the way she whipped the Lory boy yesterday. Imagine? a girl her size taking that brat down and blacking his eye!"

Maureen looked grim, bowing her head, then smiled at Matthew and Colleen and extended a hand to the bread and pan of bacon. "Eat, children!" Her wrinkled face glowed. Her white hair was tucked firmly beneath a green bonnet.

Matthew strolled forward and sat down on the opposite edge of the gate from Lawrence and picked up a slice of bread.

"Colleen—you, too. It's not much, just some shreds from breakfast—"

"Oh, Maureen, you're very kind. But I'm not hungry," she lied, smiling. She was starved, but the thought of eating salty bacon with no water to wash it down was too unpleasant to contemplate. Instead, she walked forward and put a hand on Matthew's back, watching him eat. He ate like he did everything else, lustily. No sooner was his first piece of bread gone than he'd retrieved another and slapped a thick slice of bacon in it.

"So"—Lawrence brushed his hands together to rid them of crumbs—"why the hell—er—excuse me, ladies—didn't we circle the wagons if we were going to stop like this?" He glared at Matthew.

"Well—Lawrence," Matthew answered between bites, his eyes drifting out to the dusty, windblown hills, "Sawyers doesn't think we need to."

Both men grabbed their hats as a gust of wind tore by, then Lawrence eyed Matthew skeptically. "Yer telling me the mon doesn't know we're in the middle of Injun country?"

"No, didn't say that, my friend." Matthew smiled. "Told him myself." He tugged his blue cap down over his forehead to cut some of the wind and looked lazily at Lawrence.

"Well?" O'Brian asked, waving both hands to the dry,

sage-covered hills. "There's a million places out here a war party could hide! We ought to be taking the proper pre—"

"Told him that too."

Lawrence dropped his hands, letting them slap his black pants emphatically. A loud *crack!* erupted. "Ye'd think we were being led by a blasted idiot!"

Matthew laughed that short, deep laugh that always signaled his thoughts were turning sour. He shifted positions and spoke through a long exhale. "Told him that, too. But Sawyers is convinced he's invincible. According to his lights, that makes the train invincible."

Lawrence grumbled under his breath and wiped his hands on his pants. "What are we doing floundering around out here anyway? A road through this kind of rough country is—"

"—just plain knot-headed," Douglas finished the sentence, nodding amiably, then pointed to the square buttes in the distance. "Sawyers says we're going to go north of those buttes and hit the Powder River."

"Well, there's no doubting we need water," Lawrence mumbled unhappily.

"Um-hum, water and a war," Matthew added calmly, unbuttoning his shirt to the middle of his chest.

"A . . . a war?" Maureen's voice quivered, her eyes going wide. She clutched the bonnet bow beneath her chin.

Matthew nodded pleasantly, one brow raising. "Powder River's an important place this time of year—especially for the regional tribes."

"And ye—ye think we're liable to run into—"

"I do."

"Well!" Lawrence slammed a fist into the gate. "That's all the more reason for us to be circling the wagons and taking precautions!"

Matthew sighed, his blue eyes suddenly brooding as they again drifted over the surrounding hills. "True."

"By God!" Lawrence growled loudly. "I'm going to load every weapon I've got right now!" He jumped off the gate and trudged away to pull his pistols from beneath the wagon seat. A clatter came from the front.

"Fine idea," Douglas commented, then stood and stretched his back muscles. "Well, I'd best be getting back to my duties."

He tipped his cap to Mrs. O'Brian. "Mighty fine lunch, Maureen. I'm obliged."

Colleen followed him away from the wagon, her arms crossed defensively, a frown creasing her forehead. His words about the war party both frightened and elated her. Something inside told her he was right. They were out there—waiting. That brought fear. But another voice inside whispered that the man with long black braids was with them, and that brought anxious elation. No matter how solemn her thoughts about possession, she couldn't convince herself the warrior was wicked.

"Where're you going now?" she asked, looking up at Matthew.

"Oh, reckon I'll find Williford and report on my morning debacle."

"De . . ." She blushed, tendrils of embarrassment and anger rising that he'd used another word she didn't know.

"It's—uh—very much like a travesty, my dear." He smiled, eyes mocking, then laughed as she gritted her teeth. He whispered, "It means a disaster."

"Well, why didn't you say so in the first place!"

He raised both brows quizzically. "I did."

"Anyway," she got back to the original subject, "so you'll be busy?"

"Yes." He put his arms around her shoulders and squeezed. "Why don't you get some rest, take a nap or something? The road crew will be occupied for at least a couple of hours grading that crossing. There's nothing else to do."

She sighed, staring at the tangles of sage they walked through. "All right."

As though a thought had just struck him, he abruptly stopped, put his hands on her shoulders, and leaned down to gaze into her eyes. "No solitary walks, though. Understood?"

"Understood." She saluted.

He gave her a disgusted look. "I mean it. The possibility

of finding you scalped and bloody does not fill my breast with ardor.''

"Matthew!"

"Well, it doesn't."

"I'll be careful."

"All right." He grinned as though pleased with himself for frightening her, tipped his hat, and strode away toward the rear of the train.

She turned around into the wind and looked back toward the O'Brians' wagon. Lawrence was sitting on the open gate loading a pistol while Maureen wrapped the remaining bread in a clean cloth and tucked it inside the wagon. Elizabeth ran back and forth beside the vehicle, playing some unknown game.

Colleen came up beside Maureen and smiled shyly. She'd seen Mrs. Lory come by the O'Brians' wagon early that morning and heard some harsh words exchanged, but didn't know quite how to broach the subject. Ethel Lory was such a prudish, spiteful woman that she just knew the discussion was centered on Matthew or her.

Maureen returned her smile gaily, her wrinkled face rosy and affectionate. She patted Colleen's arm and leaned back against the wagon, flowered bonnet ties fluttering up in front of her face. " 'Tis too bad the colonel wouldn't listen to yer Matthew, darlin'. One of these days we're going to get in trouble because of it."

Colleen smiled proudly and dropped her eyes. Lawrence and Maureen had not even said a word about her "improper" relationship with Matthew. Instead they'd been overly kind, going out of their way to invite the two of them to dinners and campfire talks.

"What are ye thinking, child?" Maureen asked, concerned by the look on Colleen's face. Curls of white fluttered beneath her bonnet brim. She put a hand on her shoulder and squeezed softly. "You worried about Matthew?"

Colleen laughed. "No—at least not the way you're thinking."

Maureen smiled, looking relieved. "Good. 'Cause there's

nobody can take care of himself as well as Matthew. He's a fine man.''

"You do like him, don't you?" she asked hesitantly.

"Why, of course, dear! We like both of you!"

"Maureen—what did Mrs. Lory want this morning?"

Maureen dropped her hand. "Did you hear that mess?"

"Well, no. Just some harsh voices," she replied, wrapping fingers in her tan, flowered skirt. "It was about me and Matthew, wasn't it?"

"Ah, darlin'! Don't worry your head about it! She's just a bitter old woman."

"What did she say?"

Maureen dropped her eyes and looked nervous, mouth twitching. "She was . . . trying to talk folks into . . ."

Lawrence had come up from behind and was listening. He broke in, his voice booming. "Christ, she's got a right to know!" He pointed at Colleen but his words were directed to his wife.

Maureen nodded and turned up tender eyes, then laid a hand on Colleen's cheek. "Darlin', she's tryin' to organize folks against you and have you thrown out of the train."

Colleen's eyes widened. Her skirt whipped around her legs.

"Don't ye worry none!" Lawrence bellowed, holding his hat against the wind. "Maureen told her we'd sooner she and her ugly husband were off the train than you!"

Pink flushed Colleen's cheeks, tears coming to her eyes. She forced herself to look out at the windblown plains where a herd of antelope grazed.

"It'll never happen, darlin'! She's a troublemaker, that's all," Maureen said.

"She's all talk!" Lawrence added.

"Maybe," Colleen replied. "Has she talked to the colonel about it?"

Maureen looked at Lawrence and they exchanged a pained glance.

"I'm telling you the truth, girl." Lawrence lowered his voice. "The old woman's got no backing from the train."

Colleen smiled weakly, knowing from the tone of his

voice he was lying out of kindness. She played along to make him feel better. "All right. I won't worry."

Lawrence slapped her gently on the shoulder. "That's a girl. Never fear nothing unless it's already up in your face."

She nodded and wandered away. Her heart was beating in her ears as she headed toward the jagged drainage channel. A gust of wind whipped by, worrying loose tendrils of blond hair. "Mercy!" she muttered, exasperated. Did the wind ever stop on these vast open plains?

Winding through the sage, she made her way to the earthen gorge where the road crew diligently worked. The clink-clunk sound of picks and shovels filled the air and the smell of sweating bodies rose powerfully. Across the gash, unhitched cattle mooed pathetically. The animals hadn't had a drop of water all day and were on the verge of becoming unmanageable. The bulls tossed their heads, bellowing their distress to the howling wind. Several of the horses had drifted westward toward a copse of cottonwood trees. A man on horseback lagged behind them, plodding leisurely. Colleen squinted, but the distance was too great—she couldn't make out who the rider was. He was dressed in civilian clothes, though, so he wasn't part of the military escort.

Colleen peered over the edge of the jagged channel. There was shade below. A long irregular shadow extended beneath a tan sandstone overhang. She searched the crumbling walls until she found a place she could climb down.

It was cooler in the ravine, the wind not so blustery. She strolled lazily along, letting her fingers drift over the sandy walls, Matthew's admonition completely forgotten in light of the O'Brians' words. There was something protruding from the wall ahead, but she couldn't make out what it was. She wound down the channel, unconsciously getting farther and farther from the harsh sounds of laboring men, her thoughts wandering.

The protrusion, she found, was a series of huge bones. The partial skeleton had been torn by the water in the ravine until now it resembled a snarling mouth with the teeth jutting out at awkward angles. She smoothed her hand over the cool bones. Gathering her tan skirt in her hands, she sat down and leaned against the gritty wall.

Jangling sounds drifted up the gulch, accompanied by gruff shouts of "Hyah!" She leaned forward to see the lighter wagons moving across the ravine. She frowned and put a hand to her sweaty forehead, wiping away the perspiration. Had the crew finished grading the approach already? It seemed only minutes since she'd climbed down into the jagged drainage channel. She sighed. The sounds meant she'd have to leave the cool shade soon.

Leaning back, her eyes followed the stringy clouds hurrying across the sky. They looked like wispy horses' tails. The longer she sat, staring upward, listening to the clinking of the traces as the mules dipped down into the ravine and up over the other side, the more odd she felt. It was as though her head were filling with cotton, becoming muddled and light. She sat slightly forward, a hand to her cheek, and suddenly she was dizzy. A sweeping panorama of tan dirt swelled up and she tumbled to the ground, rolling over on her back, her fingers clawing aimlessly at the sandstone. Blue sky and clouds swirled above.

The vision came rapidly, washing over her in waves of color and jagged bits of male voices. "He doesn't see us!" a voice whispered. The words echoed again and again in her mind—and then there were rustling green leaves against a background of sky—and the tall grass crept cool up her arms—"Just a little longer!"—a horse whinnied somewhere—the world whirled, and she felt nauseated, her stomach rumbling threateningly—and then the man appeared. The warrior, her warrior. He was kneeling in the grass, a rifle in his hand. Her heart cried out to him and she extended her hands. He jerked his eyes to her and his face grew suddenly terrified. "Run!" he shouted to her in Cheyenne. *"Run!"*

A spasm shook her body and she was awake, lying in the ravine, heart racing. The rattle of gunfire erupted, the cracking sounds wavering on the fierce gusts of wind.

She sat up, terror rising to choke her, and pulled herself to her feet. Gripping her skirt, she ran, stumbling over the irregular ravine bottom, her feet sliding off the sandy rocks to twist and scrape against the stones. Men shouted ahead of her, screaming orders, and over the white uproar came the piercing wolflike cries of the Indians—closer, they were coming closer.

Colleen raced down the ravine and scrambled up the rough-hewn crossing to climb out into the midst of hysteria. Men rushed pell-mell around her, screeching names or crawling in the backs of wagons for weapons or shelter. Knots of people crowded between the white-topped vehicles, trying to steady rifles. Women grabbed bawling children and dragged them beneath wagons to huddle terrified in the shadows as the warriors rode down upon them.

She was numb, her body light, as she wandered aimlessly through the violent storm of screams and turmoil. Time froze, the train becoming a still-life watercolor depicting people gaping in horror, their eternally unblinking eyes wide. She walked out away from the wagons and into the sage. The thorny branches scratched her legs until the blood ran warm into her shoes, each step through the green tangles seeming to take hours. She turned—an agonizingly slow motion—and saw them. The warriors wore only breechclouts. Red and black slashes streaked their faces and they were coming fast, galloping headlong toward the train. A solid line of dust grew up behind them. Shots rattled on the wind, puffs of dark gray smoke erupting as they shouldered their weapons and fired.

Yet Colleen could not move. Her feet were rooted to the hot sand. As the warriors charged the cavalry's horse herd, stampeding the screaming beasts, her field of vision narrowed, the periphery of the train shading black until only the warriors remained clear. And the shooting stopped. She was floating, her tan dress and blond hair billowing in the gale. She could still see warriors firing and watch blue-gray smoke rise and disperse in the wind, but only silence filled her ears—an ominous encompassing silence that left her barren, as barren as the rolling plains around her.

One warrior stopped, his horse rearing and pawing the dusty air. He turned and stared at her, black eyes squinting hard, then wheeled his horse and raced forward in a mad spattering of rocks and dirt, as if to crush her beneath sharp hooves. But her legs were leaden, her body numb. He pulled back on his reins only feet from her and gazed down, his face wild and full of hate. He wore a mustache and had a broad square face. She could smell the rich scent of the horse and the acrid odor of gunpowder.

"Where is he?" she asked, sensing this man before her was connected to the warrior in her dreams.

He cocked his head, lifting his chin to glare with one fierce eye. There was recognition and fear in his bitter gaze. Bullets spattered around him, kicking up puffs of dust. He tugged his gaze away, looking to the train. Firing had been redirected and was now steadied on him. He gave her one final glance, shrieked a war cry, and rode headlong away across the rolling plains, back toward the cottonwood copse.

Colleen stood deathly still, watching the war party retreat, listening to their triumphant cries. Her heartbeat was slow and rhythmic. No rush of adrenaline stung her veins. Only a powerful sensation of loneliness and desolation thumped in her breast. The warrior was gone, his voice silent.

Tears welled, blurring her vision. A man in blue was running toward her, shouting. But his frantic words were incomprehensible—a foreign language. She stared dumbly at him, knowing he was George Williford, but not understanding the meaning of his words. He gripped his blue cap against the wind and stabbed a finger toward the wagons.

Her knees went weak, her mind blanking out. She only vaguely noticed the captain's eyes squint suddenly, his arms reaching for her, and felt herself falling, falling.

· CHAPTER 15 ·

MAUREEN O'BRIAN RUSHED SWIFTLY TO THE WAGON AND
threw back the rear curtains to stare in at Colleen's pale
face, then frantically looked up to Matthew. He stood stiffly,
his blue eyes focused on the distant cottonwood grove, one
hand clamped over the wagon gate, the other dangling
limply at his side. His cap was low over his forehead, the
furious wind whipping his blue sleeves until they crackled.
A dark, impassive look filled his face—as though he'd seen
a ghost. Colleen mumbled incoherently, her words strange,
foreign. Matthew's fingers squeezed the wooden gate,
knuckles going white as he listened.

"Matthew?" Maureen gasped, wringing her hands as her
eyes darted over the surrounding terrain for unseen Indian
warriors. "What happened?"

His jaw vibrated softly as he ground his teeth. He shook
his head slowly, deliberately, as though it took great effort.
"Don't know."

"Did she faint? God knows she had reason, I—"

"Don't—know," he repeated mechanically, his eyes still

riveted to the trees from which the war party had emerged. There was a frightening quality to his rigid posture.

"What can we . . ." Maureen began, but stopped short when Matthew strode abruptly past her, his swagger smooth and latently dangerous, heading for a milling group of soldiers. His uniform melted rapidly into the surging sea of blue and she could no longer identify him.

Timidly she swung around to look back at Colleen. The young woman's face was tense, her head wobbling with the odd breathy words. Her flowered dress showed signs of turmoil; dirt splotched the tan fabric and blood seeped through to stain the lower hem a lurid carnelian. Maureen reached a hand into the wagon and softly patted Colleen's foot.

"It's all right, darlin'," she cooed, strain making her voice high and scratchy. "It's all right."

Behind her the gravelly voice of Colonel Sawyers called out loudly, taking roll call. Shouts of "here" and "yo!" confirmed everyone's presence except Nathanial Hedges.

"Hedges?" Sawyers cried. "Hedges!"

Only the howling wind answered.

The colonel waved a hand to a group of teamsters. "Organize a search party!"

An ominous murmuring arose as men raced to and fro, grabbing rifles and shouting orders.

Maureen looked on in dismay, a feeling of utter bewilderment filling her. Lawrence stood with his legs spread, Elizabeth's hand tucked firmly in his, listening to Sawyers' speech.

"We're safe," she whispered to herself, gaining strength from the sight of her family. A breath shuddered out of her lungs as she entwined anxious fingers in her green dress.

The search party approached the cottonwood grove cautiously, their rifles gripped firmly in their hands. Albert Holman, teamster for the road-building crew, took silent steps into the grassy copse. The sight that met his eyes made bitter acid rise in his throat. He forced a swallow.

"Holy Jesus . . ."

"What is it, Holman?" a voice called behind him. Swift steps sounded in the tall grass.

Men gathered around, coarse murmurs echoing through the party. The horrid sound of vomiting rang hollowly through the trees.

Holman clenched his teeth, his breast heaving as he looked down at the naked, torn body of Nat Hedges. The young man lay face up, his dead eyes staring sightlessly at the rustling green leaves overhead. Seven arrows thrust up like quills from his bare bloody breast. A bullet had smashed his cheek, tearing a ragged hole in his face, and a dozen others riddled his body. His skull was bare, the scalp ripped off. In the golden sunlight that dappled through the towering trees, the bone gleamed.

Holman swallowed again and whispered hoarsely, "Let's take him home, boys."

The sounds of jingling traces and clopping hooves carried on the wind as the train cautiously moved southward. They didn't stop until nine o'clock that night when they found a watery slough. Williford ordered the wagons circled and posted heavy guards. Stock was herded down to the water first. The thirsty animals bellowed and squealed their relief, wallowing in the slough until it was so muddy the train couldn't fill their water barrels for hours.

Matthew cradled Colleen in his arms and stared into the blazing campfire. Her blond hair tumbled over his chest and down into his lap, falling in thick curls to brush the sand. Darkness swelled around them like a black chilling blanket. He sucked in a deep tired breath and rocked her gently back and forth, murmuring softly in Cheyenne, telling her everything was all right. She'd said little, mumbling only that the warrior had come to her. He listened carefully to the fluent Cheyenne words she spoke, and nodded his understanding, then tried talking to her in English, but it was clear she didn't understand. Then she'd fallen silent, clutching his arms tightly and burying her face in his shirt. Her brown eyes stared up hauntingly.

His gaze drifted upward. Stars shimmered brilliantly in the cloudless sky, casting a dim gray glow over the sage and sand. Crickets squeaked like rusty hinges out beyond the circled wagons and somewhere a coyote yipped dolefully. He listened absently, his mind on the attack and the story Williford related about Colleen's behavior. Who had the warrior been who'd ridden up beside her? The captain's description sounded very much like one of the Bent brothers— George or Charley? he wondered. If the Bents, with their knowledge of white ways, were involved, the train was in more trouble than it knew.

"Colleen?" he questioned softly, smoothing his fingers over her cheek. Then in Cheyenne, he asked, "Can you tell me more?"

She stirred weakly, digging her fingers into his arms and looking up at him imploringly. "He's gone," she whispered. Every subtle inflection of the Indian language was perfect. Her eyes drifted out to the dark hills.

"Gone?"

She nodded slowly.

"Why didn't the warrior stay?"

She blinked tiredly. "The wolf—wouldn't let him."

Matthew pulled her closer, pressing her frail body to his broad chest. "Did the wolf tell you?"

"No," she said, sobs breaking out. Her chest shuddered under the impact and she pulled on his blue shirt until it came untucked from his pants, then smothered her face in the fabric.

"Shhh," he whispered comfortingly, squeezing her tightly. "I'm here."

Almost unconsciously the tune and words came back to him and he began singing a Cheyenne lullaby. It was a mourning song, a song praising the brave warriors who'd died in battles against the Shoshoni. His voice rose strong and deep in the desert silence and he felt Colleen relax in his arms, her body losing the wrenching tautness of moments before. As he sang, her tears gradually lessened, then stopped and she lay quiet and still, her breathing calming.

Douglas rocked her gently, rubbing his cheek against her forehead and singing every song he could remember until the night grew unbearably black and his campfire dwindled to dim red coals. The songs soothed something deep inside him, a wound that remained unhealed even after twelve years. Memories flooded his mind: voices echoing hollowly, moccasins on snow, weak inverted images of village cooking fires reflected in dark lakes—and icy fingers wriggled in his gut making him suck in a sudden breath.

He squeezed his eyes closed, bowing his head and tightening his arms around Colleen. "Please, *Maiyun*," he prayed softly, his deep voice barely audible, "let the punishment be mine."

Perhaps it was the combination of the battle and Colleen's near escape from death that brought back the old dream, the dream that had haunted him for twelve years. It began as it always did:

A chill wind swept down from the north, bringing huge wet snowflakes. He leaned his head against the sorrel's mane. He hadn't slept in two days and the fatigue was draining his strength—strength he needed desperately now. He patted the horse's red neck, whispering affectionately, and started back to his lodge, his legs trembling from strain. Cold sweat soaked his buckskins, making them cling to his skin. The gale howled at him, snow stinging his face like icy needles.

He threw open the lodge flap. Ducking into the warm darkness, he knelt beside his wife—his precious Enanoshe—stroking the strands of black hair from her face before slipping his arms beneath her. Though she was wrapped in five blankets, the buffalo robe on the floor was drenched in sweat. It stuck to his chilled flesh. His heart was bursting, his mind so terrified with worry he could barely think.

He picked her up, clutching her to his breast, and walked out into the freezing wind and snow, carrying her to the waiting travois. He was numb, living a horrifying nightmare from which he could not awaken. She'd taken ill three days before and now was barely alive. He stared down at her as he walked through the deepening snow, listening to the moaning of the wind through the pines. She was pale, her formerly beautiful face shrunken into dry folds, dying. Her closed eyes squinted against some barely felt pain—the disease so far along she wavered constantly between fevered bursts of alertness and coma. Her long black hair cascaded over his arms, sweeping up frantically in the wintry gale to brush his face and become entangled in his full brown beard.

As he laid her on the travois, her wasted body spasmed in agony, limbs trembling so violently he could barely keep her between the narrow pine poles. He hugged her fiercely to keep her from falling into the snow. Then her cries began—those wrenching cries that had torn his soul for two days—tortured whimpers like an animal struggling in a trap. He closed his eyes and tightened his hold, clutching her firmly to his breast, his cheek against hers. Her face was burning hot, the terrible fever still rising.

He stroked her hair, murmuring "Shhh." Tears pressed against his lids. "It's all right. I'm here."

She relaxed suddenly, her strength vanishing into the dark pit of unconsciousness. Her body hung limp in his arms. He kissed her parted lips and held her tightly for a moment longer. The bitter wind blasted his face like a sheet of ice as he reluctantly released his grip and began belting her onto the travois with leather straps.

From the corner of his eye, he saw the old man hobble out of the village, his willow cane quaking in a gnarled ancient fist. Matthew pretended not to notice, wrapping a strap around Enanoshe's legs and tugging it tight. He'd already discussed it with the old man—discussed for too damn long! There were no more words to say.

The medicine elder stood rigid, his face squeezed into hard, thick lines. His buffalo robe was coated with fresh snow, giving it the fleecy look of lamb's wool.

"You will *not* take my granddaughter from her people!" he wailed.

The snow was falling heavier, swirling madly around them.

"I must, grandfather." He slipped another leather strap around Enanoshe's chest and pulled it tight. Avoiding the elder's stern gaze.

His wife's younger brother ran out from among the conical lodges to stand weakly by his grandfather. The old man put an arm around the eight-year-old's shoulders. The boy's face was white with fear, tears streaking down his dark cheeks. He stared at Matthew as though he were face-to-face with a demon.

The old man asked, "Where will you go?"

Matthew swallowed, trying to hurry. "There is a white doctor among the Shoshoni who knows this disease, I—"

"You would deliver her *to her enemies!*" The ancient eyes blazed.

"There is no honor in harming a sick woman, grandfather. The Shoshoni will not—"

"You will not take her!"

Matthew said nothing, checking the straps to make sure they were secure. Tugging them one final time.

"No!" the boy screamed and hurled himself at Matthew, his fists flying, striking arms and chest. "Leave my sister alone!"

Grabbing the boy, he forced him to his breast, then put his mouth to the tiny ear and softly murmured, "Stop it, my brother. You must be a man."

The boy struggled briefly, burying his sobbing face in Matthew's buckskin jacket.

"Don't take her," he begged feebly as he tugged Matthew's sleeves, looking up with terrified brown eyes. "Please, don't."

He hugged the boy, stroking his long black hair. "Brother, she is not getting better. I must find help."

The old man's voice rang out like a banshee, undulating

with the wind. "If the Great Mystery wants her to live, my medicine will cure her! She needs no white magic!"

Matthew turned to look at him, pressing the boy closer and patting his back. The elder's face glowed with dark hatred, his lips trembling.

Matthew held the boy out at arm's length and met his frightened gaze squarely. "Wounded Bear, I do this for her. I must take her away to make her well. I will bring her back."

The young face puckered miserably. The boy threw his head back and ripped himself from Matthew's arms to run to his sister. He tore frantically at the leather straps, trying to break them loose, to drag his sister off the travois. Matthew reached across the travois and grabbed the child again.

"Balance, son!" the ancient medicine man called, his voice eerie. He raised a hand and flicked it at Matthew, then waited—watching. "What you take, you must give back!"

Broken Star was a powerful and dangerous man, his witchcraft legendary. It was reported that his enemies suffered terrible diseases and their families died brutally; villages were destroyed mysteriously at the raising of his hands. Though the Cheyenne elders frowned on his use of spirit power for evil—no one dared criticize.

Matthew stumbled suddenly, his head reeling. He reached repeatedly for the horse to steady himself, but fell to the snow. Nausea attacked him and he grabbed his stomach, looking up at Broken Star. A malicious smile flickered on the ancient face.

Matthew pulled himself to his feet, his legs wobbly, and braced a hand on a travois pole. He worked his way slowly forward until he could reach the reins of the horse and started walking, leading the horse out of camp, down the trail to the lands of the Shoshoni. The travois made a rough scraping noise as it dragged through the snow. Behind him, Wounded Bear's ragged screams were almost completely obscured by the hysterical cackling of the withered medicine man.

For hours he walked, forcing the recalcitrant horse to pull through deepening drifts, screaming in rage and slapping its nose when it balked, whinnying and rearing, the travois jostling violently.

But Enanoshe made no sounds—not even stirring at the animal's frantic actions. She lay deathly still, her face that of a corpse.

In the middle of the night, the snow drifted too deep to continue. Matthew pulled frantically on the horse's reins, tears of rage and futility sweeping him. He leaned into the leather, the horse screaming and fighting—but it was no use. The snow was too deep.

Dropping the reins, he walked unsteadily back to the travois, picking her up and clutching her tightly, before carrying her to a small orange rock shelter carved from the cliffs nearby.

He laid her gently on the dry floor and smoothed the damp strands of black from her face. She didn't move.

In a sudden burst of fear, he jerked her to his lap, feeling desperately for a pulse in her wrists, then moving trembling hands to her neck. Nothing, no throb of blood or heartbeat met his frozen fingers.

He cried out to the storm and the night, his voice terrified and lonely. The anguished screams echoed emptily from the surrounding hills, coming back to him. He held her tighter, seeking her cold lips and kissing them. Burying his face in the blankets over her breast, he wept, whispering her name over and over.

The Indian camp was enormous, spreading out to form an irregular oval across the low hills. The horse herd was corraled under heavy guard, fifty armed warriors pacing the perimeter, in case the soldiers of the train thought to steal their animals back. Soft neighs drifted on the wind as the horses grazed the grassy slough bottoms.

Wounded Bear let his eyes drift over the camp. Hundreds of fires glowed, undulating with the land like orange glimmers strewn over a fuzzy black blanket. A thousand faces shone golden over the flames, smiling, boasting—some worried. He looked around his own tiny fire as he fiddled with a twisted branch of sage, smoothing it down his leg and watching the tiny white scratches appear like a web over his brown skin. Across the fire, Little Deer and Gray Squirrel laughed, teasing each other about the horse raid, boasting who was braver and who had captured the most army ponies. Between laughs, they gobbled mouthfuls of fresh jackrabbit that had been roasted over the fire. A pile of bones was growing at the edge of the flames, charring and creating acrid smells. He caught whiffs when the evening breeze gusted toward him. And on his left, stretched out on one side, was Bent; his black eyes brooded as he stared across the rolling hills. He told no stories of courage tonight.

Wounded Bear sighed and tossed his sage branch into the fire. As the dried leaves caught and flared, they crackled, sending sparks whirling upward to tumble in the darkness. It was getting late, the victory celebration lasting long into the night, and he was tired. He started to push to his feet to find his blankets, but Bent's low voice stopped him.

"I saw her today."

"Who?" he asked. Anxiety crowded his heart. He gently sat down again, cross-legged, to face his friend.

"The white witch who has cast a spell on you."

"Brother, she has not—"

"She asked about you." His black eyes were probing, verging on condemnation, though his square face was bland and unreadable.

Little Deer and Gray Squirrel halted their conversation in mid-sentence to stare wide-eyed across the flames.

"She . . ." he whispered, dropping his gaze to the flickering flames. His heart raced.

"She said: 'Where is he?' " Bent propped his head on his hand and let his gaze linger on Wounded Bear's troubled expression. "I didn't tell her."

He shrugged. "She knows."

Bent's eyes hardened as frown lines creased his brow. "You will go to her?"

"Soon."

Bent turned away to nervously scoop up a handful of sand. His shoulder muscles were rigid. He poured the grains from one palm to the other, back and forth, until finally the sand had all trickled away. Then he stared at the shimmers on his fingers, swiveling them to the firelight to watch them shine. Emphatically he whispered, "Don't!"

"But I must."

"She is a white *witch* who *wants to hurt us*! Why can't you see that?" His sharp words impaled the darkness. Little Deer and Gray Squirrel exchanged tense looks.

"The raid today was successful. She cast no evil spells on us."

Bent sat forward, eyes hard. "She didn't have a chance. Our attack came too fast—but she will. Maybe tomorrow."

Wounded Bear inhaled a deep breath and got to his feet. His soul felt sore, his heart empty. Did no one understand? The wolf would not lead the woman to him unless there was a good reason, unless she would help the people in some way. He sighed and glanced around the fire at the taut faces staring at him. He met each man's gaze individually, giving each a bit of himself in the wordless exchange, then he walked away, out into the darkness.

He walked far from camp to a hill overlooking the train and sat on the cool sand. Below, the wagons were circled on the first terrace of the creek. Only a single fire glowed to cast wavering light on the white-topped vehicles. He let his eyes drift from the black starry heavens and back to the flickering orange dot. It was late and he was tired, but he wanted to look at the train, wanted to imagine where the woman was and what she was thinking. He would try to contact her later, in his dreams, but for now he just needed to gaze out over her camp. Knowing she was so close was both agony and ecstasy. The emotions vied with each other, making him ache. He plucked a leaf of sage and put it in his mouth. The bitter burst of flavor filled him.

The breeze blew up from the direction of the train, carrying smells and sounds. He extended his legs and leaned back on one elbow. Whiffs of horse and campfires mingled with the tang of sage and the musty, damp odor of the slough. He yawned, his exhaustion catching up with him, and closed his eyes. Without the aid of sight, his hearing amplified and strange sounds wafted up to him from the white wagons. He tilted his head to listen. It was singing he heard, rich masculine singing, the melody lilting on the wind, coming in fragments as the breeze gusted. He couldn't make out the words, but the tune was familiar, taking him back to the days of his boyhood when his sister had sung him to sleep when he was frightened or sick. He could still remember the feel of her tender fingers stroking his hair. He shifted positions to lie flat on the sand and stare up into the glistening stars. He was probably mistaken about the tune—no one in the white camp would know such a sweet lullaby—but it comforted him to believe it was the same.

He would listen for a while, he decided. Listen and remember.

As the first gray rays of dawn stained the eastern horizon, Sawyers gave the order to yoke up and move. People rushed to comply, dragging their oxen up from the slough and hurrying to fasten them in the traces.

Douglas walked tiredly across the inner circle toward George Williford who was orchestrating the military's actions, one hand waving, his voice rising above the general melancholy chatter of the train to shout commands.

Stopping beside the captain, Douglas put one hand on his hip and pulled his cap down over his forehead, waiting. Finally Williford turned to him and smiled wanly. His triangular face was drawn and tired, his usually piercing eyes dulled from lack of sleep.

"Insomnia, George?" Matthew asked, raising one brow.

"A little."

"Hell, I don't know why you'd have problems sleeping—

just because we're surrounded by a thousand Indians and outnumbered five to one is no cause—''

"Douglas, did you come over here to be an irritant or an aid?"

"Depends—what do you need me to do?"

"I . . ." The color suddenly drained from the captain's face and he swallowed hard, his eyes darting frantically over the hills behind Douglas.

Matthew spun, crouching and dropping his hand to his pistol. Fear laced his chest as he slid the gun out of its holster and gripped it tightly in his sweaty palm. The hills were covered with Indians, every knoll sprouting warbonnets like tall grass. The bright beadwork glimmered, feathers fluttering in the morning wind. He scanned the perimeter. No hill was bare. They were completely surrounded.

One by one the rest of the train noticed the Indians and an ominous clamor arose. A feeling of forlorn helplessness spread like wildfire through the crowd. Men lunged for rifles or to unhitch stock and herd the animals into the center of the wagon circle.

"Better do something quick, George," he said, straightening up.

"Why haven't they attacked?"

"Somebody's praying probably."

"Praying?"

"For victory and honor."

Williford nodded slowly and let his gray eyes drift over the hundreds of warriors. "You know some of those prayers, Douglas?"

"I do."

"Send a few up for us too."

Matthew nodded.

"How long before they attack?"

"Five—maybe ten minutes."

Williford turned quickly to his men. "Pile some crates up, stash your ammunition behind them and get set." He

paused, a somber light coming into his eyes as he met the
wary gazes of the former Confederate soldiers.

"Gentlemen." Williford pulled his shoulders back. His
voice was confident. "I'm no Pickett. I don't plan on losing
a single man. You are all—"

Wild howling cries split the morning as the Indians
charged down the hills, the roar of hundreds of horses'
hooves rumbling like thunder.

Men scattered. Douglas raced across the circle, gathering
his spare pistol and rifle and accoutrements from the rear
of the O'Brians' wagon, then trotting to where Colleen sat
silent, her eyes riveted to the screaming hordes that crashed
down the hills. He jerked crates out of a heavy military
wagon and threw them on the ground, kicking one open and
dragging out more ammunition. Sliding to the ground, he
lay on his stomach and steadied his rifle over a wooden lid.

"You all right?" he asked Colleen as he sighted on a
shrieking warrior riding headlong for the wagons. She was
almost back to normal, huddled in a ball on the ground next
to him, her back pressed firmly against one of the crates.

"I'm all right," she said hollowly in English. Her knowledge of Cheyenne seemed to have vanished during the night,
her face gaining back some of its rosy color. She'd braided
her hair that morning, leaving it dangling in one thick cord
down her back.

"Good." He patted her on the leg. "Can you reload for
me?"

She blinked awkwardly and murmured, "I don't want
you to kill them."

He held his fire, letting his breath out and ducking down
behind the crate, coming nose to nose with her. The warrior
rode by, firing into the wagons and whooping madly. The
blasts ricocheted to whine shrilly off into the desert.

"I'm not fond of the idea myself," he said, going rigid
as a bullet splintered a nearby crate and sent wood fragments flying. He adjusted his cap nonchalantly, giving her
a winning smile. "But I'm a selfish sort. It looks like it's a

choice of you and me or some of them. I pick you and me. Who do you pick?"

She thought for a moment. A bullet whistled by, slamming the ground at their feet and digging a long furrow. He scrambled to pull his knees into his chest as she dove for his spare pistol. Her flowered skirt flew up to reveal smooth white knees.

He cocked his head and yelled over the rising turmoil, "Trying to distract me?"

She gave him a disgruntled look, ignoring him while she hurriedly filled the cylinders of the .44 Remington. "Here!" she shouted, laying the reloaded weapon on her skirt at his side to keep it out of the dirt.

"You're a fine woman!" he shouted, hurling himself to the ground with a thump as a wave of arrows clattered off the crates, bits of feathers and splinters of shafts showering them. Jumping up, he quickly leveled his rifle and squeezed the trigger. A brightly painted Sioux brave fell from his horse, his lifeless body tumbling to the sage.

Colleen wrapped her arms over her head and tucked her knees under her. Bugles sounded from the hillsides and the clangor of shots within the wagons died down. Everyone strained their eyes, searching the plains for the cavalry—but no cavalry came. Instead, warriors rushed down the hills screaming impressive white profanities, bugles clutched in one hand and rifles in the other.

"You goddamned white bastard sons-a-bitches!" an Indian voice shouted clearly and another bugle call was played.

Matthew smiled, shaking his head at the expert cursing. The music was obviously being played to mock the whites, to taunt them into false hope. Faces within the circled wagons turned stony and shooting resumed, soldiers yelling potent oaths back at the Indians.

"Who is it out there that knows English so well?" Colleen asked. She had an embarrassed, quizzical look on her face. She was still curled in a ball, her long braid dangling over her shoulder to brush his leg.

He sighted another warrior and fired. "One of the Bent

boys, I'd wager. I'm sure their father's trading post was a good place to learn such descriptive eloquence.''

Frantic firing renewed as another wave of warriors erupted from the drainage bottom, rushing up the damp sides of the slough and screaming as they shot into the emigrant wagons. The cattle inside the circle bellowed shrilly, rushing into each other and gouging with their sharp horns. Several of the smaller bulls had bloody sides from the frightened attacks.

The soldiers, who occupied most of the emigrant section, blasted back, pushing the enemy away.

Matthew glanced at Colleen just before he steadied his rifle again. She'd grown suddenly still and quiet. Her face was slack, her wide eyes staring unblinking across the prairies. Her head was cocked as though she was listening. She nodded slightly. He swung around to follow her gaze. There, on a distant hill, was a warrior on horseback. The pony stamped the ground, whinnying at the repeated blasts. The Indian had his arms outstretched to the wagons. Colleen brought up her own arms, reaching back, and started to get to her feet.

"Stay down!" Matthew shouted at her, putting a hard hand on her shoulder and shoving her to the ground, but she crawled out from under his protective hand and scrambled to her feet to run. From the corner of his eye, he saw the warrior riding down the hill.

Colleen was running to him. Bullets whined off the crates and Matthew hit the ground, flattening himself to crawl after her, his pistol clutched in his right hand. But she was moving too fast, her tan skirt fluttering wildly in the wind. If he couldn't get to his feet, she'd make it out of the circle before he could stop her. Turning and firing three rapid shots at warriors behind him, he stood and ran as hard as he could, dodging terrified stock animals and screaming "Colleen! Colleen!"

She was almost to the edge of the circle when he grabbed a handful of flowered skirt and pulled her to the ground, then crawled on top of her, shielding her with his body, and began firing at the brightly painted faces that rode close by, pulling back their bows to let arrows fly. He only scored one hit with his last three bullets—and his revolver was empty.

"Matthew?" a frail voice called to him. "Let me go!"

Desperately she struggled against him, flailing her arms and kicking out with her legs. The heels of her boots landed hard against his shins, flashes of pain making him momentarily loosen his grip. She scrambled away, forcing him to dive for her. He wrapped his arms around her, pinning her hands to his chest, then entwined his legs with hers and started rolling for cover. Bullets spattered around them, kicking dust into his face. He slitted his eyes against the gritty onslaught and kept rolling until they hit a wagon wheel. He pulled her to a sitting position behind a new series of crates, gripping her narrow shoulders tightly.

"Listen to me!" he shouted into her bewildered face. "He may know you, but—damn it!—to the rest of the warriors out there you're nothing but a white target! You hear?"

He studied her. The glazed look was fading from her eyes, her senses returning. She reached out and wrapped her arms around his waist, pressing her face against his chest.

"Tell me what's happening, Matthew!" she pleaded helplessly, looking up at him.

He forced a smile he didn't feel and stroked her hair. "Don't worry, it's all right."

Across the circle, soldiers scrambled, hands over their ears, as Williford lit the mountain howitzer. The blast was thunderously loud. The ball sailed a hundred yards, pounding a hole in the center of a group of warriors and throwing fragmented bodies sideways. A huge splash of dust spurted into the air and silence descended, Indians fleeing up and over the hillsides. They looked like a horde of brilliantly colored ants scrambling furiously away after their hole had been kicked. Rifles lowered cautiously throughout the circle, people taking deep breaths as they watched the warriors retreat.

Matthew stared at the empty pistol still clutched in his fist. Every muscle in his body was tensed to the breaking point. He wiped a quaking arm over his forehead. The blue sleeve came back drenched in sweat. Fear welled as he looked down at Colleen. What was this thing that was happening to them? They were caught in some sort of whirlwind, being tossed and played with like rag dolls. But why? Memories threatened to rise, but he pushed them down. He couldn't let himself think of that now. If he did the fears would smother him. Sweat trickled into his blue eyes, stinging. He blinked it away.

On the other side of the circle, Sawyers climbed up on a crate and waved his arms to get people's attention. Gazes were reluctantly tugged from the hills and turned in his direction.

Over the bellowing of cattle and whinnying of horses, his gravelly voice sounded flat and small.

"Folks," he shouted, "I need every available man to help throw up a breastwork around the wagons and dig rifle pits. Who'll volunteer?"

Grim men rose from their safe positions and walked forward, a buzz of voices following them.

The earthen mound was piled level with the beds of the wagons and rifle pits were scooped out of the soft dirt overlooking the slough. People huddled in the circle, rifles propped within reach—waiting.

The Indians were still there, hiding in the windy rolling hills. They'd be back.

· CHAPTER 16 ·

"**H**ELL!" ANTHONY NELSON OF THE DAKOTA CAVALRY said, waving a piece of stale hardtack in the warm night air. "Them Injuns fired aplenty today, but they didn't hurt nothing!"

"Looky here!" John Rawze jerked up his sleeve to show a huge mound of blue rising on his forearm. "What do you call that?"

"Nothing!" Daniel Dana said disgustedly, slitting his eyes.

Nelson spat a streak of brown into a nearby sage. "That's what I mean. Oh, we got some devilish bruises and deep scratches, but nobody got killed."

Rawze sat forward, his pudgy face glowing. "They ain't got no powder, Tony. Hell! Ifn we'da chased 'em they'd still be running."

Dana scowled, commenting dryly, "You're hellaciously optimistic. You brave cavalrymen have eight horses left after the raid today. What were you planning on doing? Running down mounted warriors in your stocking feet?" He pulled a twig of cottonwood from his shirt pocket and dragged out his knife to start whittling, oblivious to the hard glares given him by the cavalrymen.

Williford held up his hands to quell the debate. "Get any ideas of heroics out of your heads. We're outnumbered five to one. We didn't get hurt today because the Indians are low on ammunition, but that doesn't mean we can outlast them."

"And," Douglas drawled, stretching out in front of the fire, "the warriors may be short on rifle supplies, but they've got plenty of arrows, and an infinite supply of tool stone out here to make more." He scanned the faces that flickered yellow. The subdued light accented the hollowness of the men's cheeks, making them look ghostly.

"What the hell does that mean—'tool stone'?" Rawze demanded.

Williford gave the man a disapproving look and crossed his arms. "You'd best ask that question properly, soldier."

Rawze looked bewildered for a moment, then shrugged. "What the hell does that mean, *sir*?"

Douglas raised his brows indifferently. "Rocks to make arrow and lance points from, like flint."

"Oh."

"Five to one, eh, Captain?" Dana asked coolly, his eyes still on his cottonwood twig.

Williford folded his arms and nodded. "Reckon so."

"Well, suh," Dana drawled slowly, "seems to me this here road is doomed if them Injuns object to our building it." He pointed vaguely to the hills with his knife and went back to whittling. The twig was almost gone.

"A sound assessment, Lieutenant."

"Ifn"—Dana turned his knife point to Williford—"the army let us fellas vote, reckon I'd put my name down for turning tail and running like a bat out of hell for the nearest military post, suh." He raised his brows and glanced around the fire, then looked back to his twig. "Course, voting don't count here—but I thought I'd let you know anyway."

Williford bowed his head and smiled. "I'll—uh—keep that vote in mind, Lieutenant."

"What else, men?" he asked, looking through the dozens of faces. "Any other questions? Do you all know what your assignments are for tomorrow?"

A wave of nodding heads eddied through the soldiers. Williford pursed his lips and nodded back, then said, "Dismissed."

Men dispersed, heading off in different directions. Matthew shoved his hands in his pockets and strolled back to his own bedroll. Not that he had real pockets left. His blue uniform with sky blue facings was threadbare, his pockets torn completely out. When he thrust his hands through the openings all he felt was warm flesh. He scratched his thighs thoughtfully.

From a distance, he could see Colleen sitting in front of the army wagon where their blankets were stowed. Her blond hair shimmered in the firelight as she threw sagebrush on the flames. She looked haggard. Her flowered dress was streaked with perspiration and smudged with dirt. Her usually lithe movements had grown sluggish.

Anxiety welled as he looked at her. He was losing her—and knew it. She'd slept restlessly last night, awakening often to reach for someone or something. He'd cloaked her in his arms and pulled her back to the blankets, murmuring that everything was all right, no one would hurt her, but she didn't hear him. Her dreams were stronger than the sound of his voice or the feel of his arms.

He balled his fists in his pockets as he walked, straining at his own impotence. When he got to the fire, he gave her a weak smile and sat down.

"You should have gotten some sleep," he chastised her softly, putting an arm around her shoulders.

She shook her head, fingers fidgeting nervously in her lap. "I'm afraid to."

"Don't be. I'm right here."

She nodded once, her tilted head and smile telling him he'd made a nice gesture, but he was ineffective against a man who could invade her dreams.

He frowned and tugged a lock of blond hair, then tipped

up her chin to see her eyes. "If I could get inside your head and stand guard, I would."

"I know," she whispered, her eyes drifting out to the dark, quiet hills.

"Will they attack at night?"

"Reckon not, 'less we put out the stock."

"Will we?"

"No."

She seemed relieved, her forehead smoothing. "Will they attack again tomorrow?"

He studied her. She was carefully avoiding asking flat out if the warrior would be there when she woke at daybreak. A tired futility swept over him, her words echoing hollowly in his chest. "They will."

"You're sure?" Her tone was vaguely hopeful.

He caressed his brow muscles and nodded. "I'm sure." His body cried out for rest, but he couldn't. He was on guard duty in an hour. He closed his eyes for a moment.

"Matthew?"

"Hmm?" he murmured, not opening his eyes, concentrating on the heavy sensation in his shoulders.

"I have to talk to him . . . do you understand?"

He bowed his head, resting his chin on his chest. Suddenly every muscle in his body ached. He shifted positions, letting his eyes survey the camp before he sighed, answering, "I do."

Out in the darkness a wolf howled, the baleful cry wavering on the wind—but it wasn't a wolf. He listened. It was a signal between Indian scouts, like shouting "All's well!" His eyes drifted over the blackness, searching. Colleen's warrior was out there.

Who was he?

The following morning the fighting was intermittent. The Indians charged down the hills, attacked for a few minutes, then retreated and stayed gone for an hour or more. In early afternoon the shooting stopped altogether and an uneasy tension settled over the train. Sawyers took the opportunity to give Hedges a proper Christian burial. It had become imperative. In the relentless heat of the desert, the man's dead body had bloated badly. People deliberately gave the wagon where he lay wrapped in a sheet a wide berth, frowning at the odor as they passed.

"Demolish that bullet-riddled wagon," Sawyers softly ordered his teamsters, a look of sincere regret on his long face.

A crude coffin was styled and Hedges' body delicately placed inside. The young man was well liked by most. Then two men shooed the cattle out of the center of the circle and dug a shallow grave, lowering the coffin and covering it up. People gathered around, men doffing hats and women putting hands over their hearts. For a few precious minutes the bustling train came to a halt.

Matthew stood beside Colleen. She had her Bible clutched to her breast. He slipped an arm through hers as the ceremony began.

"My friends," Sawyers' scratchy voice called out loud and clear. "Nathanial Hedges, a good and faithful member of this expedition has gone ahead of us to join our Father in heaven." He opened the worn black book in his hands and flipped to the rear, then looked up again, smiling wanly at the crowd. "In Paul's epistle to the Philippians, he wrote, 'For to me to live is Christ, and to die is gain. But if I live in the flesh, this is the fruit of my labor, yet what I shall choose I know not. For I am in a strait between two, having a desire to depart, and to be with Christ, which is far better.' " He closed the book, keeping a finger between the pages. "Mr. Hedges is now with Lord Jesus, his trials in this world over. In God's wisdom, he called this young man home, and though it seems untimely to us, only God knows the course of time and the purposes of life. 'In Him we live and move and have our being.' When at last the judgment comes, we will all face God and have to explain our actions here on this earth. Let us hope we can claim as pure and just a life as nineteen-year-old Nat."

A number of hearty "Amens" passed through the assem-

bly. Colleen crossed herself and murmured in a breathy
voice, "Glory be to the Father, and to the Son, and to the
Holy Spirit, as it was in the beginning, is now, and ever
shall be, world without end. Amen." Then she crossed herself again.

Matthew leaned over and whispered, "If Nat Hedges was
pure, I'll eat his foot!"

Colleen's mouth gaped. "Disgusting!"

"Um, I thought he was too."

He cackled at the horrified look on her face, paying no
attention to the indignant glares he got from the faithful
members of the train.

"You mustn't talk about the dead so—so—disrespectfully!
God will punish you!" she whispered.

"Why should I suddenly grant someone my respect just
because he's dead? If Nat wanted my respect he should have
earned it while he was able. It's too late now."

"You're definitely going to hell."

"I thought we'd already established that?"

"Oh . . ." She got a contemplative look on her face.
"I'd forgotten."

In a few hours all signs of Hedges' resting place had been
obliterated by the incessant tramping of the stock animals,
the evidence of his passing wiped cleanly from the face of
the earth.

She leaned back against a wagon wheel, letting her head
touch a wooden spoke as her eyes scanned the hills. The
sun was sinking inexorably in the west, making the clouds
glow golden, though it was difficult to tell through the thick
haze of dust rising out of the circle. The animals shuffled
constantly, kicking up dirt. It choked her, making her eyes
water. Dull streaks of mud ran down her cheeks.

Her gaze drifted over the white-topped wagons. Crates
were piled beneath the beds, children leaning against them
as they drew pictures in the soft earth. Robert was standing
across the circle, staring malignantly at her, but she was

too tired to be frightened. She stared back through blank eyes.

An owl swirled overhead, drawing her attention upward and away from her husband. The bird floated peacefully on the wind currents, drifting over the circled wagons, then suddenly dove out and away, plunging headlong toward a distant hill. She followed its erratic course. The owl halted its dive over a hill and fluttered in place. She sat forward, putting a hand over her eyes to look into the sunset—and she saw him.

The horse and rider were silhouetted blackly against the orange blaze, the animal tossing its head and stamping its feet. She lifted a timid hand—he matched the gesture. Her heartbeat pounded in her chest.

A voice called out to her, deep and soothing. She closed her eyes to listen and the world reeled, the sands spinning. She fumbled to grab the wheel to steady herself, but before her fingers could close around the spoke, she fell sideways, her cheek hitting the soft earth. His soul entered, twining around her, softly stroking her spirit, and the glistening dance took over. She floated upward with him, their minds touching, caressing, merging into an ineffably blissful union. The sea of pure light flooded around and through them, warm and sparkling—somehow healing.

"Come to me?" he asked wordlessly, his soul making the thought known to her without language. "After dark. I'll meet you beyond the wagons."

She held him tightly, her heart full and content. "I will."

And he vanished.

She clutched at the sands, her soul suddenly barren, hollow. The loneliness was unbearable, the pain of losing him like a death blow. She shuddered as tears formed on her lashes, then blinked her blurry eyes at a silver sage. Each separation was worse, leaving her more hollow and desperate for him.

"Just a few hours," she whispered to herself. Then she would go to him and they would dance and merge their souls—maybe permanently this time.

* * *

Darkness covered the sky as she fussed anxiously with the stew in the Dutch oven, her fingers thick and fumbling. Matthew watched her, noting every awkward move, every facial expression. Despite her diligent efforts to look relaxed, his handsome face showed he knew different. His eyes were alert, and he constantly caught things she dropped just before they landed in the dirt, then smiled indulgently and handed them back.

"Something wrong?" he asked.

"No!" She didn't want to tell him that tonight she would meet the warrior. Afraid even to admit the fact to herself, lest she back out.

"Tell me," he pressed, gripping her hand tightly, eyes curious.

"Matthew—I . . ."

"Douglas?" a gruff voice called from behind a series of crates. "Come take a look at this!"

"What is it?" he asked impatiently, not taking his eyes from her face.

"Something's moving out here!"

He exhaled heavily and released her hand. "I'll be back soon."

She watched him stride away, and gathered her courage, forcing her knees to be still, then she quietly slipped between two wagons and climbed over the earthen breastworks to walk out into the darkness.

The breeze was chilly, penetrating her thin flowered dress. She rubbed her hands over the goose bumps on her arms and kept walking. The starlight seemed unusually bright. Long, eerie shadows adorned the hills. She walked only a few hundred feet before she felt the gentle hand on her arm.

She turned and saw him. He was as tall and handsome as her dreams had shown her. His long black hair hung loose about his shoulders, draping to his waist and fluttering in the chill night breeze. He had high cheekbones and a straight nose, with full brown lips and large eyes. She tried to speak to him, but her voice wouldn't come.

He timidly wrapped his arms around her, as though he feared if he held too tightly she would break or vanish. His gaze was powerful as he picked her up, cradled her in his arms, and carried her farther away from the wagons to a sandy knoll, then gently laid her down and stretched out beside her, eyes locked with hers.

"I feared you wouldn't come," he whispered. His black hair formed a silken curtain around his face.

"I had to." She reached to touch his hair. The black strands were cool and fragrant. Almost unconsciously her thoughts turned to the dance and her soul reached out for him.

He closed his eyes and his muscles relaxed, but he held back, refusing to allow the merger. "Soon," he promised.

The hollowness returned to haunt her. She brushed her fingers over his smooth brown cheek.

"First—I must tell you about Sweet Medicine. A great hero of our people . . ."

She nodded and listened carefully to the story, fear growing at his words. "Like grains of sand in the wind," she repeated breathlessly.

"The road must be stopped."

"And that's why the wolf comes?"

He nodded, exhaling heavily as he caressed her blond hair. "He is a spirit helper—a messenger from the Great Mystery—sent to guide us, to right wrongs and carry out the will of the people."

"To right wrongs," she mumbled and thought to herself that that's what Jesus did—he reconciled man to God after the Fall.

Then she felt his mind reach for her and she closed her eyes to let his soul seep inside. It was like being the sand and feeling rain permeate your grains. Together they soared, spinning weightlessly in a timeless world, their souls free.

She did not know how long they lay there, locked in each other's arms. But when she awoke, his skin glistened in the light of new constellations and she knew dawn was not far away. His brown eyes were filled with as much joy and contentment as her own heart. The dance brought an ecstasy beyond words, beyond understanding.

"I have prayed for someone like you," he said as his eyes drifted over her face. "Since my sister died, I have not been able to find any woman to love—my heart has been empty."

Colleen felt his terrible loneliness in her own breast and she slipped her arms around his neck, pulling him to her. He kissed her softly, then more passionately. Their desires rose together and he untied his buckskin pants and slipped them off, then undressed her, his warm hands tender. As his body entered her, he willed his soul to entwine with hers to complete the union. Flesh and spirit pulsed in time with a universal rhythm. She never wanted it to end, never wanted to be separated from him or the eternal sea of light that swirled around their union.

When she felt him pulling away, her soul cried out, and she grasped for him, but he fled. Opening her eyes, she found him looking down at her, his face serene. The wind tousled his black hair, sending it fluttering lightly toward the dark blue sky. She touched the scars over his breasts, letting her fingers caress the mounds of damaged flesh.

"We renewed the people," he said softly, happiness glowing in his voice. "Made them whole again."

"Whole," she repeated, feeling the fragmented parts of her own being melded together in his arms.

A look of fear suddenly creased his face and he gazed away from her to the horizon. The cool wind brushed hair over his taut face. When he turned back, tears glistened in his eyes.

"You must go," he said.

"No." She wrapped her arms around his back and pulled tightly. "I don't want to."

He squeezed his eyes shut. "But you must tell the men of your train to stop the road."

In the sweetness of his embrace she'd forgotten the terrifying prophecy of Sweet Medicine, but now it came back and she nodded—she had to leave.

"We will be together soon—a few hours."

They rose and dressed, the promise of reunion lingering in their souls. They walked with their arms around each other back toward the train, stepping around sage and cactus. The horizon was a pale lavender by the time they approached the circled wagons.

He reluctantly released her and put his hands on her shoulders. Her flowered skirt flapped in the increasing breeze, as did the fringe on his pants. Then he closed his eyes and sought her soul once more. The sweet bliss of his presence pervaded her—and suddenly terror shot through her. He shoved her roughly to the ground, their union broken as a roaring blast boomed through the hills.

It happened so slowly. She opened her eyes to see him stumble, clutching a gaping hole in his shoulder. For one brief instant he stared longingly into her eyes and reached out a hand, then tumbled to the ground, bright red streaks flowing down his chest.

She screamed jaggedly, horror bursting in on her, then ran to him and pulled him to her chest; her bitter sobs shredded the quiet sunrise. And suddenly she felt him seeking her soul and his pain was hers.

She fell beside him, their souls entwined in agony.

Matthew paced in front of the fire. The darkness was fading, morning glistening on the horizon. She was with the warrior. He knew it, but couldn't search aimlessly through the night to find her. He had to await her voluntary return. Would she return?

He walked to the edge of the circle and gazed out into the gray morning light. Where was she? He saw Robert Merrill steady his rifle across the earthen breastwork. Other men, as well, were readying themselves for the possibility of attack. He cocked his head, watching Merrill closely. There was something wrong about his actions—a wrongness that twisted Matthew's gut. It was as though he already had sighted something to shoot at. Matthew trotted toward him, searching between wagons as he ran, trying to follow the man's aim. He ran faster, seeing Merrill apply pressure to the trigger.

A ragged cry was torn from his throat when he saw Colleen standing with the warrior in the hills. And he leapt for Merrill, hitting him just as the rifle blasted through the morning gray. Knocking him down, rage took over; he pounded Merrill's face repeatedly, screaming, "Who were you trying to hit, goddamn you! The warrior or Colleen?" Then his senses returned and he ran, jumping over the breastwork and racing out across the sage.

A warrior galloped down the slope. Matthew held up a hand and shouted in Cheyenne, "I mean you no harm, brother! Let me take the woman?" The Indian stopped his pony, looking anxiously at the wounded man on the ground, but motioned with his lance for Matthew to continue.

He knelt down, picking her up in his arms. She was barely breathing, her clothes soaked in blood. Frantically Matthew tore her dress, searching for a wound, but her soft white breasts were undamaged. It occurred to him that the blood on her clothing wasn't hers and he looked to the warrior. Ragged splinters of bone gleamed white in the pale morning light, blood draining to clot in massive dark globs on his chest. The wound was too high to kill, he hoped, but it was hard to tell. As he stared at the warrior's dark face and closed eyes, his memory twinged—something about the man's face . . .

The mounted Indian rode down the hill, anxious to see to his friend. Matthew stood, picking up Colleen to carry her back to the wagons.

Colleen was floating, suspended in a dark void. The warrior was there, but his mind was so weak she could barely sense his presence. She cried out to him, but he couldn't hear. Nothing moved in the emptiness. She felt as though she'd been cast adrift in a vast ocean of blackness where no light, no sound, could penetrate. Only dark stillness existed.

She tried to reach him. He floated a short distance away,

yet she couldn't touch him. Some barrier prevented their contact. She called out, pleading for him to hear—but he didn't respond. In her heart she knew he was dying, but her mind would not let her believe it.

"No!" she shouted into the stillness and listened. She couldn't hear her voice. The darkness swallowed sounds as though they'd never existed—maybe they never had? "No!" she screamed again and again.

And then she remembered the wagon train and his words about the road. ". . . blown away like grains of sand in the wind." She struggled with her consciousness, commanding her mind to climb out of the darkness and back to the train.

But she couldn't . . . she was trapped.

· CHAPTER 17 ·

MATTHEW HELD HER IN HIS ARMS AS SHE MOANED. "COLleen. Listen to my voice. Follow my voice."

Rifle blasts shook the wagon over his head. He threw his body over hers and frantically tried to unravel what had happened. She must have been united with the warrior when Merrill's bullet struck him and now her mind was suspended in the resulting void—lost. Could she escape the supernatural realm without the warrior's help? What would happen if he died?

"Live, Colleen," he whispered. "Climb out of it!"

Another blast rocked the wagon, the sound of ricocheting lead deafening. A horse thundered by, squealing, to crash into the breastworks, dead. He could see the legs of the shattered beast flailing wildly in the final moments.

"Colleen?" he called again, his voice stern, trying to project his strength to her. "Colleen, listen to me!"

He put his fingers across her wrist to check her heartbeat. It was faint, so faint he could barely feel it. But it was there.

He shook her. Her head bobbed aimlessly, the blond curls

bouncing across his blue pants. Then he tenderly pulled her back, pressing his cheek against hers and forcing his panic away. He had to remain calm, to think. What would the Cheyenne do? He strained to remember. Those visionaries granted the privilege of supernatural realms had spirit helpers to guide them, but Colleen was white. She had no . . . his eyes went wide and he stared down at her impassive face. "Colleen?" he whispered insistently. "Call the wolf! *Call the wolf!*"

Floating. She was floating through a sea of blind emptiness. She searched the sea, trying to find signposts that would point her to freedom. There were none. The void stretched infinitely around her, the blackness engulfing her, swallowing her like a single star in a vast wasteland of night sky.

"Help!" she cried out to the silence. "Help me!"

Something changed . . . she felt ripples in the sea, as though she were riding a wave, up and down, rising and falling.

"Colleen?" a deep soothing voice called.

She swam toward the sound, listening, pleading for more, for companionship in the dark ocean.

"Colleen?"

She swam farther until she could see a fuzzy white form. Its image swirled in the darkness, changing shape like an amorphous ball. She followed it—the only light in the void, the only sound.

"Here, Colleen, follow me?"

She tried to hurry to get closer, but the form stayed the same distance no matter how fast or slow she swam.

It seemed as though she moved through the blackness for months, struggling to keep from drifting back up to the warrior.

At last the form slowed. A tall brass door formed. Colleen swam closer, staring at the door and the fuzzy form. As she watched, the form took the shape of the wolf. Its huge eyes glistened black as the void in the snow white face.

A tendril of fear touched her, but she suppressed it. The wolf had saved her, guided her out of the empty darkness.

"Here," the wolf said, "when you are ready, open this door and you will be home again."

She swam closer, reaching for the door handle, but the wolf drifted over to block her path. She stared into the black wells of his eyes, silently questioning why he stopped her.

"Tell them," he said, his deep voice lilting in the darkness, "tell them Fort Connor has been built. They must go there immediately and take the Bozeman Trail to Montana. For if they do not leave the sacred grounds of the Cheyenne—they will be killed. All of them." He stopped and his words hung in the air like flakes of snow swirling in the wind.

She nodded, gazing into its eyes. The black depths bore holes in her.

"The warrior?" she pleaded. "Help him?"

The wolf nodded its furred head. "Of course, he is a man of the people."

Colleen turned and reached for the door handle.

Matthew mopped her sweating brow with a cool damp rag. Her long blond hair was wet from the moisture seeping out of the cloth and clung in thick strands to her neck. She seemed to be fighting something, her eyelids fluttering as her body jerked spasmodically. He put an arm beneath her neck and raised her head.

"Colleen?"

Abruptly she was wide awake, her eyes so streaked with tiny red lines they glowed crimson. Her breast heaved as though she'd just run a hundred miles.

"Battle," she muttered, blinking her eyes at the booming shots that rattled the wagon over her head. The shots were intermittent, as though the warriors were playing with them, keeping them off balance but really not trying to kill them.

"Yes, we're still fighting," he said, running fingers through the dark hair over his forehead and sitting back in relief. He'd piled extra crates around the wagon bottom to better protect her, but only now did it strike him how dark the sanctuary was. He couldn't quite make out the frown lines on her face.

"What happened?" he asked, putting a hand on her arm.

"I was trapped . . . floating." Her voice was low, her thoughts focused inward.

"And?"

"Oh! Matthew, it was terrible!"

"And?" He pressed not because he was uninterested in her subjective experiences, but because her sudden awakening meant someone or something had helped her escape, and "helpers" usually had reasons. He noticed vaguely the shooting had stopped. Had someone wisely decided to parley?

She blinked thoughtfully as though remembering. "And . . . we must stop building this road!" She whirled around to face him, her eyes wide. "We must go to Fort Connor and from there take the Bozeman Trail to Montana."

"Why?"

She twisted the fabric of her skirt nervously. "Because if we don't the Cheyenne will die."

His mind rumbled with fragments of voices and scenes, memories long forgotten because they were too painful to recall. He closed his eyes and rubbed his forehead. Yes, of course, how could he have forgotten?

"Sweet Medicine's prophecies?"

She nodded, searching his face.

He nodded too, exhaling heavily. "And where is Fort Connor?"

"I—I—don't know. The wolf didn't—"

"It's all right. It must be on the Powder. Bozeman Trail crosses it."

He leaned forward to crawl out from under the wagon.

"Wait!" She clutched his navy blue sleeve, fear rising. As long as he was close she wasn't afraid. But the thought of him leaving was like a sharp poker in her belly. "Where are you going? Don't leave me—"

"I'm going to go threaten the commander of our expedition, my dear." He raised both brows, smiling impertinently. "You mustn't stop me while I still have the courage."

"Don't be silly," she chastised, her heart fluttering. "You're the bravest man I've ever known."

"And have you known so many?" he asked, cocking his head as though inordinantly interested.

"Well . . . no, but—"

"That's what I thought." And he was gone, sliding out from beneath the wagon and walking quickly away.

She peeked between the crates that formed the walls of her sanctuary to see him adjust the pistol hanging at his side and then weave through the cattle, slapping their haunches and uttering rough words. He climbed over the earthen breastworks on the other side of the circle and she lost sight of him.

She blinked at the darkness. The shooting had stopped and a soft hum of excited voices eddied through the train. Idly she wondered what was happening but she was still too disoriented and frightened to crawl out and see. Instead, she slid to the far corner of her "room" and leaned tiredly against a wooden crate, her thoughts returning to the warrior and the wolf.

The noon sun was hot, baking his skin relentlessly as Matthew worked his way across the circle and over the earthen breastworks. Even before he climbed down to the flat plains, he heard George Williford's usually calm voice bellowing "No, Colonel!"

Williford was red-faced, his fists clenched at his sides as he faced Sawyers and the Indian chiefs. Obviously a parley was in session and not going well. Douglas sauntered up to within ten feet of the captain and stopped, crossing his arms to listen.

"Captain!" Sawyers growled through clenched teeth. "I'm in command of this expedition!"

Williford tugged his cap down low over his eyes, apparently attempting to quell his anger. "Sir"—he lowered his voice, and turned his back to the Indians—"the tribes cannot be trusted. If we give them supplies they're liable to run off for a few hours and hit us harder tomorrow."

Sawyers glanced sideways at the chiefs. Red Cloud's long warbonnet fluttered like angels' wings in the wind, the red and blue beads on the headband glistening. Dull Knife's porcupine quill shirt looked like an armored breastplate. The dozen lesser chiefs stood in the background, their faces impassive, black eyes blank. Only George Bent, who was dressed in an army staff officer's uniform, looked emotional, his face taut and nostrils flaring as he translated for the chiefs. Sawyers scratched his salt and pepper beard and hooked his thumbs in his belt.

"Your opinion is noted, Captain," he snapped, glancing over his shoulder to Bent. The Indian was listening as intently as if he had a hand cupped to his ear.

Dull Knife mumbled something to Bent, who responded hotly, shaking the rifle in his hand at the soldiers, then turned to Sawyers and Williford.

"You will not build this road!" he ordered, his square face growing more tense. "The chiefs demand you head west and take the Bozeman Trail."

Dull Knife nodded slowly, meeting Sawyers' gaze. The colonel tried to stare bravely back, but the chief's face was so cold that he dropped his eyes to stare at his own boots. With his head bowed he responded, "That'll take us out of our way. We're going north."

George Bent clenched his fist and shook it at Sawyers. *"Then you will die!"*

Williford gave the Indian a cool, hard stare. "If it's fighting you're after, friend, we'll oblige."

From somewhere in the surrounding hills, a voice shouted to Bent, "Tell the goddamn bastards they must hang Chivington for his murder of our people at Sand Creek!"

A cynical smile crept over Bent's face. He smoothed his mustache with his fingers and nodded. "That's part of the price—hanging Chivington."

Williford looked as though he'd burst. His jaw dropped

and he took a step forward, blue sleeves fluttering in the wind. "Our people have laws, Bent! Chivington will be tried in a court and if he's guilty, he'll be punished—but not before!"

Bent slitted his dark eyes. His voice was low and threatening. "You don't punish baby killers—not if they killed *Indian* babies."

Sawyers interrupted the standoff. "I assure you, Mr. Bent, I have friends in high places in Washington. I'll do everything in my power to see that rogue brought to justice."

"What?" Williford was astonished. He shook his head as though trying to clear the statement from his memory. "Colonel!" he whispered, turning sideways to keep Bent from hearing, but it was a futile attempt; the Indian walked closer. "Do you know what will happen if you lead these people to believe that Chivington will be punished and then he's found innocent of wrongdoing? Jesus, man! The next train that takes this road will be cut to pieces!"

Sawyers gritted his teeth, his eyes drifting back to the Indians. "We must be on our way, Captain. I'm sure you understand—"

Bent shouted for all to hear, waving his rifle over his head. "If Chivington is not hung, my people will ride down on every train that dares to cross this land! We will tear your women apart with our lances and chop your children to bits before the eyes of their fathers!" His eyes gleamed in savage anticipation.

Sawyers' jaw slackened, his face going white. He opened his mouth to speak, but no words came out.

Dull Knife and Red Cloud conferred briefly, then waved Bent over and spoke in hushed tones. The lesser chiefs in the background walked forward, gathering around to hear. Warbonnets rustled. When the discussion was finished, a shrill war whoop went up and the lesser chiefs raced away to the hills to dance and sing. Bent walked back to Sawyers, a disagreeable smile on his face.

He halted in front of Williford and held the captain's sharp gaze for a few seconds, then turned to Sawyers. "You will stop this road and head west—now!"

"But," Sawyers balked, pursing his lips, "the Congress of the United States has authorized—"

"Damn it!" Williford erupted, throwing up both hands and shouting at the top of his lungs. "Your military escort just resigned, Colonel! I will do everything in my power to protect my command and the best way to do that is to head back to Fort Laramie. If you're going on through Indian country, then you'll do it without military support!" He spun around and started to tramp away. Sawyers stopped him.

"Captain, General Dodge ordered you to escort—"

"You *imbecile*!" Williford roared. "There aren't enough soldiers in the whole damn world to protect you if these Indians decide to band together to stop this expedition! You'll—"

"And we will!" Bent threw his head back and shrieked a war cry and howling sprouted from every hill, sounding like the wailing of banshees.

Williford and Sawyers both looked up, eyes hauntingly alert. Warriors danced and cavorted over the sage, screaming, rifles and lances thrust toward the sky.

"It's up to you now, Colonel. Decide!" Williford tramped back toward the circled wagons, his triangular face tensed until it looked like a dried apple.

Douglas walked up beside him as he climbed the breastworks, kicking up dust with his rapid retreat.

"George, we've got another option," he said coolly. "Fort Connor is built and—"

Williford stopped, eyeing him seriously. "What the hell is Fort Connor? I never heard of it."

"New fort, George," Matthew said. "It's over on Powder River just off the Bozeman Trail."

"Built by one of Connor's columns?"

Matthew nodded. It made sense. "Way I figure it, it's got to be a hundred miles closer than Laramie."

"I knew they were talking about building one in these

parts." Williford rubbed his chin, blowing out a breath and looking skeptically at Douglas. "But tell me how you know about a fort I've never heard of?"

"I . . ." He thought hard, his eyes quickly drifting over the soldiers and Indians outside the circle. George Williford was a bright man, but it was doubtful he'd believe a spirit wolf had relayed the information. "The Indians have been talking about it. They say it's only manned by a handful of soldiers."

Williford stiffened. "You believe them?"

Douglas nodded.

Williford put a hand on his hip and stared at the ground for a few moments. "The Indians talking about attacking the fort?"

"Didn't hear 'em say so, but if they're attacking us, I doubt the fort is safe."

The captain shifted uncomfortably, squinting. "A handful, huh?"

Douglas nodded again. "Reckon those boys could use some help."

"Reckon . . . how do we get there?"

"Go southwest, pick up the Bozeman and head north. 'Less we can spot the tracks of Connor's column."

"All right," he exhaled the words. "I'll tell Sawyers that's where we're headed and he can come if he wants—"

"Think he will?"

Williford hesitated. "Doubt it. Man's got a brain like a rock."

"Yes, suh."

They both turned as Sawyers climbed over the breastworks, puffing, his face red. He made an airy gesture at Williford and shouted to the teamsters. "Holman, load a wagon with all the flour, sugar, coffee, and tobacco we can spare, then roll it out to the Indians."

"You made a deal?" Williford charged loudly.

"Of course, Captain! Once you were out of the way the Indians grew very cooperative. In exchange for supplies, they've agreed to let us be on our way. This expedition is heading north to Montana!''

''You—''

Matthew's loud, contemptuous laugh interrupted the debate. ''We'd better get the hell out of here and leave the colonel to his expedition, Captain.''

''Why?''

''I reckon we got 'till about sunrise before the next attack comes.''

Sawyers stepped forward haughtily, his translucent eyes arrogant. ''What are you talking about, soldier?''

''Well, Colonel.'' Matthew fixed the man with a bold glare. ''The deal you made must have bought off a few of the lesser chiefs, but—''

''Who agreed?'' Williford demanded.

Sawyers fumbled for words. ''Well . . . there was some dissension but I smoothed the ruffled feathers and—''

''And bought off a couple of lesser chiefs!'' Matthew said, shaking his head.

The captain eyed Sawyers askance, his brows lowered. A creaking wagon loaded with hundreds of pounds of supplies jostled by them. Holman looked disconcerted as he led the mules over the breastworks and out to the waiting Indians. Matthew scanned the Indians standing by the white parley flag. Neither Dull Knife nor Red Cloud were present. He nodded to himself. The chiefs had demanded the road be closed and when Sawyers continued spouting patriotic gibberish about Congress, they'd left. The deal had been made with the remaining lesser chiefs who were greedy and figured they could get some grub for free.

''Lieutenant,'' Williford ordered softly, ''organize guards for the train tonight.'' Then he turned to Sawyers. ''Tomorrow we'll be heading for Fort Connor, Colonel. You can follow if you like.'' He turned and strode away.

Sawyers turned to Douglas. ''Fort Connor? Where's that? I never—''

''New fort on the Powder.''

Sawyers looked contemplative, considering something.

Douglas stood for a few moments looking at him, then spun and walked the other direction, leaving the colonel alone with his thoughts.

He strolled around the camp again, growing more irritated with each new circumambulation. Finally he spotted Daniel Dana leaning up against a military wagon and headed in that direction. The lieutenant looked bored, yawning and gazing out to the sunset. The sky was shading a subdued yellow, giving the few drifting clouds a golden halo.

"Dana?" he called, lifting a hand in greeting. "Where the hell are Nelson and Rawze. They're on the roster for guard duty tonight and I've hunted—"

"Hell!" Dana spat, puckering his face. "Last time I saw them they was out jibing with the warriors."

"What for?"

Dana scratched his belly and spoke through a yawn, "Said the savages was flashing rolls of greenbacks and asking for powder."

Matthew straightened up, his face tightening. "Are you telling me they were trading ammunition to the Indians!"

Dana threw a lazy arm over the side of the wagon. "No. Just saying that's the last place I seen 'em."

"Jeezus!" Douglas growled, eyes drifting over the barren hills. The Indians had vanished after collecting their booty. "You don't think those jackasses would arm the enemy, do you?"

Dana shrugged. "Never thought either one of 'em was particularly bright, Lieutenant."

"Let's organize a search party!"

The party walked the hills in groups of four, winding methodically through tangles of sage and prickly pear as the night sky grew darker and stars began shimmering overhead. Coyotes yipped in the distance, their dark bodies poking up like sentinels on the hills. The squeaky voices of young pups added an element of the macabre to the serenade.

Dana stopped to listen. The dogs were silhouetted blackly against the background of dark blue sky, their noses tipped to the heavens as they yowled. No Indians were in sight—but that didn't mean they weren't there. He gripped his rifle more tightly and started off down the side of the hill when a voice called out, "Over here!"

He spun and trotted back to the edge of the hill to look down toward the voice. As he got closer, he could see a young infantryman kneeling beside a crumpled mass of blue and knew that at least one of the men had been found. He slowed his pace and took a deep breath. The scene didn't look good.

"Tony Nelson," the blond boy explained nervously, wiping sweaty palms on his pants. "I—I guess—"

"Yep," Dana finished for him, "guess so."

The boy nodded quickly, then looked away to the undulating plains.

Nelson's body was riddled with arrows. He lay face up, staring blindly at the darkening sky. Flecks of dirt had blown into his eyes and sprinkled the wide brown orbs like tan leaves mired in mud. He was pinioned to the ground, a long pole protruding from his belly, and his once blue uniform was so stained with clotted blood it looked purple.

"Damn it!" Dana cursed under his breath. He'd seen a lot of death and dying during the Civil War, but he'd never gotten used to it. His stomach still lurched when he looked into the eyes of dead men.

"Get out of here!" he yelled to the young blond, waving a hand. "Go on back to the train and tell Williford we found one of 'em."

"Yes, suh." The private saluted and stood rigid until Dana heaved a sigh and returned the gesture, then the soldier charged off down the hill to the wagons.

Dana breathed a disgruntled sigh and stared into the sightless eyes. "Goddamn you, Tony!" he murmured, grinding his teeth as he looked at the arrows and pole. "Well, hell, somebody's got to . . ." His voice trailed off and he resolutely bent down to break off the arrow shafts.

Nelson's body wriggled after each crack. Snapping off the last shaft, he stood, gripped the lance, and jerked hard. The body made a sucking noise as he released his pull and wiped his brow. The lance was firmly rooted in Nelson's gut. Bending over, Dana wrapped fingers around the base of the pole. Lukewarm blood oozed up to stain his hands. He pulled again and continued jerking repeatedly, trying to get the spear point past the fibrous tissues, until finally it ripped out. Fresh crimson blood flowed, welling through the jagged hole.

He straightened up and threw the lance across the sands, watching it catch on the sage and tumble, then he put his hands on his hips and took a deep breath. "Damn fool!" he muttered and suppressed his desire to kick the corpse. What kind of a man would run out and sell ammunition to the enemy? Some low snake . . . he halted his thoughts, caressing his chin. No one had proven that's what Nelson and Rawze were up to—but he'd seen the glow in their eyes when they talked about the thick wads of greenbacks. He folded his arms and swallowed the lump of hate rising in his throat.

Gazing out to the sands, he spotted several men still searching for Rawze. He lifted both arms and waved, yelling, "Search party? Rendezvous here!"

Men in blue trotted to the tops of hills, rifles dangling from their hands, then ambled down over the edge toward him. When everyone had been accounted for, Dana cleared his throat and bowed his head briefly, swallowing hard. "Boys, widen one of them rifle pits. That'll be Tony's new home."

Men scurried to dig. Once the pit was scooped out to about five feet deep, Nelson was lowered down into it. His limp body lay twisted against the irregular earth, his sightless eyes still staring. The shuffling of feet began. No one wanted to hold the shovel that would fill the grave.

Dana looked around. "Well, who's gonna volunteer?"

Surreptitious glances passed from one man to the next, but finally, Miles Latcher, a redheaded eighteen-year-old with big blue eyes, stepped bravely forward. "I will," he said simply, taking the shovel.

The dull thudding of clods on the body sent an eerie chill through the men. Faces tensed, some bit their lips, others frowned awkwardly. In everyone's mind the phrase ". . . but for the grace of God . . ." echoed—and Dana knew it, could sense it in the hushed whispers and hollow stares.

"All right, boys," he soothed, tugging a red kerchief from his shirt pocket and mopping his brow. "Let's tramp it down and be done with it. We don't want Nelson to get dug up by wolves."

Soldiers shifted uncomfortably, afraid to step into the pit on top of the body. Silent questions were exchanged in anxious glances. Finally one timid man stepped cautiously on top of the soft dirt and tramped halfheartedly.

"Jeezzz!" Dana muttered. He strode forward and shoved the man out of the pit, tramping it himself. A sinking feeling invaded his gut as the soil compacted deeper and deeper.

Yellow Leaf pulled the blue tradecloth dress from the rushing waters of the river and wrung it out, then shook it and hung it over the branches of a small aspen tree to dry. Wiping her hands on her red cotton dress, she reluctantly went back to her washing. The old women washing clothes near her gossiped loudly, exchanging stories of who would marry next and who was expecting a baby. They gathered around her, she knew, as a show of disapproval. Their words about marriage and children were meant as both a slap and a nudge. She ignored them, her thoughts on Wounded Bear. Was he all right? Ever since the soldiers had left the village to go and fight the wagon train, she'd been having nightmares—nightmares of him dying.

She picked up a white shirt and pounded it lightly with a rock, then shoved it beneath the water and rubbed it between her hands.

"You're a silly girl," Old Woman Walking Stick leaned over and whispered. She was a very old woman, over sixty summers, with short gray hair—cut in mourning—and deeply wrinkled skin. But her faded brown eyes were still sharp as a hawk's.

It was as though she was trying to keep those nearby from hearing. That puzzled Yellow Leaf. Only five minutes before, this old women had been the most vocal in discussing the horrid lives of old maids—not mentioning Yellow Leaf by name, however.

"Why do you say that, grandmother?" She pounded the shirt with the rock again.

"You are twenty summers old. Soon the men will stop asking for you." Her aged head tottered in a nod.

Yellow Leaf dipped the shirt in the river again, swishing it around to free the dirt. She said nothing. An emptiness swelled in her heart.

"Wounded Bear doesn't want you," the old woman pointed out bluntly, waving a negligent hand. "Why do you chase after him?"

She stopped, red flushing her cheeks. Anger mixed with her hurt. "I do not chase, grandmother," she said stiffly.

The old woman cackled, slapping her aged knee. People along the bank turned to stare. "You chase like a child crying for the moon!"

Yellow Leaf clamped her jaw and looked out to the rushing river, watching the waves wash over the rocks. She laid the shirt in the grass and stood up to leave.

Old Woman Walking Stick reached out and grabbed her red skirt, tugging. "You sit back down," she ordered.

Yellow Leaf debated for a few seconds, heart beating thunderously, then sat down again, her face turned away. It was rude to disobey an elder, but she would if she had to—to keep from crying in front of the others. Her heart was bursting.

The chattering along the river had stopped completely, everyone straining to listen.

The old woman lowered her voice so no one else could hear. "Lame Deer is going to send horses to your father, and blankets. He wants you badly."

Yellow Leaf did not speak. Lame Deer was a good man—

a great warrior—but she had already told him "no." Her heart obliged her to another.

"Don't be a silly fool," the old woman whispered. "Lame Deer is twice the man Wounded Bear is."

At this Yellow Leaf looked up, fire in her eyes. Her hurt faded. "Grandmother, I respect your wisdom, but I will not listen to you—"

"Hush, child!" the woman admonished, leaning forward until her ancient eyes were only inches from Yellow Leaf's. "Wounded Bear is addled—or under the spell of that white witch. He acts like he has no relatives!"

The accusation was startling. It implied he acted contrary to the needs of the people.

"You are wrong, grandmother. He works every moment for us."

"He works for no one but himself," the woman charged, squinting. "Himself and that witch!"

"That is *not* true! Wounded Bear loves his people, he is out fighting the wagon train now to show how much he—"

"Ha! He is out at the wagon train to find that witch." Old Woman Walking Stick leaned back, raising one brow and nodding.

Yellow Leaf dropped her eyes to the river, watching white caps form and disappear. Was that what he was doing? Was fighting the train just an excuse to get him close to the yellow-haired woman? Hurt constricted her throat.

"Ah, now you see." The old woman smiled knowingly. "Everything about him, his fighting, his healing, even his visions, come from the witch. His power is gone!"

"No!" Yellow Leaf shouted and stood up. "That is a lie!" It was a terrible sin to say such a thing to a respected elder, but she couldn't help it. Harsh whispers ran up and down the riverbank. "He has power and it comes from his spirit helper, the wolf."

She turned, hands trembling, and started to walk away, but the clopping of hooves stopped her.

She frowned, wiping a hand over her sweaty brow, and waited. The sound came from the tableland above the river.

In only a moment, dozens of riders crested the ridge and swept down into the river bottom.

Women and children grew suddenly quiet as the warriors raced into camp in a whirlwind of dust and dismounted.

Seeing George Bent, she ran forward through the tall grass and grabbed the reins of his horse, her eyes imploring. "Is it over?" The horse stamped, rearing its head against her hand.

Bent's black eyes were hard as he met her gaze. He was dressed in a soldier's uniform and looked bitterly tired, damp hair hanging in thick strands over his ears. "We need food. The Dog Soldiers are riding on."

"But . . ." she insisted, reaching out and gripping his blue sleeve as he tried to walk away. Her eyes searched the other riders. She didn't see Wounded Bear. "Did we win?"

"The road is stopped."

She smiled suddenly, relief showing in welling tears. "We are safe, then?"

Bent stared for a moment at the dried grass. "For now. But the soldiers will come after us. The fighting isn't finished."

"Oh!" She dropped her eyes.

He softened his voice, shifting awkwardly. "There are wounded to be tended."

She looked up, searching his face. His intimate tone told her more than his words. He squinted and gazed out through the cottonwoods.

He struggled with the words. "Wounded Bear . . ."

Fear prickled through her. She swallowed, twining fingers in her red skirt. "A—Alive?"

"I'm not sure—he was badly injured. Little Deer is bringing him."

The scraping sound of travois met her ears, she whirled. Horses came down the hill, dragging the wounded behind them. Little Deer rode near the front. She dropped the reins of Bent's horse and ran through the trees, her fear so strong she could barely breathe.

Little Deer halted his horse beneath the thin shade of an

aspen. Dismounting, he walked to the travois and began hurriedly unstrapping his brother.

Yellow Leaf stopped a few feet away, her eyes riveted to Wounded Bear's pale face. He was murmuring softly, tossing his head back and forth. The striped red and blue blanket he was wrapped in was soaked in sweat, clinging to his skin.

Little Deer tenderly picked him up and eased him to the ground in the dappled shade of the tree. The wind tousled Wounded Bear's loose hair, sending it fluttering over the dried grass. Sunlight speckled his face.

"Help me!" Little Deer commanded urgently.

She forced her leaden feet forward.

"The canteen on my horse." He pointed. "Bring it."

She ran to untie it. It had U.S. written on it. Taken from a soldier? She rushed back and handed it to him.

Little Deer opened it and took a swallow, then poured some onto a cloth and washed Wounded Bear's fevered face. Yellow Leaf leaned down beside him and took the cloth from his hand.

"Let me."

He gratefully conceded, nodding as he straightened up. His face was grave. "His shoulder—is bad—festered."

"I'll take care of him," she whispered, unwrapping the blanket to stare horrified at the wound. Pus oozed from beneath a hardened yellow crust, black clots of blood forming an irregular halo around the infection.

"Go and rest, Little Deer," she said, her heart in her throat. "I'll stay with him . . . tend his wound."

He shuffled his feet. "I . . . tried to clean it."

She looked up into his tense face, forcing a confident smile. "He'll live. Don't worry. But you must rest."

He gave her a stiff nod, then turned and tiredly walked away, heading toward the group of warriors in the center of camp.

She looked long at Wounded Bear's taut face, then gently brushed his dark hair back from his eyes.

"Here!" he muttered, reaching out with his good arm.

"Here, take me! Don't . . . don't . . ." The words became incoherent.

"You're a great medicine man," she whispered to him. "The people need you. You must live."

"Medicine, medi . . ." he repeated so lowly she almost couldn't hear.

Quickly she walked to Little Deer's horse and pulled off the blanket, then draped it over the thin branches of the aspen, deepening the shade over Wounded Bear. The golden speckles of sunlight on his face vanished. There was a knife tied to the horse. She unsheathed it.

Kneeling beside him, she whispered, "I have to clean out the infection, my warrior." She smoothed her hands over his dirty face. The sands of the desert had mixed with his perspiration to create muddy streaks. She'd never been able to touch him like this; it salved her hurt soul, made her long to feel his arms around her.

Wounded Bear stirred only a little, digging fingers into the grass at his sides. His breathing was shallow and labored, body fighting the infection.

She lowered the iron blade to the yellow crust on his shoulder and began scraping away the infection. The pus was thick, flowing down to stain the blanket beneath him a dull yellow. The stench of the wound grew stronger as she worked, until she had to turn her head away, letting the river breeze freshen the air in her lungs.

"Why? Why!" he cried, gasping and reaching out to the warm wind.

"Shhhh, my warrior," she cooed, stroking his fevered brow. "It's all right. Your medicine is stronger than the whites'. The infection will go away, just as they will."

She sliced off a piece of greenish flesh and threw it out to the grass, then murmured, "You must live." She brushed a timid hand down his bare chest and patted his side. "I need you to live."

He seemed calmed by her touch, relaxing. She patted his arm. "Don't worry. The people have faith in you. They need your wisdom. Someday you will be the greatest Tsistsistas medicine man, a man to guide us through the hard years ahead.'' She pushed Old Woman Walking Stick's words out of her mind.

The blanket in the tree flapped softly in the breeze. Ants crawled up from the grass to dart over Wounded Bear's limp arms. She blew them off and returned to his damaged shoulder. Some of the reddish flesh beneath the infection was showing through.

''Do you know I love you?'' she said softly, touching his fevered forehead. ''Love you more than—''

His eyes fluttered open, staring obliviously at the turquoise sky. ''Come back,'' he murmured, reaching out yet again. ''Come . . .''

''Here,'' she whispered. ''I'm here.''

He reached over with his good arm and clasped her left hand fiercely, pulling it to his chest. ''Stay?'' he murmured mournfully.

''I'll never leave you,'' she answered tenderly, knowing it was the yellow-haired woman he spoke to, believed he held. She disentangled her hand from his grip so she could continue cleaning the wound.

''I'm right here, my warrior. But you must sleep and get well.''

''Sleep . . .'' he mumbled, closing his eyes. His tired head lolled limply to the side.

She reached for the canteen Little Deer had left under the tree and uncorked the lid. Pouring water into the wound, she washed away the welling blood.

''The elders think you're under her spell,'' she whispered, barely audible even to herself, ''that your spirit power is gone.''

She gazed at his closed eyes. His lids fluttered. ''But I know that's not true. Your power is unharmed—only your heart is gone.'' The frail sound of her own voice made her look away from him to the rustling aspen trees.

She moved to sit above his shoulder, her thigh resting beside his pale face. ''Does she make you so happy . . . this yellow-haired woman?''

Stroking his damp hair, she returned to the wound. The infection was mostly gone. White splinters of bone protruded. Carefully, as though working on a patient who could feel each touch of her fingers, she picked out the splinters.

"What is it that she does to make you happy?"

He seemed to have dimly heard the question. He stirred, murmuring incoherently, head moving weakly to rest against her thigh.

She put her hand to his face again, caressing the hot skin. "I would share my soul with you—if I could. Teach me how."

He murmured again, pressing his cheek against her red skirt. It sounded vaguely like "wolf."

"Is he there with you?" she questioned, stroking his chest. "Tell him the people need you—that you must live. Tell him . . . I need you."

She flushed the wound with water again and went to gather the dried stems and leaves of a blood-root plant from her parents' lodge. The plant was used primarily to dye porcupine quills for adorning dresses or shirts and was always on hand. It was also a powerful poultice for wounds.

Her steps were heavy, legs leaden with fear and pain, as she walked back to the aspen tree. Picking up the canteen, she poured water over the dried root in her palm and stirred it with her finger until it formed a thick paste, then plastered it over Wounded Bear's injured shoulder.

Sitting down beside him, she laid his head in her lap and mopped his face with a cool wet cloth.

He reached for her again, his arm waving weakly, searching. She clasped his hand and he brought it back to his chest, squeezing her fingers with all his dwindling strength.

She talked to him the rest of the night, sitting awake, stroking his chest, answering when he called for *her*.

Colleen was curled on her side beneath the wagon when she heard Matthew's distinctive catlike steps. She sat up and smoothed her hair, knowing the gesture was futile. The tangles were knotted and dirty.

He knelt down and peered beneath the bed into the blackness, whispering, "Colleen?"

"Yes!" She crawled forward until she was only inches from him and could see the camp beyond. People knelt around campfires. Orange flickers danced across the covered wagons. Matthew's face shone softly golden.

She noticed the animals were gone. Earlier she'd heard mooing. "They moved the stock?"

"Herded them down to water."

He offered a hand and pulled her out into the bright starlight. She looked up at the twinkling stars. Charcoal clouds blotted segments of the sky.

Walking a few paces, Matthew sat down and leaned back against the wagon wheel. She followed, sitting beside him and watching as he untied a canteen from his belt. She frowned, recognizing the dented metal; that canteen always carried whiskey.

"Humm," she murmured, pulling up her knees and cradling them in her arms.

He smiled and filled a cup. "We'll have to share," he whispered conspiratorially, handing it to her. "You go first."

She put out a hand to block the transferral. "I don't need a drink."

"Not now . . . but you will."

"I will?" she asked in confusion.

'Um-hum, by the time that cup takes effect, I suspect you'll need another one." There was an amused glint in his eye, and seriousness too.

She reluctantly took the cup and sipped. His mouth was pursed awkwardly, as though he was fighting some inner battle, and his blue eyes looked hesitant—almost fearful. He stroked his brown mustache and extended one leg, then gazed up at the night sky.

"What is it?" she asked.

He fumbled with the canteen in his hands. "Can you feel it yet?"

She blinked, not sure. There was a fire in her belly and

her limbs were beginning to numb, but the sweet, reckless feeling was missing. "Not—really."

"I'll wait." He propped the canteen against his hip and fidgeted with his fingers, lacing and unlacing them.

"What's the matter with you?" she pressed, frowning. "You're as nervous as a bride on her wedding night." She swallowed a good gulp of whiskey. Whatever this thing was, it was hard for him and that meant it would be just as hard for her. She took another swallow.

He bowed his head and adjusted his blue cap, then, almost as an afterthought, took it off and beat it lightly against his sky blue pants. His mouth was pursed again.

"An apt analogy," he muttered hesitantly, rolling his cap up and pounding it against one palm.

She jumped at the sharp slapping sounds. "Are you doing that to make me nervous?"

He didn't look up. "No." He sighed and flipped his cap open, then put it on again. Exhaling audibly, he reached over and tipped her cup down to look inside. It was almost empty. He looked up hopefully, brows arched.

She blinked. "Yes, I feel it."

"Good, then I'll take the cup back if you don't mind." He reached out.

She handed it over and watched him pour it half full, then bolt the contents in one throw of the hand.

He closed his eyes and caressed his brow. "There'll be difficult parts—this'll help."

"Help me or you?"

He paused, his mouth slightly ajar. "Me more than you—but both of us, I think."

"Matthew," she said, putting a hand on his muscular thigh and squinting to see his dimly lit face. "What's this all about?"

He picked up her hand and kissed the palm, then clutched it to his damp blue shirt. He was dripping perspiration. "Colleen, my dear, I'd like to tell you about my wife."

· CHAPTER 18 ·

SHE PULLED HER HAND BACK, HER MOUTH OPEN. "YOUR *wife*!"

"Yes, I—" He reached for her hands again.

"Stay away from me!" She hid her hands in the flowered folds of her skirt.

It briefly occurred to him to dig them out, but he decided against it.

"It's not what you think."

He closed the fingers of his outstretched hand and slowly brought them back to his lap, silently absorbing every movement of her face, the twist of her mouth, the pinched expression. He nodded briefly and refilled his tin cup, pouring the liquid with a concentrated nonchalance.

"I was eighteen, Colleen." He sipped gingerly at the whiskey. "She was almost seventeen."

Memories long forgotten swept through him. He could see her dark gentle eyes teasing him, could feel the tender touch of her fingers on his face. He closed his eyes, astonished by the strength and clarity of the memories.

"We spent only nine months together before her death from cholera in 1853." The words rang with an empty resonance.

"Oh—she's dead!" Colleen said in relief, the smile coming back to her face.

He frowned. "Your tenderness is truly touching, my dear."

"Well, Matthew, it's just that I thought—I mean I was afraid she was—well, you know—alive."

"Only here," he said, tapping his chest.

She bowed her head in sudden understanding and fiddled with her skirt. "You still love her?"

"Never stopped."

He looked around the camp, watching people. It was dinnertime and the smell of baking bread filled the air.

"What was her name?"

"Enanoshe," he whispered.

There was a short silence while he shifted positions, extending both legs and snuggling his back against the uncomfortable hub. He felt odd, haunted, as though Enanoshe was somewhere close, just out of his reach, her black hair blowing in the wind as she reached out for him. But he couldn't see her, couldn't reach back. He hardened his thoughts. Like a damned soul awaiting the final judgment of God, he stood defiant before the golden throne. Blue eyes contemptuous—unrepentant—he was certain his actions had been right even if the divine decision didn't reflect the fact—knowing it wouldn't.

A melancholy smile brushed his lips as he played with the tin cup in his hands, flipping it over and over.

"She was—Cheyenne?" Colleen asked.

He nodded, fixing her with hollow eyes.

"Why was it difficult to tell me?"

He sighed. "There's more to it. Some folks blamed me for her death."

"Were you responsible?" She looked at him from beneath her lashes, blond curls falling over her shoulders.

"No."

"Then why are you being so hard on yourself?"

He frowned and pushed the cap back on his head. Dark, damp locks fell over his brow. "Don't know, really."

She shook her head. "Since when did you develop these honorable tendencies toward martyrdom?"

"Martyrdom?" he questioned indignantly, wiping his moist palms on his sky blue pants. "Me?"

"A little late in life for you to develop such nobility—don't you think?"

He thought of a suitable answer, but never had a chance to use it. "I—"

"Are you finished unburdening your conscience?"

"Uh . . . yes."

She got to her feet and extended a tiny tanned hand to him. Her face glowed yellowish in the dim light of nearby fires.

"Good, I'm so tired I could sleep a hundred years." She yawned, stretched her arms over her head. "Let's go back to our tent?"

Confused, he stood and put an arm around her shoulders. They walked in silence.

He jerked awake, a sharp cry slipping from his throat. His lungs heaved; cold sweat had soaked his blanket. The darkness in the canvas tent was stifling. He rubbed his face with trembling fingers. The dream of Enanoshe had come again.

Colleen rolled over sleepily and patted his broad back. "You all right?" she murmured and sat up next to him.

"Yes," he whispered. His eyes drifted to the eastern horizon. There was a very faint brightening over the rolling hills. He sighed as he lay back down, staring blindly at the darkness. Colleen put her head on his chest and tucked the blanket around him.

"Bad dreams?" she murmured, squeezing his arm.

"Um . . . what?" His thoughts were far away.

"Dream?"

"Yes—just a dream," he said, caressing the tangles of blond hair that sheathed his chest.

Wounded Bear struggled to open his eyes, but his lids were too heavy. Pain seared his chest at the meager effort. He clamped his jaw to stifle the cry bubbling up in his throat. His body felt prickly, as though some demon thrust a thousand burning arrow points into his flesh. The agony was a fire that burned in waves over his breast.

He concentrated, tugging repeatedly at his lids until they opened. He was lying in a clump of cottonwoods, the thin leaves quaking lightly in the breeze. The grass beneath his bare back was cool. He commanded his forefinger to stroke the blades. Then tried to close his palm around them, but pain jabbed wickedly, forcing a groan through his clenched teeth.

Someone stirred beside him and he saw Yellow Leaf's beautiful face lean over. She looked tired, eyes puffy. Had she been sitting there for long? Her long black hair draped over his chest.

"Wounded Bear," she said, gently mopping his forehead with a damp cloth, "you must not move. I have your shoulder tied tightly in rawhide straps."

"Water?" his dry voice croaked. He bit back against the pain the utterance brought.

"Here." She lifted his head and tipped a gourd of water to his lips. He drank greedily, most of the cool liquid splashing down to drench his neck.

"You are lucky," she murmured as she laid his head back against the grass. "The ball caught you high on your shoulder. Nothing vital was smashed, though I fear you will never have full use of your arm again—but you will live—if you lie still and let the wound mend."

Wounded Bear smiled faintly. He had known he would live. The vision granted him by the wolf in the dark void assured him of a few more years. He closed his eyes. The image of the wolf brought back memories of his night with the yellow-haired woman and he could see wisps of hair dancing in the wind and could feel the softness of her skin beneath his fingers. When he was stronger, he would seek her mind again. Soon, he promised himself. He let his memories of her fill him, sweetening his mind, dimming his awareness of the staggering pain. He had held her in his arms—she carried his child. Though she would not yet realize it, he knew. The *maiyun* had granted him a vision during their last embrace. He had seen the union take place and knew the baby to be male.

His thoughts wavered, sleep forcing dreams, dreams of his son.

The train had barely yoked up when the attack came, Indians screaming down the hills, bullets and arrows smashing into the wagons.

Williford's horse spooked, bucking stiff-legged. He clung tight, waving the wagons by him. They rushed to find safety, but by eleven o'clock in the morning the attack had forced them to circle the wagons on a low, sage-covered hill.

So the attack had come, just as Douglas had said. Williford was outraged; his ragged blue shirt was drenched in sweat as he strode across the circle to Sawyers. The colonel was already shouting to the assembled crowd.

"Volunteers, men! Who will volunteer to ride out and find General Connor's troops?" He held up both hands, palms open, his long face pinched.

"What for?" Williford yelled from the back of the crowd. People turned to stare at him.

One of Sawyers' brows raised, his expression going hard at the sight of the captain. "With more military support we can travel farther into Indian country and complete our mission."

Turmoil rose, voices chattering wildly.

Williford looked around at the faces of his men. The soldiers looked back with questions in their eyes, some kicking dirt to avoid his gaze. No one wanted to volunteer for a suicide ride.

"Fifteen men," the colonel continued, shouting over the clamor. "Just fifteen!"

Williford walked forward, anger and indignation winding through him as he shouldered between whispering road-builders and wide-eyed worried emigrants to stand ten feet from Sawyers.

"Fifteen men, Colonel?" he asked, aghast, and waved a hand to the hills where the Indians had momentarily re-treated. "Against a thousand Indian warriors?"

"Captain, the bravery of our men is beyond question. They—"

"Hell, man! Bravery isn't worth a damn against bullets! Fifteen men wouldn't make it more than a hundred yards before they were cut down!" He was tired, dead tired. His fuse seemed to be getting shorter by the minute, violence welling hotly in his veins.

Sawyers glared and ignored his observation, looking over Williford and back to the crowd. "Who will volunteer for this mission?"

An uneasy quiet settled and Williford let his eyes drift back to his men. They'd go if he ordered it, he knew that. These "White-Washed Rebels" were a dedicated and cou-rageous group of men, but he couldn't order anyone to un-dertake a mission with such odds. The soldiers waited, their eyes fixed on him.

"You're not getting any volunteers, Colonel," Williford announced, frowning and crossing his arms.

"Captain." Sawyers stepped forward and lowered his voice. "I order you to select fifteen men for this mission."

"You have no authority over me, Colonel," he replied flatly. "My men are going nowhere."

A loud cheer rose from the men in blue, hats flying into the air like tumbling balloons. When the ruckus died down, Sawyers was trembling with rage.

He glared out over the soldiers. "I didn't realize," he charged at the top of his lungs, "that your men were as fainthearted as you, Captain!"

Insane anger gripped Williford, he lunged, fists frantically seeking Sawyers. Someone grabbed him from behind before his blows could land. He struggled against the iron arms around his chest.

"Damn it, George!" Douglas said in his ear. "Stop it! It's not worth your career!"

He relaxed and shrugged off the muscular arms. If only he weren't so exhausted. He'd gotten no more than eight hours' sleep in four days and his ability to think was nil. His mind worked constantly on half power—his emotions racing full-time. He turned around to nod his gratitude to Douglas. The lieutenant looked worried.

"Colonel," he exhaled the word in one disgusted breath. "The only place my men are going is Fort Connor at the earliest possible moment." He turned and started walking away through the crowd.

"You're a stinking coward, Williford!" Sawyers shouted. *"A filthy stinking coward!"*

He stopped dead in his tracks and slowly turned around, wanting a fight—needing one. But Sawyers had vanished, fled immediately on seeing him turn.

"Indians!" someone screamed.

Williford whirled, drawing his pistol. The hills came alive with piercing wolflike cries as warriors rode down upon the train, trying to stampede the stock. People crisscrossed through the wagons, rushing for safety and rifles, as bullets whistled around them, splintering wood and furrowing twisted patterns in the soil.

The attempt failed, the warriors retreating over the hills to await their next opportunity.

Before dawn the following morning, Sawyers ordered four members of his road crew to locate Connor's column. Two days later they returned, sneaking in under cover of darkness.

"Colonel?" Charlie Sears wheezed as he pulled back the flap of Sawyers' tent, then fell into a coughing fit, his lungs clogged with dust from his hurried fifty-mile ride.

"Come in, Sears," Sawyers said, laying his pen and paper aside.

He complied, ducking through the flap and standing awkwardly before the colonel. The expedition's leader was seated at a plank table writing, a lamp burning next to him.

"Found Connor's trail, sir," he informed, choking back another coughing attack.

"But no soldiers?"

"No, sir."

Sawyers exhaled heavily and leaned back, his face tense, brow furrowed. "Where did the trail lead?"

"Didn't follow it out all the way, sir, but I reckon it goes straight to Fort Connor." He took off his dusty hat and slapped it on his hip. Puffs of dirt hung on the still air. "My advice, for what it's worth, Colonel, is to follow that trail, no matter where it leads."

Sawyers sat rigid, defeat plain on his long face. His salt and pepper beard wriggled as he spoke. "Not much choice, is there?" His voice had gone hollow.

"Reckon not."

"All right," Sawyers breathed, lightly pounding a fist on the plank tabletop. "Tell the crew—and . . . let Captain Williford know."

Sears bowed. "On my way, Colonel."

The news spread like wildfire.

· CHAPTER 19 ·

Six days later Colleen ambled leisurely through the towering cottonwoods that lined the Powder River. A cool westerly breeze blew, sending waves rippling through the tall grass. The sound of rushing water roared in the stillness. On the east side of the river, cone-shaped hills sprouted from flat plains. On the west side, perched high atop a sage-covered tableland, was Fort Connor. The train had made camp on the east side of the river because there was more grass for the stock. She looked back to the fort. It wasn't much of a fortification, really. Only days old, the square log stockade had barely been completed when the train arrived.

She shielded her eyes and looked back toward the post. Soldiers milled outside, sawing cottonwoods for the new quartermaster depot and laughing with the newly arrived infantrymen. The post had only had a handful of soldiers before Williford's command made its surprise appearance and the fort was overjoyed with the additional manpower.

She turned back around and continued walking, her gaze on the shining sands beneath her boots.

Spying an oddly shaped piece of driftwood, she knelt down and retrieved it from the muddy water. Her hair followed her hand, leaving the golden strands wet. She brushed them over her shoulder and sat down on the bank to unbutton her shoes and slip her hot feet into the cool water.

She sighed in pleasure, pulling her skirt higher to bury her knees beneath the rippling surface. A breeze teased her hair, making it curl in front of her face. She closed her eyes and leaned back against the sandy beach, letting the sensations of muddy toes, fragrant air, and cool water penetrate her body. The river was a tonic for her exhaustion. Several minutes passed while she daydreamed and watched the clouds drift in the sky above.

Soft, sand-muffled footsteps caught her off guard. She abruptly turned, half expecting a war party. Instead, the tall, lean figure of Matthew towered over her. His face was deeply tanned. He had his blue sleeves rolled up over his elbows and a wry questioning grin on his face. His eyes glittered at her bare legs.

"Must you," he said in a sinister voice, twirling his mustache, "expose yourself so?" He knelt down beside her, eyes rudely appraising.

"Expose? Matthew, there's not another living soul for a quarter mile!"

"Indeed?" He nodded in quizzical omniscience, then pointed a finger south to the fort and whispered, "Do you see that clump of trees?"

"Of course."

"Have you ever heard of field glasses, my sweet, naive, little vamp?"

Her mouth dropped open and her arms flashed out to tug her lavender hem down, embarrassment flushing her cheeks. "Oh, Matthew! I—"

He put his hands on his hips and threw his head back to laugh. His cackles were so loud that she knew the soldiers at the fort could hear him.

"Hush! Tell me you were just joking."

"Why, my dear"—he stifled his amusement, smiling maliciously—"the kind soldiers even offered to let me have a peek."

Her sharp intake of breath sent him reeling into another tirade of laughter.

"You threatened them, I'm sure!" she said triumphantly, visualizing his stern reproach for their vile actions.

"I did not. What kind of brute do you think I am? Well"—he held up a hand as her mouth opened to answer— "never mind that. My point is that these poor boys are stranded in a virtual wasteland and the sight of your lovely legs will fuel their dreams."

"Dreams . . ." she muttered, her voice trailing off as her eyes widened. "You don't mean—"

"But of course, I do. You think these men inhuman?" He cocked his head impertinently and whispered, "Your angelic image will soothe many a frustration, my dear.

"Now come here and let me kiss you."

"I will not!" she objected, timidly leaning past him to gaze back at the fort. "What if those blackguards are still watching?"

He reached over and forcibly dragged her to him, then soundly kissed her, despite her ferocious attempts to escape.

"You rascal!" she said. "What did you think—"

"I thought I'd let them know you're taken and they're not to make silly fools out of themselves trying to woo you."

"They wouldn't—"

"Do be realistic, dear. Men lose all their senses except one around beautiful women." He gave her an impetuous smile. "And the one they retain is purely glandular."

She got to her feet in a huff, wishing he spoke English. "Matthew Douglas . . . you're infuriating!"

"Not disgusting?" he asked, blue eyes wide.

"Oh, well, that too!" Thoughts were roiling in her head. "Disgusting" and "glandular" were somehow related. She felt better knowing that.

He laughed like a fiend, then stood up beside her and wrapped an arm over her shoulders. Together they started walking down the sandy edge of the river through the wavering shadows of the cottonwoods. As they walked, she could sense his mood changing. His mirth was gone, replaced by a subdued seriousness.

"I came to tell you something important," he said hurriedly, as though he wanted to get it over with. "There's a Cheyenne camp near here." He pointed northward with his chin, his eyes flitting over her face.

Her heart hammered. Was the warrior there? A soft reverie smoothed her face, her mouth quivering. She clutched handfuls of lavender organdie to still her careening emotions and dropped her gaze to the sand.

"Is he—"

"I don't know," Matthew responded with unguarded impatience, a sharpness in his voice. "The fort has been monitoring the village, but they've shown no hostile intentions. There are women and children there, so it's doubtful it's the same group who attacked us—though"—he exhaled—"the wounded might have been taken there."

"Matthew—why did you tell me?"

"Because—if . . ." He swallowed and tightened his grip on her arm until it verged on being painful. His face had grown hard, unreadable. "Honey, have you had any dreams of the warrior since the road was stopped?"

"No, I—I haven't," she said, straining to keep the disappointment in her heart out of her voice.

He stopped walking and released her, stammered briefly on the verge of saying something, then thought better of it and jammed his fists in his pockets—staying silent. After a few seconds, he muttered softly, "Maybe it is over, then."

"What?"

He lifted his eyes to meet hers and for a moment she thought she saw a flicker of fear in the blue depths, but it vanished quickly, as though an impenetrable curtain of lead had been dropped. He laughed shortly, a dry unemotional sound, not like his normally gay mirth.

"It's not important," he said, putting his arm back over her shoulder. His self-confidence was back, his mouth curled into a grin. "I just thought you'd like to know is all."

"Thank you," she whispered uncomfortably, knowing there was more.

Wounded Bear struggled to mount his horse. With his right arm still bound tightly, he couldn't seem to get the leverage necessary to swing his leg up and over the creature's back. The pony whinnied at his awkward efforts and sidestepped.

"Ho, little one," he said, patting the animal's flank.

The pony calmed some, swatting him absently with its tail. He sucked in a breath and tried again; twining his hand in the white mane, he threw his leg up. The horse moved again and he fell painfully to the ground.

He leaned his head against the animal's back. Sweat streamed down his face. Backing away, he wiped his brow and licked his lips, then slapped the pony on the haunches. It blew softly and trotted a short distance away to graze on the thick, dry grasses of the river bottom.

Even the slight exertion was more than he could bear. He swayed on his feet, his vision blurring. He grasped for a nearby cottonwood branch, but only managed to snap off a few twigs. Staggering, he fell to the ground, landing on his right side with the world spinning around him. He clutched at the browning grasses to steady himself and crushed his eyelids together. The pain in his shoulder swelled powerfully.

Soft harsh words startled him. He looked up to see Yellow Leaf running quickly through the trees. She was dressed in a bright red dress made from tradecloth. Her black hair was loose and flying out behind her.

"I told you," she admonished, "that it would be another week!"

Wounded Bear smiled and wiped the sweat from his face. "I thought maybe I could hurry things."

She puckered her face, pouting, and sat down beside him in the tall grass. "Why are you in a hurry? The train has stopped building the road. Our people are safe."

Wounded Bear did not answer. His people thought he'd been freed of the woman's witchcraft and he didn't want to tell them different. But the wolf had come in his dreams and told him she was near, at Fort Connor. He'd sensed her presence in his heart, but hadn't tried to contact her. He was saving his strength for their next meeting. He smiled inwardly, knowing it would not be long until she knew she carried his child. She would need him then. He had to force his uncooperative body to work.

"Tell me again about the bullet bruise?" he asked her, hoping the knowledge would gave him a better idea of healing time.

Her voice was tender. "It was bad. Your muscles were purple from the shock, your shoulder blade broken."

Wounded Bear imagined the torn muscle tissue and fragmented bone. Cautiously he took a deep breath and forced his thoughts away from his physical condition to the woman. In his mind he felt her lying softly beneath him, her golden hair glistening in the starlight as their souls entwined and danced. The images called to him. Perhaps in another week he could try to contact her.

Yellow Leaf shifted uncomfortably and bowed her head to gaze absently at the brown grass. Her voice was thin and fragile. "You're . . . going to her, aren't you?"

He met her soft eyes. The hollow look of guarded hurt made him drop his gaze. He fumbled with the grass.

"I must."

Colleen crouched before the evening fire, lifting the cast-iron lid on the Dutch oven to check the bread baking inside. The antelope steaks were already cooked and keeping warm in the pan propped on the coals. Matthew had gone with Captain Williford to the fort—or rather, been summoned by Colonel Kidd, the commanding officer—but he'd promised he'd be back by sundown and it was almost nine o'clock.

Anxiously she gazed up at the stars and hugged herself to fend off the evening chill. Crickets squeaked rustily in the darkness and mosquitoes buzzed over her head. She spent more time shooing them away than she did worrying about Matthew. The hearings must have just taken longer than he thought, that's all.

A coyote interrupted her thoughts, yipping mournfully; the wail drifted across the river, then the entire pack joined in to fill the hills with baleful whimperings. She smiled and listened. A variety of sounds met her ears, but one was different, a soft rhythmic pounding, like a faraway heartbeat. She closed her eyes and concentrated on sifting that one sound from the rest, but the more she strained to listen, the fainter the beating became until it vanished altogether.

Matthew's deep laugh brought her back and she opened her eyes to find him. He was standing at the edge of camp, talking with another officer. He looked in her direction and winked. The other officer turned too, tipping his hat to her. She smiled shyly and nodded to him, then went back to her loaf of bread, lifting the cast-iron lid to check inside. She looked up again when she heard Matthew say, "Good night."

He walked lazily toward her, a broad smile on his face, his blue eyes dancing.

"Well, Lieutenant, what did Colonel Sawyers accuse the captain of and did Colonel Kidd believe him?"

He laughed out loud at her bluntness, giving her a reproving look. "It was all very profane, are you certain your delicate female ears won't melt?"

"Don't be a goose. Tell me."

"Well, Sawyers accused Williford of negligence, insubordination, and cowardice—among other quaint phrases I'll spare you."

"No! Tell me!" She tugged his blue sleeve.

"My dear," he said, one eyebrow arching. "Your interests have truly improved under my tutelage." He pulled her closer, whispering, "He called the captain a lily-livered son-of-a-bitch."

Her mouth dropped open and she pulled her head back in disbelief. "Really?"

"Yes." He grinned.

"And what did Captain Williford say?"

"Oh, George was quite professional about it all, if painfully straightforward. He laid the panorama of our sufferings and deprivations out on the table and humbly requested we be reassigned to Fort Connor and Sawyers provided a new escort."

"Did Colonel Kidd agree?"

"Of course. Though God knows how the new cavalry escort will handle Sawyers' bombastic priggishness—"

"So—we'll be staying here?" she interrupted, clutching his sleeve. Anxiety welled inside her.

He studied her nervous actions, his expression changing. "Don't you want to stay here?"

"I—I want to stay with you," she replied tentatively, her long hair draping over her face to shield her from his probing scrutiny.

He reached over and pulled up her chin, making her look at him. His eyes were hard as iron. "The warrior?"

She nodded.

"He's contacted you?"

"No, but—"

"Colleen, I am assigned to this post for the remainder of my service, which is three months. I can't go gallivanting off with you in search of—"

"Matthew, I'm only asking—"

"They call it desertion, my dear. It's greatly frowned upon."

"I wouldn't ask you to desert!"

"Good!"

She squirmed, twining fingers in her lavender skirt. She'd planned on leading into this discussion more delicately, but now it seemed she had little choice. Her cheeks flushed crimson and her gaze dropped to the campfire. He watched her closely, frowning.

"Matthew . . ." She paused, eyes going uneasily over

camp. "It's—it's past my time." She said it quickly and found that once it was out it wasn't nearly as painful as she'd thought. She glanced up at him from beneath bristly lashes. He had a dumbfounded expression on his face. Dear Lord, was she going to have to be more specific?

He stared blankly for a few seconds, curiously watching her abashed movements, then his shoulders suddenly stiffened and he sat forward, his eyes flitting over her flushed face. "Past your . . . Colleen, are you trying to tell me you're pregnant?"

"Yes!" she whispered, peering uncomfortably at passersby.

He sat motionless, blue eyes riveted to her face, hunting for something which he did not find. His Grecian-statue features were as stony as the marble figures he reminded her of. She shivered under his penetrating gaze, wishing he'd say something, but not willing to demand it. So hard were his eyes that she couldn't hold his gaze and she bowed her head to stare numbly at her fumbling hands. The lavender organdie beneath her clammy fingers was growing more and more wrinkled.

Finally he swiveled to sit facing her and put a rough hand beneath her chin, turning her face so she couldn't avoid his scrutiny.

"Mine?"

He said the word stiffly and it occurred to her for the first time that he knew about her night with the warrior, had read her transparent face like a book, but never mentioned it until now out of some private sense of honor. Her pointed chin quivered against his hand.

She considered giving him a decorous lie, but knew he'd see through it and knew more certainly that if he didn't now but found out later, he was likely to do something irrational, like stroll in with a grin on his face, bow deeply, and drawl, "You sweet little cheat, shall I slit your throat now or would you prefer dueling pistols at twenty paces?" Just the thought made her blood run cold.

"Matthew, I . . . wish I knew for certain—but I don't."

She swallowed convulsively, her throat bobbing against his hand, and chanced a glance into his eyes. The blue had warmed some and a dark amusement sparkled in the depths. He released her chin.

"However, sheer statistics are overwhelmingly in my favor. Is that right, dear?"

She blinked. It took a moment for her to realize what he meant, but when she did, she lunged for his hand, gripping it tightly, and blurted, "Oh, yes, Matthew!"

He sighed, raising his brows, and squeezed her hand back. "I appreciate your candor. And, since I love you, I'd just as soon start believing the child is mine now."

A sweeping feeling of breathlessness came over her. She clutched her lavender bodice, eyes wide.

"Are you sick?" he asked, concerned.

"No, I . . . Matthew, you said you loved me."

He pulled back a little, squinting in mock disapproval, but there was a twinkle in his eyes. "You'd hoped I was toying with you so you wouldn't have to take me seriously?"

"Oh, no, I—"

He kissed her, pulling her tightly against him.

· CHAPTER 20 ·

THREE DAYS LATER COLLEEN STOOD OUTSIDE THE FORT IN the hot sun and watched Sawyers' expedition pull out of its cottonwood camp bound for Montana. The cavalry escort kicked up a trail of dust as they clopped along. A twinge of pain flashed through her as the emigrant wagons jostled by. She'd had a tearful good-bye session with the O'Brians, Lawrence clutching her hands tightly and murmuring sincere moral advice: "Lassy, it don't matter a whit to me, but it does to some folks, so you ought to marry that boy. You know?" he'd stressed, his cheeks flushing. "Make it right?" She'd mentioned in a hushed voice that Matthew hadn't asked, but Lawrence only frowned a little and granted, "Well, he's not really your average fella, is he? Don't worry, it takes some men longer."

As she watched the train disappear in the thick cottonwood groves down the river, it struck her that she hadn't seen Robert's wagon. A moment of fear tingled in her veins, but then it occurred to her that she'd missed the very start of the train and perhaps the cavalry had reordered the wagons. He was probably farther up front.

A warm gust of wind shoved her backward. She gripped her lavender skirt and leaned into the gale to steady herself. Her blond hair whipped around her throat, cascading over her eyes. She waited until the gust ceased, then gathered the curls together and pulled them over her shoulder.

It was a clear day, the sky cloudless and pale blue. She turned her back to the wind and looked westward. Cool blue mountains rose in the distance and her heart fluttered. They weren't exactly like those in her dreams, but some element was the same, some wispy ethereal quality to their hue. She stared curiously, the sight comforting and at the same time foreboding. But then she dismissed it—forcibly bringing her mind back to the sage-covered tableland and rough-hewn fort behind her. She didn't want to think about the dreams. The warrior hadn't contacted her in over three weeks and, though his absence was like a blow in the stomach, she was growing reluctantly accustomed to the idea that he wouldn't be back. The chasm that had yawned when he first disappeared was closing up and she felt more stable now, though she suspected there would always be a hollow place inside her that only he could fill.

She tugged on her hair as another gust of wind splashed across the plains, then sighed and turned to walk back to the fort.

It was early evening when she started down the ridge to the river, strolling quietly along the edge of the tableland and peering at the trees in the river bottom below. The sunset blazed ruby red with a pale blue halo, making the storm clouds drifting down from the north glow like pink slate. Two weeks had passed quickly, she mused, threading her way through the sweet tangy sage. Quickly and peacefully. So peacefully in fact that sometimes she wondered if it all wasn't just a dream from which she would be rudely awakened someday. But that thought was too painful to think of and she spent most of each day reading her Bible, playing card games with the soldiers at the fort, and talking with Matthew.

Thinking of Matthew made her laugh. Since she'd told him about the baby he'd grown remarkably silly, refusing to allow her to lift anything weighing a pound or more and tucking so many blankets around her at night that she thought she'd smother to death. When once she had protested, kicking them off and saying sharply, "I declare, Matthew, if you don't stop being such a ninny I'm going to think you've lost your mind!" he'd responded by throwing her a supercilious sideways look and since that moment it seemed she never had blankets. She'd awaken in the middle of the night, freezing, to find him rolled up like a mummy in every blanket they had. Of course, he always innocently maintained it was an accident, but she knew better.

Her thoughts shifted as she reached the narrow dirt path that led down to the river bottom. Twining her hands in her yellow skirt, she lifted it lightly off the ground and proceeded down the steep path, her blond hair fluttering in the wind that swept up the river. Shadows caressed the soil, wavering as the wind blew the leaves of the trees. Reaching a flat sandy cove filled with towering cottonwoods, she dropped to the ground and pulled up her knees to gaze at the muddy river. It flowed by in a dawdling, unhurried fashion. Foamy tufts washed up on the sand at her feet, clinging to the bank like some ephemeral dirty moss. She touched the foam, feeling cool bubbles break beneath her fingertips, then drew her hand back to study the grayish film on her skin. As she sat, studying her palm, a wave of dizziness rolled over her. She clutched aimlessly at the huge tree trunk beside her, but the world spun like a child's top and she knew the warrior had returned.

The dance began and she was floating in an ocean of light, cloaked in his gentleness, her soul reaching for his and finding it. Together they whirled, meandering through the other, communicating wordlessly as the light bathed them in an eternal stillness.

And then it was over—the warrior disappearing like a

bubble bursting—and she found herself lying on her stomach on the cool sands, river water washing over her right arm. The loneliness swelled, the chasm yawning wide again as tears blurred her eyes. She dug her fingers into the cool grains and cried.

Soft footsteps touched the sand behind her, but before she could look up, a voice called softly in Cheyenne, "It's all right," and a tender hand touched her shoulder. "I'm here."

She rolled over to look up into the warm eyes of the warrior and her soul calmed. He was dressed in heavily beaded buckskins, concentric red, blue, and yellow diamonds covering his chest. But there was an anxiousness about his manner.

He extended a hand to her, his gaze drifting over the tableland leading to the fort. "Hurry," he whispered urgently. "We must go before they find us."

She took his hand.

Matthew stood uneasily before the campfire. It was getting dark and rain had begun to fall. It was a light misty rain, but from the looks of the scudding clouds, when the storm arrived it would be violent. Already lightning flashed brilliantly to the north, sending bellows of thunder rolling down over the fort.

He folded his arms and spread his legs, staring intently across the tableland. Smoothing his mustache, he let his thoughts wander. Where could she be? Several soldiers had said they'd seen her walking leisurely southward. Had she gone down to the river seeking solitude? He shook his head, jammed his fists in his pockets, and started pacing nervously, his eyes darting over the sage and down to the trees. Colleen was one of those women who demanded time alone to sort through inner thoughts. Usually he gave her that time—but tonight he balked. The storm was only minutes away and daylight was fading quickly, casting a blue hue over the land.

He clamped his jaw and turned his back to the increasing

gale. As the storm approached, the wind whistled violently, tearing at the sage and whipping his blue sleeves. He tugged the cap down tighter over his forehead. How much longer should he wait before going to find her?

A brilliant bolt of lightning struck a hill across the river and the simultaneous cackle of thunder hit him in the face like a fist. An icy shiver played up his spine as he remembered that night weeks before when Colleen had gone out into the darkness and not come back until the following morning. The face of the Cheyenne warrior filled his mind—hauntingly familiar.

Desperately he tried to place the man's strong features, but a dim voice in the back of his mind told him he didn't really want to. He fought the awareness, searching his memories.

The rain was coming down harder, pelting him in huge wet drops and soaking his blue uniform.

"Damn it, Colleen," he murmured insistently, then picked up his feet and trotted southward, through the endless tangles of sage.

The clouds pulled a black blanket over the fort and sent jagged swords of lightning slashing against the surrounding hilltops as he rushed just ahead of the darkness, his eyes glued to the ground, searching for her boot prints. Thunder crackled wickedly in his ears, the repeated roar drowning out all other sounds, bombarding him with wild vicious cackling. His steps faltered, his legs going suddenly weak. The memory struck him like a cold wet wave and he staggered. The old medicine man—and the boy.

The boy! his mind screamed at him.

"Wounded Bear?" he shouted and started running again, his whole body numb.

"No!" he screamed. "My brother, no!"

The shrieking wind and roaring thunder swallowed up his cries as he ran blindly across the tableland, heedless of the tearing sage at his feet and growing darkness. He stumbled forward, tumbling to the ground as a brilliant flash of lightning spun an eerie luminescent web around him. The major shaft of silver light seemed to point to a place at the edge of the sage flat. Were the *maiyun* talking to him? using the voices of the wind and rain? He stared upward into the sky, blinking as huge raindrops splattered his face, then pulled himself to his feet and ran for the edge of the flat. He found them, found her boot prints. The rain had not yet erased evidence of her passage. He hurled himself headlong down the steep dirt path toward the river bottom, racing against the torrents of storm and time.

"Colleen?" he shouted into the moaning cottonwoods, his lungs heaving. *"Colleen!"*

The wind slapped wetly into his face, shoving him back and forth, making him weave as he ran through the thick grove of trees. Thunder boomed so loudly around him he had to put his hands over his ears before it dashed his hearing. He called her name until his throat ached.

Halting his frantic steps, he waited for the next slash of lightning and the next, searching the sand until he found her heel prints and tracked them to a small cove. The huge cottonwood tree had sheltered her prints from the storm. The sight that met his eyes made the air still in his chest. He straightened up slowly and stared out into the dim night, clutching the brim of his cap against the chilling sheets of rain. Surrounding her prints were soft moccasin impressions. Matthew squeezed his eyes shut, his mind reeling in terror. The rain was washing away their trail. How could he follow? Was this what Broken Star had meant? Had Colleen's death been planned long ago by the spirit world?

"No!" he screamed in rage, shaking his fists at the heavens. "Take me!" He dropped to his knees on the wet sand and pleaded, *"Take me!"* A boom of thunder was his only answer.

A frantic wave of rage and futility swept him. He turned his face up to the black sky and spread his arms wide. His voice was choked. "I'm the one responsible, *Maiyun!* Let the punishment be mine!"

Kneeling there, his uniform wet, body cold, the wind howling through the towering trees, his tortured mind put

the puzzle pieces together. He shivered and dropped his
arms, then got to his feet and ran, ran with all his might
back to the fort to pack his pistols and saddle his horse.
When he rode out into the terrible raging storm, he knew
where he was going. The spirit powers were carrying out
an old man's instructions, playing him and his world against
a screen of pain and hatred.

The sandstone rock shelter would be waiting. There, the
threads would be pulled tight.

Robert Merrill watched Douglas ride out—man and horse
lit up by brilliant flashes of lightning—and smiled faintly to
himself. He'd seen Colleen and the Indian earlier, too, but
hadn't been quick enough to follow them. Yet he knew
Douglas would and he *could* follow Douglas. He grinned
broadly, tightening the cinches of his saddle. He'd hidden
his wagon in a pile of brush and bided his time, knowing
his chance would come eventually. Colleen and Douglas
wouldn't always hang close to the fort. And now he could
even the score.

He laughed out loud as he mounted his horse and kicked
it into a trot, staying just far enough behind that Douglas
wouldn't notice his presence.

Colleen shivered. They had been galloping through the
rain and thunder all night. As sunrise seeped dully through
the black clouds, she could see the terrain had changed
dramatically. Sparkling snow-capped peaks rose up before
them, stretching endlessly to the north. She'd seen these
mountains a hundred times in her dreams, but their crystal-
line beauty had never come through. As she gazed up to the
ragged blue mountains, she felt oddly as though she were
coming home.

The warrior slowed the pinto pony to a walk and they
began to climb toward forested slopes. He dropped a hand
to hers and stroked the fingers that laced over his stomach.

"Almost there," he said softly, turning halfway around
on the horse.

Colleen tightened her grip. Throughout the night they had briefly let their souls entwine so that now her heart ached for the union to be permanent. Matthew kept coming to her mind, his tall, muscular form swaggering toward her with that insolent, taunting smile on his face. He loved her and would follow if he could. But could he? she wondered. The storm had been so violent, scrubbing the face of the world clean and wiping away all tracks. It would be difficult if not impossible for him to find her. She hugged the warrior tighter, feeling his strong brown hands gently caress her arm in return, and pushed thoughts of Matthew out of her mind, trying desperately to avoid the pain they brought.

She gazed out at the snowy peaks, letting her eyes wander across the pines and tall grass, the sage and juniper.

He stroked her arm again, his voice softer and more confident. He pointed to a distant cliff face that shone red in the dull gray light of the cloudy day. "Our home is there," he murmured.

"In the red rocks?"

"Yes, next to a deep canyon that's streaked with bands of gray, red, and orange. A cold stream rushes through the bottom. The fishing and hunting are good."

He turned around to gaze into her eyes and a wealth of conflicting emotions stirred her. There was warmth there and tenderness, his love evident. She smiled and raised her hand to caress the muscles of his chest. Because their souls had shared the same space, she knew this man, knew his strengths and weaknesses in a way she could never know Matthew's. God had made the right choice, she thought, in fating her to this warrior. Still, it would hurt. She missed Matthew.

He kicked the tan and white pinto and they rode higher, climbing up into the mountains.

Matthew held his hand up to shield his eyes from the driving rain. With each flash of lightning, he searched the landscape. A horse with two riders, that's what he sought. He'd caught a single glimpse of their tracks before the rain washed them away. The hoof prints had been deep, the animal carrying a heavy load. They'd have to go slower than he because of the extra weight, but that fact didn't help much. No man could force his horse to gallop full tilt through the slippery mud and endless tangles of sage.

He wound northward, memories flooding over him. Enanoshe's face, pale and drawn, sprang up clearly. The bitter cries of her brother tore his mind. He felt as though he were living over that terrible day so long ago. Broken Star's voice cackled in his ears, "Balance, son. What you take, you must give back!" The last two words echoed again and again through his hollow breast, leaving him sick.

Water ran in rivulets from his mustache, streaming down his blue shirt. The wind had grown forceful and wintry, penetrating his uniform until he shivered constantly. How long would it take him? he wondered. He forced his memory of the land to work. He'd ridden the same path a dozen times, but it had been almost twelve years. How far was it? Thirty-five miles, maybe forty? Could he reach the canyon of the Middle Fork of the Powder River by nightfall? He nodded to himself, almost certain he could.

The lightning storm raged around him, jagged flashes making the horse whinny and bolt.

"Hoshah," he soothed, stroking the animal's red mane. "The storm will break soon."

The afternoon light dwindled as they climbed the slope. Wounded Bear studied the twisting pathway, guiding the pony ever upward. The rock cairns appeared, marking clearly the old trail used by his people for centuries. He reined the horse to a stop and offered the woman a hand to help her down. Pain stabbed through him, his bandaged shoulder crying out at the exertion. He dismounted and took her by the hand.

"See these?" he asked, pointing to the long line of rock cairns that dotted the trail, sprouting up from the rocky ground like enormous, chunky anthills.

Colleen walked to the closest pile of stones and knelt down, touching the rocks. "What are they?"

He came to stand beside her, smiling warmly. "The Old Ones made them. We must add stones. They tell the spirit creatures that we hold this path sacred." He bent down and collected several small bits of sandstone and she did the same. "We will throw one stone on each cairn as we climb."

She nodded.

He strolled a short distance away to stare out over the blue peaks. The southern Big Horns sparkled white with new snow, the tallest peaks cloaked in masses of dark rumbling clouds. Winter was not far distant. Soon the ground would be covered with snow and the hunting would become difficult. In his mind he was already planning how much meat to dry and how much pemmican the two of them would need. His heart grew happy, his thoughts drifting to the *maiyun*. The spiritual powers had seen his heartbreak after the death of his sister and sent him the yellow-haired woman to fill the chasm of loss. He spread his arms wide and prayed, thanking them for taking pity on him—for blessing him so abundantly.

He stopped and lowered his arms as he felt her tiny hand on his back. He turned. Rain was falling, patting lightly on the needles of the evergreens and sending a sweet pungent fragrance winding through the mountains. He wrapped his arms around her and focused his mind.

The dance began, her soul touching lightly at the edges of his, growing closer, swaying, entwining, as they floated in the bosom of the Great Mystery. Whispers of eternity called, the sea of light brightening to spread tentacles throughout the universe and, in a dazzling flash of white, the boundaries of their selves dissolved, leaving them one with the light—one with all things. The One pulsed as the universe breathed, moving in perfect rhythm with the flow of time. They lingered there, listening to the celestial heartbeat—being the pulse of existence—until the dance began to slow and their union was broken. Wounded Bear could feel the woman grasping frantically for him, but he had to pull away. The time had not yet come for the final culmination. The wolf had told him to wait—that he would tell him when the moment was right.

The breeze touched his skin and he opened his eyes to see tendrils of windblown blond hair covering his face. He smoothed them away and looked down at the woman. When their gazes met, it was as though all of time had been compressed into that one moment. Nothing else moved in the universe, except the flow of life between them. He clutched her to his chest and then slowly walked back to the pony, his heart full.

As they rode up the slope, the canyon appeared, its streaks of multicolored sandstone vivid and dark through the shower of rain. The splotches of evergreen trees glowed blackly against the red background.

They rode through a narrow defile and out onto a broad sage flat overlooking the canyon. A small orange rock shelter, perhaps twenty-five feet long and a dozen feet wide, was scooped out of the cliff behind them. Wounded Bear guided the pony to it and helped the woman down, then dismounted himself. They ran laughing into the shelter to escape the rain, leaving the pony to graze on the hillside.

A pile of gnarled pine branches darkened the corner of the orange shelter. The irregular ceiling showed signs of eons of fires, charcoal streaking the orange. Wounded Bear dug out the blackened coals filling the fire pit in the floor and built a new fire. The rain was coming down harder outside and the wind blew chillingly over the high country, but they huddled together before the flickering flames and were warm.

Matthew stopped before he rounded the corner. The darkness was heavy, the chill wind biting into him. He would have to walk the rest of the way lest the horse make his presence known before it was right. He tethered the animal to a juniper and mustered his courage, clenching his fists.

"Be still," he commanded his jittery mind, trying desperately to push the wrenching memories of the place away.

He stiffened his back and walked forward, haunting images attacking him before he'd even cleared the narrow defile. He stopped and took a step backward, shutting his eyes and ordering his ragged breathing to return to normal. His anxious lungs refused to obey. Even through the darkness and storm, he could feel her presence—could see the dark eyes smiling longingly at him. He swung around to face the sandstone cliff that loomed darkly beside him and pounded his fists viciously into the gritty surface, trying to bring his mind back under control, to quiet the raging emotional torrent that tore his soul. His fists quivered as he lowered them and leaned his shoulder heavily against the rock face.

Memories forced themselves upon him: Once again the snow was falling and he had to stop the horse and pick her up in his arms. The freezing wind slapped at his body as he carried her to the shelter and laid her beneath the overhang. His mind screamed at him! *Why had the spirits chosen this place!*

But he knew. His eyes drifted forward to the crevice beside the rock shelter and a wave of calm spread through him. She was buried there, resting safely in the arms of the cliff.

"My Enanoshe," he breathed hoarsely.

The rain fell harder, beating him with its fury. He sucked in a halting breath and tugged his cap low over his eyes, forcing his reluctant legs forward. When he rounded the bend, he saw Colleen nestled in Wounded Bear's arms. The shelter glowed golden in the light of the crackling fire. He stood silent for a moment, surveying the situation, his muscles rigid. Broken Star's words echoed hollowly through him. ". . . must give back . . . *give back* . . . GIVE BACK." He allowed the echo to filter through his entire body before he stepped forward.

"Wounded Bear, my brother," he greeted, a tension and sorrow in his voice. "We must talk."

The warrior shifted suddenly, lurching for his rifle.

Douglas stepped into the light of the fire, his hands spread wide, showing he did not have his weapons drawn. Wounded Bear relaxed only a little, laying the rifle across his knees.

"Who are you, white soldier?" he called suspiciously.

"Matthew!" Colleen cried, staring at him with wide pained eyes.

Wounded Bear got to his feet. "Who are you?"

"Can I share your fire, brother?" Matthew asked softly. The warrior reluctantly waved him in out of the rain.

He knelt facing Colleen as Wounded Bear quietly took his place at her side. The two men never let eye contact waver.

Wounded Bear tilted his chin up, eyes squinting. "You have been in my dreams, soldier. Why?"

Matthew's mind drifted back twelve years. The boy had indeed grown to be a man. His shoulders had broadened and hardened, displaying bulging muscles and sun-bronzed skin. He let his eyes wander over the man. Yes, his little brother was a warrior now. A feeling of pride meandered through his breast, mingled with a tragic sense of loss. He shut his eyes tightly against the pain. When he opened them, he found the warrior staring at him with hostile reservation.

"You have grown to be a fine man, little brother."

The warrior sat still, watching him, then, as recognition dawned, astonishment filled his face. Matthew stood and walked away from the fire, turning his back, making himself vulnerable if Wounded Bear wished his life. Footsteps sounded behind him. The hand on his shoulder was strong.

"Brother?" the smooth Cheyenne voice called.

Matthew turned halfway around and, seeing the brown eyes become soft, embraced Wounded Bear as he had that freezing night twelve years ago. The strong arms around him felt comforting, as though some wrong had been righted.

Pulling back, Wounded Bear met his gaze. "Her death was not your fault, Howan."

Matthew smiled dimly at the use of his war name, giving a bare nod.

"Where is she, brother?" Wounded Bear asked.

He swallowed—grief rising to choke his utterance—and pointed to the crevice with his chin. "There."

Wounded Bear turned and gazed long at the vee-shaped gash now filled with windblown earth and pine needles. Somber light filled his eyes, as though he suddenly understood the plans of the spirit powers. He nodded slowly and took Matthew by the arm, leading him back out of the rain and into the shelter.

"Come," he said tenderly. "Sit with me by the fire. We will talk."

Gratefully Matthew nodded. Maybe, the *maiyun* had forgiven him. He looked up at the starless sky, fear still fluttering in his stomach.

Robert Merrill crawled on his stomach through the mud to the rock pile in front of the sandstone shelter. There, he steadied his rifle over the large stones. Chuckling, he pulled both pistols from their holsters and laid the weapons next to his right hand. From the looks of things, he might have to make three fast shots. He wiped rain out of his eyes and squinted through his sights, the firelight gave him clear targets.

Douglas and the Indian were standing outside the shelter, talking. They blocked his view of Colleen. He grumbled coarsely, "Damn it!" Then, "Ah, there!" They were walking back inside. Wiping rain out of his eyes again, he lined his sights on Colleen's white chest. Her breasts heaved erratically when she looked at the two men beside her. Damn filthy whore! he spat to himself. One man wasn't enough for her!

He started to squeeze gently on the trigger, then a new thought struck him. He stifled a hysterical roar of laughter. Why hadn't he thought of that before? Justice would ring much truer if she had to watch Douglas die first.

He shifted his sights to Matthew's broad muscular back.

From across the fire, Matthew studied Wounded Bear, then let his eyes drift to Colleen. She looked back anxiously, love written clearly on her face. He sensed she wanted to come to him, but was torn between him and Wounded Bear. He gazed at her for a few moments, drowning in the familiar warmth of her eyes.

"You all right?" he asked tenderly, smile slightly reproachful.

"Yes, Matthew," she said worriedly. "I'm sorry I—"

"Is the baby . . ."

A rifle shot blasted the stillness. The bullet slammed into his side, jerking him. Colleen's screams bristled in his mind as he fell, clutching his wound. He rolled swiftly, bringing up his pistol as another shot boomed. From the corner of his eye, he saw Colleen fall. *Was she hit?* Desperately he tried to steady his revolver on the location of the last flash, but his body trembled so violently from wound shock—he couldn't. As if alive, the sights refused to line up. Then he saw the bearded man rise up from behind the rock pile.

"Hold it!" Robert gruffly commanded. He held a pistol in either hand as he walked cautiously forward.

Wounded Bear let the rifle braced against his injured shoulder drop. Matthew reluctantly lowered his pistol; it slipped from his grip as he rolled over to put a hand to his side. His fingers came back coated with thick hot blood. He stared fearfully at it, knowing what it meant. *Dear God, not yet. Not yet. Give me just a little longer.*

Merrill cackled hysterically at the scene, head thrown back. "Thought you'd shamed me, did you, Douglas?" he roared.

Matthew rubbed a fist into his eyes; a gray haze swallowed the edges of his vision. Destiny closed in around him. *Let the punishment be mine . . . mine.* The words rang like the trumpets of Judgment Day. For a brief moment he cast his gaze heavenward, speaking silently to the *maiyun*, asking defiantly about justice.

Merrill took another step toward him.

"Robert, don't!" Colleen screamed. "*Don't!* Please, I'll—"

"Shut up, you damned whore!"

A wave of relief washed through Matthew at the sound of her voice. He turned feebly to lock eyes with her. Tears traced lines down her cheeks. She struggled to escape the protection of Wounded Bear's arms and come to him. A splash of crimson stained her skirt, growing wider with each moment.

If he could just reach his other pistol and drag it from the holster before . . .

Merrill's eyes shifted suddenly to something over Matthew's shoulder and his face grew ghastly pale.

A chance. Matthew grabbed for his revolver. From the edges of his mind he heard Merrill's pistol cock as his own fumbling fingers slipped upon the Colt's polished grips.

A low keening moan froze them, echoing from the hillsides. Matthew watched as a huge white wolf leapt from the crevice, its lean body stretched out as though in flight. It hit the ground, bounded once, jaws gaping wide, and vaulted for Merrill.

Disbelief twisted Robert's face. The pistol fell from his fingers, his eyes widening in terror as he screamed and turned to run.

The wolf slammed into him—snarling, gleaming teeth bared. Knocking the man to the wet ground, it clamped huge jaws around his throat. A brief shriek impaled the night . . . then gargled into eternal stillness.

Matthew lay immobile. The beast had torn Merrill's head from his body and thrown it a short distance away; it still rocked as though animate. The wolf licked its red lips and looked at Matthew, black eyes glistening. A silent communication passed between them and *from somewhere . . . somewhere, a voice called his name, sweet and familiar, as warm as it had been twelve years ago.*

"Enanoshe?" he responded feebly.

Had she waited for him all these years? He tried to turn and look at the crevice, but his tired body refused. *She was there. He knew it. If he could only . . .*

Colleen screamed raggedly and tore herself from Wounded Bear's arms to run to Matthew's side. Standing over him, she gasped in horror. The gaping wound in his side poured blood, soaking the moist earth. She stopped breathing.

Slowly Matthew lifted a hand to touch the widening spread of red on her skirt. "You . . . all right?" he whispered.

Warm blood ran sticky down her thigh from her leg wound, filling her boot. Her movements were agonizingly slow—as though she walked in a horrible dream. "I love you," she whispered.

Matthew reached weakly for her again, and a sob welled in her throat. She dropped to her knees, clutching his fingers tightly, smearing the blood from his hand to hers. His breathing was labored, the hole in his side spewing red bubbles when he exhaled. Drops of blood rose to his lips. Gently she caressed his fingers. He shuddered.

"Matthew?"

Wounded Bear knelt behind her and rested a hand on Matthew's shoulder, shaking his head, pain choking him.

Matthew's half-closed eyes fluttered as the wolf threaded through the grass. Red streamers coursed down its white chest. Methodically the spirit creature examined each of their faces, resting for a long minute on Matthew.

"It's over . . . grandfather," Matthew murmured, exhaling unsteadily as he gazed into the beast's black eyes.

The wolf slowly nodded. "The old man's magic was strong, Howan."

A faraway tinkle of girlish laughter drifted to Matthew on the wind, warm, beckoning. "Helper, let me . . . Enanoshe?" He gazed anxiously toward the crevice.

"Seyan waits for you," the wolf assured. "Go."

Colleen squeezed Matthew's hand as a soft smile crept over his sweating face. Leaning down, she kissed his bloody mouth, trembling when his lips touched hers.

Matthew's body jerked slightly—stilling.

Colleen stared emptily at the big tanned hand that released its grip on hers.

"No," she whispered hoarsely, shaking Matthew. "No!"

"Colleen," Wounded Bear murmured, wrapping strong arms around her and pulling her away. "Don't."

Tears blurred her vision. She pressed her cheek against Wounded Bear's and held the wolf's glistening eyes. The creature examined her curiously a moment before turning away to lay a huge paw on Matthew's broad bloody chest.

"Warrior," the wolf said, "it is over."

Wounded Bear nodded and gripped Colleen tighter, pressing her so close she could barely breathe. "Now, Colleen," he whispered, stroking her hair. "Forever, this time."

The warm gentleness of his soul swirled around hers, twining through her, soothing her pain. The dance began, the eternal sea of light washing up around them.

• EPILOGUE •

"*THEY WILL TEAR UP THE LAND!*"

The old man wiped a tear from the corner of his eye and lightly pounded the rickety pine table. Lavender rays of sunset glimmered through the cracks in the walls of his tiny Indian Agency room, streaking his seamed face. Around him, haunted Cheyenne eyes gleamed in the candlelight.

"And *you*"—he wept, stabbing out a gnarled finger—"you will let them!" He closed his eyes, head tottering in a grim nod. "We fought . . . we fought . . . but you will not . . ."

A murmur filtered through the crowded room, people bowing their heads in shame. What could they do? Caged and starving, they were tired. Only the bluecoats brought them food now, scant and rancid; it made the people sick unto death.

"Listen to me, children," the old man pleaded, running a hand through his graying black hair. His odd eyes flamed. "I see the whites bringing huge shovels to rip chunks from the earth . . . I see you . . .'' He took a deep halting breath. "I see you doing it with them.''

His shrill sobs pierced the room, drifting to the soldiers standing guard in the cold outside. They turned uneasily, waiting.

"You will become crazy. You will all die off . . . *die off* . . . because you've forgotten the prophecies of our fathers!''

Suddenly he reached out to the wide-eyed man nearest him, staring up imploringly, "Don't forget, my son. *Promise me you won't ever forget.*''

Wounded Bear, 1897

• HISTORICAL AFTERWORD •

SWEET MEDICINE IS THE TRUE CULTURE HERO OF THE Cheyenne tribes. They say he came to them "many centuries ago," at a time when the people were living lawless lives, murdering and hurting each other. Sweet Medicine changed that. He brought the Sacred Arrows and taught them how to use the arrows to renew the world and cleanse the people.

From a scholarly perspective, it is difficult to say whether Sweet Medicine truly lived or not. If he did, it was probably, as the Cheyenne say, "several centuries ago." One of his alternate names is Rustling Corn Leaf, implying he lived long before the Cheyenne came to the plains, when they still lived along the Missouri River and grew corn. Sweet Medicine taught and performed miracles among the People for many years. It was just before his death that he prophesied the coming of the horse and the rifle ("something that makes a noise, and sends a little round stone to kill"). He prophesied the search for gold and the sicknesses that would decimate the People. And he foresaw the coming of the whites. "There will be many of these people, so many that you cannot stand before them. On the rivers you will see things going up and down, and in these things will be people, and there will be things moving over dry land in which these people will be." Wagons, perhaps, following the twining roads that would eventually lace the west.

The tribes of the Great Plains believed that the overland trails had a mystical power. They called them *"medicine trails."* History supports their claim. The road system changed the face of the country. By 1850, these routes had become pulsing arteries of transportation leading emigrants to the western territories, miners to goldfields and military troops to the newly established posts in the Far West. When the massive migrations began to slow around 1867, perhaps 350,000 people and 10 million stock animals had traversed the plains. The impacts on the land and to the Indian way of life were immense. Grass and wood supplies were critically depleted, game animals were hunted to near extinction along the routes. Thomas Fitzpatrick, Indian Agent for the Upper Platte and Arkansas region, wrote that the roads were responsible for the "entire ruin" of the Indians' territories. He declared in 1853 that the Sioux and Cheyenne were actually in a starving state. "Their women are pinched with want and their children constantly crying out with hunger."

Pushed to the edge of destruction, the tribes had no choice but to fight back.

In 1857, Lieutenant Kimble Warren led a pack train of army topographical engineers on a reconnaissance of the Black Hills in Dakota Territory. He'd made it only halfway when a Sioux war party rode down on him. Through a torrential rain storm, he sat his horse arguing with the chief. Black Shield told Warren if he didn't turn around, he and his entire detachment would be killed. "The Great Father asked us for a road along the Platte, and we gave it to him," Black Shield explained. "We gave him one along the White River and another along the Missouri . . . This is the last place left to us, and if we give it up we must die. We had better die fighting like men.''

By the time James Sawyers' expedition crossed Warren's path in 1865, the tribes were desperate. The Niobrara road slashed through the heart of the final sanctuary of the buffalo—their chief food source. Surely, though history doesn't record it, Sweet Medicine's prophecies must have been ringing like warning bells in the heads of the Cheyenne.

No matter the cost, the road had to be stopped.

While Colleen Merrill, Wounded Bear, and Matthew Douglas are fictional characters, the background events portrayed in this book are real: Sawyers and Williford were locked in constant battle, hurling bitter accusations throughout the journey. After the siege that began on August 15th where ''a few thousand Indian warriors'' surrounded the train, Williford knew his men were overwhelmingly outnumbered and he balked. Sawyers wrote in disgust, ''Our escort commander began to grow faint-hearted and all the officers . . . were clamorous for the abandonment of the expedition.'' He, of course, disagreed, ordering that they push onward. The train was attacked repeatedly thereafter. Dull Knife and Red Cloud, through their interpreter, George Bent, demanded the road be stopped. Finally, when Williford refused to order any of his men on Sawyers' ''suicide mission''- to find Connor's troops—it ended.

General G. M. Dodge credited Williford with saving the train. An officer with a distinguished war record, Williford had seen almost constant battle from Shiloh to the end of 1864 when he was mustered out to recover from wounds and exhaustion. A coward he was not, and Dodge knew it.

When Sawyers at last arrived in Virginia City (after being attacked several more times by the Arapaho), he found the military's assessments had preceded him. He was greeted by allegations of incompetence. He immediately went to Washington to answer congressional charges of mismanagement of the expedition and of private interest in the Hedges' freight business.

Though he successfully defended himself, his road was

never used by emigrant wagons again. The inhospitable terrain and Indian resistance effectively destroyed the usefulness of the Niobrara Road.

To this day, the Northern Cheyenne wage a constant battle against white destruction of the land. Only four years ago they resisted the United States government's plans to mine their reservation in Montana for coal. One of their central reasons was a fear that Sweet Medicine's prophecies would come true.

May the *maiyun* continue to guide them.